Scandalous Affairs

A Pleasure Garden Follies Anthology

Layna Pimentel

DEDICATION

To my husband. Without you, my world would be nothing but an empty shell.

ACKNOWLEDGMENTS

This book couldn't have been possible without the many people involved behind the scenes. Tracy, Jessica, Kali, Sara, S.J, Lisa: You girls kept me grounded and sane in some of the craziest moments in 2015, and here's to many years of friendship. To my editors who worked on each of these stories: you have my eternal gratitude for breathing new life into these novellas. Last but not least, Teresa at BMB Designs: I couldn't have imagined a more beautiful cove

Scandal at Vauxhall

CHAPTER ONE

London, England, 1818

The opulence of Lord and Lady Sinclair's ballroom borrowed many Italian influences, to the artwork, chandeliers, and even the fabrics selected. Young ladies lined up on the one side as randy gentlemen scouted their amusement for the evening. And yet again, Her Grace, Isabel Griffith, the Duchess of Brimley, attended another high society event sans her duke.

Henry Griffith, the fifth Duke of Brimley, had always been known as a notorious rake, from the countless affairs he'd had with married women and dalliances with some of London's most sought after courtesans, to coveting another duke's wife, even after their nuptials.

Some days Isabel wondered if her father even cared that he'd wedded her into what would become a lifeless, loveless, and solitary union. One that benefitted the family name only, but made everyone involved despondent.

If only her family had been patient enough for Nathaniel's return. She could have married into status as her parents desired, *and* she'd be happily in love. Isabel often wondered whatever happened to the marquess.

On a night like tonight, however, she was thankful for the lack of her husband's presence. These types of occasions always put him in a sour mood. He'd wind up playing whist and lose. Then, he'd drink himself into a stupor, drag her away from whatever conversation she was having, take her home and bed her roughly, only to fall asleep before giving her any pleasure in return.

Pfft. What is pleasure anyway? Yet, while she didn't have much experience in the ways of lovemaking, it was highly unlikely most marriage beds were like hers. Especially during these moments, she wished she had the courage to run.

Is married life supposed to be like this? Leaving me feeling filthy, unworthy, and so lonely? She hadn't the slightest clue about what she'd ever done wrong, but the pang of regret over not standing up to her husband made her frailer with each passing day.

Distracting her from such sad thoughts, Lady Balfour approached, fanning herself with expediency. "My dear, have you heard? The Marquess of Stoughton has just arrived. My word, he hasn't aged one bit, and he's looking quite fit."

Nathaniel! He's alive. Isabel's heart pounded in her chest as her gaze settled on him.

She hadn't seen him since he'd told her he was leaving on business for the war office. Her pulse kicked up furiously to the point that she felt light-headed and breathless. He was still a sight for sore eyes. His dark hair and piercing blue gaze stood out in the crowd. The sheer breadth of his shoulders framed his muscular size. She watched as he stopped and spoke with other gentlemen, his back now facing her and Lady Balfour.

My God! He really is here. Would he even recognize me? Hardly. He's probably here to fetch his mistress for the evening. Why would he even pay me any mind? Besides, she was a duchess, very much married, and obliged to keep up appearances.

"My, would you look at the size of his thighs," Lady Coxley announced as she approached the ladies, garnering a few giggles from prying ears.

Isabel smirked, knowing all too well in what direction this conversation was headed.

"They are wonderfully built, but I'm sure some other lady has laid claim on the marquess."

"You haven't heard, have you, Isabel?"

"What haven't I heard?" she asked. *Her breath hitched and her pulse raced. What could I have missed?*

"Come away with me to the terrace. I wish to speak to you in private. We can't have half of London listening in."

She followed Lady Coxley outdoors, leaving behind the sounds of merriment to be embraced by the shrouded darkness of night and silence.

"They say the marquess will not marry until he's found her."

"Until he's found who?"

"The one who broke his heart. But in all honesty, everyone knows it's you. With any luck, perchance some horrible fate will happen upon Henry."

If I were only so lucky. "You shouldn't talk like that! And for the record, the marquess and I were done long ago. Remember, he's the one who left me."

"Isabel, you cannot expect me to believe that you haven't thought about that man— at least once or ever—during the course of this sham of a marriage of yours. The haute ton in its entirety knows where he is right now. And you'd be a fool to think Henry gives two ninnies about your welfare." The sound of someone clearing their throat interrupted them.

"Excuse me, ladies, but I was wondering if perchance I could steal Her Grace for a dance."

Good grief. Did he hear any of our discussion? I cannot believe he's actually here.

Heat coursed through Isabel at the thought of holding him once again. She nodded and held out her gloved palm for him to take. "I'd be honored, My Lord."

"The pleasure is all mine, Your Grace."

Leaving behind Lady Coxley, she followed his lead inside for a waltz.

"It's been too long, Isabel. I've missed you terribly," he whispered as they took a turn about the dance floor. Nathaniel bowed and took her hand. His touch warmed her, and the gentle squeeze that followed reassured her that the flame they once had was still there.

She and Henry hadn't danced since their wedding and even then, he quickly discarded her to dance with the Duchess of Downsbury. If she'd only known her dismissal that evening would be the first of many others. For the most part, her husband had two left feet, but Nathaniel whisked her away gracefully to the tune. She wished to kiss him again and remind herself of their time together. *Good heavens, Isabel. You're married. Enough of this foolishness!*

Isabel felt him pulling her closer as his arm at the small of her back pushed her in. His head dipped down, and, naturally, she looked up at him, ignoring every stare and whisper as they moved together. She finally cringed and mustered the courage to ask him the one thing weighing heavily on her mind. "Why did you take so long? Why didn't you come sooner? Nathaniel, there hasn't been a day I haven't thought of you."

As the music wound down and the dancers departed, Isabel locked her eyes on his and felt a tear escape. "You've been missed greatly, My Lord."

His thumb swiped away the drop. "My dear, there hasn't been a day, hour, or dream you haven't occupied."

Her chest tightened with his admission. *Could he have really wanted me all this time?*

"Nathan—"

Shouting from the foyer bled into the main ballroom as a squire and a number of other gentlemen made their way through. Recognizing one of the men as her footman, Isabel rushed toward him. "Stanley, what is wrong?"

"Your Grace! I'm so glad I found you. The duke...he was caught...something about a duel in Hyde Park."

Slightly unsteady, she wavered on her feet, only to be caught by the marquess, who approached from behind. "I'm not sure what you mean, Stanley. What exactly was he caught doing?"

The footman lowered his voice to a whisper. "Your Grace, you know— the rumors of your husband's affair with Her Grace, the Duchess of Downsbury. Well, apparently the duke found them in the duchess's chambers when he entered to claim his husbandly rights."

And there it was.

The world seemed to fade away upon hearing his words. However, she had always known of her husband's infidelities, so she refused to swoon. "Thank you, Stanley. I wish to leave now. I'm sure all of London will know of this by morning, if they haven't heard by now." She turned to the marquess. "Thank you for the dance, My Lord. I bid you a good evening."

With her head held high and her stomach in knots, Isabel departed the ball, fearing what the dawn would bring. Would she wait at home for her husband to stumble back after victory, or would she be delivered the news of his demise? Given the heartache Henry condemned her to, and the embarrassment he'd wreaked on his family name, perhaps she should attend.

Before the door to her carriage closed, she reached for the footman's hand. "I'd like to stand witness to the duel."

"But, Your Grace, no lady should view such wicked displays."

"It couldn't be any more humiliating than finding out your husband was caught by another. A fellow peer, no less."

"I'll see what I can do, Your Grace."

Her attendance would mean going against all protocol and decorum, but she needed to see it, if for nothing more than closure.

Nathaniel wondered what exactly had pulled Her Grace away in a hurry. As he walked around the ballroom, he listened to the whispers until he reached the games room. Lord Broxton waved him over to the whist table. Lords Avonlea and Rutledge cast an amused glance.

Both had gone to Oxford with him and hadn't spoken to him since his return to London. It was interesting. After his trip from the continent earlier this month, all the ladies still sought him out, but not his friends.

"Come now, Lord Thompson, we still have room for one more, and the betting has just gotten more interesting."

"How so, Rutledge?" he asked.

"Well, it all started with fifty guineas and you following Her Grace, the Duchess of Brimley, onto the terrace. Fifty guineas gets you in, and another says you'll bed her before the year is out."

Nathaniel raised his eyebrows. If he were a gambling man, he'd have played along. But tonight he wasn't. Something about the way Isabel had been trying to maintain her composure told him that things were going awry one way or another.

"Rutledge, you may bet all you want on what I do in private, but I wager I'll have my boot so far up your fob arse before the night is out."

The table broke out into a fit of laughter. "Game on, Thompson. I'm almost certain you'll lose the bet."

The cards were dealt and all had played their hands when Lady Rutledge came up behind her husband. "My dear, the most intriguing news. His Grace, the Duke of Brimley, was called out by Downsbury. The duel is at daybreak. Apparently, he caught Brimley with his wife."

So that was what had her rushing out of here. This didn't bode well for Isabel. Downsbury was an expert marksman, and Brimley didn't stand a chance. Isabel could very well be a widow before breakfast, and the thought had to have frightened her. The worst thing about the entire scenario was that he couldn't offer any assistance until he knew of the outcome. Scandal already sat at her doorway, and it was only a matter of time before all of London heard.

Lord Broxton chuckled and didn't appear the least bit fazed by the revelation. "I wouldn't worry about it, my dear. Her Grace, the Duchess, should be happy her tyrannical husband does not stand a chance. And if the rumors are correct, I imagine Downsbury will still remain a cuckold and very much at the center of bets at White's, as his duchess has been stringing around several lords."

His wife gasped mockingly then giggled. "Oh my! She has certainly been a busy body, hasn't she?"

"My dear, if there is nothing else of import, please let us gentlemen return to our game."

"Certainly, My Lord." She practically skipped away with the new information to gossip about.

Heartache swelled in Nathaniel's chest. Lady Broxton's announcement certainly explained much. Had he not been sent off via the war office's command, and married poor Isabel as he had intended, he could have spared her this grief and embarrassment.

In fact, he found it quite shocking that society should take so much pleasure in observing and commenting on everyone's lives as if they were a Greek tragedy or some ridiculous play at the theatre. Mocking and ridiculing, subtle but harsh, ruthless and relentless. The follies of those who took pleasure in another's misery should be eternally punished.

Nevertheless, the more he pondered on the matter, the more he wanted to see Isabel and lift her spirits. Yet, he could not. She was above his station, and married, no less. It was bad enough his mother had many dinners planned and balls to attend.

The dowager had an agenda of marrying him and his sister off. However, no respectable peer would go near his dear, naïve, imprudent sister. Thus, the future of his family estate was now left entitled to him. To keep the other two women in his life content, in addition to this conundrum, would prove to be his greatest feat ever.

The game of whist lasted all of a half hour when Nathaniel excused himself from the gaming table, only to be met by his mother and sister on his way out.

"Where do you think you're going, Nathaniel?"

"Nowhere of any import to you, Mama," he whispered, removing her stiff hand from his wrist.

"Come, dear brother. I shall not be deprived of at least one dance."

Nathaniel huffed, knowing what they were up to. "I think not. I have something I must do right now."

"Pish posh, love. White's is no place for a man in the marriage mart. Lord and Lady Sinclair's ball is, and you're leaving far too early!"

"I think not," he repeated. And without giving either woman a second glance, he abandoned the ball to find out more about Brimley's dealings with the Duchess of Downsbury.

Isabel dressed in her riding habit, prepared to go on horseback if needed. One way or another, she would witness the proof of her husband's betrayal.

"You're mad, My Lady!" the butler exclaimed. "You cannot attend. No respectable lady attends a duel. If you wish, I'll make an appearance in your stead and return once it is over to deliver the news myself."

"Absolutely not. If you desire to accompany me, then do so. Otherwise, I ride alone."

The servants begged and pleaded for her to stay behind, and deep down she knew she'd regret her decision, but one couldn't blame her for wanting closure. Isabel slipped out the back entrance, racing toward the stables before her footmen could intervene.

"I'd like my horse readied immediately," she commanded the stable hand.

When her mare was brought forth, she climbed up, accepting the young man's assistance, and bolted willingly from the stall. No one, not even Providence, could stop her from watching her foolish husband make the biggest mistake of his life.

The unfortunate thing was that she could only watch from afar. Rows of beech trees with lush foliage rustled in the early morning breeze. She dismounted her horse and wrapped the reins around the fence. Walking around the tree line, she attempted to remain out of sight. At the sound of men shouting, Isabel halted beneath an oak and peered around the trunk for a better look.

Her husband and Downsbury stood angrily facing each other, their seconds hovering to ensure they didn't start before the surgeon arrived. When he finally showed, he crossed the green, and the count began.

"Five. Four. Three. Two."

The hair at the nape of her neck rose, and her lips trembled. Yes, her husband had many faults, but none should be punishable by death. *Lord have mercy on his soul.*

"One." The pistols went off, followed by some shouts. Isabel's heart hammered in her chest as she gripped the bark harder. One shot executed with precision would inherently and irrevocably change her life for the better. Yet, how cruel she was for thinking such dreadful thoughts. Ladies weren't bred for such wicked sentiments. Sentiments that would have never been born if she'd married the love of her life in the first place. She dared not witness the dreadful scene, but clung to the same mental image over and over: a heap of flesh and muscle fallen, sometimes breathing or not. A surgeon's declaration.

Guilt washed over her in waves, much like high tide. She shouldn't be here, but summoned the strength to finally witness the results of such a barbaric tradition. Actions such as these might soon provide her with freedom from a loveless and childless union. *Freedom.* She squinted to find her husband on the ground, lifeless. His silvery-blue waistcoat was unmistakable. A chill washed over her, and her eyes began to well up with tears. The surgeon lifted his limp arm to check his pulse and loudly pronounced his death.

Isabel inhaled sharply and backed into the tree, pushing a branch out of her way. It flung back and smacked her in the face. She bit back the sting, thankful for the momentary distraction. Hooves galloping away caught her attention. As she stepped out from her hiding space, heavy hands caught her unawares.

"What do you think you're doing here?" a deep, burly voice questioned her. She spun on her heels to face her inquisitor. The man gasped. "I'm beggin' your pardon, Your Grace! I had no idea...you shouldn't be here," Henry's solicitor growled, drawing the attention of the gentlemen that remained behind.

No, I shouldn't. Her life was about to change. She was stunned, horrified, and suddenly feeling very alone, the uncertainty of her future swallowing her whole. Before she could even speak, the surgeon approached. *Would it be too much to ask, to be left alone? I cannot possibly deal with them right now.*

He tipped his hat and cast a downward glance. "Your Grace, I offer my condolences. Can I have someone escort you home?"

Isabel shook her head. "I think I should be able to manage."

"Well, at least let me escort you back to your mare. I had no idea Your Grace could ride." He tucked her tense, gloved hand into the crook of his elbow. Once they were close enough, he assumed position to help lift her.

"Thank you, sir."

"You're most welcome. Please, if there is anything I can do, let me or my wife know, Your Grace. We would be most honored to assist you in any way we can."

"Thank you kindly, sir. Should a need arise, I will call on you."

Within minutes, Isabel reared her horse back and rode home hard, only stopping when she reached her front door. Passing the reins to a surprised footman, she stepped through the threshold, collapsing onto her knees.

The butler rushed forward, hollering for the housekeeper to come quickly. "Your Grace, what's happened?"

"His Grace, the Duke of Brimley, succumbed to a fatal gunshot. What will become of us?"

"Your Grace," he bent down to help her, "I know I speak out of turn when I say that we're sorry for your loss, but no matter how uncertain all may be now, just know we— the staff—support you fully. We will be here for you no matter the challenge. You have my honor as a servant. No harm shall come to you. Now, if you'll follow Mrs. Cooke, she shall see you settled into bed."

Isabel sighed, feeling a weight lift from her shoulders. *But what will they do if I can't afford to keep them on?* She'd hate to see them leave, but the harsh reality was this: what would be left to her with Henry's passing would be determined by his solicitor. A man she wouldn't give two farthings for, and who had the manners of a pig.

CHAPTER TWO

Ten months later.

Isabel paced to and fro from the dais to her garden window, facing the back of her townhouse. Uneasiness had her on guard, but she hadn't the slightest clue the cause of her anxiety. The skies were gray and the clouds shifted in strange, hard angles above, threatening to unleash some sort of God-given punishment. Nevertheless, Isabel found her thoughts and paranoia distracted once again by Cecily's incessant chattering.

While she enjoyed the frequent visits by her closest friend, Miss Cecily Turner, their teatime had turned into a weekly accounting of London's wagging tongues and scandalous mischief. For the most part, their conversations had been light and humorous, yet as of late their talk had been dark and unsatisfactory. Three times this month already, Cecily managed to bring up the Marquess of Stoughton, and every time his name was mentioned, Isabel's heart broke.

She had written to Nathaniel on at least half a dozen occasions to seek his council on some stately matters—as her late husband's solicitor sorely neglected her—and not one letter received a response. Disappointment summarized her life in light of recent events, especially after she had poured out her heart to him at the ball. Isabel glanced over to her companion then looked away as a single tear trickled down her cheek.

She missed Nathaniel.

Cecily scoffed, drawing her full attention. "I just find it utterly distasteful how the dowager countess continues to declare the marquess's affections for Lady Eloise Morton, and insists the marriage would be most advantageous. Even more shocking is the age difference! Why, she's barely out of school, and he's a man in his prime. A man his age with a wife so young is a disaster of a match. The affairs, illegitimate children...the list

9

goes on," she ranted.

Isabel dismissed the words with a wave of her hand.

"Darling, what in heaven's name are you thinking about?" Cecily asked, setting her tea down. "My brother will be here soon, so we must finish making our list."

Isabel cocked her head to the side. *What in the devil is she talking about?* "What list are you going on about, Cecily?"

A pounding on the door, followed by men shouting, alerted the women, and they sat there staring at the entrance. Smith, her butler, finally made face until he was pushed out of the way by the Duke of Downsbury. The duke marched toward her then halted as soon as Isabel rose to address him.

"You, sir, have crossed the line!" she said staunchly.

"And you, My Lady, are going to be ruined! I want what is owed, and I'll not stop until I have it."

Isabel sucked in a breath, trying to find the patience to avoid blurting out unladylike expletives. "My Lord, would you care to explain? How is it exactly that I'm going to be ruined? Far be it from me to mention that all of London is still talking about my inability to keep my own husband in my bed. Or shall I remind you of with whom he was cavorting?"

Richard Waite, the Duke of Downsbury, stood before her with his fists at his side and paled.

"Edmonds! Please escort His Lordship to the gate and see that he never returns."

Her butler moved to guide him out when Richard turned and viciously snarled, "It was just as well that your husband lost the duel, but mark my words, My Lady, you will lose everything by the time I am done. He owes me far more coin than what is recorded in the books at White's, Your Grace.

"Once I am finished, you will be reduced to a pauper. A word of advice, madam— you may even be able to restore some power if you brush up on your skills. I hear Madam Martine is on the hunt for new courtesans."

Isabel's limbs went limp. Her chest constricted, and the need to weep overwhelmed her every sense.

"Do what? What could you possibly do, Richard, without further embarrassing yourself?" the new, but familiar, voice asked from the door.

Shock coursed through Isabel's veins. Her knees quaked and soon she found herself unable to breathe.

Nathaniel. He's here were her last coherent thoughts before swooning.

Nathaniel stood in the doorway, taking stock of the situation. Isabel and her guest looked positively aghast and Downsbury even more annoyed now that he'd been interrupted.

"Thompson! What in the world are you doing here? Is the dowager of Brimley your latest conquest?"

Nathaniel nearly erupted at the accusation. Instead, he crossed the floor in three large strides and grabbed the overzealous duke by the neck, only to lose his grasp when Downsbury kneed him in the jewels. Pain radiated down his legs, and his groin throbbed, but that didn't keep him from finishing this.

Downsbury sidestepped, but Nathaniel ran straight at him, tackling him into the side board. Tea cups clamored as they smashed to pieces on the parquet flooring. Isabel's companion screamed. Nathaniel's face ground into the floor as Downsbury attempted to wrap his clammy, wiry hands around his throat. He craned his neck to where he saw the ladies last, and his heart plummeted at the sight of Isabel on the floor, her friend huddled over her, shielding her from debris.

"Enough!" Nathaniel roared with all the compunction he could summon. "If you fail to cease this harassment, Your Grace, I will be sure to have a full investigation launched into all your comings and goings at White's. And let me reassure you, there will be nothing left to your fortune by the time *I'm done*."

He heaved off the desperate duke and rose his feet. "Smith, see that His Grace finds his way out immediately."

The uninvited guest staggered from the parlor.

Just how much trouble is he in? Nathaniel rushed to Isabel, falling onto his knees.

"Don't just stand there, miss. Go find Edmonds or the housekeeper. Immediately!" He stroked Isabel's hair.

The grim news of her marriage to Griffith had made it all the way out to the field, sending him into a bloody rage and boxing two agents while he wallowed in his regret. And now, here she lay in his arms. Who knew what she'd been told about his whereabouts, then and these last few months.

His heart crushed at the thought of her being told he was dead, or that he'd finally settled with a dim-witted chit who couldn't have been more ill-matched than his own parents. Perhaps her father had convinced her that Griffith was a better match. With that idea, his frustration escalated, and the only thing he could do was stroke her cheek. "Come on, love, wake for me. Let me gaze upon those beautiful violet eyes."

She stirred for a moment, her ruby lips murmuring gibberish. Her companion entered the room, dragging a maid along. "The stable boy has run for the doctor. He should be along shortly." Miss Turner blushed, kneeling next to him and gently taking Isabel's hand into hers. The housekeeper paced frantically by the door.

"You should know, My Lord, Bel was told you'd met your fate while you were in the service of the Crown. So you can imagine how surprised she was to see you all those months ago," Miss Turner declared while gathering the folds of her skirt.

"Of course she was told that, Miss Turner. I suspect her father arranged the match then?"

She nodded.

It was as he expected. Though, he suspected more to the tale then just what the *haute ton* read into.

Nathaniel leaned forward, placing a kiss on the crown of Isabel's head. Her eyes fluttered open. Miss Turner and the housekeeper squealed with joy. But Nathaniel was still distracted by his vengeful thoughts.

Should Downsbury attempt to make further contact, he'd be sure to expose the duke for the very swine that he was. *What kind of lord threatens the widow of the man he'd shot six months prior?* No matter what happened, he would keep his love safe.

"Wh-what happened?" Isabel pushed off the floor but fumbled, her legs still weak. She glared at the girls, trying to recall the last few moments. "Oh, good Lord!" she gasped. She'd been on his lap. *What would my parents say if they saw me in such a position?* Isabel summoned the gumption to stand on her own two feet, regardless of her knees shaking furiously, and turned to face him.

"You—you're here." She crossed her arms, lips twisting into a snarl. "What in damnation took you so long? All those letters and not one single response. What did I do to be punished so?"

He followed suit by rising, but instead of replying, lifted her into his arms and carried her across the room to the dais. "You, my dear, are unwell. Rest first. Scold later."

Of all the nerve! "A slight bit presumptuous, are we? And precisely what makes you think there will ever *be* a later, Nathaniel?"

But for all the anger slowly simmering, seeing him again made her soft, warm, and light-headed. Many a night, she lay in her bed chambers, dreaming of all the wicked things she wanted to do with him. To him. Wicked temptations. Temptations that only Nathaniel could satisfy. If only they had married as planned, and she had not been told that he had died during his service to the Crown.

During the few evenings that Henry had come to her chambers to claim his husbandly right, she had imagined and replaced his cold detachment for the warm caress of Nathaniel. Stolen kisses in the moonlight, naughty exchanges, and gentle strokes of forbidden flesh.

Her fondest memory was the time that he climbed through her window in the middle of the night, coaxing and teasing her to join him in the grove.

That night had sealed her fate.

Or so she'd thought. He had kissed her slowly, instructing her on how two people in love communicated with touch alone, his gentle ministrations keeping her maidenhead intact.

Good Lord, how is it even possible to become damp with only memories?

This man, for as deeply as she loved him, had given her much pain and grief with his absence. He hadn't written to her once. For her that was unforgivable. Though he could try to make amends, they weren't foolish children any more. They had responsibilities. Their time together had most certainly passed. And even if they were so fortunate to be blessed with another chance, she'd have to wait the full year before any such affair should become public.

"I have no idea why you're here, Lord Thompson, but I assure you, you needn't have wasted your time. Your presence here is not required. And while I thank you for your concern and assistance, I think it's time you left."

"Leave us," he ordered Cecily and the staff who hovered by the door.

How dare he! Isabel bolted from her seat. "You, sir, are impertinent. You cannot just waltz in here and command my guest to leave!"

Nathaniel closed in, blocking any route of escape. "And you, My Lady, need your rest. Once you have recovered and the doctor issues a clean bill of health, I am taking you away from here. I suspect Downsbury will not cease until he's fully embarrassed himself and embroiled you in another unnecessary scandal."

"And you think that leaving with you, after my husband's passing only six months ago, will not create a scandal of its own? You are mad."

"Well, you can't very well stay here."

His logic had merit, but no respectable widow would consider entangling herself in an *affaire de coeur*. But the solution was simple enough. "Very well, My Lord, you have made your point. I shall travel to Bath then perhaps I will stop for a bit at Vauxhall."

"Alone?"

She refrained from laughing at the ghastly glare he gave her. "Of course not. Robert Turner was planning on taking Cecily for her birthday. I think I shall accompany them. That way I will not be alone, and it would be impossible for me to find myself in the embrace of another scandal."

He rolled his eyes heavenward. "Why do I get the impression, Isabel, that nothing has changed?"

What does he mean that nothing has changed?

"Changed? What in the world is that supposed to mean? You...up and left, without so much as explaining to my parents what your intentions were. Do you have any idea how many days I spent hating you, loathing the day you were born? You were the one who did not have to endure Henry's cruelty!

"Much has changed, Nathaniel. The only difference is that you are not centered around it. You say you thought of me often while you were on the continent, but pray tell, how many women did you spend time with? Wait. Don't answer that. I have no desire to learn of how many maidens you took or exotic courtesans with which you fornicated." Anger boiled dangerously, and for a woman who barely raised her voice, Isabel neared her point of no return.

"My dear, I have no desire to give you an account of all my comings and goings. I should be the one to ask, while you were married to the cad, did you not think of me? And why all the hostility? Darling, I mean to ensure your safety. Downsbury was being positively outrageous with his claims. I will not have him patronizing you in any way."

"You give yourself far too much credit, Lord Thompson."

"Frankly, I don't think I give myself enough. Right when I think I am doing an honorable gesture, I am shot down. I have no idea what I have done to earn such poor behavior, but if I have offended you in any manner, you have my deepest apologies."

Pfft. "Have no idea? You only barged into my home, manhandled the duke—who happens to be a fellow peer—and threw him out of my house."

"I did not like his tone," he growled. "Isabel, he was out of line!"

"He might have been out of line, but I do have staff to ensure my safety, My Lord. Now, if you are quite finished, I would like to get back to my company."

He stared at her as if she had three heads. "If that is what you wish, then I will depart, but before I leave I should impart to you some words of wisdom. Whatever he is up to reeks of mayhem and disaster, and this is far from over."

Nathaniel stormed out of the parlor, the front door slamming behind him. She had injured his feelings. There had been hurt and regret in his eyes. Now that he was out of sight, her stomach turned. How she wished she could take her words back. She owed him an apology.

Isabel glared at Cecily, who now stood only steps away, shaking her head disapprovingly. While today was a new day, yesterday's excitement had weighed heavily on her mind, keeping her from a restful sleep.

"You know if it were not for the kindness and interference of His Lordship, Providence only knows what would have transpired." Cecily shifted her eyes to the very same doorway out of which the Duke of Downsbury had been escorted the day before. "Furthermore, I daresay, if it weren't for His Lordship's quick wits, not even vapors would have brought you out of the state you were in. I, for one, am glad for his intrusion."

Isabel wanted to agree with her, yet refused to concede. "Honestly,

Cecily, in all the years we've been friends, you have never once abandoned me. And now, here we stand, and you have all but taken his side in the matter."

"What matter, Isabel?" She closed the distance between them, wrapping her arms around her. "My dearest friend, you will always be the sister I never had. I would never forsake a friend for a man, let alone the Marquess of Stoughton, but believe me when I say he wants to make amends, if not more."

Isabel desired nothing more than to push away the mere thought of her and the marquess entangled again. *No.* Her time to prove to herself that she did not require the approval of her parents, friends, or the *haute ton* was now.

Being a widow would yet prove most advantageous to her independence. She would not have to rely on a man approving household changes. She could move out of the city to wherever she wished. She could even travel to the continent or the Americas.

In a feeble attempt to stray from the seriousness of the discussion, she pulled away from Cecily's embrace and smiled. "I assure you, my darling, I am fine. I will recover and move on as I did when Henry passed." She sighed and fiddled with her gloves. "I can't believe you managed to convince Robbie to take us," Isabel whispered.

"Really, Isabel, did you think my brother would miss the opportunity to escort us— you—to Vauxhall and Bath? I think not. I dare say, the moment I suggested it, he was positively beaming."

Oh. Isabel had entirely forgotten how smitten Cecily's eldest brother was with her.

Robert Turner the Third had only just returned from the war in hopes to finally marry his betrothed. What he had not expected to find was that she had gone off to Gretna Green and eloped with some other fool.

Unfortunately, Robert would not find happiness with Isabel. She liked him well enough, but never saw him in a romantic way. Though, he was handsome and had the Turner family's charming dark brown hair, bright blue eyes, and dashing smile.

Contemplations about the kind of life she and Nathaniel could have had intruded her mind once again, never giving her an ounce of peace. Would they have had a brood of children by now? Or taken up residence in his family estate? What would it be like to feel his lips against hers after all this time? His hands raking her body up and down? His wicked tongue delighting her in ways she had only read about in the French novels her friends often shared?

An unfamiliar feeling washed over her, desire mixed with fear and possibly envy. They could never be. Proper etiquette dictated that she wait a period of one year for mourning. *But why should I?* Her late husband would not have hesitated to leave her funeral and find himself in bed with his mistress.

The sound of horses outside aroused her attention. She approached the window and spotted six magnificent speckled grays tethered to a beautiful, black-lacquered carriage.

Both ladies stood in silence, waiting for the occupant to emerge.

They glanced at each other, speaking at the same time. "Who do you think it is?" Time seemed to drag for an eternity before another carriage appeared down the lane.

"Robbie!" Cecily squealed excitedly, recognizing their family carriage, only to be silenced as the Marquess of Stoughton stepped out from the first one.

Gasping, Isabel groaned. "Good Lord!"

"It is about bloody time, if you ask me!" Cecily cheered.

Isabel's heart thundered in her ears, and she could barely find her breath. *Why is he here?* He knew full well her intentions, and truthfully, she had never known him to make such house calls with a team of horses. *What is he up to?*

Nathaniel made haste in exiting the confines of his carriage. He hated the damned thing and disliked even more to be brought to such lengths in demonstrating his affections. For him, there were better ways to show a lady appreciation and admiration, to declare undying devotion without having to ride a team of horses to the steps of a dowager's door.

Yes, he loved her now, as much as he did then. He would do anything to secure her confidence. And heaven forbid anyone get in his way.

The moment he had found out about the arranged marriage her father had made for her, the overwhelming fear of never seeing her again had pummeled his heart down his throat and into the pits of hell. And only Isabel could rescue it. He did not want to spend the rest of his life with anyone other than her.

He was bound and determined he would finally make Isabel, Lady Brimley, his. Now would be as close as he could get to a second chance. He was certain there would never be another opportunity as such.

Adjusting his cravat, Nathaniel noticed the curtain fall into place in the parlor. *Is Isabel watching from the window? Or maybe a servant?* With no previous arrangement, he truly hoped Isabel would receive him. Allow him to escort her to Vauxhall and, perhaps, further on to Bath.

They could use the sojourn to become reacquainted in more than one way—just as in their youth—in complete and total abandon. With no need to fret over disappointing either set of parents, nor risking his title, they were free to explore as they wished.

As Nathaniel was about to knock, the door opened and her butler stood before him, flashing an amused grin. "My Lord, the ladies will see you in the drawing room."

He wondered who exactly was here, but given Isabel had been in the company of a female companion the night before, perhaps she had returned to check on her. They would surely protest his return and his mannerisms from the previous night. Not that anyone's opinions mattered, as Isabel's well-being was a priority, next to her pleasure, of course.

Led away from the foyer, he was received in the same room as yesterday, only today Isabel sat quietly with Miss Turner at her side. Both ladies rose and curtsied. "To what do we owe this pleasure, My Lord?"

He found the flush of her face fascinating. The thought of sliding his fingers across the rosy flesh made him wonder if her entire body would blush the same way. *What an ill-timed thought. Get a hold of yourself, man! You are here to strengthen your bond with the woman.* He smiled. "Well, Your Grace, it was my desire to speak with you. Alone, that is."

The instant grin on Miss Turner's face was infectious. He smirked in return, only to have Isabel leap from her seat. "You cannot expect me to ask my guest to leave."

Miss Turner giggled and waved her gloved hand. "Hush, darling. Think nothing of it. I shall step outside briefly to see if Robbie is ready to depart." Slightly turning, she curtsied and rushed out of the door.

Scrutinizing the wary glances Isabel delivered, he stepped toward her, capturing the faint floral scent encapsulating her. Isabel's beauty mesmerized him, increasing his need for her exponentially. Her devilish, violet eyes scorned him for the interruption, yet the way she colored from the apple of her cheeks to her neck denoted a much more fiery reaction to his presence.

His eyes moved to the swell of her breasts, distracting him even further. He shifted his stance to accommodate the increasing bulge in his pants.

"Well now, I hope you are satisfied, Lord Thompson. Not only have you succeeded in bullying your way in for a bit of privacy, you have managed to clear the room in a mere few seconds. You may sit. Shall I ring for refreshment?"

She waved for him to sit opposite of her, but Nathaniel chose to sit next to her instead. He dragged another chair from the lone table in the far corner of the room and moved it next to hers. "Tea would be nice but not necessary. We will be leaving shortly.

Have your butler summon my footman to take your things to my carriage."

She stiffened, and her eyes widened. "Have I misunderstood you, My Lord? Did I just hear you say you will be taking me to both Vauxhall and Bath in *your* carriage?"

Yes. You heard me well. I will not leave your side ever again, he wanted to say, but only grinned and winked at her.

"I assure you, madam, your hearing is in perfect health. Yes, I will escort you. Nevertheless, you will still be in the company of Mr. and Miss Turner. I would not dream of your dismissing them so easily. Though, I am rather thankful for the opportunity for us to be reacquainted." In truth, Nathaniel was ecstatic, his nerves threatening to reveal his true feelings.

"My Lord, this is highly improper—" Her outburst was cut short as Miss Turner returned with her brother.

"By the by, this is a pleasure, My Lord!" Robbie gleefully smiled. "So we're a party of four, then? Well, we must not tarry."

Nathaniel rose from his seat and offered a hand to Her Ladyship. "Madam, if I may have the pleasure of escorting you?" Both men bowed to each other.

Isabel's eyes narrowed. "You may, for now."

"Smashing. Now come along, we shall not keep the Turners waiting." *And I really cannot wait to get you alone. I have waited so long.*

Isabel stood in the middle of the path in awe. "Oh, Robbie, it is beautiful here."

Cecily fanned herself incessantly as she took in the general splendor of the grounds: ladies in all the fashionable wear the times had to offer, dapper gentlemen escorting them, and simply the general liveliness surrounding them.

Nathaniel bent his head, whispering into Isabel's ear, "Not nearly as beautiful as Your Grace, I might add."

Isabel blushed, simply replying with a coy smile. She turned her attention to Cecily. While she adored her most cherished friend, Isabel feared the giddiness ready to burst would draw unnecessary attention. "Calm yourself, sister. Or half of London's elite will vouch for us to be denied entry. We wouldn't want that to happen, would we?"

Cecily walked with her brother while Isabel took the marquess's arm and followed their lead.

Vauxhall's reputation for being elegant and enchanting certainly rang true. Then there were the Pleasure Gardens. *Why exactly do they call it that?* she wondered, trying to avoid any scandalous images the mere title brought on.

Her eyes fixed in the direction of the orchard and would not move, as if drawn to some mythical landscape where knowledge, escape, and trouble awaited. It would be rude of her to abandon Robbie and Cecily, but on second thought, branching off might not prove to be a bad idea. Cecily would experience London's favorite playground, and Robbie would perhaps meet a lady or two who might elevate his status.

The barrister, elder by two years, had always been interested in her, yet seemingly more in the idea of settling down. Unfortunately, his designs on her had been met with disappointment. Her secret betrothal to the Marquess of Stoughton, then her marriage to the duke, had made each of their meetings tense, even if it was for only moments at a time.

"Isabel? Lord Stoughton? Shall we head over to the amphitheater?"

Isabel barely registered Cecily's question. "I beg your pardon, I seem to be lost in my thoughts."

"I can see. The amphitheater. Shall we attend?"

The temptation of the gardens struck Isabel like a musical chord on the harp. Or maybe it was like a siren, drawing a sailor into his own demise. But, surely, nothing could happen to her while she was here. This was, after all, civilization. *Or could it?* With Nathaniel by her side, "expect the unexpected" should be her motto.

"Robbie, you take Cecily on ahead, and I will find you both later. I would like to walk around for a bit."

"My Lady, you cannot expect me to leave you alone with the marquess?"

"Robbie, I will be fine. Now go ahead and escort Cecily." Isabel lowered her voice.

"You might even find her a handsome rogue to whisk her away."

A light of amusement flickered in Robbie's eyes. "As you wish, Your Grace."

"Lord Thompson?" Isabel turned to find where he had wandered off to, but did not see him anywhere. *So much for asking him to join me.* Shrugging, off she went in search of what was so splendid about the gardens.

Nathaniel's heart rate quickened with every step Her Ladyship took toward the more secluded area of the Pleasure Gardens. Blood rushed to his groin, and he was eager to find out where she was headed. Engaging in a public flirtation like that one outside the amphitheater earlier would not compare to the embarrassment she would soon discover if she kept walking on the path ahead.

Would she encounter lovers moaning, completely in raptures over erotic touches and sweet words, or the suckling of a rosy bud from an exposed creamy breast? Mayhap, she would stumble into a shrub head first, finding herself propositioned to participate as a third party. Good grief, he had to stop her from continuing on any further, or at the very least, convince her to partake in their own scandalous adventure. *Time to get off this main path.*

Nathaniel reached the entrance lined with ancient oak trees and hedges. *What will it take to convince her that we belong together?* He turned his head side to side, noting the sparseness of people occupying the park. With any luck, he would catch her before the maze.

Proceeding along, he halted by a bench where a couple affectionately held hands, completely engaged in their own seduction, when he discovered an odd shadow opposite of them. Intrigue and his swollen cock led him on, curious to see if the shape belonged to Isabel. And if it did, what in the world she was doing?

He closed in, quietly taking cover behind a tree. A smirk crossed his lips as he watched the woman spying on the intimately involved pair.

There had not been a moment these last twenty-four hours when the duchess did not occupy his thoughts. He dreamt of disrobing her out of those ridiculous layers of clothing, palming those beautiful round breasts, giving them the proper attention they required. Then, he would bury his face between her silken thighs, delving into her slick folds, edging her closer and closer to ecstasy as her eventual release shook him to the core.

Nathaniel shifted slightly to adjust the bulge in his breeches when he stepped on a twig, snapping it. The splintering wood drew the woman's attention in his direction. Attempting to conceal his location, he moved into the shade, where he could not be found. Nevertheless, he had finally found her. *The devil take it!* Isabel, of all people, stood there, observing the couple lying down.

Nathaniel approached cautiously, to avoid alarming the duchess, until he stood behind her. She turned to face him, her belly fluttering with nerves. He locked her wrists above her against the trunk, leaving her nowhere to escape his assault of tender kisses. Lowering his head, he nipped at her lobe and dragged his tongue down the side of her neck.

"Darling, you do realize what you are doing is called voyeurism and is quite illegal." He released her hands, only to wrap his arms around her, pulling her into chest. Her derrière firmly pressed against the throbbing ache of his manhood.

"Nathaniel!" she whispered angrily. "Release me this instant, you oaf!"

"Not on your life, Your Grace," he quipped. "Had I known you were interested in such wicked things, I would have indulged you sooner. There are several establishments in London catering to those particular needs.

"On the other hand, my love, I will have you know, I can attest to my skills at pleasuring women. And I can assure you with the utmost certainty there will be no need to scandalize you further by taking you into such establishments. No proper lady should be in attendance to begin with."

Were it not for her growling, he would take her right there. "Isabel," he murmured. "What you have been watching so intently is beneath you. Allow me to show you, in private, what pleasure—as you observed—would be like. We would make music, love. And you, darling, would never desire another."

She relaxed into his body, allowing him to give pause to the moment, until she turned to face him. A flush swept across her cheeks, and her chin dipped down, her stare no longer holding his. "Nathaniel," she stammered. "I had no idea sexual congress could be that way. Henry...Henry never applied such ministrations when bedding me."

Nathaniel tensed at her admission. No lady should be denied, and even though Isabel had been deprived of such pleasures by the poor excuse of her late husband, he most certainly would not abandon her in her time of need.

"Sweeting, I need you to look at me." He lifted her chin with two fingers until their gazes met. When those glossy violet eyes stared back, his heart broke. "My love, your husband was a coward, a sham, and far from being considered a man. The only thing honorable about him was the duel that ended his shallow existence."

Lord, how he wanted to take her right there. But then he would be no different than any other randy rogue, looking to flip a skirt for the sheer scandal. "Isabel, a proper gentleman always ensures his lady is well taken care of before his own release."

Unable to contain his desire any longer, his mouth crushed to hers. She tempted him, much to his own ire, like Odysseus's sirens. Isabel called to him in a way so primal, nothing could stop him. Not even Poseidon, the commanding ruler of the seas.

Somewhere along the line, she wrapped her arms around his neck, following his lead as his tongue swirled beyond her luscious lips. He lowered her with the intent to conceal themselves from other curious visitors of the gardens. Once nestled onto the carefully manicured lawn, his control vanished.

He slipped his hand beneath her skirt, sliding it along her long, silken legs. Reaching her stays, he cupped her mound as she squealed. "Shh, darling. Let me take care of you." Nathaniel's fingers dipped into her drawers, and he could not have been more delighted to find her damp.

His intangible need to drive an explosive release from her made his cock swell to an uncomfortable level. The only thing he focused on was the beautiful vision beneath him. Her head tipped back as he rubbed her engorged nub. Her breasts threatened to burst from the confines of her corset.

Using his free hand, Nathaniel released her stays. He dipped his head to take the pert, pink nipple between his teeth, gently nipping at the one before gradually moving to the other. She bucked against him.

While taking great care not to cause her pain, he plunged his fingers into her. Tormenting her with each second passing, he brought her closer and closer to release. She trembled and squeezed around him. Ceasing his assault on her senses, he slid down her body, kissing and caressing until his lips met the apex of her thighs, and her skirts rested over his head.

Nathaniel continued his seduction by lapping at her folds, his fingers delving deeper. The sounds of other visitors to the gardens faded as Isabel's moans intensified. Her muscles tensed, and her groans grew louder. His relentless focus on her core sent Isabel into release. She quivered, tensing around his hand while he indulged in her juices.

When she finally steadied her breathing, he found himself pulling out his own member. He stroked to the image of one very sated duchess, who would soon be his in every possible way. Nathaniel closed his eyes, picturing her lips around the crest of his cock, teasing his thickness while she squeezed his tight sac. *God! What you do to me...*

His heart thundered in his ears as he pumped faster and faster. She was naked and bathed in the moonlight, in the comfort of his chambers, whispering naughty things and playing with her God-given assets. If there was ever a pair of tits to be seen, hers should be modeled. An alabaster bust of envy, placed on display in his dressing room, where only he could appreciate it.

She would play with her precious cunt, showing him what she could do to herself while thinking of him, her tiny, delicate fingers rubbing her clit and delving them into her sticky wetness. She would then withdraw those same dangerous digits and pop them into her mouth. She would suck one by one slowly, as she did with his cock—being the relentless tease that he knew she was.

His body went rigid. Blindness struck him, and his breath escaped. "Isabel," he groaned, before exploding into his palm.

He waited for what seemed an eternity before opening his eyes, and his heart rate restored to an even beat. *Damn.* He had never intended to subject Isabel to a compromising situation. Nevertheless, he had enjoyed the pleasures given and could not remember the last time he had taken his own pleasure, thoroughly enjoying the vivid imagery he created.

Surely, now Isabel would see there could never be another. He would be the only one. Not because of their indiscretion, but because of the power of their connection.

Isabel was blushing something fierce. "Guess I need to do something about this mess," Nathaniel declared. Before he could reach for his handkerchief, Isabel offered hers. "Thank you, love. I suppose we should get you back to your friends before they start to wonder where we have run off to."

Her violet eyes fixed on his, soft and glowing. He had most certainly satisfied her, but would it be enough? After helping her up, Nathaniel insisted on adjusting her bodice, but she swatted his hand away.

While he did not know the first thing about fixing hair or gowns, his only concern was to be supportive. His expertise was unraveling those tight and stern buns women wore, until cascades of waves fell seductively around their breasts, and efficiently removing evening dresses, so pleasure would be met with expediency.

She stood there, waiting for him to lead them out from their seclusion, but all Nathaniel desired was to undo her gown again. "Well, darling, you do realize that was only the beginning?" He took her arm and steered her back to the path, when they were met by an unwelcome face. Stiffness settling in his neck and shoulders, he released Isabel and clenched his fists at his sides.

"Downsbury, what are you doing here?" Nathaniel pulled Her Ladyship behind him. "I should have known that a rat would eventually leave town."

The duke regarded Nathaniel with even more disdain than the previous day. "I assure you, Lord Stoughton, I came to take some air and get away from the tedium of daily duties. What I did not expect was Brimley's widow to be here of all places…much less with you. I hope the risk was worth it, Your Grace." He smirked. "Your Grace, My Lord, excuse me. I have business to attend to."

Before Nathaniel could reply, the duke rushed off to speak with a gentleman leaving the park. He turned to Isabel. "I do not trust the man. He is up to something. Let us go. I will return you to Mr. and Miss Turner, and we will depart shortly after that for Bath."

CHAPTER THREE

Isabel tucked her arm into the warmth of her escort's. Both she and Nathaniel quietly walked toward the amphitheater without as much as a word spoken. While the consequences of their actions flitted through her head, tension pulled at her neck. *Perfect! Not only do I have to worry about our reputation. But I could certainly do without this pain, and the grumbling of my belly.*

The afternoon sun, while not entirely at its peak, managed to impair her vision. Her head throbbed as if a mallet had fallen upon her tousled locks. Perhaps Nathaniel was just as worried as her about what the duke might have seen. *Or is he disappointed with me in some way?*

If Downsbury played witness to their indecent behavior, would he sell the story to the gossip column of the daily? Or would he use it to blackmail her further? The mere thought made her flush. She stumbled onto the lush lawn face down, wishing to die an instantaneous death.

"Darling, are you all right? Are you hurt?" Nathaniel asked as he crouched down to take her hands into his.

Heat seared her cheeks. Sickness settled deep within her belly. *What in damnation is wrong with me?* More embarrassed than anything, she pulled away, lifting herself from the ground. She straightened her skirt, still feeling faint.

Isabel wavered, her body temperature rising to an increasingly uncomfortable level. Nathaniel's reputation in the House of Lords would be tarnished irreparably if such a scandal were announced. Moreover, should the duke proceed with his claims in a court of law, and the justice ruled in his favor, she would be turned out into the street. She couldn't let this go on any further.

Before she could even utter a word, Isabel's reality faded. Leaden, she sank uncontrollably into the marquess's waiting arms. *Providence have mercy on me.* "We're both ruined," she muttered as darkness closed in.

When she regained consciousness, she felt herself being carried and laid upon a bench. Opening her eyes, she saw a crowd forming behind Nathaniel. Isabel sat up slowly, fanning herself, when she overheard the whispers.

"Maybe she is with child?"

"Her husband has not even been cold in the grave for a year!"

"How scandalous!"

Nathaniel turned around to face the gathering, "A little privacy, if you may!" The group disbanded swiftly, and he returned his attention back to her. "My darling, what hurts? Shall I summon my physician?"

Isabel shook her head then lowered her eyelids and smiled. She relaxed, releasing a shallow sigh, remembering the time she had tripped down the hill attempting to meet with him in secrecy years before.

He had run to where she had fallen, taken off her walking boots to examine her ankles, and then placed a kiss gingerly on each. The memory warmed her, and she giggled. "Nathaniel, do you remember that time on the hill?"

He stared at her as if trying to comprehend what she was asking. His eyes narrowed, and his lips thinned. "Madam, have you lost your wits? When did you last eat?"

Humph. Is he deliberately avoiding my question? Isabel turned her head in an attempt to ignore him when she felt his hand brush again her knee.

"Yes, I remember the hill, my dear. I also remember those delectable ankles of yours. The question is, when will I see them again?"

Breathless and hopelessly eager to answer, Isabel returned her gaze to his. *He must be mad. To imply that we will...It is impossible.* "To answer your first question, Nathaniel, the last time I ate was at breakfast. I could use a spot of tea, maybe a sandwich. As for your second inquiry, I really do not think we should continue."

"Very well." He rubbed the back of his neck. "We will walk across the lawn to there." He pointed in the direction of the tea house near the entrance to Vauxhall. "From there, we will find the others. And I will still escort you to Bath. We could use the time in my carriage to clarify a few things."

"What could we possibly have to clarify, My Lord? After our indiscretion in the park, we should avoid being together for a while."

"Not bloody likely. If you think for one moment I will abandon you when the *haute ton* has a field day at your expense, you are wrong. Now come along and let us find Mr. and Miss Turner."

Nathaniel could not believe his ears. Did she honestly think she could be rid of him so fast? *No.* Not on his life, his honor, his family's name. She would be his bride. And the sooner the better. His lack of propriety had led them down this path, and she tempted him every moment of the day. How could he not stake his claim? He never anticipated the duke would go to such lengths to tarnish Isabel's reputation. But he would deal with

Downsbury soon enough.

After they reached Bath and retired for the evening, he would send a note to his secretary with detailed instructions on how to proceed. Nathaniel needed to know how much money the duke was after, and if there was any chance he would be awarded what he claimed.

From the safety of Bath, he would be free to orchestrate a plan to remove Downsbury from his shadow. Considering the duke's neglected wife played a role in this debacle, he would not be surprised to discover just how mismatched the two were. That alone would be sufficient in resolving any blackmail Downsbury was plotting. Both would pay dearly for turning his beloved Isabel's life topsy turvy.

In the meanwhile, only Isabel's safety, reputation, and health mattered. The sojourn to Bath would benefit them both. Perhaps he might even convince her marrying him would help alleviate some of this mischief.

Yet, something still nagged at him, at how wrongly he could have underestimated this state of affairs. For all anyone knew, Brimley could have instigated this situation, knowing all too well what it would do to his dowager duchess. Such cruel intent would mean there were other troubles—financial woes—the staff did not know about. *Had Griffith paid their wages regularly? Had suspicious characters visited their townhouse in recent weeks?*

So many questions crossed his mind, and time was limited. He would investigate as soon as he returned, but for now there was no use in jumping to conclusions.

Once seated comfortably in his carriage, Nathaniel reached for a blanket and tucked it around Her Ladyship. The simple sandwich and tea may have restored her senses for the time being, but he did not want to take any more chances. "Drive on!" he shouted.

He moved to sit next to her. She had closed her eyes and leaned into the side uncomfortably. Taking care to not wake her, he shifted her position to rest on his shoulder. The long silence while she slept gave him the opportunity to rehearse in his head how he would propose to her. However, an unsettling feeling that they were being followed nagged at him.

Nathaniel twisted his body to push the drape away from the window, which was currently concealing them, and did not spy anything suspicious, only lone riders and the horses traveling at a normal speed behind them. Even so, the feeling lingered, making him wonder just how desperate Downsbury was to gain what he wanted, and why he would want to bring down Isabel so badly.

If the law granted Downsbury restitution, the woman could easily find herself homeless and without a cent to her name. He loved her—had even worshiped the ground she walked on when they were younger. Now, she faced a scandal so large that he wanted to shield her from the possible cruelties she could encounter.

Moreover, his body ached to join with hers. *To be finally reunited with you, my love. Absolutely no one will come between us this time.*

Nathaniel, deep in thought, barely noticed her stir until her eyes popped open. How he delighted in her gaze. Every time he stared into her deep dark pools, he found himself completely blind with love and lust. Leaving no room for a rebuttal, he bent his head and kissed her. He was close to losing his composure again.

To his surprise, Isabel cooperated and took the time to mimic the swiping of his tongue and nip of his lips. *Ah, an avid student. The things I can teach you.* He twisted to lift her on his lap, pressing her against the burgeoning bulge in his trousers, and continued his seduction.

"Nathaniel," she whispered breathlessly. "We should not."

No, we should not, but could either of us really wait? "I know, love, but I cannot stop."

She shook her head and lowered it to take his mouth again. Her eyes were heady with desire, and a blush so pink swept across her face and down her neck to the valley of those sweet, sweet breasts.

"Darling, if this is truly what you desire, there is no going back."

Isabel responded with a nod, repositioning herself. She straddled him then reached behind and undid the fastenings of her gown. Nathaniel reached out to assist, but she pressed her hand against his chest. "No, my love. Sit back and watch."

Whose seduction is this? It had certainly started as his. But out of nowhere, the bold woman decided that she wanted to take over. After undoing her dress, Isabel let it slip down, exposing the fine-boned corset and her bust ready to burst. She was heaven to watch, but he knew from the mischievous gleam in her eye that she was far from finished.

Those creamy curves begged to be caressed. His groin ached to a fevered pitch. How he wanted to bury himself, deep and hard, between those ever so tempting thighs. *Damn it all to hell!*

Nathaniel refused to wait any longer. Regardless of any inkling he had about them being followed, this was about as private as it was going to get. The moment they arrived in Bath, there would be far too many gossiping London folk about.

He pulled Isabel closer, crushing his mouth to hers, reveling in the sweet lingering taste of tea and cakes. Her plump lips took the brunt of his passion, which would only serve a hint as to what lay ahead for her. Nathaniel reached for her hands, planting them on his shoulders, releasing her from his kiss. "Do not move your hands. Am I understood?"

She nodded, and her eyes glossed over with arousal.

Nathaniel lifted each breast out of the confines of her corset and lowered his head to take the peak of one rosy bud into his mouth. He sucked sharply, creating the desired effect of one very stiff nipple before duplicating the attention to the other.

"Sweetheart, I would love for you to lift just a moment, while I undo myself." When she did, he unbuttoned the front of his trousers to release his manhood. More than anything, he wanted to hear her scream out his name, but once again, they were in a situation that required the utmost discretion. He made quick work of lifting her shift out of the way.

Then, urgency drove him to drop her on his waiting cock.

She was so tight and accommodating, it took every ounce of patience not to thrust with speed. Surely, Isabel would kill him, before they could get married, if their encounters continued to be so intense.

She gasped as she tipped her head back, her breasts shifting forward as she arched. *This is what it feels to be in heaven.* She moved with grace and confidence as she rocked against him, elevating him higher. Nathaniel's legs tensed and a bright light blinded him. He peaked into a colossal release.

Nathaniel opened his eyes to find hers burrowing a searing gaze into his soul. He smiled and she did so in return. "You, my love, were incredible."

"Why thank you, My Lord. Though I dare say, the next time around should be in a much more comfortable environment."

Now that is food for thought. He snorted and dug out his handkerchief. When she rose from his lap, he realized he had not taken precautions. *Egads!* Not only would this be the scandal of the century, she could very well be with child as a result of yet another indiscretion. This woman was forever making him forget himself.

Isabel had taken her place next to him, righting herself while he did the same. They were close enough to the city of Bath that if they did not hurry, the doors would open and all the visitors and residents would notice what had transpired during their travel.

Nathaniel's carriage slowed to a trotting pace. Noise now seemed to occupy the space outside of the transport. They had arrived, and within a few hours, her friends would soon join them. They came to a stop. His footman opened the door and waited for them to climb out.

"Your Grace, once we are settled into our suites it would be an honor to escort you to dinner."

"The honor is all mine, My Lord."

Nathaniel tucked her arm into his as they strode to the reception desk, the footman behind them with their trunks. And now began the arduous task of damage control. They both needed a miracle to survive the next few days.

The hotel's servants were quick in getting Nathaniel settled. His valet, Evans, managed to get his things in order and even saw to it that he was not disturbed by tedious troubles. Setting the quill down and blowing a quick breath on the drying ink, he re-read his missive.

Bartholomew, follow these instructions with haste and be sure you keep with the utmost discretion.

It has come to my attention that the Duke of Downsbury holds a particular interest in acquiring the estate of His Lordship, the late Duke of Brimley. I would like you to find out exactly what he is after, his debts, his and his duchess's coming and goings, and anything else that might be of use.

You should also be aware that he may sell information to the daily of a recent dalliance I have had.

Please notify me most urgently should anything appear. A certain respectable lady's reputation is at risk. She has already been through far too much grief for me to allow any further damage to press.

~N.S.

Excellent. Now all he had to do was sit back and wait for society to unleash its wicked forked tongues and wreak havoc. Nathaniel suspected he would not have to wait long before his secretary replied.

"Evans! Come quickly."

His valet attended, standing rigid, his hands clasped in front of him.

"Be sure this is sent to my secretary of affairs, Bartholomew Winters, by express. It is imperative that he receives this tonight."

"Absolutely, sir. I shall see to it right away."

Upon second thought… He rose from the desk. "One more thing. Evans, has there been any movement from Her Grace's room?"

Evans smirked. "None, sir. As far as I know, things have been quiet since her dinner was served in her rooms."

"Very well." So Isabel had opted to dine in her chambers, instead of with him. "Now, be gone."

Lost in deep thought over their indiscretions, Nathaniel pondered what Downsbury stood to gain from blackmailing them. He would have to be in a bad way financially to risk any kind of exposure into his affairs.

Taking a swig of his brandy, Nathaniel returned to the desk to pen another note, this time to his estate. His staff could use the time to prepare the manor for the arrival— hopefully—of a new mistress. However, his mother ran the house with such fluidity that no stone was left unturned.

When he was young, no child was put to bed without her love and affection, and everything was left in a state in which his father would be pleased. The late Marquess of Stoughton had provided a firm hand in assisting his mother. But for the most part, the man had participated in most of the games he and his siblings played.

One day he aspired to be just like his father. Have a slew of children running through the estate, Isabel chasing after them and hosting parties and tea. There was not a dream about his future that did not include her. Isabel inspired him daily to be the very best he could. If it were not for his fond memories of her, he might have not made it back to England in one piece. Yes, soon Her Grace would be the matron of his family's estate.

Nathaniel stood staring aimlessly at the fireplace for what seemed hours, poring over his thoughts of what was in store for them, before deciding to check on Her Ladyship. *How will my family react to her becoming my wife?* Surely his sister wouldn't mind in the least having someone closer to her eighteen years to converse with, but his mother…his mother would take to the vapors once she heard.

She will simply have to make do with my decision.

"Excuse me, miss."

The young lass entered, with a shy blush sweeping across the bridge of her nose. "Your Grace."

"Fetch me my dressing gown, and you may be dismissed. I have no intention of entertaining this evening."

"But, Your Grace—"

"No need to worry, my dear. I'm not an invalid, nor a crone in need of assistance. Enjoy your evening. I assure you, I will be in perfect health tomorrow. I promise."

Without the bat of an eyelash, the young maid retrieved her gown and held it out while Isabel stepped from the cool bath water.

Since their arrival in Bath, she had wondered how long it would be before Nathaniel joined her. Yet the overbearing man had avoided her since escorting her to the elegant suite. Clearly he'd gotten so caught up in other affairs that all thoughts of eating had fled from his mind. What could possibly be keeping him from visiting, tending to her needs? From the moment he had laid her upon the park green and fondled her in the most loving and sinful ways, she had burned for him.

Dampness pooled between her thighs from thinking of those delicious moments. She ached to have him buried deep within her, driving himself in until the only thing she could see were heavenly constellations. Both would be coated in sweat and their release, biding their time until need drove them into an all-consuming lust.

Damnation! Of all the men to drive her to distraction. Only ten months had passed since her husband's death. Their connection was a scandalous one, and no matter how she tried to imagine things working out in the end, the situation would not resolve amiably. She would be excluded from society affairs. A pariah. The hazard was all hers to bear, and it would take her months, maybe years to repair the gossip. Inevitably, their dalliance would have to stop, quickly and quietly.

Isabelle sat by the fire, brushing her hair dry, running through her mind what to tell him. If the determination burning in his eyes at the gardens gave any clue, Nathaniel was a man used to getting his way. He would not simply accept that she was not interested in pursuing this relationship of theirs any further. No, Nathaniel would see to it that he did his duty, marry her to preserve his family's good name.

Good grief, his family. What might they think of this mess?

A gentle knock at the door startled her. Isabel set down her brush and craned her neck to get a view of who would enter. However, from where she was seated, she could only see the sitting room.

"Enter," she called out, pushing away from the vanity and walking toward the entrance to her apartments. "Did you forget something, young lady? I am sure I gave you my utmost assurance that I will be fine for the remainder of the evening."

Isabel adjusted the wrapping of her robe without so much as glancing up, stumbling into a wall of muscle, sweetly-scented and familiar.

"And I am positively convinced you should have someone with you, myself excluded, of course," Nathaniel drawled, making her stomach flutter with excitement and nervousness. He lifted her chin with his fingers until their eyes met. His gaze penetrated her soul, right down to her core, promising so much more than what she had already tasted.

"But excluding you would take all the fun out of this trip, My Lord."

He smirked and stepped back. "I trust you had an agreeable dinner?"

"I did indeed, My Lord."

Nathaniel walked past her toward the fireplace and adjusted the logs to make room for more. "That should keep you cozy until morning. In the meanwhile, your companions are set to arrive later tonight, and I hope to enjoy breakfast with all of you. Now, I suggest you get on to bed, and I will get back to securing our future, Your Ladyship."

He deliberately swatted her derriere. While she did not understand what he meant about securing 'our' future, she had to find a way to talk to him before he made any plans. However, before she could even speak to him about quitting this nonsense, he had left her apartment with but a shred of hope. She had to stop him before they made even bigger fools out of themselves.

When her trip to Bath concluded and she returned to London, she would have to contact Henry's solicitors to confirm if the Duke of Downsbury had any claim to her husband's estate. That would be difficult, as her husband's barrister had a notorious reputation for not wanting to deal with women.

Their last discussion had been via post, to disclose her inheritance—albeit a minimal one, but one that would permit her to continue living in her present residence with pin money to last for several years.

Isabel had never been one for grand expenditures, nor was she lavish in spending her husband's money. Henry had made most of his fortune in gambling and seizing debts. *Is it possible Henry owed Downsbury? Where would I go if Downsbury is found in favor with the justice?*

Isabel quivered, knowing all too well she would be fortunate enough if she ended up in some dowager's house. Though, she had managed to save a small fortune of her pin money so that she could purchase her own cottage—nothing too grand, nor would she keep the full stock of staff.

Perhaps this was the change she needed to move forward. Once she returned to London, she would send out inquiries to see if there were any country homes for purchase and permanently move out of London.

Nathaniel was bound to be cross with her, but she needed to put distance between the two of them if either wanted some semblance of peace.

CHAPTER FOUR

Nathaniel blinked furiously at the stream of sunlight concentrating on his face. His head throbbed from the bottle of brandy he had indulged in. How else was he supposed to keep clear from Isabel until the issue with Downsbury was resolved? All this scandal was ruinous to everyone it touched.

He desired nothing more than to drag her into his suite and make sweet, passionate love to her, over and over until neither of them was conscious. The distance between them killed him.

Nathaniel fumbled with his sheet and promptly covered his head with the blasted thing. Waking up alone in bed was bad enough, but when having numerous dreams of Isabel over the course of the night left him as rigid as granite, there was but one way to resolve the issue.

Before he could even take matters into his own palm, a harsh knock on the door came, followed by footsteps into his bedchamber.

"My Lord, forgive the intrusion. You need to see this right away!" The valet fumbled with a rolled up paper in his hands.

Nathaniel sat up with haste, the sheet falling away, exposing his nudity. He reached out to accept the daily, unfolded it, and groaned at the headline.

Scandal At Vauxhall.

He could not help but read further.

Reliable resources indicate that over the course of last weekend's festivities, Her Grace, Lady I., was found in quite the scandalous and compromising position at the Pleasure Gardens with Lord S. It is speculated whether the affair had been ongoing prior to His Grace's demise. To think his wife would go against all decorum and be so bold. I daresay, ladies, you shall not want your daughters in such company. Keep a close eye on your girls, and prohibit any interaction and affiliation with either of them. Trouble and scandal follow them as second nature, and the season is far from over. Be on your guard.

Nathaniel pinched the bridge of his nose, sucking in a long, deep breath. *How am I ever going to explain this to Isabel, let alone to my associates?* Not that his associates would care. In fact, he would not be surprised if they applauded him for his indiscretion making the front page.

However, the article was another matter entirely. He had hoped to make her his wife before the year was out, but at the rate the gossips ran in London, he would have to procure a special license before the end of the week.

First, he would source out where the information came from and have a letter of apology published in lieu of the damaging post. And then attempt to provide damage control upon his next visit to the House of Lords. He would need to have an explanation regarding the situation. Yet to ascertain how exactly they would react, Nathaniel could not be sure. And to be frank, he could not care less what they had to say on the matter.

"Evans, get my things together and have my coach readied. We leave within the hour." *Bartholomew better have started the investigation. Things are about to get even busier for the poor man.*

"But, My Lord—"

"There are no buts, Evans. It is imperative that we be on our way. I must speak with Her Grace immediately."

Nathaniel stalked toward the washstand without haste and inhaled deeply. *I will succeed, and we will overcome this. Why did they not teach in school how to deal with delivering ill-timed and embarrassing news?* 'Twas a good thing her friends had arrived earlier this morning. He could not bear the thought of leaving her alone until these shenanigans were put to a stop.

Isabel, already dressed and waiting in the morning room of her apartments, reminisced over the last few days. Cecily and Robert would join her soon, but she had enough time to enjoy her first cup of morning tea at her leisure.

In another day or so, she would return to London and begin the stressful, yet mandatory, steps to procure her safety and secure her future. In the end, her title meant nothing to her. She had married the duke at the hands of her parents. And while her papa had been a baron living as a wealthy merchant and spared no expense in pushing her into the elevated circles, nothing about the extravagance had won her over.

What is the point of being happy with pretty baubles and residing in an enormous estate without a husband or children? The only difference was that now she could choose to live alone, against the odds and the world, it seemed.

Nevertheless, the thought of Nathaniel's touch and how he made her feel alive washed over her and settled deep within her soul. There was no point in denying the magic he held over her. Wanted. Sensual. A woman. Since that ill-fated night at Lord and Lady Broxton's ball, the way he held her hand, escorting to the ballroom, he had opened the floodgates that once kept her memories locked away.

Perhaps in another lifetime, she had told herself nightly. He had vowed they would be together again, renewing their love for each other. And in that other lifetime, she would cherish him and be the woman he wanted.

About to pour another cup of tea, Isabel heard heavy footsteps entering her chambers. "What in God's name is going on here? Whoever it is, your manners are—" Isabel spun on her heels and found Nathaniel standing only a few feet away.

"I apologize for the early call, Your Grace, but this simply could not wait." His stance was rigid, his jaw set, and his lips formed a thin line. *The man looks positively grim.*

He passed her the daily, and she read the headline. *Good Lord! And so it begins. Who? How? Why? Downsbury!*

"I will be heading into London for damage control. I think it would be best if Your Grace continued your stay in Bath. I will write to you as soon as things have been resolved."

Her eyes welled up with tears, and her hands shook. The room suddenly did not feel large enough for both of them. "Nathaniel, you cannot mean to handle this situation yourself?"

They were surrounded by madness. Downsbury's determination to tarnish their reputation, all in the name of getting money—or whatever he was owed—would cost them everything. Her husband's gambling had been a wretched waste of time, bringing nothing but heartache and grief into their lives.

More footsteps entered, alerting them that they were no longer alone.

He tipped her chin up. "I promise, Isabel, I will fix this."

Before she could respond, he kissed her hard, passionately, and with the promise of his return. He stormed out the door, not glancing back. The voices of Cecily and Robert Turner pulled her back into reality.

"Isabel?"

"Your Grace."

"Why in the world is there such chaos outside? Is the marquess really leaving?"

"He is." Without disclosing much more, she handed her friend the daily, observing her pale at reading the headline.

"Is it true? Oh, wait, please do not answer that. This is rather all too shocking and exciting all at once."

"Would you be quiet, Cecily, and give me that." Even Robert winced.

"Cecily, how could you say such a thing? Can you not tell how grievous this situation is?" His quizzical gaze returned to Isabel. "Your Grace, how may I be of service? While I am new as a solicitor and have not had the opportunity to develop meaningful contacts, my employer might be able to assist in some damage control, or at least offer some advice on how to proceed."

Though hiring her own solicitor would be perfect, the last thing she desired to do was create a larger problem for Nathaniel to fix. Instead, Isabel sat on the dais, defeated.

"Your offer is too kind, Robert, but I must regretfully decline. The Marquess of Stoughton has offered to investigate. I think it would be best to allow him to continue in his efforts." She heaved a sigh, knowing her next statement would take even more willpower. "I think the best thing I can do is stay here for a few days and then return to London. I completely understand if you remove yourselves from my company during this time of speculation."

"Absolutely not!" Cecily cried and childishly stomped her foot. "After what we have all been through, I will not leave you like this."

Robert's offer had been generous, but if too many people outside of the scandal involved themselves, the likelihood grew for the situation to get further out of control. Robert desperately needed to get Cecily as far away as possible. "Think about it, Robert. If you let her stay here, this could potentially ruin any chance for her to marry well. Then what will you do? Support a sister who is a spinster as a result of being associated with the likes of me?"

The sadness in his eyes was her acknowledgement that he understood and agreed. There was no use in ruining two innocent lives over this foolish behavior by the duke.

"Cecily, Her Grace is correct. If we stay here, what do you think will become of your season? We simply cannot afford any scandals." He returned his attention to Isabel. "Your Grace, I'd like to request a private audience with you."

"Robert, whatever you wish to say, you may do so now. The longer you tarry, the more people will speculate."

"As you wish." He cast a wary glance to his sister then began. "We have known each other a long time now, and while I do not have much to offer, if you came back to London with me, I would make a decent husband. I earn an honest living, and while I do not live extravagantly, I think I could make you happy."

Isabel's heart broke, knowing that she had to reject his offer. She would only give up

her independence for one person, and right now, that person was knee deep in this scandal.

"Robert, please. Not another word. I will not have you waste your life on a mistake I have made on a whim. Besides, you deserve someone who is sincere and loving and respectable. I have no doubt you will find that lady one of these days."

"Very well, Your Grace, I will leave you for now, but my offer will stand. I will stop by the townhouse in a couple of days to check in. We will discuss this more once you have had a moment to recover from your travels."

He bowed then led Cecily out of the room. Isabel's stomach flipped with unease, and she wished for her company to stay along with her. But sometimes the proper thing to do was to let things go. And she would have to do just that when she left London permanently. The coming days would be challenging, and once she set foot in London, life would become even more difficult.

Nathaniel rode hard, not stopping once. By the time he reached his estate, his man of affairs was already there, deep in discussion with an unfamiliar gent and his old university friend Lord Avonlea. *Why would he be here?*

"So nice of you to join us, My Lord. This is Marcus Williamson, a runner from Bow Street, and Lord Avonlea you already know."

"To what do I owe this visit?" Nathaniel reached out to shake Mr. Williamson's hand.

"A pleasure to meet you, My Lord. It would seem we have a bit of a problem. There are rumors of the unsavory kind that the Duke of Downsbury is heavily in gambling debt. There are also whispers that there is a bounty on him, should he not pay by week's end.

"Then, in the middle of my investigation, your man here found me and wanted me to look into a potential extortion case. Lo and behold, it is about the same gent I am working for. I will not lie. I find the accusations of extortion entirely false, yet given the dire straits in which the duke finds himself, we are going to have to find a way to resolve this quickly. Preferably before we find a body floating along the Thames."

Nathaniel's felt his lips twitch at the image. *Hmm…so now Bow Street is involved. And yet, not one word is mentioned about the gossip rags.*

Surprisingly, Avonlea spoke up, and not so unexpectedly, out of turn. "Or my thought is this—protect the Duchess of Brimley and let the cad fight his own battles. If the duke perishes, then it is of his own negligence and irresponsibility."

Avonlea did raise a good point, but he could not publicly agree without sounding unsympathetic. Well, not until this debacle was resolved. If Bow Street Runners were already investigating death threats against the duke, then maybe there was an alternative way to rein him in and leave Isabel out of this.

"Mr. Williamson, I dare say, the gambling hells are usually the first place where gossip of who owes whom becomes public knowledge. Just how much in debt is the duke?"

"My Lord, you know very well that I am not in the position to divulge that information so freely. I can, however, be persuaded…"

Brilliant. On top of a sticky situation, he was dealing with a crooked runner. "I mean no offense, Mr. Williamson, but I think I can use my own resources to get the information. I imagine Downsbury is already paying handsomely, not including your existing wages with the office."

"Do not think for a moment about interfering in my investigation, Lord Thompson. If you so much as stick your nose where it does not belong, I will beat that bloody smirk from your face, and have you incarcerated and declared an accessory to the threats. And for a gent in your position—after the gossip column—that would be considered suspicious and damaging to what remains of your reputation."

Avonlea snorted behind them. He knew all too well that Nathaniel of all people did not respond to intimidations. Not even the Bow Street office would be able to hold him back if he decided to set the record straight with this crooked little bastard.

"What a preposterous threat, Williamson. You honestly think you can take a man of my size and strength, and walk away unscathed? I'm willing to bet fifty guineas you'd lose in under a minute," Nathaniel cautioned the fool.

Cowardly, Mr. Williamson decided to leave and backed away. "This is not over, gentlemen!"

No, it is not. Not by a long shot.

"My Lord, forgive my impertinence, but that did not go very well at all," Bartholomew mumbled.

"I suppose it did not," Nathaniel quipped. "Gentlemen, why don't we go indoors and discuss this further? I could use a drink and a moment to sit down."

The three men walked in the front doors, and there stood his butler, completely unhinged. "Master Thompson, the dowager countess is waiting for you in the parlor. She was adamant that she would not leave until she saw you. She has not stopped barking orders, nor has she ceased in expressing her displeasure with the décor. She keeps going on about an engagement party."

His man of affairs and Avonlea chuckled loudly and offered to wait for him in the library.

"Do not fret, old friend. I happen to like the décor, and I will see to setting her in her place," Nathaniel quipped with a smile.

Good Lord, what could the woman want? He had only been in town for a few minutes, and he had already managed to chase off a Bow Street Runner and now, he must do the same with his meddling mother. Such luck he had. And if he knew her right, she had already read the daily.

Entering the parlor, Nathaniel found his mother pacing to and fro by the window. He slowly crossed the hall and poured himself some port at the sideboard. "Would you care for some, ma'am?"

"Hurumph! You know very well, Nathaniel, I will not drink that. 'Twas what ruined your father, and I will not have the same thing happen to you."

"What are you going on about now, Mother? Father drank in the evening when he played cards with his chums."

"Or when he was with his mistress. You know, with each day that passes, I see more of him in you. For instance,"—she tossed the paper at him and continued her rant—"is that what really happened, or did she convince you to do worse?"

She had heard all right—the most scandalous and butchered version of events.

"No, it did not happen like this. And for the record, I love her. Were it not for her parents passing her off to the Duke of Brimley, she would have been my wife the moment I returned to London." He wandered the room, ignoring the dowager still sitting in his favorite chair, looking regal but possessed. "Yes, we had an indiscretion, and it was completely my fault. Had I just waited until we were married, none of this would have happened."

"Married?" the middle-aged woman croaked.

"Yes, Mother. Married."

"That trollop's husband has not even been dead cold in the ground for a year, and you are going to marry her? I will not stand for it. Your sister's reputation depends on you doing the honorable thing now. Discard any notion of marrying *her* this instant. Find yourself a respectable bride, or I will."

"No." Nathaniel clenched his fists to keep himself from throwing a nearby object.

"No? You are mad, Nathaniel!" the crone shrieked.

"I am not, and I will not tolerate you throwing more insults my way. If you are quite done, please see yourself out. Do not make any attempt to create more havoc than what already exists, or you can be sure I will make you pay."

"You would make your only sister pay for your sins? You tread on dangerous ground, Nathaniel. You may be the Marquess of Stoughton and can flaunt your power and prowess around, but I assure you, this is not the last of this conversation."

He dragged his hands through his hair and held his breath for a few moments. *Just what is it with everyone today, wanting to have the last word with me?* He crossed the room before glancing back. "I trust you can see yourself out."

Storming down the hall, he entered the library, slamming the door behind him. He took a seat across from both men by the fireplace and stared into the flames. "Well, gentlemen, it would appear that we will have to take things into our own hands. Though, I am surprised by your presence here, Avonlea. What is amiss?"

"Life has been dreadfully boring abroad, not to mention a certain widow keeps following me around. I have no desire to get wrapped up with money-grubbing widows. If I wanted a fancy lady who would cost me a pretty penny, I would much rather find the most extravagant courtesan to spend my money on and still leave with my cock attached."

Ah! There is that randy sense of humor that I knew of back in Oxford. "You don't say. Well now that you are back, you should check out Madame Martine's establishment. I hear they are quite reputable, and if I am not mistaken, you will probably see an old chap or two from school. All hiding from the doting mothers at the season's balls."

"No doubt."

"So, what is first on the agenda?" Avonlea asked, his fingers tapping the arm of his chair.

"Finding out how much the duke owes, and whatever else we can find out. Bartholomew, I would like you to dig into the family's history, and the comings and goings of him and his wife. There could be more trouble at the home front. Something we could use against him. Avonlea and I will visit White's and Barnaby's this evening. I

would not mind finding out just how much in trouble the cad is in." He grinned. *Maybe even torment the bastard a bit…*

CHAPTER FIVE

Nathaniel walked into White's expecting a full house, but found only every other table filled. None of the men were recognizable, until one called out to him from a side room.

"Lord Thompson! We were just discussing you," Lord Ashbrooke announced. "Come and have a drink with us, so you may settle a slight disagreement."

Nathaniel winced yet accepted the man's invitation, coming to the instantaneous realization that other members from the House of Lords would be present and would no doubt question the column in the post.

Of all the times for them to call me over. He was filled with trepidation, but the quicker he finished with them, the faster he could inquire into the books and bets previously made against Brimley and Downsbury. He did not doubt the bets were vastly amusing, though he remained troubled by what he might find in there about his dowager duchess.

He entered the private area with skepticism and sat next to Ashbrooke. "So what kind of clash of opinions are you gents having this evening?"

The Earl of Sheffield coughed hoarsely, pausing to take a swig of his port. "If you would be kind enough to declare what the daily has posted is nothing more than an idle rumor, then you are free to carry on about your evening."

"Gentlemen, while I do not feel the need to justify everything I do, what I will say is what the daily posted is not entirely true. But it is not false either. Yes, I was with Her Grace that afternoon. Nevertheless, I fail to understand how it is anyone's business." "Do you mean to say the two of you were caught alone, in a compromising situation? Or was this a planned outing blown out of proportion by a jealous suitor or female competition?"

Nathaniel shook his head in disbelief. "The outing was planned, and I hardly see what business that is of Parliament's."

Ashbrooke slammed his fist down. "There you have it, men! The dowager duchess did not wait a full year. Fifty guineas say, before the year is out, she will be a mistress."

What in damnation…"Just hold on a moment there, Ashbrooke." Nathaniel vibrated and strained against the natural instinct to lunge at the Earl and beat him senseless. He had expected this behavior and nothing more, yet the mention of Isabel reducing herself to someone's mistress boiled his blood.

He gripped the table and rose. "I'll not sit here and be a party to such nonsense. Her Grace will serve as no one's mistress, and she deserves far more respect than you are granting her. If there is more talk of anyone expressing an interest in pursuing her, consider this a warning. I will call out anyone who dares touch what is mine. Her Grace will be my marchioness. Mine. Am I understood?"

"Settle down, Thompson. I speak on behalf of everyone here when I say that no one will pursue her. Nevertheless, she is marred by her husband's scandal. He owed a great deal to the Duke of Downsbury, especially the deed to his country estate.

"The greater issue is that Brimley is rumored to have fathered the child that the Duchess of Downsbury now carries. The books are betting how long before Downsbury sends his wife into the country and puts the child up in an orphanage. Others say it is only a matter of time before she is shipped off to the continent."

Christ. There has to be more to this story than what Ashbrooke is saying. "Is there anything else I should know about Downsbury's troubles, gentlemen?"

"Well, other than your mother confiding in my wife that you and Lady Eloise Morton will be married by year's end? I should tell you, several hundred pounds have already been placed in favor of the match. She is quite fetching, too, do you not think?"

Nathaniel pinched the bridge of his nose. "Of course my mother would feed such nonsense to the wolves…No offense, Ashbrooke."

The Earl raised his hands and chuckled heartily. "I'll be the first to admit my wife is dedicated to the pursuit of gossip. More often than not, finding herself in more trouble than necessary."

"Gents, this has been a most enlightening discussion, but I must be going. I have other engagements requiring my immediate attention."

Nathaniel walked away annoyed, yet amused, at how easily he came across the information he required. Though some of the bets made were not in the least bit pleasant, he enjoyed that the men could at least discuss them with some civility. However, none of the talk did anything to reduce his anger. He could not shake the disgust of the men betting on Isabel becoming someone's mistress. If one thing was certain, the only mistress she would be was over Stoughton Manor and his children.

Isabel cocked her head to the side, observing the exasperated expression on her butler's face. She had only been home for an hour when callers began showing up. With each visitor, he politely turned away the lords and ladies calling. They had all read the gossip columns, and she could only imagine the bets running around in White's about who would bed her next.

Henry must be turning in his grave. Not only had she succeeded in further disgracing his family name, but she had managed to embroil and embarrass another prominent household in the process.

"What is it this time, Edmonds?"

"I have come to give you an accounting of the visitors thus far—that is, if you are ready, Your Grace?"

She chuckled. "Do not just stand there, go on."

"Lord and Lady Broxton arrived inquiring about your health. Mr. and Miss Turner also stopped by, as did Lords Avery, Banham, and Stokes. Oh, yes, a Lady Eloise Morton also came around. She was quite put out when I made it clear she would not be received."

Edmonds bowed. "Is there anything I can get you, Your Grace?"

"That will be all, Edmonds."

He bowed and quickly left her in peace.

Good grief. Overnight, her life had turned into a tragedy. Bad decisions, lustful temptations, and the uncanny habit of landing herself in a world of trouble seemed to be her calling in life. Not only was she doomed to be kicked out of her estate, she would not be entirely surprised if she acquired offers to become a mistress to some of the peerage. She sighed. *Why does the name Eloise sound so familiar? Ah! Yes, that damned woman the dowager countess desires her son to marry.*

Her housekeeper barreled into the room, huffing and puffing, vibrating with what seemed to be excitement. The floor boards shook, and her silver brush rattled on its mirrored tray. "Your Grace, he is here!" She wrung her hands and stood on her toes, excitement plastered all over her face.

"Who is here?"

"The marquess. Who else would come? He is looking even more dapper than usual, too."

"I will be right down. Please make sure Edmonds sees to his comfort until I have made myself right." Her heart fluttered. But the fact that her hair was still disheveled from removing her hat, and the fatigue of stress had irritated her usually clear complexion annoyed her so. She changed into comfortable satin slippers, pinched her cheeks until they were rosy, tucked away a few loose strands of hair, and prepared herself.

The last few days had been awkward and lonely, not being able to speak with him. During these emotional times, she wondered just how sincere and committed he was to her cause. Alone, in a time where most people would have thrived on company, the solitude provided her with a much-needed pause from life. Yet, she had missed Nathaniel terribly.

Once upon a time, she had worshipped the ground he walked on, envied his ability to experience freedom away from this pretentious society. And while serving the war office was no pleasant adventure, he had still managed to see the world and experience it very differently. While he never married, she suspected he had thwarted life-threatening situations and did what he must for his country, no matter how insidious the actions may be perceived by a lady.

In the end, she had come to terms with and accepted the cards they were dealt. She went on to marry a philanderer, who wound up beaten at his own game. And Nathaniel now pursued her once again, much to her chagrin.

"To what do I owe this pleasure, My Lord?" she said, walking downstairs. *I wonder what news he brings. The debt is probably larger than what I originally expected.* "I honestly did not think you would return, as I have not received any word from you in well over a week." She studied Nathaniel as he stood guard by the window, rigid and watching the driveway.

He turned to face her, leaning against the sill. "I have come to take you for a drive so that we can discuss my findings and come to an understanding about a few things."

"Honestly, Nathaniel, I am tired. I have only just arrived, and I am in no mood to argue nor contemplate a fantasy future with you, let alone go for a drive. Can we talk about such things here?"

His face reddened. "Like hell!" He spun on his heels and strode toward her, closing the space between them in seconds. He reached for her wrist, pulling her toward him.

Isabel winced in pain and pounded his chest. "Nathaniel, you brute. That hurt."

"Now, as I was saying, come along. My driver is waiting for us."

"Good grief! Have you gone mad, Nathaniel? I am exhausted. Quite frankly, had I known you would be so bull-headed, I would have had Edmonds decline your entrance, too!"

He stared at her blankly before tossing her over his shoulder like she was a common tavern wench. Too appalled to even scream, Isabel folded against him. It wasn't as if she could run from him. He would only find her and repeat his barbaric actions.

Uneasiness surged through her every nerve ending, from head to toe. He walked past Edmonds and the housekeeper, who both only smiled. *They better not have had a hand in this.* And out the door they went, garnering the attention of the footmen and the drivers of other carriages passing. *Just what exactly did the marquess discover that requires such privacy?*

Nathaniel closed the carriage and rapped on the window for the driver to move. *Why the hell does she feel so unsafe with me? Doesn't she think I can keep her safe?*

For the life of him, he could not understand what caused this sudden shift in the dowager duchess's behavior. She grumbled the entire time, and even called him a barbarian. He shifted so his knee brushed against her skirt, close enough that he could feel the heat from her on this rainy and dreary morning.

"What has you on edge, darling? Have I ever given you any reason to think I would harm you?"

She frowned. "No, but we should not be doing this, Nathaniel. Haven't you had enough of this scandal?"

"And what exactly are we doing, love? We are only going for a ride through Hyde Park. There is nothing scandalous about that...well, other than the way I carried you out of your house." *And the next time I do that, I will be tossing you into our marriage bed.*

"No, but there is a matter of those unsavory rumors...about the two of us. Have you even managed to stop into the House of Lords to explain your behavior?"

Nathaniel groaned. He owed an explanation to no one. Not to Parliament, his mother, Avonlea, or the *haute ton*. He burned to have her again, but he would only take her to his bed once they were married and out of public scrutiny. In the end, they would only have to answer to the good Lord for their sins, though they had less to answer for than her late husband.

"My dear, when I said I would see you soon, I certainly meant it. I did not wish to inflict any unnecessary stress until I had all my information straight. Would you like to hear what I have learned?"

She immediately faced him and paled. *The poor, dear woman is probably horrified enough that her husband's sordid affairs are common knowledge.*

She nodded. "Well? Don't keep me waiting, Nathaniel."

"It would appear that while your husband was engaged in pleasurable activities with Downsbury's wife, he, too, was being duped. It is rumored that she also strung along Lord Wycliffe. The chaps at White's and several other establishments have heard through their wives that she has also been out of sight.

"The last time anyone has seen her was at a ball a few weeks back when one of the ladies commented on her weight gain. When asked when the child was due, she left the ball at once, in a rage. It is unsure if she is truly with child. And even then, whose child is she carrying?"

She gasped, though the twinkle in her eye denoted amusement.

"I am not even close to being done. Your late husband also lost a sizeable fortune to Downsbury. But not nearly enough that you would need to consolidate your husband's holdings. He apparently lost the deed to your country estate. With your permission, of course, I could have my man of affairs act in your stead to meet with Henry's solicitor and see what other debts might be outstanding?"

She sat back, shooting a wary glance. "You would do that for me? Even after all the trouble you have gone through to get this much information?"

Nathaniel pulled her into a tight embrace. *I would do anything for her. Why would she question my honor now?* "My dear, I would cross pirate-infested seas, battle the fiercest of warriors in the East, and walk over hot coals if it meant I could be with you. When we get to the bottom of this, Isabel, it is my deepest wish to right the wrongs of our past. No matter who objects, I will not settle for less than you."

"Are you sure, Nathaniel? This is too risky."

"My dear, risky was our liaison in the gardens. What was said on the matter will soon be nothing but a shadow. Considering the Duchess of Downsbury will have her own scandal posted soon, I would not give it a second thought."

The carriage came to a halt. Some shouting ensued, and he shushed her. *Who the hell is stopping our carriage to engage in a very public argument?*

"I desire to speak to my son, this instant!"

Nathaniel gave her grace a displeased frown. "I am truly sorry, in advance, for anything that comes out of that woman's mouth."

"Do not say that, Nathaniel. She is your mother!"

"She is my mother all right, and as insane as they come. I suppose we should get this over with." He hated being put on the spot and even though they were in public, his dear mother would not hold back her wicked tongue. Was it any wonder that she drove his father to drink? He patted Isabel's leg and knocked on the window, acknowledging he was stepping out.

The moment the door opened, his mother already stood there, preventing his exit. She pushed her way in and glanced over to where Isabel sat quietly, wide-eyed with shock. He looked behind to see his sister, mouth gaping wide and speechless by their mother's forwardness.

"My Lady, it is highly improper to bully yourself into one's carriage," Nathaniel growled.

The countess snorted. "I will do as I wish, and you will not say another word until I am finished." Pointing her wiry finger at Isabel, she continued her berating, "You...you...miserable excuse for a duchess! You will never have him for a husband, and that you can be sure of!"

"Enough!" Nathaniel barked loud enough that all of Hyde Park could have heard. He gritted his teeth, barely able to stand another syllable from the intolerable woman. No one had the right to talk to Isabel that way, no matter their station. "Get out, Mother, before I

toss you out. If you do not cease this nonsense immediately, I will have my sister removed from your care, and then we will see what you have to say." "You would not dare," his mother scowled.

"I would."

Without so much as another word, the dowager countess exited the carriage.

Relief washed over him. "We are ready. Drive on." He sat back and released a heavy breath. "Well, I for one am glad that is over. You have my humblest apologies, Isabel. Once the old bat gets started, she tends to carry on."

Isabel smiled as she rested her head on the window closest to her and closed her eyes. It had not occurred to him how tired she might be. And to think, he had carried her out of the house as if he was some ancient Celt, stealing himself a wife.

Good Lord, he had behaved so barbarically. He had not shown her an ounce of consideration. Next time, he would plan them a picnic with the help of her staff.

Her butler rubbed the back of his neck and pressed his lips together.

"Edmonds, what is the matter with you? You look as if you have been caught doing something you should not have. Out with it."

He blew out a long breath. "Well, Your Grace, it would appear that Lady Broxton has arrived again, and I…permitted her entry."

Isabel winced. *Will this day not end?* "Please, Edmonds, no more visitors after Lady Broxton leaves. I do not feel very well. I am beyond exhausted, and I really need the time to think everything over."

She took a step forward and swayed on her feet. The corridor would not stop moving. Her head spun, and gravity pulled her forward. Her vision clouded, and she gasped for air.

"Your Grace!" Hands came to her aid, steadying her.

"I am fine. I am fine." She swatted Edmonds's hands away. "As I said a moment ago, I am quite exhausted."

Lady Broxton ran out of the parlor. "Your Grace, let me assist you to the dais. I can imagine how exhausted you must be, so I will not keep you for long." Her guest took her by the elbow, leading her into the room and seating her in her favorite seat by the fireplace.

"Thank you for your assistance, Lady Broxton. My curiosity is piqued, and I am dying to know why you are here a second time today. Surely whatever news you bring could have waited a few more days?"

"I am truly sorry for the inconvenience, Your Grace, but sadly, it could not. There really wasn't enough time. The invitations had gone out while Your Grace was out of town, and our garden party is tomorrow. I came with haste to invite you, that is, if you are feeling well enough?"

"Thank you for the invitation, Lady Broxton. If I am well enough, you can rest assured I will attend. Although, I am sure you are aware that my attending such an event before my year of mourning is over might be cause for even more scandal."

"Pish, posh. All of London, one way or another, is involved in their own scandal. And if you are not aware of it already, Her Grace, the Duchess of Downsbury, is rumored to be with child. Though, secretly, we all know it is not the duke's, either." She winked.

Isabel's head pounded relentlessly while her guest went on and on. Finally, she coughed and rose from her seat. "Lady Broxton, while I would love to converse some more, I really must lie down. I am not sure if it was a lack of rest, or perhaps something I ate while at Bath. I have to ask you to leave."

"Of course, Your Grace. Do be seated, and I will see myself out. Thank you for your time."

Once the front door closed, Isabel collapsed into her chair. *I just need to close my eyes for a bit. I am going to be all right…*

CHAPTER SIX

Isabel squinted as morning light flooded her bedchamber, illuminating every corner and bouncing off her looking glass on the dressing table. *Good Lord! I feel as if I have slept for a century.*

Stiff, parched and light-headed, she rang for assistance. She all but managed to slide out of bed and wrap herself in her silk robe when her housekeeper came barreling in. She loved the woman dearly, and praised her for her efficiency, but every time she ran, the bloody floorboards shook.

"Your Grace, you are awake!"

"Of course I am. Why wouldn't I be?"

The housekeeper only started at her with wide eyes, lips pursed.

"Oh, never you mind. I have Lady Broxton's garden party that I must get ready for. I could use some tea and a bit of toast."

The woman only gawked then curtsied. "Yes, Your Grace. Right away."

Isabel's day was only beginning and something did not feel right. She did not fear facing some of London's notorious wagging tongues today, but she did not relish the fact that she had to sit with them for tea.

Her personal life and misadventures would surely be the main subject. She did not doubt, even for a moment, that the dowager countess had gone to work in attempting to further damage her reputation. And to think, Nathaniel insisted on making her his bride. His mother would certainly have an apoplectic fit.

Nathaniel's threat to remove his sister from their mother's care also gave her pause in how doting of a brother he could be. Both his mother and sister were fortunate that, unlike some other young men around town, he cared very much for his family, no matter what controversial things they had done. *Why, it was only weeks ago that he had heard of what his sister had done after he had left the ball six months ago.*

Isabel giggled, remembering the horror splashed across Lady Balfour's face.

"Good heavens! She actually beat Broxton at vingt-et-un. The wager was set at twenty-five pounds when Lady Thompson realized what she had done. Poor Lord Broxton never had a chance to escape the sound tongue-lashing her mother gave him on propriety."

"Your breakfast is ready, Your Grace."

"Thank you. Could I trouble you to bring me today's edition of the daily?"

Isabel enjoyed the comic relief that came at the expense of foolish young ladies. Nathaniel's sister clearly did not enjoy being confined to the strictest of rules when it came to proper decorum and imagined she was quite the handful at the best of times.

She had overheard the ladies talking one evening regarding why young Miss Thompson had been discharged early from the academy. While the details were sketchy, apparently hitting another young lady with a fan, and then pulling said girl's hair, nearly incited a riot. The antics resulted in candles being knocked over, a small fire being started, and the headmistress losing her only wig to the flames. The child was a magnet for trouble, maybe even more so than she.

Her housekeeper slipped into the room, quietly dropping the news near her tray. The warmth of her tea soothed the dryness in her throat, but the toast was hardly sitting well with her. Isabel scrunched her nose at the aroma. "This smells awful—"

Then as if receiving a blow to her delicate stomach, Isabel fled to the water basin. A cold shivering sweat coated her silk-covered body. Her muscles contracted, and for the first time since her childhood, she succumbed to a wave of nausea. In between heaving, both the butler and the housekeeper rushed in behind her.

"Your Grace—"

"Enough of this nonsense," the butler announced. "I'll fetch the physician myself."

When Isabel finally quit, she slid back under her covers, curling into a ball. *It was only toast.* Never in her life did a crispy piece of bread elicit such a reaction. The sounds of Mrs. Pitts's feet shuffling while cleaning up her dreadful mess washed away with slumber, striking her fancy once again. But before—*heaven forbid*—she was granted any rest, the edge of her bed dipped, and the warmth of her housekeeper's hand rested on her forehead.

"Your Grace, you have not had your monthly yet, have you?"

Isabel blinked, furiously trying to remember when her last cycle passed, and the more she thought, the more she was coming to the same conclusion. *Good God! The day in the carriage—it would have been the only time—*

A single tear fell, followed by an onslaught and a steady stream. *What will Nathaniel do? Will he cut all ties to me? Will he wed Lady Eloise Morton?* She had certainly gone and mucked it up now. But she was certain of one thing. She would never give the child up and no one could make her. Nor would she allow the child to be raised by a woman as self-serving as the dowager countess.

Nathaniel paced the morning room, undecided on what to do first. He had not heard back from his solicitor, nor had he received a response from Isabel. He expected he would have heard from her by now, but his instincts were beginning to confirm his earlier suspicions of someone in Isabel's household keeping his letters from her. *But who? And what could they possibly gain from keeping me away from her?*

A carriage pulled up the drive, and his mother, on cue, floated past him. "Ah! Just in time. We pay the servants handsomely, why in heavens are they not outside?" she shouted.

Their butler and two servants rushed to the door, opening it in perfect synchronization as the footman was about to knock.

"Ladies Eliza and Eloise Morton, Your Ladyship!"

Nathaniel blinked and swallowed a lump the size of a brick. Clearly the butler had a sense of humor. *Why on earth are they here? Mother.* Mother and her scheming, and of course, he had already heard the rumors and read the bets in the books at White's. He approached the entrance casually, glaring daggers at the matriarch of the Thompson family.

"Ladies." Nathaniel strained to smile and offer them the courtesy of a simple bow. "We are delighted to receive you. What would be the occasion?"

The elderly Lady Morton disregarded his comment and turned to his mother. "You said things were settled."

He craned his neck to listen in on what the ladies were discussing, but to no avail; the moment they caught him watching, they began whispering. *Will this never end? The last I checked, I was head of this house!* Ignoring the nonsense and the lone Eloise, who now stood down the hall ordering the servants around, Nathaniel rushed out the door.

He needed information, and he needed it now. Once business with his solicitor was clear, he would stop in and visit Isabel. If they would not let her respond, then it was up to him to show everyone that he was not to be trifled with.

Nathaniel had only reached his horse when a willowy shadow blocked his exit. "You know, most people would find your behavior inexcusable. But I find it part of your devilish charm, Lord Thompson."

"Lady Morton, I need you to step out of the way. I have errands that I must take care of."

"I am sure you do, My Lord. However, it would be highly irregular were it known our host ignored us, let alone kicked us out to the curb. In pursuit of a ruined dowager duchess, no less." She stalked toward him like a cat in heat, waiting for the precise moment to pounce.

"I mean no disrespect, My Lady, but I have business with my solicitor." He walked his horse past the arrogant chit, knowing all too well what kind of disaster awaited for him when he returned home.

"Her Ladyship invited us, but many others are expected. It would be terribly foolish for you to leave right before all your guests arrive."

Nathaniel stopped dead in his tracks. *What in the world is she talking about?* His stable master approached and reached for the reins. Nathaniel nodded, allowing him to take the beast back to its stall. "Just exactly how many people did my mother invite?"

She paused and pursed her lips. "Well, I do believe she mentioned some of your available friends from Oxford would be in attendance, as well as the Duke of Downsbury, Lord and Lady Broxton, and a few others."

He cringed as anger mounted in him. *She invited Downsbury! How could she?* The woman was hell bent on forcing him to his knees. Perhaps he should consider retreating to their family's hunting lodge and plan an extended trip to the continent for his mother. He returned to the house, bracing himself for the tension beginning to plague his neck, and only stopped as he pulled his butler aside privately.

"I need you to send word to my solicitor. I would like to meet with him in my library within the hour and not a minute later."

"Yes, My Lord."

Nathaniel shuddered at the thought of what he would do with so many visitors. His limited privacy would impede his efforts to sneak away. Unless he waited for his guests to retire for the evening, but then again, he must do his best to avoid more scandal. Tonight would surely be interesting, and the only thing he looked forward to was keeping an eye on Downsbury.

Isabel's heart sank, and the tears wouldn't cease flowing. Henry's physician confirmed her pregnancy, and in the same breath, he had delivered the strictest of orders she was to rest. Thankfully, he had enough sensibility to not question who the father might be. She did not think she could handle the embarrassment of acknowledging Nathaniel having played a part in her condition.

Not to mention the unfinished business with Downsbury and the family's country estate. As soon as the matter was dealt with, she would leave London permanently and live in the country. Somewhere she could raise the little one in peace and away from money-grubbing dukes.

The thought made her wonder sadly about the status of the Duchess of Downsbury. *If she really is with child, who had fathered the babe? Was it Henry, or another gent of nobility and wealth?* The mere thought of her being shipped off to remain hidden until the child was born, only to have to give it away, made Isabel want to weep.

"Your Grace?"

"Come in."

"Well, now that the worst of it is over, we will need to have some new gowns made up for you and prepare a nursery."

"There will be no need to clear out one of the rooms. I have no intention of remaining in London. Once I have received clearance, the townhouse will be sold, and I have every intention of moving to the country. I have no desire to raise a child in a home that harbors nothing but terrible memories. No. We shall embark on a new life, in a new home."

The housekeeper paled at the news. "Your Grace, but what of the staff?"

"I will not have a need, nor the room, for a full staff in a country cottage. I will offer everyone a handsome compensation for your years of service, but I think it is time I do something for myself. Once I am settled, I will send word to my parents, who, hopefully by then, will have forgiven me for my course of actions."

"Your Grace, while I understand your need to do things on your own, you are not thinking clearly—in your condition, you should not be making drastic decisions," the woman exclaimed.

While she had a point, Isabel simply could not sit idle any longer. Days had passed without any word from Nathaniel, and the pain, mixed with longing, confused her to no end.

Nathaniel's appointment with his solicitor had gone better than expected. Isabel's country estate had been the only casualty of her late husband's idiocy, which meant everything went to her, as he had no heir. Absolutely everything had gone to Isabel, and he doubted she even knew how much his fortune spanned.

Estates on the continent and in Scotland, to investments in the Americas, all monies belonged to her. And for a woman who prided herself on her independence, she was about to become the wealthiest dowager duchess he had ever known.

Such a pity she had to endure the humiliation of her husband's affair, and even their own tryst at Vauxhall. Nothing would ever take away that embarrassment. He had never once considered Isabel a conquest. Yet, he never stopped himself from leading them into compromising situations.

He eased into his seat in the parlor when Downsbury spoke up.

"So, how exactly does one get away with scandalous affairs at the Pleasure Gardens, My Lord? I am vastly amused at how quietly the House of Lords has been handling your indiscretions."

Nathaniel choked on the port he had been sipping and cleared his throat. Everyone from Avonlea, his mother, Eloise and her mother, and the various other guests were silenced.

"Your Grace, while I am not one to listen to what the wagging tongues of London have to say about anything or anyone, I will remind you once again, I do not discuss my personal life. Not in private, nor in public. And I find it particularly rude and inconsiderate of you to even bring up such a discussion before delicate ears.

"That said, I think everyone present would love to know how your lovely duchess is doing. Pray tell, why hasn't she yet graced us with her presence?"

The duke sneered, only regaining his composure when the dowager countess approached Nathaniel from behind and whispered, "What in the devil are you doing?"

"Do sit down, Mother. I am only asking what the entire is room is dying to know."

"My wife is unwell and has decided to rest in the country for a bit."

And there it was. The duchess was surely in confinement, and to keep from further embarrassing himself, he had rushed her off to the country. *How typical.*

"Of course she did," Nathaniel muttered before setting his glass down. "Well, I wish everyone a good evening. I am exhausted and would like to retire before my sensibility escapes me."

Eloise threw herself into his path, blocking his exit once again. "Surely, My Lord, I could entice you with some cheery music."

"I am sorry, Eloise, but I would much rather retire for the evening. Perhaps another time."

On cue, Avonlea retrieved the eager, husband-hunting Miss Morton from his sight. A heavy knock on the front door drew everyone's attention from the parlor. A panicked voice pleaded and begged for entry. Approaching the foyer, his butler barely managed to keep the visitor put.

"What seems to be the issue?"

"The Duke of Downsbury…where is he? I have urgent news!"

"What news?" the duke asked, joining the party in the foyer.

"Her Grace's carriage. There was an accident. Her body has been washed away."

Gasps could be heard from the other room. *Well now, this evening has certainly gotten more interesting.* If he heard right, the duke only snorted. "You are positive her remains could not be found and that she has indeed died?" The messenger nodded furiously.

"Run along now. Thank you for the message."

Nathaniel's butler closed the door behind the boy. The marquess shook his head when the duke ordered everyone into the other room and requested more drinks. The man clearly had no heart, simply dismissing the fact that his wife had died. No grief. No questions asked. *What kind of man went on with life without a moment of introspection?*

Nathaniel could not believe he had just walked on by and did not let the loss of his wife move him one bit. He marched back into the parlor and stood in the entryway. "That's it? That is all you are going to say on your wife's death? Did you slip on your way here and lose half your wits? Your wife is dead, man. Go home and at least put a half decent effort into fooling the public that you are grieving!"

"Why on earth would I do that? Her Ladyship and I have much to discuss." And it was the sinister smile that the duke gave Nathaniel's sister that threw him over the edge for the final time.

"You had best set aside any notion of making her your next duchess. I will not allow it!"

"And you are in no position to make demands. The girl isn't your charge. And I am quite sure your mother will have no objections to the match, will you, Eleanor?"

His mother smiled and nodded to the duke, and his sister swooned right into the arms of Avonlea. This night had gone from terrible to a living, breathing nightmare. *I'll kill him if it's the last thing I do!*

CHAPTER SEVEN

Nathaniel's sister bounded down from the terrace steps and threw herself into his arms. Tears stained her face, and she trembled beneath his embrace. "Nathaniel, you cannot allow Mother to marry me off to that unfeeling, cold toad! His poor wife! And he could not even be bothered to leave and verify it was true."

"I know, darling. I shall see what I can do to prevent it from going any further. Now run along inside and do try to stay out of sight. The less Mama and Downsbury see you, the less distraction you will pose."

Anger boiled to a fevered pitch, forever sealing Downsbury's fate. Nathaniel would call him out just as soon as his guests had departed. And his mother had also secured a permanent holiday to the continent.

Nathaniel struggled to understand what the duke was up to.

Then there was the matter of Isabel's country estate. Downsbury would not stop until he had it, and from the news his solicitor delivered yesterday, Downsbury was indeed heavily in debt. Perhaps that is why he had announced inconspicuously in the parlor his intention for Emily's hand in marriage.

Her dowry was substantial and more than enough to lure any greedy man. The only unfortunate thing was that she was an impertinent brat, and for many reasons he had been grateful that she had not been married off as soon as some of the other young ladies from the academy she attended.

He had to find a way to end this lunacy. *But how?* The only way out for Downsbury was a duel or debtor's prison. The thought of the duke being locked away at Newgate was enticing, though Nathaniel doubted he would end up there. As sneaky as the bastard was, he would probably flee the country if he got wind of such a deal.

But then again, maybe that was the angle the duke operated on. Take what he could from Isabel, marry Nathaniel's sister, and then flee the country. Once the cad was gone and out of sight, though, what would he do with Emily? Leave her discarded in the streets of Venice or Paris? *Good Lord!* His imagination ran wilder with each passing moment.

A duel it is.

The next morning, Nathaniel fought a yawn as the excitement from the night before left him restless and pacing the grounds until now. The servants bustled about and his mother's scolding voice could be heard in the distance.

A sigh escaped his lips when Avonlea approached. "Dare I ask what has her in such a foul mood this early?"

"Could not sleep, I see? She is perturbed by the fact that you could not be found in your quarters this morning. She has got the Mortons all in a dither as she remarked you might have gone to see *the whore* again."

Nathaniel lost his breath and winced at the label. He punched Avonlea in the face and grabbed him by his lapels. "Do not ever in my presence use that word to describe the future marchioness of this manor! Am I understood?"

"Get a grip on yourself, man. I was only repeating what your doting mother said, you dolt!"

He released Avonlea, brushing his jacket where hands were imprinted. "Apologies.

But if I hear Isabel referred to as that once more, I just may have to kill someone." His friend chuckled at his admission, though he did not seem to think it funny. Another yawn escaped while he stretched his tense muscles. He needed sleep, but he also desired to gain some hold over Downsbury. "I have a proposition, Avonlea. If you are ready for your day to start, I would like to go and make some acquisitions. Without them, I do not think I will stand a chance in ridding Downsbury of his ridiculous notion of marrying my sister."

"If this is your way of asking me for aid, you should know subtlety is not your forte. I will be glad to assist in any manner that I may, but do you not think you are being rather hasty? Besides, that bratty sister of yours has just received the shock of her life. Do you think she might start acting like a lady?"

Nathaniel snorted. "Not in the least, but it might stop her from doing foolish things like winning a public game of whist with Broxton."

Isabel jumped out of her skin when she heard the pounding at her door. *Please don't let it be Downsbury. I cannot deal with him right now.* She descended the stairs to find Edmonds giving entry to a gentleman.

"Your Grace, this would be Mr. Smith. He is Lord Thompson's solicitor."

"A pleasure to meet you, sir. Let us speak in the morning room. Edmonds, see that some tea is brought in please."

The solicitor followed closely behind, only stopping when shown where to sit. He must have been sent by Nathaniel. His arrival meant things were ready to move along, though she would have much rather had Nathaniel present for this discussion.

"Your Grace, I am so glad I had the opportunity to work on your behalf. Your late husband would not have approved, but I am thrilled, nonetheless. Nathaniel wished to be present, but he is otherwise occupied with a house full of unexpected guests. He entrusted me to speak with you."

"Go on."

"The late Duke of Brimley, as far as I could find and verify with his own solicitor, only owes the deed to his ancestral country estate. I have also been advised that considering the Duke of Downsbury is too in an abundance of debt, all of his holdings have been acquired to pay off the remainder. It is my understanding that a portion of any monies left over will be forwarded to an orphanage in memory of the Duchess of Downsbury's death."

"Oh!" Shock of the news made her shudder. *How could she have died? She was with child!* Isabel shuffled to the edge of her seat, struggling to find words of sympathy. She pressed her hands against her belly.

"Don't despair, Your Grace. From what we know, her carriage careened down a hill during some horrible weather. The carriage ended up in a swelling river, twisted and smashed. She would have succumbed fairly quickly to the frigid temperatures, if she did not break her neck first."

His last words made her cringe. The poor dear had been forced to leave her menacing husband, and while Isabel did not condone the duchess's adulterous actions, she could not bear the thought of what it must have felt like to be exiled in such a manner.

Contemplations of her own predicament made her wonder just how safe she was in her newly independent ways. While she had given much thought to what it would mean to live alone in the country, how would her actions impact the life her son or daughter would have?

Isabel did not know what hit her when tears rolled furiously down her cheeks. She wanted Nathaniel. She felt helpless and alone. And why on heaven's earth was she crying? Her emotions ran high and low, and she despised not having any control over them.

The solicitor stood and walked over to where she sat on the dais. "There, there, Your Grace. Lord Thompson has assured me that all will be fine once this matter of Downsbury is completed. He also asked I deliver this note to you." He slid the vellum script into her hand and bowed his head. "I must be going now, but please feel free to send for me if you are in need of anything else. No matter the measure, I will do what I can to assist you."

Isabel sniffled, keeping the tears back. "I am most grateful for your kindness, sir."

Nodding to Edmonds, she watched as her butler escorted the man out of the room, leaving her alone with her thoughts, worries, and wild imagination. Nathaniel's solicitor had revealed some perplexing and disconcerting news about the duke's financial straits. She did not care if the country estate was lost to him—in the end, Downsbury would never see an ounce of the money he needed.

Who was this mysterious person who had acquired and paid off the debt? There were so many questions and not enough time to pursue them. Her first order of business would be to look into which way to travel first.

Nathaniel and Avonlea sat with Lord Broxton and several others in the gaming room at Almack's, gambling and discussing the latest bets placed at White's. While Broxton's wife meandered about, giggling and gossiping with the other ladies, he watched the endless procession of young ladies and randy gents dance away their evening merrily.

Then, the shrieking of women had all the men rushing out into the main ballroom. Gentlemen shouted, and out of the corner of his eye, Nathaniel carefully followed the swaggering, stumbling, lean shadow that belonged to Downsbury, who shouted obscenities at anyone blocking his path.

"Where is he? Thompson! Show yourself, you bastard!" he bellowed.

Nathaniel approached cautiously, nodding to the footmen who flanked him, ready to toss the duke to the curb. "I have it, gentlemen. Please see to the needs of the ladies who are distraught." He addressed Downsbury. "You have found me, you drunk, now what do you want?"

"Why did you do it? I have had enough of your interference!" the duke sputtered.

Ah. So he has just found out. Good. Challenge me, you fool.

Downsbury stepped forward but tripped over the leg of chair, landing face first into the game table. Cards scattered about and glasses shattered into a million shards on the floor. Avonlea and Broxton now flanked him, pulling him to his feet.

"Honestly, Richard, you need to stop. It is bad enough you tarnished your own reputation with your debt, and I pity the humiliation you faced with your wife becoming pregnant by another man, but what I will not tolerate is you pushing your bad fortune onto my future marchioness, nor onto my sister. What I did was to ensure your place was kept at the furthest possible distance from my family."

The duke snorted and pushed the men away from him. "I will not pay you a pence back. You will never get it out of me."

"Ah, but Your Grace, that is where you are wrong. Your debt has been paid, and all the notes and deeds to your various estates and businesses have already been transferred in my name. You are penniless. The only thing saving you is the donation made in your name to the local orphanage in memory of your wife."

Downsbury paled and roared, "I challenge you at first light, you worthless excuse for a peer. Your family is ruined. And when you lose our duel, and you have breathed your last breath, I will take your sister and her dowry. No one will find us."

Nathaniel's hair rose on the back of his neck. *Why can't I just do him the favor now?* "First light it is. Avonlea, see that he is tossed out."

Nathaniel exhaled a long and controlled breath. Isabel would kill him, and never mind what his overbearing mother and sister would say. But Downsbury was finished one way or another.

Isabel wrapped her arms around him, refusing to release him.

"Settle down, sweeting. I will take care of the duke. All you need to do is remain calm."

Pfft. Stay calm. How could anyone in their right mind stay calm? She was with child—illegitimately at that—and he did not know about the pregnancy. He was leaving for a duel, and Henry's solicitor was due to arrive with the details of her settlement.

"Nathaniel, please," she pleaded. "Do not do this! I will leave if I must, but I will not let you risk your reputation in the House of Lords over his issues with my husband's indiscretions."

"Isabel, it is the least thing I could do. Besides, once this is over I will procure us a special license, we will have a private ceremony, and live out the rest of our days as it once had been intended."

The man is mad. He departed with a swift bow, leaving her a mess in the worst way. *How could he?* The infernal marquess would stoop to a new low and possibly kill a man. Isabel began to sway on her feet, all this foolishness, her nerves. It was too much to take in.

"Your Grace—"

Isabel quivered head to toe as her eyesight washed away and all her weight came crashing down beneath her.

"Gentlemen, please have your seconds in place and take your positions."

Nathaniel inhaled before turning around. No matter how this morning ended, Isabel would be his now and forever, and not even his family could tear them apart.

Fear and determination were the only things keeping his head afloat.

About to turn, he heard one shot go off then a second. Nathaniel barely raised his own pistol before Avonlea stepped between the two men.

"Enough," he shouted, drawing the attention of passersby. A small, curious crowd moved closer. "Lord Thompson, you're injured!"

That was when Nathaniel noticed the pain radiating in his shoulder. *Hell.* Isabel would surely be with him once she saw he was injured. Lucky enough, his townhouse was not far from Hyde Park, and he could change. "I will be fine. To hell with this interruption! Downsbury called for this duel, now let us finish this blasted thing. I haven't got all morning!" he roared.

"The duel has been called off by His Grace. When he misfired, I approached him, and that is when he dropped his firearm and took off with his second. Why in the world would he abandon the duel and ruin whatever honor he had left? He will never be able to show his face about town any time soon." Avonlea adjusted his cravat then patted Nathaniel on the back. "I will only be a moment. Let me see what is keeping your driver so long."

No, the duke would not return. He had lost all credibility now, and if he thought for even the briefest of moments that he would gain Emily's dowry, he was wrong. Now that the debacle was over with, he had run the bastard out of London, hopefully for good. But now, Nathaniel had more property than he cared to own, and quite frankly, did not have the time to manage it. He would have to see about selling those newly acquired assets.

He shrugged to release the built up tension in his shoulders and winced.

"My Lord, I can tend to your wounds back at your house, or would you prefer to summon your own physician?" the surgeon asked, while examining his shoulder briefly.

"I would rather we did not have it looked at. What I need is to wash up, pack the wound, change, and check in on Her Grace."

"My Lord, if your wound is not thoroughly flushed, it could fester. It needs to be attended to with expediency."

Avonlea approached and stared ice-cold daggers. The look sent a shiver down Nathaniel's spine. Avonlea could intimidate a lion if required, and truth be told, he envied the man's size, but he would never admit to it. "Do not be a fool, Thompson! You are in need of medical assistance, and that is that. I will ride with you, as I have already summoned for your carriage. He will meet us at your townhouse."

Nathaniel growled. *How can everyone fret at a time like this, when I have so much to do?* White's would be in an uproar over Downsbury backing out, and that was one sight he looked forward to. He followed Avonlea into his waiting carriage.

The door closed behind him, and the two gents sat in silence briefly.

"Thompson, I am not going to pretend that I understand the sort of madness that leads a man to duel a duke over a dowager's property. I will, however, give a word of advice. If you intend to do the honorable thing, do it soon. I will assist where I can, but your mother is making a muddle of things."

"I am sure by now, Avonlea, you know all too well that I do not back down after my mind is made up. Isabel is my match in every way. And while my eagerness to reacquaint with her made a mess of things, I plan to make her my wife. And the sooner the better. I would cart her to Gretna Green tonight if it meant I could have her now."

His friend sat there stoically, smiling as if he were a cat that swallowed a mouse.

"What is so amusing, Avonlea?"

"Nothing. Well, other than the fact that I am remembering what you said our last day at Oxford."

How could he ever forget the day he denounced marriage. How it was only meant for—Ancient history did not matter now.

The carriage came to a halt and the footman opened the door. He stepped out with Avonlea behind him and entered his manor, only to find his servants rushing about. Orders were being shouted and bonnets were strewn about in the main hall. *For heaven's sake, what in damnation is going on?*

Nathaniel and Avonlea slipped further into the hall when all became clear. *Of all the times the dreadful woman had to stop by, she chooses now.*

"Benson!" his friend shouted, drawing not only his physician's attention but his mother's and sister's as well. Pressure built up behind Nathaniel's eyes.

"Nathaniel!" both women squawked. "You're injured!"

Benson and Avonlea closed the space between them. "Benson, I will join you and Thompson upstairs. Ladies, I do believe we have everything under control. Lady Thompson, you are looking lovelier as each day passes. Miss Thompson," he bowed.

"How is it that I have not seen you this season?" Avonlea declared.

Nathaniel rolled his eyes heavenward. "Come along, Benson, I am sure you do not have all day, and I have much to do myself."

All three gentlemen ascended the stairs to his bedroom. Nathaniel tossed his jacket on a nearby chair and sat at the edge of his bed, stripping out of his shirt. The wound looked worse than it felt. The flesh was torn and the blood surrounding the gash had begun to dry. But the only thing weighing heavily on his mind was finalizing the necessary arrangements.

"This should not take too long, but I wager you will need to rest."

"Rest is for the dead, Benson. Get the bullet out, sew me up, and name your price. I have to leave before the Archbishop finishes his appointments today."

"What the hell would you be needing to see the Archbishop for, Thompson?" Avonlea queried.

"You know why, or have you wasted too many of your nights in more than one tankard?"

He tried to continue speaking, but the pain blinded him and stole the very words from his mouth.

"Listen, Thompson, sit tight, and I will see what I can do."

Nathaniel patiently waited for the doctor to finish pulling through the last stitch and bandage up the area. "There. Now be sure to get some rest, My Lord."

He went to stand up, but the room spun and threw him off balance. Evidently, he had miscalculated his own tolerance for pain and loss of blood. Faint and woozy, Nathaniel laid back and closed his eyes. *I only need a few minutes.*

Isabel opened her eyes to find herself in her bed alone, no one in sight, and with a fearsome headache. Her last recollection was that of Nathaniel leaving her for a duel. He had promised he would be back and swore nothing would happen to him, yet a sinking feeling in the pit of her belly told her otherwise.

Something had gone amiss, and she did not know what. Now if only she could summon the strength to see what news might have arrived after his departure.

She stepped off the platform and tiptoed across the floor in search of her slippers.

She slid them on, and as she was about to leave her room, the housekeeper caught her.

"Your Grace, you shouldn't be out of bed. The physician said in your condition, you need every ounce of rest you can manage. Not to mention, you needn't burden yourself with grief."

"More grief? I assure you, madam, I am quite capable of walking, and I am feeling much better. Has there been any news of Lord Thompson?"

She watched the housekeeper's ruddy cheeks pale, eliciting even more questions. "Your Grace, allow me to assist you back to bed, and I will tell you what I know."

Isabel sighed and rested her palm on her belly. "Do the rest of the staff know of my condition yet?"

"Yes, Your Grace. Though, while we were quite pleased to find out that there will be the pitter patter of tiny lord or lady feet through the house, we are all quite worried about you." The housekeeper helped Isabel into bed, tucking blankets around her small form.

"A friend of Lord Thompson's stopped by the house, shortly after your swoon, to advise that the duel was over, but that Lord Thompson was injured. The injury he sustained was not life-threatening, and he was being tended to by a private physician.

"The gentleman, a Lord Avonlea, asked for your whereabouts and we, Edmonds and I, told the man you were resting. He asked us if your affections for Lord Thompson were true, and we answered truthfully they are. Upon his departure, he assured us you and Lord Thompson would be free soon enough from this scandal, and he was positive a marriage between you both would certainly be blessed."

The sheer thought of Nathaniel being injured over her honor broke her heart in many pieces. She had no idea how one man could make her senseless. And to hear that he still wanted to pursue marriage, despite ruining his family's good name, baffled her. *How on earth can I ever repay him?*

"Your Grace, there was just one other thing. I do not mean to be so bold, but there are strong objections to your match with the marquess. It is rumored that his mother is in the process of formally announcing an arranged betrothal to a certain Lady Eloise Morton."

Isabel's stomach dropped into the pits of hell when the housekeeper confirmed her worst nightmare. They were better off separated. Society would never accept their union, much less a child out of wedlock. Her mind was made up—once she was deemed fit enough to travel she would venture off to the country in search of a smaller estate to live out the rest of her days.

"Please ask Edmonds to prepare my carriage and pack some of my belongings into a trunk."

"For how long, Your Grace?"

"I expect we will be gone for a fortnight. I think it is time for me to seek out my new home."

"But, Your Grace—"

"Run along now, we haven't got all morning."

This time she feared they would never have another chance. This child was a miracle, but would be a constant reminder of her love for him.

Nathaniel clenched his fists, searching deep within not to lose his temper with her servants. "What in the hell do you mean, she is not here?"

The butler stammered. "My Lord, Her Grace said that she would return in a fortnight, and that they were only going into the country."

"Is there anything more you could tell me about where she could have gone?"

"I overheard the maids whispering about Her Grace finding a smaller country estate."

So that was it. *She's running, the imp!* Isabel must have heard that his mother announced the betrothal to Lady Morton. Quite frankly, he could not blame her for wanting to take the high road, but no matter where she went, and no matter what hijinks his mother pulled, he would always find his way to Isabel.

"Very well, my good man, I will see what I can do to find her. Before I go, though, do you have a preference in what manor you serve Her Grace in?"

"I beg your pardon, My Lord, I am not sure I follow."

"My good man, I am about to make Her Grace the Marchioness of Stoughton. Would you prefer to stay here in this residence, or could I persuade you to join us at my estate?"

"My Lord, your offer is quite generous. Had I been much younger, I would gladly accept, but it was my wish to retire soon. With Her Grace now being cared for by you, I do not see why I am needed any longer."

Well, it was certainly good to know his affections had the approval of the staff, but good servants such as Edmonds were hard to find. "I am sorry that you will not be joining us. Should you ever need anything, come see me immediately. I will ensure you are taken care of."

"Absolutely, My Lord." Edmonds nodded and passed his hat to him.

Nathaniel turned to leave, nearly running into Avonlea. "What is the rush, old chap?"

"We are on a mission."

"What kind of mission?"

"The kind of mission that requires an oath of silence. The kind that will send my mother into a fury, and the kind that will infuriate a certain duchess."

"Sounds like my kind of adventure, Thompson. Where are we headed? "To the country."

"Your Grace, I am sorry, this is the only room I have left."

Isabel glanced around. It was passable, accommodating the needs of every traveler. A bed, fireplace, a table and chair, and a chest of drawers. Besides, while it was the furthest thing from extravagant, she would only spend the night here.

"Are you sure there is nowhere you could place my driver for the night, ma'am?"

The woman pondered for a moment before replying. "There be a loft in the stables. I am sure m'husband will not mind if he rests up there. I will get m'boy to show him the way. Your Grace, I am honored you are spending the night here. I will be sure you get the best breakfast the county could provide ya with."

"That will be all, madam." The innkeeper's wife retreated.

Isabel released a heavy sigh. By the time Nathaniel even realized she was gone, she would have a new cottage bought and paid for. She slipped out of her gown and draped it over the chair, neatly tucking her shoes underneath. Clothed in nothing but her stockings and shift, she scurried to bed and blew out the candle that illuminated the south side of the room.

Isabel tossed and turned, her thoughts swimming around what her hardships would be like over the coming months. If anything good came out of her tryst with Nathaniel, this child would be loved like no other.

As soon as she found a place she could call home, she would write to Nathaniel. He would be welcome to visit her and the child anytime, but their son or daughter would stay with her. They were safer that way. Free from vicious gossip and a meddling grandmother. Perhaps one day, once she had forgiven her own parents for the colossal mistake of passing her to Griffith, she would introduce them to their only grandchild.

That day would not be anytime soon. She could spend a lifetime healing from her loveless marriage and almost marrying the man she should have to begin with. Fate had been cruel to her in many ways, but her pregnancy would soon make up for the faults.

Isabel could not find the driver of her carriage as she walked into the inn's dining room.

"There you are, Your Grace!" the innkeeper bellowed. "Please have a seat. Milly will be right out with your breakfast."

"Thank you, sir."

Only a scant second later, a platter of eggs, toast, ham, and a side of porridge and tea was placed in front of her. All were her favorites, but what she would not give for a minute of company. Isabel hated to dine alone and often found comfort in dining with the servants when Henry spent the night out.

She finished eating and rose to pay the innkeeper. "Your Grace, the pleasure was entirely ours. I do believe your driver is outside waiting. Allow me to escort you."

Upon arriving at the carriage, Isabel saw a local woman there talking with the driver. She blushed. "Your Grace, we will leave just as soon as you are inside. You will have to change carriages in a few hours, but I assure you all will be fine."

"Is something wrong?"

"No, not at all. It is only that the road we must take is rather bumpy, and I fear for your safety. A more suitable mode of transportation has been arranged at no extra cost."

"Well, if it is so terrible, then why are we taking it?"

"Your Grace, it is the only road in that direction," the driver declared.

Isabel sat down, finding the situation entirely too suspicious. *What exactly has transpired in the time I have woken up to the time I managed to get out to the carriage?* Pretending nothing was amiss, she sat there silently and smiled. *I will figure out what you are up to, and then we will see who is clever.*

After visiting two villages, she still had not managed to find the perfect home along the way. They stopped in a field for the luncheon the innkeeper's wife had packed before they left. Isabel leaned against a tree and closed her eyes briefly. She missed Nathaniel with all her heart, but she knew leaving him would be best for them both. He would be free to enter into an acceptable marriage.

"Come along now, Your Grace. We will be changing just up the road from here."

She awoke to a start, not even realizing she had fallen asleep. Isabel stood, brushing off the grass from her skirts and climbed into the carriage. *Just how bad is this road that we have to change carriages?*

Two hours later, the sun began to descend and they turned onto a gravelly road and stopped. She heard a quiet exchange of words, and the side door opened. Her driver smiled. "I am afraid I will not be continuing on, Your Grace, but I assure you, arrangements have been made once you have reached your destination."

How odd. She climbed into the second carriage and waited for it to start up again. She managed to doze off, only to awaken and find Nathaniel sitting across from her.

"Hullo, love."

Moments passed as reality set in. He really was here with her. Isabel leapt from her seat into his lap and embraced him. "But how did you find me?" she whispered before pressing a kiss to his lips.

He chuckled and returned her affections. "Sweetheart, it would not have mattered where you escaped to. I would have followed you to the ends of the Earth."

"Nathaniel, where are we really going?"

"To see a certain blacksmith."

Isabel tried to conceal her shock, but could not. "We are going to Gretna? Your mother will be furious. We really should not do this."

"As head of our family, I am sure she will eventually get used to the prospect. I want you to be my wife, my marchioness, and I will not settle for anything less. Isabel, please tell me that you will marry me. Nothing and no one will get in our way, ever again."

Tears of joy streamed down her cheeks. "Nathaniel, I would not have you any other way. I accept, but we *are* going to have to find a way to deal with your mother, sooner or later."

"Leave it to me, love. I will do anything for you and to preserve our little secret." Nathaniel patted her belly and gave her a wink.

CHAPTER EIGHT

Six months later

Stoughton Hall was filled to the rafters with family, with the exception of her mother-in-law. Isabel's parents wished to be present when their grandchildren made their entrance into the world. The first set of cries carried throughout the halls, announcing that little Edward was here. Thirty minutes later, a soft cry emanated from their chamber, this time revealing Abigail Marie.

Isabel looked over at her husband while he held their son and she held their daughter. Nothing could be more perfect. Their lives could not have been more complete. The family estate would soon be overwhelmed with visitors from London. Friends, associates, and the non-believers would all descend upon Stoughton Hall to bear witness to the two tiny miracles that they had been blessed with.

"Love, you should pass Abigail to the nurse. You need your rest. It is not every day that a woman performs the herculean task of delivering twins."

"I am quite all right, dear. If it is all the same, Dr. Benson, I desire to have the children stay with me a little longer."

"Of course, My Lady. Lydia, come along, let us give the family a little privacy." He turned to Nathaniel. "My Lord, we will be along in a bit."

Then there was the matter of the dowager countess and her underestimating Nathaniel. Nathaniel had paid passage for her to tour the continent, and thankfully, she would be departing in a few short days. Isabel giggled and wished she had been present when Nathaniel delivered the news. She figured there was more to the discussion, as her mother-in-law had packed hers and Emily's things for the hunting lodge.

"Isabel, have you ever seen children more beautiful than ours?"

She turned to him and returned a loving smile. "No, love, I cannot say that I have."

"I do hope Emily gets to spend time with us. I think it would be wonderful for her to be around the children."

"I am sure she will be a doting auntie to Edward and Abigail."

Once things were settled in Stoughton Hall, she would sit with Emily and plan the season. With her meddlesome mother-in-law away, she was certain she would be able to find her new sister-in-law a suitable suitor, not one who was simply interested in her dowry.

The dowager countess scowled at her young and naïve daughter.

"Mama, you cannot be serious? Lord Avonlea would never take advantage of me! Nathaniel would kill him!"

"Would he now? He is too busy with that farce of a wife and two babies to even notice the desperation we are in."

"Mama, if you would only concede. Pride has no place in this world. And you are just as entitled to see your grandchildren as any other. You only intervened out of love for him."

"You tell that to your brother and his wife, and see what kind of response you receive." The dowager countess sighed and stretched across the dais, contemplating her next steps carefully. She needed to find Emily a husband and fast. There was no way she could afford to keep up appearances without further assistance from the marquess.

The door rang, and she watched the butler rush forward in the hall. Just as quickly as the door opened, it closed, and the footsteps drew closer. "My Lady." The butler passed her a letter, bowed, and took his leave.

The countess opened the note, and after reading it twice, she folded the vellum and smirked. *Well, well, well. We are saved after all.*

"Emily, pack our trunks. My trip to the continent will have to wait. We are heading to London. This season is starting to look up."

"What are you about, Mama?"

"This letter is our ticket. Yours. Your future, my love. And if I am not mistaken, you could be the next Duchess of Downsbury."

She watched her young daughter pale. "Are you thinking of pawning me off to the same cad who wished harm to my sister-in-law and showed no remorse in his previous duchess's passing?"

"It matters not, love. At some point in time, we all make sacrifices."

"If that is so true, Mama, what in heaven's name did you ever sacrifice?"

"Love, darling. Love has no place in our society. You will learn eventually. Now run along. I would like to be in London by this eve, and I will not tolerate being late for our first ball of the season."

"A ball! Mama, have you gone mad? I have nothing that will suit."

"Yes, you do. Wear the cream gown. Eleanor will assist with your hair while I make the final arrangements."

Nathaniel may have married that scandalous twit, but my daughter will certainly marry well. Then she would see who finished on top. Her daughter would finally be a duchess, and there wasn't a damned thing her son could do about it.

The End

A Sinful Education

CHAPTER ONE

Sussex, England, 1819

Charles Avonlea, the Earl of Bridgeton, sat behind his desk just as sour as the weather plummeting from the sky. Heavy rain, thunder, and flashes of lightning had shaken every window in his family estate for over two days. And with the precipitation came his mother, who escorted his elderly Aunt Agatha from the country.

His family's estate on the outskirts of Sussex offered many commodities, but not the one he desperately needed at this moment. Solitude. What he would not do to return to his townhouse in London, away from his doting relatives. Both women meant well, but when they put their minds to it, they embarrassed him deeply. Especially when the season came around.

Their conversations always started and ended with when he would marry. As far as they were concerned, he was wasting time. They incessantly reminded him they did not have much left, though he would wager differently.

While his mother pretended to put on airs that she was lonely, he had heard her giggling with some of her lady friends about gentlemen who came to visit every so often. The mere thought of her engaging in activities with a man at her age made him shudder.

Who would have guessed women in their advanced years still wish to—?

Why in heavens name am I thinking about that?

Suddenly, the front door slammed shut, and his aunt cursed aloud for all of the manor to hear about her aversion to being drenched.

"Now, now," his mother chided as he pictured her passing her belongings to the butler. "If I remember correctly, Aunt Agatha, you were the one who insisted on traveling right away. I would have been happy to have waited out this dreadful weather."

Avonlea's eyes rolled into the back of his head. *And so it begins.* He rose from his seat and walked around to the desk when his mother's displeased tone echoed down the corridor.

"Where is that ungrateful son of mine? And would someone bring me some tea before I catch my death?"

He stood there, pondering what could have her in such a mood. He stepped into the doorway, leaning against the frame, and folded his arms across his chest. "Mama, I would say welcome home, but you look as if you wish you were not here."

She gave him a frightful scowl, swatting at him. "Pish posh. Can't you see the condition us crones are in? We are tired, hungry, and most of all, wet. Be sure the fire is nice and hot, for when I return to the parlor with your aunt, we have much to discuss. Now run along, I won't be but a few moments."

Avonlea could already imagine the conversation they would have. *You must take a wife. I am not getting any younger. Your father's legacy demands you produce an heir. What on earth is taking you so long in choosing a wife? Are you secretly a molly?* Oh, yes, he could hear them both now. Niggling at his delay. But the trouble was not of what his dear mama thought.

His difficulty lay with his lack of trust in anyone, or anything, these days. That, and the fact that he had a deep feeling his past would come back to haunt him.

Shortly after graduating from Oxford, both he and the Marquess of Stoughton were enlisted by the war office. They only spoke of their time in university, and their assignments overseas were kept in silence. Nathaniel had been sent on one mission, while Avonlea was stuck spying for the crown in France and Italy.

He had traveled many places, witnessed the poorest of living conditions, and overindulged too frequently. Lady Fortune had been good to him so far—that news of his romps when he should have been working had not made it to London. But that day would come. His visits to brothels and smoke houses would make for good gossip, the war office would question his honor, and his family would be scandalized.

Then, there was the matter of falling in love with a fallen girl, who had been expecting a child last summer. In the midst of making preparations to return to England, she had disappeared from his apartment and was later found in a back alley, not far from the smokehouse he had patronized.

'Twas in that moment he concluded his work for the war office, advising them there was nothing left to discover, and returned to England. The thought of falling again, much less to marry, only brought back terrible memories.

Avonlea stalked toward the fireplace, added more logs, and then shifted the others at the bottom. Ash plumed upward, the dust making his nose twitch. The crackling of the additions drowned out his previous thoughts.

Life was unpredictable, much like a fire. A slight breeze could whoosh in and wreak mayhem. And that mayhem, at present, was called Mother.

She entered the parlor, gossiping away with his aunt.

He stood, holding out a chair for first one and then the other at the small round table facing the front yard. The sky was still quite dark and dreary, but the rain seemed to have stopped for the time being.

When he sat, his butler poured the ladies some tea and a port for Avonlea. "Will that be all, sir?"

He nodded, though he was tempted to find some excuse to keep the man in the room with him.

The butler left the parlor, closing the doors behind him.

"So, ladies, how can I entertain you this evening? I imagine it won't be over a game of whist."

"You, young man, are remiss in your duties. We expect an announcement by the end of the season. We are tired of waiting, and…and if you do not choose a wife this season, we will arrange to have your inheritance amended." His mother glared daggers at him, a cold and empty gaze that penetrated to his soul. He knew in that instant she meant every word and would not hesitate in wielding what power she had left as a dowager countess.

He downed the contents of his glass as if they were his last. Avonlea preferred to enjoy the sweetness of the deep purple tones of the liquor, but it seemed the conversation would end up making him crazed. Every muscle from his neck down tensed to a frightfully uncomfortable level. *Christ. She cannot be serious?* "Mama, Aunt Agatha, I do not take threats well. I understand you mean well, but I am not ready to take on a wife."

"Who said one has to be ready? You marry, and then you carry on with your affairs of the estate. Besides, what are you waiting for? Love? 'Tis a female inclination, not a man's. And hear me now—I do not threaten the inevitable. I simply remind of what's to come, if no action is made."

Avonlea supposed his inheritance could be amended, but that would take months, even years. *And who exactly does she think I will lose my estate to? Hmm.*

There was always his cousin, Albert, who was presently taking up residence in his expansive manor in Scotland. Would the man really trouble himself in coming so far? Besides, while Albert made his own riches at gambling whenever he sought out the tables, his family's fortune afforded him the security and comforts of the privacy he required upon his return to England. Perhaps it was best not to tempt fate.

His mother set her teacup down with a clatter. "There are a handful of young ladies I have my eye on. Would you take care in paying attention? I will only mention their names once, and I will begin arranging for some informal meetings."

Avonlea's innards twisted and gnarled with anxiety. Would fate be so cruel to make him go through this again? The painful memories were too much to even give thought to in the presence of his mother and aunt. At least the woman had suggestions. Though, he could not wait to hear what prizes she had to offer. "What if I had my own list of women I was considering?"

His mother scoffed. "Pray, amuse your ailing aunt and I, who is on this supposed list?"

Of course, she'd ask me for examples. "There is Lady Emily Thompson, the Marquess of Stoughton's sister. I have also considered—"

She gasped loudly. Her bright blue eyes widened with visible shock. The look alone spoke volumes. He was in trouble. "You will not tarnish our family's reputation by bringing in a Thompson. Scandal will only follow. Or did you happen to miss last season's events?"

How could he? It was as if the devil had his hand in the unfortunate and untimely deaths of the Duke of Brimley and the Duchess of Downsbury. He could not have been happier that Nathaniel and his marchioness finally were together.

And then there was the marquess' sister. Emily was an attractive girl. She had somehow managed to get under his skin. He had thought of her on occasion these last few months. He had even departed Madame Martine's without finishing the evening's festivities. There were moments whenever he saw a redheaded young lady, when he somehow wished it had been her.

Yet here was his mother exclaiming how much she disapproved, even though Emily had played no part in the scandal. "If that is your only objection to the girl...her familial relations cannot be helped. One cannot be at fault for who they have for a mother. Pity that. Though, you have piqued my curiosity. Pray tell, who do you think would be my match?"

"At the top of my list of recommendations is Lady Eloise Morton."

"Was that not the chit Lord Thompson's mother tried to pawn on him?"

"How eloquently put, you clod. More politely put, she was jilted. She's nice, comes from a good family, and she's pretty enough."

"Pretty enough! What in damnation does that have to do with anything?"

"A pretty one is easier to take to bed than an unsightly one."

While his mother spoke the truth, he was beguiled more by a woman who spoke her mind. He needed a companion who was sharp-witted, one who did not cower at the first sign of a challenge.

"La! Do not tell me you prefer slightly unconventional girls, Charles?"

"No. Though, a plain girl would not make many demands, nor have high expectations," Avonlea chided while he tapped the edge of the table, waiting for his mama's reaction. When she swatted him, he only laughed in response.

"My dear boy, I am simply considering our lineage. Think of the excellent structure you have. Were it not for the inheritance of my mother's eyes, and your fathers very appealing...never mind that. Anyway, I have the most handsome of men for a son, who's an Earl at that. So, begin to behave as one."

Avonlea smacked his forehead. "Mother!"

"What? Besides, think of the darling children the two of you would have." His aunt nodded at the comment. The conversation had clearly gone too far.

"Mama, Aunt Agatha, I am going to my chambers now to forget everything you've just said. If I find a wife, it'll be on my own. The day I need my mother to find me one is the day I take a vow of celibacy. Am I understood?"

He got up and strode out of the room, slamming the door behind him. His mother's words rang loud in his head. *A pretty one is easier to take to bed than an unsightly one.* What would ever possess her to say such a thing? Though his vow of celibacy was nothing but malarkey, he wanted his mother to stop meddling, so he needed to act right away.

"How precious they are, Isabel. They rival any other babies I have seen!" Emily crooned, cradling the female twin. She envied her glowing sister-in-law, and the brood she and her brother had created. One day she would be a wife and have children, mayhap a whole house full of little ones. Warmth washed over her—content children meant a happy mother and household. *One day this could be my family.*

"Your brother mentioned this was your first time around young children, but I will take your saying so as a compliment."

"I do hope I will get to see them often. Mama is in such a state, still. I hope she gets over the fact you are the new marchioness. She has only had months to get used to the idea." Mama would never get over it. Emily knew her far too well to expect anything less. The woman was likely to take her vengeance to the grave, if permitted.

"I do too, but for the meanwhile, I have other matters with which to occupy my time." Isabel winked at her as she rubbed her son's arm.

As Emily leaned back into the chair, a nursemaid lifted the sleeping babe from her arms. She was jealous of her brother and his wife. They had found each other and happiness, even after all the interference and scandal. She hoped one day to have a husband who would love her the same way.

But the question of the hour was whether her mother would ever approve of such happiness. The dreadful woman would niggle her way into Emily's life, and somehow find a way to hinder progress. Were it not for the fact that her mama was her official guardian—for the time being—she would have found a way to stay and live here at Stoughton Hall with her brother, his wife, and the twins.

Another nursemaid entered to collect the second twin, and Isabel rose with a stretch and yawn. She held out her hand to Emily. "Come now, my dear. You and I shall take a walk in the garden. I need to talk with you about some rumors I have heard and could use the fresh air."

Emily followed her sister-in-law out the side door and down the path where the roses lie.

"So, it has come to my attention—well, at least the rumors—that the Duke of Downsbury has returned to town. The servants have been whispering about his intentions to find another duchess."

"What does any of that have to do with me?"

"Well, my maid told me in confidence that she heard your mother discussing it with one of the servants when you were dropped off this week. Apparently, she's kept up communication with his grace the entire time he was gone."

"I thought he had gone off to the continent?" Permanently, she had desperately hoped.

"He had for a time, but he's been back for a fortnight. I suspect your mother has been a busybody."

That was not a first. Her dear mama, up to no good, when she was probably kneedeep in sheep's manure. *Of course she has…Would she dream of doing anything else?* Emily grumbled to herself.

"What was that?"

Heat seared Emily's cheeks. She could not believe that she had spoken aloud. "Oh, nothing. Mama just has a tendency to interfere where she doesn't belong, and knowing her, she's plotting something devious."

Isabel giggled. "Between you and me, I am ecstatic at her desire to no longer live here. Albeit, it came at the cost of your departure. I know if Nathaniel could have you here, he would. I will broach the subject with him tonight. Surely, there is something he will be able to arrange."

To live here would be a miracle, but so long as her mother lived and breathed, there'd be no chance of her relinquishing Emily's care to her brother. "So, what do you propose we do in the meanwhile? Plan a picnic and have some fun, much to her ire? Or should we host a dinner party and make her the guest of honor? We will invite some of her female companions and secretly make fun of them."

Isabel hooked her arm with Emily's. "What a splendid idea. We could name the dishes after her and her friends."

Emily was lost in a fit of giggles when her brother approached.

"Pray, what evil plot are you ladies conspiring?"

"Absolutely nothing meant for your ears, my love." Isabel unlatched her arm from Emily and wrapped it around her husband, kissing him feverishly.

Emily adored them both, but seeing the two of them behaving like lovesick fools did nothing but make her stomach turn. There were things to be seen, and this was not one of them.

"My, my, such an expose for a married woman. I do not think my dear sister wishes to be scandalized in such a manner."

Emily snorted in the most unladylike way. "My dear and unsuspecting brother, I dare say there isn't much of anything you could do that would shock me."

"On the contrary, Emily, there is much in this existence you do not know as of yet. But with the right partner in life, the experience is limitless. Now, run along upstairs. I am sure I heard your name being called." Nathaniel winked. "I would like a moment alone with my wife."

Of course he did. They were married, after all, and she was a guest in their house.

Emily turned toward the estate and walked at a leisurely pace. She could not help but admire the stroke of luck her brother had when he and Isabel were reunited. While she was much younger at the time, only she knew of her brother sneaking off to meet with Isabel in clandestine. It was all so romantic and exciting…and so beyond protocol. *If our father had ever known…*

"You could, of course, use this time to get ready!" "Ready for what?" she shouted back at Nathaniel.

"A ball, of course. I will be escorting you fine ladies to Almack's this evening."

Emily shook her head. *Almack's? Good Lord! What in heaven's name am I going to wear?*

"Oh, Lord Avonlea, you are quite the dancer." Lady Morton gushed all over him, her blush giving her unladylike intentions away. "Do you think my mama would notice if we slipped outside?"

Her hand wandered further down his chest. The Earl of Bridgeton cleared his throat as he gently lifted it, holding it in his own for a moment. "My dear Miss Morton, while you are making it abundantly clear you take me for some randy rogue, I will do the honorable thing and depart once I have returned you to the company of your mother. I assure you, your advances have not gone unnoticed. I do not have any intention in misleading you to a courtship beyond this dance floor. Now, come along, we should not tarry."

Your mother, after all, is potentially waiting for us to be caught in some sort of moment of passion. And there is no way in damnation I would entertain that thought in this lifetime, or the next.

She started to protest, but instead whimpered at his intentions made clear.

He crossed the floor and delivered the eager girl to her mother.

"Did you kids have a great dance?" her mother questioned the young Lady Morton, whilst giving him a wary glance.

"I did, Mama, and he promised me another before the evening is out."

He opened his mouth to correct Lady Morton when her mother cut the words from him. "Outstanding! Lord Avonlea, you are beginning to exceed my expectations. Very well, you have my permission to collect Elizabeth for the quadrille."

All Avonlea could do was nod. He bowed and took his leave, heading in the direction of where the other gentlemen waited for their ladies to finish chirping.

That is when he noticed the Marquess of Stoughton.

Diverting his course, he strode toward the seat next to Nathaniel. "It has been far too long, Nathaniel. How are your marchioness and the offspring faring?"

"It has. You should stop by and see, or you can ask the marchioness yourself. I think I see her heading this way with my sister. I am sure you remember Emily?"

Avonlea gave his chum a wry look. Nathaniel was not exactly known for his humor, but Avonlea knew of his dry sense of fun. "Yes, I remember her. I was, after all, the one who caught her in your library when she swooned, after the duke learned of his duchess' fate."

"Ah! I hope you do not plan on bringing up that business again?"

"Absolutely not, but I also hear he's back in town. You would think he would have had enough sensibility to leave London life behind. Do you think he'll make an appearance tonight?"

The marquess snorted. "Here? At Almack's? I think not. I am sure he would not dare set foot in here."

One could not be too sure about that. The man had connections everywhere and would not hesitate to pull out all the stops to get what he wanted. He did not possess an ounce of scruples and did not give a farthing for the worth of a life. His honor had come into question, too, after disappearing from the duel with Nathaniel last year.

Avonlea dreaded the moment when he would have to address the duke the next time his grace was present, and in his high opinion, he desperately hoped that would be no time soon. As the ladies approached them, the singular, emerald vision before him caught his breath.

Fiery red ringlets fell past Emily's shoulders. Piercing blue eyes shimmered in the candlelit ambiance of the room. Her gown accentuated her delicate size, and the brilliant shade of green with a gold sash completed the heavenly image. Suddenly, the earl longed to hold her again.

Avonlea's blood rushed to his loins, need filling him. *Damn. Out of all the ladies here tonight, Emily makes me burn.* A rosy blush swept across her cheeks, darkening the little specks of freckles. His thoughts were interrupted when someone tapped his arm.

"My lord, have you suddenly become deaf and mute?"

"Lady Thompson, I offer my apologies." He bowed and took her hand, pressing his lips to the tender skin on the back. "It has been too long, my lady."

"It has, my lord. Do say you will join us soon for dinner. I can have Duncan assemble a dinner party in no time, and if I were the wagering type, I would say you would have a grand time. Please say you will join us on Saturday. Besides, I have it on good authority that Emily will be dining with us as well."

He turned to observe Nathanial's approval splashed across his face in the form of a grin. The marquess crossed his arms and now leaned against the wall. "Do you intend to keep my wife waiting?"

"Forgive me." The earl returned his gaze to the marchioness, who now smiled as if she had ensnared him in a trap. "You have my word I will attend your dinner on Saturday."

"A wise choice, my lord. I would hate to resort to drastic measures to secure your presence."

And what in the world is that supposed to mean? Did she mean to have me drugged and dragged to Stoughton Hall? "My lady, I assure you, no force will be needed. I will be there."

"Most excellent, my lord. Then, I suppose you'll be pleased to know that we will have one of the loveliest young ladies London society is privileged to have joining us, too. Oh, Nathaniel, dinner will be wonderful!"

Avonlea smiled at Emily, trying to contain a light-hearted laughter. "What is the matter, my lady? You appear quite flushed." He had seen a rosy blush sweep across her cheeks when the marchioness referred to her as "one of the loveliest young ladies…" and here she was being coy.

"I am quite well, my lord. Thank you for your concern." She had risen up on her toes to whisper something into the marchioness' ear and then returned her attention to him and the marquess. "If you gentlemen will excuse me, I need to step away for only a moment. Nathaniel, my lord."

He bowed and watched how her hips innocently swayed. Lord, the woman…girl…Christ! He could not think while he was around her. Avonlea watched her every step of the way until she joined a group of women her age.

"Ahem," the marchioness teased, "I suppose that means you are pleased with who will be joining us on Saturday?"

"Indeed, my lady, indeed." *My night could not have gone better.* "Well, my lady, I must be going. I look forward to dinner this weekend." He turned to Nathaniel and reached out to shake his hand when another touched his shoulder.

"There you are, my lord! I have been looking all over for you. My dear Eloise has been waiting for some time, and you have not yet collected her for the quadrille. I must say, I am quite put out."

Of course, you are... "My apologies, my lady. I shall rectify the situation at once, but I must also warn you, I do have to leave right after. I mean no offense by my quick departure."

"I will think nothing of it. I am so glad for your attentions, sir. I feared after last season's debacle, my poor Eloise would never make it this season, and you have by far exceeded our expectations."

Avonlea choked on his spit. "Ma'am, I should be clear as to what my meaning is. That is to dance and nothing more. While I hold you and your daughter in high regard, I do not have any intention of pursuing this friendship beyond the hall."

The woman stopped and turned to face him. Her face quite red, the matron appeared she would detonate at any given moment. She licked her lips and opened her fan, moving the air between them as if giving him a warning signal.

"My goodness, my lord, that is quite unfortunate. I could not imagine how any young lady would feel inclined to entertain you given your inability...Ah! Excuse me, I do think I see Lord Broxton's nephew."

Lady Morton had turned on her heels and abandoned him, leaving him to question what inability she implied. *Unbelievable.*

"What was that all about, Charles?" the marquess asked.

The earl shook his head and exhaled loudly. "That, my friend, is a disappointed and scorned matron. To be frank, they should have warnings posted at these functions. They are all quite the same." *No matter how the bread is sliced.*

"You should have seen his face, Emily. I swear it—the man is smitten with you." Emily's sister-in-law gloated. "Oooh, and did I mention how unruly Lady Morton was behaving last night. Something about his manners and being a cad. That her precious Eloise was made for royalty, and the earl was not worthy of the gift her daughter was."

She gasped, Cecily echoing the reaction beside her. Suddenly, the world was cast in a different light.

Once upon a time, she never would have dreamed that one of her brother's friends would have paid her any mind. Her heart fluttered to hear that Lord Avonlea certainly noticed her. He had always been handsome, in a rakish sort of way, and the ladies had always wanted to be in his good graces and company. Though, she had always wondered if he had ever seen her as more than a girl, as his friend's sister.

Emily had ventured off with the marchioness after breakfast for a walk of the grounds, meeting up with her bosom companion, Miss Cecily Turner, for a picnic.

"I, for one, am jealous," Cecily stated dryly. "The earl is a dream. Imagine the babies that man will produce. Goodness, he is simply made for sin." "Cecily!" Isabel scolded.

"Pshaw. I have only stated what everyone else is thinking. See what I mean?" She pointed at Emily. "If Lady Thompson was not thinking of it, would she be blushing?"

Emily, despite the heat that coursed through her veins from embarrassment,—*or was it really just that?*—knew that Isabel's friend was right. His lordship, the Earl of Bridgeton, certainly oozed an air that most men in his circle did not possess—charm. *Well, that and an incredibly toned body given the size of his masculine…err…wellformed legs and backside.*

Heavens! I really should not be giving such thought into the male anatomy, much less his. Mother would have an apoplectic fit if she knew. Nevertheless, the man turns the heads of every female. Why should I be any different?

"Isabel, I have to admit, Miss Turner does raise a valid point. Good heavens, the man is simply…" A shadow cast over them as she was about to continue. She looked up, only to gaze upon the object of their fiendish and scandalous discussion.

"Ladies, I do hope I am not interrupting an important debate?" Lord Avonlea asked, who was joined by her brother a few moments later.

Emily and her companions shook their heads. "Certainly not, my lords. Is anything amiss?"

"Not at all. It just so happens my mother is riding with my aunt, and I am in need of practicing my evasion tactics. Besides, 'twould be bad form, if your brother and I noticed you and did not stop to visit with you. That is, if you do not mind. If you are expecting anyone else…"

Without even realizing it her hand had left her side, Emily reached out to his leg. "You are welcome to join us, my lords. Here, there is enough room on the blanket as well."

For the briefest of moments, her heart stopped when she touched him. He stared down at her and their gazes held for a moment. He sat next to her, and as he righted himself, Emily handed him a sandwich that Duncan had prepared. "Would you care for a bite, my lord?"

"I would indeed. You are most kind."

"'Tis our pleasure, my lord."

"Nathaniel, why are you still standing?" Emily queried, ready to pass him a biscuit.

"No, my dear. I think I shall head on back home. I did promise Isabel I would be home on time this afternoon."

I am perfectly fine with that. I would not care for you to watch how foolishly I behave around this fine specimen of a man. "Pity. I was looking forward to discussing dinner plans on Saturday."

"If you are at all concerned with what is going to be served, I can assure you that Isabel is quite capable of handling the arrangements. Do you doubt cooks ability in serving all of us?"

Emily gasped at the horror of how she must have spoken. "My apologies, Nathaniel, I meant no offense."

He chuckled at her. Heat seared her cheeks with embarrassment. Her brother certainly knew how to jest with her. She glanced over at lord Avonlea and found him smiling at their banter, while her companions fluttered their fans, hiding their amusement.

How in the world will I deal with having dinner near him on Saturday? I cannot think straight, nor can I have a conversation that does not include a vivid image of him charming me. I am simply besotted. If Mama every found out—Perhaps the only place for me is the nunnery.

CHAPTER TWO

"So tell me, Lord Avonlea, have you heard the news yet?" The marchioness raised her eyebrows, sipping on her wine.

He imagined she was making reference to the Duke of Downsbury's return. The very thought of the man made him gag.

Nathaniel cleared his throat, obviously hoping to deter his relentless wife, but the woman continued.

"His grace, the useless and deplorable Duke of Downsbury, has returned to town, and he is apparently still in the marriage mart, something I hear you have in common with him."

Christ. His mother had certainly spread the word he was looking for a wife. He looked up to find Emily glaring at him. She pursed her lips, a crimson flush sweeping across her cheeks. When their eyes met, she turned away. "Yes, I have heard he has returned, and while I disapprove of his being permitted to find a new bride so soon, it is hardly a matter any one of us can control." "Here, here," Nathaniel muttered.

Emily cleared her throat. "I, for one, am appalled at his lack of insensitivity. How does one not mourn the loss of their spouse? When two people enter the sacred union of marriage, they become partners for life. How dreadful, that even if their marriage wasn't as it should be, he could not at least put on airs."

"That may be the case, but we still have no business to involve ourselves."

"On the contrary, my dear, we should be interfering. I shan't name my source, nevertheless rumor has it, he has his sights set on our very own Emily."

Emily gasped, cutlery slipping out of her hand and clamoring to the floor. "I have no idea what would have given you that impression, Isabel, but surely you are mistaken. I would never marry such an unfeeling clout."

"And you, my dear sister, do not understand the power Mother wields when it comes to making deals with the devil. She is, after all, your legal guardian." Nathaniel tossed his napkin onto the table.

Emily gazed at her brother with a pensive expression for a brief moment then she looked down, cleared her throat, and ran from the room. Her sobs echoed down the hall.

Avonlea could not blame her for losing her composure, for surely, if he was in her situation, he would most certainly find it grave. He could not think of a single female who would want a cold and unfeeling duke to prevail upon them. She pulled at his heart. Something in her blue eyes called to him.

Charles quietly observed the usually upbeat family dynamic suddenly change into something mournful and serious. He could not recall a single time when he had seen them all this distressed, other than many months back. "Now, now, there is no need to spoil what was a cheerful evening. My lady, dinner was outstanding, but I do regret I should depart. There is a young lady in need of consoling. I should hate to impose further."

"My lord, you would not be imposing, as I was the one who invited you. And do not worry a moment over Emily. The silly gel is worrying over nothing, and I shall soon ease her anxiety. Besides, I am sure the marquess would not mind time alone with you." The marchioness gazed kindly at her husband while she pulled away from the table. "Excuse me, my lords, I have a young lady to console."

Avonlea nodded and turned to face his host. "Honestly, Nathaniel, I do not want to keep you from explaining further to your sister on what your wife's meaning was."

"It is no trouble at all, old friend. Let us move into the library and get more comfortable."

Avonlea followed the marquess, his nerves frayed and sanity questionable. He paced by the fire, feeling more on edge than ever before. Nathaniel poured them some port. He reached out and took the glass. "Thank you."

"I have been meaning to address some concerns, Avonlea. Up until that nasty business with Downsbury, we had not had a chance to discuss your return from the continent, nor mine. I imagine you completed your assignments? You returned to London at least a month before me. You were not hurt, were you?"

Avonlea chose his next words wisely. Here he stood with one of the only men he trusted with his life. What would he do with the information about Celine, the baby, the opium? Would he expose himself for the true cad he was?

Somehow, he doubted it, but that same feeling that the ground would disappear from beneath him loomed again, just as when his mother and aunt had berated him for not having found a wife yet. Only this time, he sat on the floor trying to regain his senses whilst the world tipped on its axis.

He looked up to find Nathaniel on his haunches before him. "Are you all right, Charles?"

He sighed, and with resignation, told his story to the bitter end. "So now, do you comprehend why I stayed away? If the war office knew that I never completed my assignment, I would be finished."

"Not necessarily, old friend. To some degree, in your circumstances, some would have considered you unfit to complete the mission, and they would have retracted you immediately. If it had come to the question of your honesty, I would have gladly stood by you. But sadly, we were not on the same assignment."

A pity that. But mayhap, it was for the better. "'Tis a good thing to know you still value our friendship." But would the rest of society understand? His mother and aunt could not begin to comprehend the complex emotions he kept hidden, and he certainly could not expect another woman to feel second rate, either. There simply was not an easy answer on how to move forward.

Nathaniel rose and squeezed his shoulder. "And you, my friend, were at my side during one of the most difficult times of my life. I will stand by yours, if there ever is a need."

Avonlea eased back into his chair. Relief washed over him, and with comfort finally settling him, he swallowed the remainder of his drink. "What other concerns do you have, Nathaniel?"

"Lord Wycliffe, in particular. I am not quite sure as to how deep his attachment with the former Duchess of Downsbury goes, but what I do know is, in his present state of madness, he'll soon no longer be permitted into White's if he cannot get his drinking under control."

"And that is just the beginning." Charles snorted and stood to help himself to another port. "Can I get you another? For I am sure we will be needing a few more before we are finished."

"Certainly."

Avonlea set the decanter down and walked toward the marquess with their glasses. Whatever troubled the earl would soon pass, or so he hoped.

Avonlea groaned at the sight before him.

Lord Rutledge and a few others sat amused, watching a member of their circle make a total and utter fool of himself. The server attempted to leave a drink on the table for Wycliffe, but the clout kept reaching for the other glasses on the tray.

"My lord, those aren't for you", the scrawny young man said, holding back the plate. "Those belong to other patrons. If you would like, I will drop by again in a few moments with another for yourself."

Wycliffe mumbled an obscenity and went back to his own beverage.

Avonlea reached over the table and swiped the Earl of Wycliffe's scotch. The man had clearly imbibed enough already. And he suspected it had to do with the former Duchess of Downsbury's untimely death.

"Give me my blasted drink back!" Wycliffe hiccupped.

He simply shook his head. "I will not. Get a grip of yourself, man. I understand you are mourning, but enough is enough." Avonlea swirled the contents, eliciting a groan from Wycliffe. "This will not bring her back. It is time to move on."

Wycliffe snorted. "I cannot simply go and find someone to replace her. You would not understand. I have needs, and only she knew exactly what I required."

This surely could not be all about bedding a woman. Just what exactly is he in to?

His comment had garnered some attention, the other gents chuckling in their seats.

"I assure you, if you take the time to visit Madame Martine's establishment, you would be pleasantly surprised at how accommodating her ladies are," the earl quipped.

The drunkard grunted in disgust. "If you won't give me my drink, and the staff here at White's won't serve me, I will find myself a hovel. Luckily for me, London has many."

He rose, knocking over his chair, and ran into a server, sending his tray clattering to the floor. The contents spilled and stained his pants. "Ugh! Get out of my way." Wycliffe growled, staggering out the door.

"Well, that was a joy. When do you suppose the Earl of Wycliffe will get his head out of the bottle and heed his father's wishes?" Lord Rutledge asked while taking the glass from Avonlea's hand.

"Never, at the rate he is going. Wycliffe has a duty, and the only way he can get out of this mess is with help."

"Help? Stop being ludicrous, Avonlea. You should know it is every man to his own at this point. There is too much going on right now, none would dare meddle in personal affairs."

"What are you afraid of, Rutledge? That your own skeletons will come tumbling out of the servant's quarters?"

Rutledge, whose portly belly stuck out more than a woman in confinement, stood and wagged a fat finger in his face. "Listen here, you impertinent fool, I will not tolerate your insolence."

"Insolence? You, my fat friend, will be one of the first pigs to be roasted on an open spit for your negligence. Quite frankly, I think I will follow Wycliffe's direction and have a swig of some cheap vile from a hovel in one of London's finest." Avonlea departed, leaving Rutledge and the other gentlemen to wager and gossip like women.

Why does life have to be so black and white? He had heard of Wycliffe's attachment to the duchess, as others did, but to think there really was more to the association. What if he and Emily were in that situation? Married to other partners, but visiting each other secretly. What a ruinous conundrum in which to be. To be besotted with someone who happens to be married to another.

Not too long ago, he had assisted Nathaniel, and now he would do the same for Wycliffe. *Why does it always fall on me?*

He walked down the cobblestone street until he reached a young lad in cut-off pants. "I have a guinea with your name on it if you will tell me what direction a tall, muscular man passed by. He has dark hair, though I doubt anyone would notice given the hour it is. He is also wearing gentlemen's clothing much like myself, and he might have been mumbling. Did you see any man of the sort?"

"'E went that way, sir. He was grumbling like a madman, something 'bout being gipped a scotch at White's and 'eaded in the direction of them fancy ladies. I think the establishment is called Martine's."

So the bloke was headed for Martine's place after all. It would not hurt to keep an eye on him. The man clearly needed a release in the worst sort of way. *Well, so do I, but every time I close my bloody peepers, all I can see is Emily.*

The earl reached into his pocket and handed the lost child his compensation. "Now, run along home. There is no need for you to be out here for the rest of the week with that sum."

Beneath scraggly hair kept untidily under a dingy cap, dark eyes peered back at him. "You are mistaken, sir. My mum needs more than this to keep out of debtor's prison. But if you ever need anything else, this could be my corner."

"Pray tell, what is your name, child?"

"M'name is Percy."

"After your father, no doubt?"

The child snorted. "M'father ran off with a whore in Whitechapel, and his name sure as hell ain't Percy. He took off before I was born."

Avonlea surmised this was a common story from the slums of London. A tragedy really. Children were the future of this country, and sadly, this one would be lucky if he made it to twenty. "Either way, lad, stay out of trouble. Understood?"

"Yes, sir!"

He treaded through the gas lit, cobblestone street until he happened upon the tallest house in the lane. He approached the door when a lone, burly guard, who wore the stench of piss and ale, blocked his entry.

"There be a fee for late entry into this evening's festivities, guvnor."

"And what would that be, sir?"

"A guinea for entry and another for my silence."

He pondered a moment what the gent meant. If the oaf thought Charles was shackled by marriage, then he was sadly mistaken. The day he took a wife was the day he ensured the woman could handle him in every single way. "I will give you the guinea for entry, sir, but nothing more."

The idiot grunted and held out his grimy hand while Avonlea dropped the note, pushing him out of the way to enter the establishment. For a bawdy house, Martine had gone out of her way to make the surroundings more like home. Men were seated in lavish chairs, decorated in the finest fabric, while some of the girls sat on their laps in nothing more than a silk robe, loosening their cravats.

There was a time in his life where the sight of women dressed as such would have excited him, but the mere spectacle of them made him flaccid as the day he was born. He only wanted one woman, and she happened to be the redheaded miss that would land him in a heap of trouble, and irritate his mother so.

A serving girl handed him a tankard, and another, the topless one, led him into a parlor already buzzing with activity.

"My dear, while I am thankful for the drink, that is not why I am here. Where is your mistress? I wish to speak with her."

She blushed and stared at him blankly. "She is with a client, sir."

"Then interrupt her, please. I have need to speak with her."

The wench bowed and looked displeased at his words. "If you would not mind waiting here then. I doubt the parlor would suit the mood you are in."

A few minutes later, the girl returned with a very annoyed and disheveled Madame Martine. Her corset had been done up roughly, so that even more of her generous cleavage stuck out, and her flaxen hair was mussed. Apparently, whatever client she was entertaining at that moment was not in the mood either. "You requested my presence, my lord?"

Her hands wandered aimlessly down his chest and straight toward the band of his pants. "Leave it be, Martine. I came here for Wycliffe. Now, where is he?"

"Surely, you do not mean the useless and drunken clod I just left?"

"Considering he left White's in that condition, then I imagine we speak of the same gent."

"Ugh. Take him out of here. I no longer want him to visit this establishment."

"And why is that?"

She scowled and made an unladylike gesture of disgust. "That man is not right in the head. Have you any idea what he likes to do? None of my girls take any interest in being abused in such a manner."

"Other than drink, Madame, I assure you, I have no interest in learning about his past time with the ladies. In or out of the bed. What he does in his own time is of his own affair. Now, if I may."

"He's right through there, in Daisy's room." She pointed to the room she had vacated. "I will not issue a refund, either. He's been more trouble than he's worth. See that he is removed, immediately. I have other clients who would appreciate our services this evening."

Avonlea sighed, imagining just how awful he had treated Martine. He reached into his pockets and pulled out another note. "For your trouble, Madame."

He stalked into the room and found Wycliffe asleep at the edge of the bed, hanging onto a loosely tied neck cloth at the bedpost.

What have you gotten yourself into now, Wycliffe?

For someone intent on trying to move forward, he was doing a smashing job of ruining his reputation. The foolish man would eventually have all of London talking if he did not sober up.

Avonlea bent down to loosen Wycliffe's necktie from the bedpost and tucked it into his pocket. He shook the earl until his arms flailed from the disturbance. "Come on, old chap, It has time to catch some air."

From the dead weight of Wycliffe, came gurgling and then talking, as if he were dreaming. "She did not want to be bound. She hit me with her fan…"

"Come on, Wycliffe. Up we go." *There is hope for you, yet.* He heaved the man up and walked him over to a chair. The earl opened his eyes as Avonlea splashed some water from a washbasin onto his face.

Wycliffe waved his hands to keep him from tossing more water and growled. "Enough of that! I am awake, man!"

Good thing, too. What would the daily say, come morning, if they read about him carrying the earl out of the bawdy house? His dear aunt would have a fit of the vapors. *Just what I need.*

Emily pouted from her chaise. Her mother had supported the match since the Duke of Downsbury announced his interest in her at Stoughton Hall, all but nine months previously. "But, Mama, this is utter madness. His grace has not even proposed, and you are already planning a wedding?"

"Yes, dear, I am planning an extravagant wedding. After all, my only daughter is going to be a duchess."

A duchess who will no doubt be terrible at all that will be expected. Releasing an exasperated groan, Emily pulled herself up and righted her gown. "Mama, if you had half a mind, you would know, just as the rest of the ton does, that the duke has only just returned from the continent. In addition to your lunacy, his marriage was recently annulled."

Frankly, Emily was surprised and disturbed that Lady Cordelia Waite's death had not been investigated further. The duke's lack of emotion when his wife died certainly perplexed not only her, but many others. If she married him, would he treat her in the same regard, or would he be as doting as her brother and his marchioness?

To be as happy as Nathaniel and Isabel. Maybe I will be so lucky to find the same thing. "Mama, I would like to go for a ride today. I hope you did not have anything planned?"

Her mother gave her a bemused glance and tapped her nimble fingers on a silver platter. "Actually, I did have plans for us, my dear. I am expecting some deliveries, and we need time to get you ready."

What on earth is she talking about? "Mama, what exactly are you referring to?"

"There is a formal dinner and ball being held in your honor tonight."

"Mama, I do not understand why, though."

"The duke, of course. This is our way of a short, but formal courtship."

The truth slapped her in the face. How could anyone so shallow and empty want to court her?

Their portly butler entered the parlor and bowed. "My lady, this just arrived for the youngest Lady Thompson."

Emily eyed the large parcel and hesitantly took the package from him. "I wonder who it is from." She unwrapped the red velvet ribbon, lifted the lid, and gasped. "Good heavens!"

Sitting in the nearest chair, she extracted the loveliest gown of silk and muslin in the prettiest pink she had ever seen. The sudden need to weep overwhelmed her. "It is…beautiful, Mama!"

She pressed the dress to her chest as the remainder of the delicate fabric swept across the floor. Its coloring complimented her pale flesh and would go perfectly with the drop pearl necklace her papa had given her a year prior to his passing. Perhaps the ball was not so much a bad idea. If the duke had gone to such lengths to ensure she dressed properly, it could only be a sign of future thoughtfulness.

"What time is the ball tonight?"

"His grace informed me seven o'clock sharp. Dear, it appears in your frazzled state, you dropped a card."

Butterflies fluttered about in her belly, and she shook from excitement. Emily bent down to pick up the vellum.

My dearest Emily, I apologize for not having consulted you before picking out the gown. I was assured by the modiste that it is very much the fashion, and I am profoundly confident that you will look ravishing.

She should have been content with his gift, but was ravishing a word to use on a girl who is new to society? *He could have at least tried to woo me with something poetic, but a duke really doesn't have time for that, does he? He is too busy with managing his duchy. Nevertheless, how could he say something so crass? So insensitive…*

Emily looked over at the time, wondering how much of it she had wasted on trying to decipher what the duke had meant by his note. *Perfect.* She had time to compose herself and check the state of her hair. *What will he be like?*

Emily sincerely hoped her brother and sister in-law would make an appearance, yet doubted the marquess would be inclined to have his wife in the same room with the duke. She doubted the duke would even invite her brother after their trouble.

Never in her twenty years had she ever considered herself marriage material, much less a duchess. Her belly sank with fear. She did not know the first thing about running a household, nor had she been permitted to attend such formal parties. If she had to accompany the duke on matters of business, what would be the expectations? Her head swam and drowned with possible scenarios and terrible outcomes.

Emily lifted the garment from the box and passed it to their butler. "Alfred, please have my maid prepare a bath, and I would like some tea and biscuits brought up. There is too much to do and such little time to prepare for this ball. I doubt I will have time to dine before we leave."

Alfred bowed then quickly turned and left the parlor. *Tonight can't come soon enough.*

The Earl of Bridgeton cringed at the sight of young ladies eyeing him. They fluttered their fans and giggled as he passed, their chaperones scowling at him. Normalcy. So this was how the season would begin. His inheritance made him such a high prize. Unfortunately, what the ton did not know is that marriage was the furthest thing from his mind. *Though that will never stop Mother from encouraging this farce.*

Emily had invaded his thoughts these last few days, as well as her impending betrothal to that scathing arse Downsbury. Since that nasty business with her brother, the thought of the duke laying his hands on that innocent, yet devilish chit incited his fury. From the moment he had caught her, swooning, in the marquess' parlor, her softness had appealed to him in the most primal way. Simply put, she made his cock twitch.

Her youthful and creamy complexion was most desirable, and the fact that she was new to the seasons of London meant she was not corrupted by its indecency. The one thing he detested the most was an over-confident girl who possessed the intelligence of a fly. A mule had more sensibility than half the women in front of him.

Out of the corner of his eye, he spied Emily standing at the duke's side. He painfully watched as the cad's hand slid down from the small of her back to caress her bottom. Her eyes widened with shock, and Charles observed her polite smile as she swatted Downsbury's hand away.

Fury rushed through his veins. The duke did not deserve her.

Then, Downsbury leaned in and whispered something that must have revolted her.

Emily's lips pursed, and she shivered. Avonlea was about to rescue the chit and ask her for a dance, but the duke cleared his throat and raised a glass that he took from a servant. "If I may have everyone's attention, I would like to make a toast." The guests surrounding him sighed and shushed the other attendees.

"To Lady Emily Thompson."

Emily delivered a shaky smile and curtsied. Yet once everyone finished cheering, her smile curved into frown. She slipped her hands into the folds of her gown, he imagined to conceal their trembling.

Time to rescue the poor girl. Hopefully, she's had some dancing lessons.

Avonlea crossed the floor and stopped before the newly engaged couple. "Your grace, my lady." He bowed. "I was wondering if you would mind if I stole your lovely companion for a dance, your grace?"

The duke simply slipped Emily's hand into his. "She could use the practice, Lord Avonlea. Go ahead, my dear, I have some plans to discuss anyway."

Charles led the way to the dance floor and bowed as the musicians commenced the waltz. Her hand rested on his upper arm, and her gaze never left his. His heart momentarily stopped, giving him pause. Something in the air around him ignited a passion and desire for the young woman. And to think, their dance would be short-lived. "Do you want to talk about what the duke said that had you so offended?" he asked.

"Aren't you the bold one this evening, my lord. Why ever do you think I was offended? He simply made promises—albeit shocking ones—I do not think I have ever heard spoken so publicly."

He must have said something lewd, for her response left more questions than answers. "And just what exactly did he say that was so shocking?"

She snorted. "My lord, you'll forgive my impertinence when I say, that it would be improper for me to repeat such things, let alone reveal the intimate discussion I had with my betrothed."

Intimate, my arse. Why, if I had to guess, he probably scandalized her by telling her what he was going to do to her. And now, he is surely off shagging another guest while we are dancing. Everything about the man was detestable. One could not trust a snake while it slithered about London, much less at his own party.

"Emily…My lady—forgive my manners—but I am a man in every way and maybe more so than the duke will ever be. I know the signs and the physical reactions when a person—a woman—is repulsed at the suggestion of doing something beyond her comfort level. What did he say?"

Her eyes widened, and she turned away to gaze upon others dancing around them. Some of the guests chuckled, their attentions focused on the pair.

"You know, you do not have to marry him. Nathaniel will ensure you are well provided for, until you are ready."

She halted and released him the moment the music stopped. He waited for her to scold him over his presumptions. She would not make a scene here of all places, but if she admitted her feelings for the duke, he would let her go on about her business and not dare to interfere. But something about this situation did not smell right. Avonlea was a man who followed his instincts, and his skin crawled with a sensation indicating danger was close.

In a time when the country's finances were uncertain, as war had taken its toll, he trusted his sixth sense. Emily was in danger, to put it plainly, and if she thought for one moment the duke meant well, she was wrong. Were Charles a betting man, he would wager his estate that Downsbury was up to something sinister.

As soon as Wycliffe sobered up, he had to speak with the man who'd coveted the duke's wife. If anyone knew how evil the duke could be, it would be him.

"My lord, I really must be leaving. His grace will wonder what is taking me so long." She curtsied and left him in a rush.

His gaze lingered on the curves of her gown and settled around her bottom. He had fantasized about her derriere since the night he had caught her in his arms. Images of her bare arse sinfully occupied his thoughts more and more. As she disappeared down the hall, another man stepped in next to him.

"She is quite the catch, that Lady Thompson. A spitting image of her mother, too. I envy the duke," the tall, stout, and balding gentleman stated. "I wonder, though, if she'll be enough to keep him interested. The good Lord knows, the previous duchess carried on so many affairs, it was not any wonder that she ended up dead. All of our sins will come to the forefront, and we pay for them in this lifetime. Pity she lost the child as well."

"What are you talking about, and who, might I ask, are you?"

"The duchess was with child and not of the duke's, if you gather my meaning. And I was the one who pulled the dilapidated carriage out of the river. Sadly, her body was never recovered. It was just as well. The pariah would have never had a proper burial. His grace was quite annoyed."

Of course, Avonlea had been uneasy that was never found. How else would Downsbury have been able to obtain an annulment? It would be rather amusing if her grace were to make a miraculous return from the dead. The duke would surely have an apoplectic fit.

He was about to respond when he caught the wisp of Emily's skirt go by. She stopped at the terrace, glanced back to see if anyone had followed her, and slipped out into the shadows of the moonlight. He bowed to the stranger. "Excuse me. I have just remembered something I must do."

Walking toward the terrace, Charles happened to notice the duke headed in their direction, adjusting his cravat and walking down an empty corridor. *What the devil has he done?* Closing the door behind him, Avonlea found Emily sitting on the bench, sniffling. He crouched down before her and offered his handkerchief. "There, there, sweeting. Tell me what happened."

She bent forward into his waiting arms and sobbed. "He...he..." She trembled.

"He being who, love?"

"The *duke*. When I departed the ballroom earlier, I went in search of him and found him with another woman."

"Surely, they were only discussing—"

Emily released the most unladylike growl. "What could have they been discussing, when she was on her knees with her mouth over his...?" She pointed to his groin.

The fact that the duke was already beginning to show his true colors, before they were even married, solidified that these two were ill-matched. The marriage was doomed even before it started, and she would never be anything more than his chattel.

"Are you sure it was even him you saw?"

"I cannot believe you are doing this to me. Stop patronizing me! Yes, it was him I saw. And to make matters worse, he acknowledged my presence by announcing that, in no time, I would be doing the same."

His heart lodged in his throat. "Emily—"

The terrace door opened and slammed shut. "What do you think you are doing with my intended? Alone, out here, where there is no one else? How dare you!" Downsbury questioned, huffing and puffing.

'Twas as if the duke had slapped him. "Me?"

There they stood behind the poplars in the darkness, silent other than the sound of crickets chirping. The earl shielded Emily from the duke, and it took every ounce of patience to not strike the insolent fool.

The door opened and closed again. "Oh my. What on earth has happened?" Lady

Thompson asked. "Emily, what have you done, you impossible girl?"

"Yes, what have you done, my dear?" Downsbury added with a hiss.

Between her mother and the idiot, Charles was not sure he could handle much more of these games. All he could think about was whisking her away from this madness.

"Lord Avonlea, I believe this would be your cue to take your leave. This is a private matter and doesn't involve you," the dowager countess quipped.

Oh, it involves me all right. "While that may be true, if I come to find out that you've done something to harm Lady Thompson, duke or not, I will call you out. And do not think for one moment the Marquess of Stoughton will not hear about this."

Charles turned toward Emily and bowed. "My lady, courtship to this man is a mistake, and any notion of marrying him is even more ludicrous. I may not have the power of a duke, but I assure you, even men of my stature would be able to provide you a good home and be a loving husband."

Egads. He could not believe he had uttered those words. But there was no way in Dante's seven circles he would let her fall prey to the coxcomb nor her mother's machinations.

He focused on the older Lady Thompson. "You, as a mother, should be ashamed of what you are putting your only daughter through. Of all the directions you shove her in, you place your daughter's love and happiness in a man who will never be content with a wife, much less with one woman."

The earl stormed off the terrace and, ignoring the guests, he passed by while the dowager countess followed hot on his heels.

She managed to catch him just outside the door and pulled on his jacket. "You should be ashamed of yourself, Lord Avonlea. This whole party was in honor of their betrothal," she yelled. "What were you doing with my daughter out on that terrace? I demand you tell me this instant, you…you…*rogue.*"

Avonlea pinched the bridge of his nose, struggling with every force in him not to shout at the old bat. "Madame, I assure you on my father's honor, I did nothing to disgrace your daughter or family name. I was merely consoling her."

The matron scoffed at him and poked her wiry finger into his chest. "They only had a disagreement. Couples do that. People argue all the time, and certainly do not need rescuing of any sort from the likes of you. You, sir, will maintain your distance from Emily and not meddle in their affairs. Secondly, you'll not involve my son in this, either. The marquess is far too busy with the twins and that whore of a wife."

He could barely breathe as anger boiled beneath the surface. "You'll not address her ladyship in that manner ever again. Am I understood? If any harm comes to Emily, you madam, will rue the day you were born."

"Pray tell, what exactly do you plan on doing? Abducting my daughter? Shipping me off to the Americas? My lord, their union is now a legal arrangement. If anything happens to the future Duchess of Downsbury or me, you *will* be held accountable."

Grinding his teeth, the earl cracked his knuckles. "If we are quite done, Madame, I have places to go."

As he was about to descend the first level of steps, his mother called out, "Charles!

Do not think you can leave this party without even stopping to talk to me."

"I am, and I will."

"But where are you going?"

"To see a marquess about his sister."

Nathaniel had to know something was not right about this marriage, and if anyone could stop it, it would be him.

CHAPTER THREE

"I do not know what possessed you to wander off to the terrace by yourself, young lady, but going forward, you'll not embarrass me further," the duke snarled.

Emily could not believe he was scolding scolded her for running away after catching him in the middle of his indiscretion. Her stomach sank as hurt swallowed her whole. "Is this the way it will always be? For if it is, I will have you know, I will not accept your proposal. I will not be a party to your scandalous dalliances. Enough people have been harmed by them, and I will not stand for it. Me, embarrass you, your grace? I was not the one whose mouth was so indecently—"

"You poor innocent," he chided, closing the distance between them. He smirked at her before pulling her into a tight embrace.

Emily nearly lost her breath when he held her pressed against his chest.

With his free hand, he took hers and rubbed it over his hardening member. Her knees wanted to buckle beneath her. Rage began to consume her, and she could not help but feel violated and repulsed by his touch.

"You need not be afraid of this, nor be jealous of any other women. Once we are wed, those beautiful, pouty lips will be wrapped around my cock in no time. And if you do it right, I just may keep you around longer than I was expecting. But I am positive, given enough time and training, you'll even be open to the idea of another woman joining us, or entertaining others."

Emily gasped at the notion of sharing her future husband and was astounded he had suggested it with ease. Before she could speak, he freed her hand, only to pull down her bodice and expose one of her breasts. Fear riddled her body, and she felt a single tear drop down her cheek.

Much to her chagrin, they were still hidden on the terrace, and no one thought to come looking for her.

"While your tits are not of the size I normally prefer, they will do." He pinched her nipple and chuckled.

A sharp pain from his aggressive touch forced her to step back. "Your grace, you should not be touching me like this in public. We are not even married."

"Nonsense, love. Many men and women before us have done far more sinful things than this before entering the church. Perhaps I will move you into my house once our engagement is announced, and spend some time in the evening educating you on a subject far more carnal."

Emily tried to pull away, but the duke maintained his hold. "And where do you think you are going, love? Into the arms of Lord Avonlea? I think not. That man will no longer be permitted to speak with you."

He released her and gave her bottom a hard squeeze. "Now, run along and clean yourself up. You look affright, and I will not be cuckolded by your inability to keep up appearances. You are about to be made into a duchess, so you may want to start acting as one and learn to do so with perfection."

Heat seared her cheeks. How could anyone be so crass? Her mother was marrying her off to the devil incarnate. And the earl was right. Marrying anyone else would be better than being paired off to his grace. He would never love her, and she was certain he had not loved his previous duchess.

Their marriage would only be in name, and all because her dear mother wanted to be elevated in her status. *Mama*. She needed to find the woman and leave. Nausea washed over her in waves. *Nathaniel, I need you.*

She picked up her skirts and left the terrace whilst the duke laughed abruptly behind her. Haphazardly, Emily pulled the rim of her bodice up, hoping no one could tell what had almost transpired moments ago.

"Run, poppet, because in no time at all, you won't even be able to do that."

The nerve, the audacity. She wanted to run all right. Straight into her brother's house and never return to London. Suddenly, the notion of becoming a spinster did not sound so bad. Frankly, the thought was becoming more appealing by the second.

But then again, she had an earl practically pleading her not to court his grace any longer. In that moment, she had seen a very different man than the boy who had gone to university with her brother. Not only was he handsome in a devilish way, but honorable.

La. That trait certainly stood out the most and made her insides warm.

Not paying any attention to her direction, she collided with the butler.

"My lady. Forgive me."

"Nothing to forgive, sir. I was entirely in the wrong. Have you seen my mother?"

"Yes, my lady. She just came back in the front door. I believe she just finished scolding one of the guests."

Of course she was. *Poor Avonlea.* She would never forget how kind he was, nor how warm he felt when he shielded her from the duke. "Thank you, sir." About to turn down the next hall, Emily found her mother.

"There you are, my dear. Where are you going?"

"Home. I am unwell and very tired. I am sure all I need is some rest."

"Why, of course, dear, let me get my things, and I will go with you."

"Oh, Mama, stay and enjoy the gathering. 'Twould be a perfect opportunity to mingle with some of the men in the duke's circles. Perhaps you will find yourself a randy and wealthy gentleman to take care of you as well." *And keep you from meddling in my life.*

"That sounds like a lovely idea, dear. Are you sure you'll be all right?"

"Yes, Mama. Go."

Giving her a wary glance, her mother turned and left her alone. Perfect. Now she could stop at home and pick up a few things on the way to Nathaniel's. *This time, I will have to find a way to stay even longer.*

"You know…right when I think I finally have peace in my house, you show up at my door and drag me to Wycliffe's. What in bloody hell is keeping Wycliffe, Avonlea?" Nathaniel asked, drumming his fingers on the wooden arm of the chair.

The earl continued to pace by the fireplace when the bloke decided to make an appearance, completely disheveled and clothed only in his breeches.

"What on earth are the both of you doing here? It is after midnight."

"I am not quite sure either, Wycliffe, but *he* will explain." Nathanial scoffed, pointing at Charles.

Why do these two always make me out to be the villain? "Wycliffe, once you tell us the information we seek, we will be out of your sight. I want you tell us what you know of what transpired before the duchess's exile into the country, and any other useful information you may have."

The drunkard stumbled into the seat behind his desk and propped his feet up. His long, dark hair covered the dark circles around his eyes and hid the fact that he had not shaved in days. "If you gents neglected to notice, I drink to forget about *her.* The last thing I want to do is remember how vile and despicable the duke is, let alone think of the duchess's time spent with that clod."

"Why do you say he's vile?" Avonlea asked.

"Go on," Nathaniel added.

"He's a dirty bastard, you know. He knew all those things about Brimley were wrong, but he led the haute ton to believe Brimley was fucking her. Then, there was the fact he threatened to ship her to the continent and leave her in some institution. Though, I have my doubts about where he was planning on sending her. Bah." Wycliffe slammed his fist down. "Enough of this interrogation. Get out of my house now. Both of you. I want m'sleep," the Earl slurred as he rose.

"Fine, we will leave, but I will be back in a few days to check on you. Wycliffe, this isn't right. You need help. I can take you into the country for a few days for some hunting, if you wish."

Once upon a time, the earl would not have considered offering such assistance. Yet, considering the man still grieved for a woman he held dear, 'twas a position Charles knew well. Wycliffe required time to heal, but he still needed to move forward, and mayhap a hunting trip might bring the man to his senses.

"The answer is no. Now, leave me be. I trust you'll find your way out."

Wycliffe left him and Nathaniel staring at each other. "Well, you heard the man. Off we go."

They had not made any progress in obtaining the information Avonlea had hoped for, but Wycliffe's feelings and character assessment assured him that they were correct in their suspicions. Downsbury was the last man on God's earth who could be trusted.

Climbing onto their horses, he grunted and muttered an oath. "Nathaniel, your sister is not safe with him. I can feel it in my blood."

"Avonlea, I simply cannot stop anyone based on a hunch. I need proof. If Emily is in any danger, I need something solid and significant. One doesn't summon Bow Street on domestic matters. Unless you can find something else, I cannot do anything to undo the duke's engagement to my sister."

Frustration mounted, and if there had ever been a moment where he felt useless, now was the occasion. They needed more evidence, anything that would rouse the suspicion of the magistrate.

"Listen, we've known each other since Oxford, and our friendship has been tested in many ways over this last year. I will not have you ride home alone and drink out of anger. Come stay with me at the manor. I am sure after a good nights slumber, we can find another way."

"What would your bride think of me intruding upon your abode at this ungodly hour?" Avonlea asked.

"Hardly anything. Hopefully by the time we slip in, the entire house, including the twins, will be sound asleep."

Thirty minutes later, he followed Nathaniel in through the entrance to find his wife napping on the dais in the hallway. When they entered, she woke with a start. "Good grief, I had not meant to fall asleep out here."

The earl turned away, wanting to avoid embarrassing her in the manner she dressed.

"What are you doing down here, my love?"

"Emily arrived a short while ago. Quite exasperated, too. The poor dear, I fear, is falling prey to your mother's machinations. I am not quite sure she should be marrying the duke, Nathaniel."

The marquess sighed. "Avonlea, please make yourself comfortable in my parlor. I will join you soon."

Charles meandered off in the direction of the parlor, quietly contemplating the marchioness's proclamation. Thank goodness, he was not the only one who could see past the duke's influence.

Moments later, Nathaniel joined him by the fireplace, stoked the fire burning out, and went to pour them some port. "You have to understand, Avonlea. I simply cannot put an end to this nonsense without considering how it will ruin Emily's chance of being marriageable. Think for a moment, if you will, if we were to end this engagement. Name one reputable gent who would offer for my sister. They'd all think she was defective in some manner, and I will not have her name tainted."

He took the glass Nathaniel passed him and watched the deep, rich tones of purple swirl by the light of the flames. "I am not saying you have to ruin her in the process. We could simply make him go away. To be frank, if you ask me, I think he proposed the match because of her dowry."

"While that may be true, it still does not mean I have the right to ruin her reputation. I was true when I said I will stop this marriage from being pursued, but only when we have more to go on. This isn't some conspiracy theory we are working on for head of state, either. We are talking about bringing down a member of the peerage. There will be consequences to our meddling. And I, for one, will not risk the reputation of my children and wife."

The earl knew all too well what this could do to their family. Peace had only just returned to their lives. And what he was proposing would disrupt things once again. "I would never ask you to do such a thing, and I can see now that I should have never returned here."

"Nonsense. Henry will see you to the guest wing. I am sure by morning we will all be in better spirits."

One can only hope.

Emily tossed and turned for what seemed an eternity. Hearing Lord Avonlea's voice in the darkness roused her from slumber each and every time she closed her eyes. Tonight's turn of events certainly left a bad impression of what her pending nuptials to the duke would bring. Even if she confided in her mama of how lewd he was, the woman would never believe her.

She had never dreamed of the day she would marry, much less to a duke. His grace, while he was not entirely attractive, had a charming air about him. Perhaps it was his wealth, or maybe his confidence, that attracted others into his circle. She would hate to be known as the only one who did not particularly care for his sexual prowess or finances.

Emily shuddered to think that people actually enjoyed such demeaning acts. Then the image of that woman on her knees, sucking hard and fast on her betrothal's nether regions invaded her mind again. She had heard of the act plenty of times from attending plays and reading those French novels her friends had stolen off the headmistress. There were other positions they'd often joke about as well.

One night, she and the young ladies giggled in the darkness, when they should have been sound asleep, of how some enjoyed it from behind. That is, until one of the schoolmistresses had walked in on Agnes Miller saying she had watched her eldest brother take a woman that way not too long ago. It had been utterly scandalous!

Several lashings later, Emily had been removed from the school. And thank heavens her mama had never found out about the discussion, as Nathaniel had been the one to collect her. While he had been told a more fabricated version of events, she suspected he knew more than what he led on.

She had always been curious as to what kind of pleasures a woman could receive. Most of the ones illustrated in those novels had been for male release, so what did that mean for her? From what she walked in on, she hardly saw how a woman could enjoy being on her knees, her mouth so full. *How on earth did a person breathe like that?* So many questions and no one to ask.

Well, there was. But would she really get an answer? She could not very well ask her brother and his wife. And her mother was out of the question. Perhaps the answer lie with attending more plays, or maybe even asking another gent. But who? Even more, how to begin such an inappropriate conversation without a man taking it as an invitation?

I am an imbecile. No one would believe her. She was a girl, and her only real value was whether she could bare an heir to his grace's title.

All these thoughts had her in a tizzy, and she was wide-awake. Dawn would not be for hours, and her tummy grumbled from not having eaten during the evening. All in the name of fitting into that ridiculous gown that exposed far too much of her bosom.

Slipping out of bed and wrapping her robe, she lifted a candle from the bureau and crept out of her room. The hall was dimly lit, and the house was asleep. Almost. An old man servant walked the lower level.

Emily stepped off the final, hardwood step and sat the candle down on the table against the wall of portraits. She slipped into the kitchen and knocked on the sideboard to announce her presence. The last thing she desired was put dear old Duncan in his grave long before his time.

"Lady Emily, I had not been informed of your arrival here at Stoughton Hall."

"Well, I imagine not, as I did not arrive until well after midnight. What has you up at this forsaken hour, sir?"

The old man chuckled. "In my old age, dear, I fear I do not sleep much. Though, I had come down in hopes of having some warm milk to help settle my nerves."

"Oh, that sounds wonderful. Could you warm some for me as well, please?"

Duncan had served here ever since her papa was a lad. Three generations was a long time to be a servant, and sadly, even having spent many years in this home, she did not know much about him. *How was it possible to share a house with so many people and never really know any of them? What a sad state of affairs.* Her mama had spent so much time barking out orders and demands, she wondered if she even knew their names.

Before she returned home, Emily wanted to get to know the staff, even spend a little time with her niece and nephew. Up until a month ago, when her mother had dragged her out of this house, she had not had a moment to visit the babies at all.

"There you go, young miss. I hope it settles whatever is bothering you tonight."

She laughed. Nothing could settle what bothered her unless her wedding was called off. "That, I doubt, sir, but I am willing to try anything."

"If I may speak, miss."

"Certainly, Duncan."

He gave her a warm smile. "The staff and I heard through the grapevine you are to be the next Duchess of Downsbury. Is the news true?"

I wish it were not. "Yes, it is. Though, I am not confident I am the best choice for the job. Trouble seems to find me no matter where I go."

"Well, one cannot argue with that, but I daresay, you are young and beautiful. What more can a duke ask for other than male heirs."

"They should be getting an obedient wife, who will be submissive to the bone. I do not have such talent." Emily chugged the last of her drink in the most unladylike manner and rose from her chair. "Duncan, I think this was just what I needed. If you do not mind, I would like for you to take me on a walk of the grounds tomorrow. I would love for us to talk some more."

"Certainly, miss."

CHAPTER FOUR

The Earl of Bridgeton stood glaring at the marchioness with shock. His mouth dropped, and his speech had gone for the moment. "But, my lady, I really should not be going. Nathaniel should be the one to escort you and Lady Thompson to Vauxhall."

"Pish posh! It was Nathaniel's suggestion. He said for you to ask him if you did not believe me."

Charles groaned. *Of all the places to take them.* This, by far, was sure to be a colossal mistake. If the duke ever found out he was there with Emily, his grace would have his hide. "Fine. Just this once."

Considering Emily had not risen yet for breakfast, he had time to go for a change of clothes and return. "Does our future duchess know yet?"

"I imagine not. She only arrived an hour or so before you two. Besides, she'll be fine with it, I assure you. She did mention she owed you some kind of apology for the way her mother behaved, so this outing will provide her with the opportunity."

He had wondered when he would see her next. At least, he knew she would be safe from the duke's advances for now. Though Vauxhall's entertainments were surely a bad influence, he hoped nothing too shameful would be on display in the theater. She had already seen far more than she expected in the duke's care, and he pondered what her thoughts were on the act itself.

The pleasure of having a woman's lips engulfed on one's cock was incredible. The warm, slick heat. The constant movement of a tongue swiping, sucking. The kittenish sounds aroused him.

Heaven help me... The urge to pull out his manhood and see to his relief was maddening. Thinking about Emily doing the same things with her tousled red locks, and her pouty red lips swollen from him kissing her...*Jesus.* If he kept these thoughts up while he was on his horse, he would be walking funny by the time he returned to collect them.

It was truly a pity he could not find anything to break Lady Thompson and Downsbury's engagement. For if he could, he would consider asking for her hand in marriage. He doubted she would accept his offer after the sham of a betrothal with the duke, but Charles longed for a woman to challenge him and make him burn the way she did.

The gel was high maintenance without a doubt, but she had a certain amount of naiveté that appealed to his more masculine tendencies. Instructing her would be a delight. Showing her that not all rakes were total coxcombs and hare-brained was something he felt she needed to see and experience.

In all his years of being a bachelor, not once did he *not* take a woman's pleasure into consideration. Women were not just vessels, but divine treasures who should be idolized. Loved. These were the things women had taught him over the years. It was not until he came into his title, did he learn that the most important rule was that a woman's pleasure came first.

When widow Haverford first approached him after he returned to London from Oxford, she had taught him a wealth of information. For a woman of her experienced years and eccentric tastes, she had instructed him in order to gain favor.

He was not one to brag, but over the years, his lady companions complimented him on his length, girth, and how he used his tongue. While such comments pleased him, they did not do a thing for the loneliness occupying his days of late. He did not like the feeling of being used, and while once upon a time he would not have cared, now life had changed significantly.

However, all of his thoughts these days focused around Emily. She made him burn. Nathaniel would have his arse if he knew of the sinful thoughts Charles had about his sister.

Avonlea stopped outside of his townhouse. His doorman opened the door. "Edward," he called out to his butler. "Once I leave, please have a change of clothing brought over to the Marquess of Stoughton's manor. I was hoping to be home today, but the marchioness seems to have other plans."

"Certainly, sir. For how many days do you expect to be gone?"

"One, maybe two at the latest?"

"Very well, I will have Brandon deliver the items himself after your departure."

Avonlea turned to leave just as his butler called, "This came in for you earlier. It has his grace's emblem on it. I think you should read it right away."

Christ. What does he want now? He broke the wax seal and opened the vellum.

You will stay away from her. If you do not cease your harassment, I will ensure all measures will be taken to secure you. Permanently.

She. Is. Mine.

His grace,

Richard William Waite, the third Duke of Downsbury

Charles crumpled the paper and tossed it to his butler. "Hastings, the next time you receive a missive from his grace, do us all a favor and destroy the damned thing immediately. I am not easily intimidated, and I will not stand for it." I would rather spend time in Newgate for assaulting the duke before submitting to idle threats.

Slamming his chamber door shut and coming out of clothes, he stood by the washstand, conveniently stationed near his bedroom window. Standing stark raving naked, washing his hands and his face, he began to think of Emily. Again. His cock swelled, and his thoughts drifted to her gown the other night.

The way the silk had caressed her maidenly curves. The swell of her small, but perfect breasts revealed she did not need a corset in the least. Easy access. Perfect. Her beautiful, wavy red hair falling just above them. Sweeping to and fro, enticing the male eye, and making his blood rush fast and hard.

The earl caressed his thick, hard cock and pumped.

A noticeable pink swept across her cheeks and down her neck. Would the rest of her body be pink with arousal? Rosy and pert nipples responded to the flicks of his tongue, a moan of delight rising from her throat as he worked between her thighs, lapping up her very essence.

He could barely maintain his stance without using his left hand to grip the washstand. He was so close to release.

He would swipe his tongue until she loosed all her juices. Dripping, sopping, glorious honey. He would rise above her and fuck her until she cried out his name. Charles. Charles.

Breathless and mindless, Avonlea came. Jets of his seed hit the side the basin as he tried to regain control of his own passion. The woman drove him mad, and she had not the faintest idea of what she did to him. Perhaps he should tell her and see what her reaction would be.

Would she run, or would she embrace him? But they would never be as long as her mother was in the picture. And there was not a damned thing he could do about it.

Using the water from the washstand, he cleaned up any evidence of his release and changed his clothes. Vauxhall would be interesting, and he would be lucky if he survived being in the same carriage with her.

Emily hummed for most of the ride to Vauxhall in the carriage, while her sister-in-law prattled on about the twins. She and his lordship laughed at the fact that her brother had stayed home, but when the subject waned, all returned to silence until they arrived at the venue.

Charles cast glances at her and genuinely smiled at Isabel's prattling. But every once in a while, he stared down at his lap and fumbled with his fingers. He gulped hard and exhaled, as if he were deep in thought about something tremendously serious. She would give anything to know what had him so engrossed.

"If you do not mind my saying, I am dying to see the theater. It has been some time since I was here, and I really wanted to see it the first time around."

They both looked at the marchioness in astonishment, when Emily piped up. "Well now, if you and my darling brother had not been so busy with your own scandal, then I would not have the world's loveliest niece and nephew."

Isabel cast an amused glance at Lord Avonlea, and he put up his arms. "The lady said it, not I."

When the carriage came to a halt at the entrance, Emily carefully watched the earl exit and hold out his hands to each of them. Isabel descended first then she, but something strange happened when they touched. His fingers lingered a moment, and he gave hers a gentle squeeze.

Her heart leapt at the sensation, which flowed right down to her toes. Fortunately, they were covered in her slippers, or someone would sure notice them curling. She observed a change in him since the last time they had spoken at the ball.

Emily hooked her arm with Lady Isabel and dragged her toward the theater, his lordship following closely behind. They entered and were greeting by a portly and aged doorman.

"Welcome, Lady Thompson, Lord Avonlea. And who might this darling young woman be?"

Emily flushed. She did not hear compliments all that often, and found it delightful someone had called her a woman without being crass. "I am Emily Thompson, sir. Lady Thompson's sister-in-law."

"Forgive my ignorance, miss. Shall I have one of my lads escort you to the balcony?"

"I believe I know the way, sir. Thank you for asking."

The earl led the way, and she and Isabel trailed after. Emily's heart raced as her eyes followed the curve of his lordship's bottom. This had been the first time she had looked at him so thoroughly, and her imagination ran wild. *What would he be like? Touching me the way Downsbury did?* Would he be gentle and soothing, or would he be gruff and callous? His thighs were thick and shapely in his riding breeches, and she wondered what his bare back would look like.

An unfamiliar warmth crept up her back, and seared her cheeks. Wicked thoughts of the two of them in an intimate embrace. Emily shook her head. Even viewing that woman on her knees with her soon-to-be-husband, she had barely caught a glimpse of his grace's appendage. *Do they all look the same? What does Lord Avonlea's look like?* Her face burned once again as the scandalous musings returned.

When they reached their balcony, Isabel entered first, then she, followed by Charles. He sat next to her.

"Are you all right, Emily? You look piqued," Isabel asked as she turned.

"Oh, I am quite fine."

"Are you sure, Miss Thompson? I can arrange for a glass of water to be brought up," his lordship queried.

"Nonsense. It is a tad warm here, so I shall rectify the situation by removing my shawl." *Good lord. If they only knew what has me so out of sorts.* The musicians finished tuning their instruments when the actors came out.

"Excuse me. I do believe I need to use the…convenience," Isabel whispered into her ear.

"Shall I accompany you?"

"No, dear. Sit and watch the play. I shan't be but a few minutes." Isabel tapped her shoulder and slipped through the curtains.

She was finally alone with Lord Avonlea, but would he indulge her questions, or would he find them too scandalous and report to her brother? *No, he would never do that. Nathaniel would shoot him.*

"Is her ladyship well?" he asked.

"Yes, she is fine. She'll be along momentarily."

"Are you enjoying your outing so far, Emily?"

She could not pay attention to anything other than the fact the gentleman next to her roused her curiosity perilously. "Yes, my lord. Pray, Lord Avonlea, would you mind indulging my ignorance for a moment?"

His eyebrows shot up, and he cleared his throat. "What is on your mind?"

"Do you recall that night at the ball when I confided in you? About what that woman was doing to his grace?"

"Yes." She noticed his body tense.

"Well, I had some afterthoughts, and was hoping to understand a few things." Her breath hitched.

"Emily, I am not entirely sure you should be asking me questions of such intimate nature, but I will do my best to answer in the most delicate way."

"Excellent, my lord. I was hoping you would agree. The first thing I was curious about was that compromising position I found that woman in. Is it normal practice for a woman to pleasure a man that way? And how does it feel? Do they all look the same?" Lord Avonlea shifted back in his seat. His mouth opened to speak, but she observed the shock splayed across his face. "Have I offended you, my lord?"

"You have not. It would take much more than that to surprise me. Emily, I think you should talk to her ladyship about this."

Emily frowned, wondering why he wanted to redirect her question. "Whatever are you afraid of? No one is here to listen upon our conversation."

"Fine. But if I get caught saying these things, I will make sure it is known that the scandalous nature of our conversation started with you." He pursed his lips and groaned. "The act you happened upon does occur in marital relations, and more often in extra-marital ones. The practice itself is not common, and most women find it repulsive."

She for one, could certainly appreciate how offensive the act was perceived, but if it was perfectly acceptable in a man's eyes, would it be the same for a woman? "How long does it take before a man releases, and do they spill into a woman's mouth? You still have not told me if it is truly pleasurable."

"The time it takes for a man to release, I suppose, is a matter of how well a woman is performing. It is expected that a man spills into her mouth, as well as the woman to swallow." By now, he had crossed his arms, and his leg went over his knee. He looked positively cross at her, and it was his turn to flush.

"As for how pleasurable it is, I can assure you that if it is done correctly, then the level of satisfaction would be evident. Each man's member is not like anyone else's. They vary in lengths, girth, and—Emily, truly, you must cease asking me such inappropriate questions."

Just as he shut his mouth, her sister-in-law returned and stood before them. "Is everything all right, you two?"

"Just wonderful." The earl turned away, returning his attention to the curtains closing for the first act.

"Emily? You look like a cat who swallowed a caged bird."

"All is perfectly well, Isabel. You need not worry."

"If you are positive. Lord Avonlea, Nathaniel had made a request earlier, and it slipped my mind until now. He would like you to stay on at Stoughton Hall until the end of the week, if it is not too much trouble."

His lordship mumbled and nodded. "Excuse me while I catch some air before the entertainment begins again." Then, he disappeared.

I have offended him. She had the reputation for being the most obstinate chit London had ever laid eyes upon, and now, she had become the most scandalous one as well.

CHAPTER FIVE

Emily lay in wait for the old grandfather clock to chime twelve bells on the main floor of the manor. While Stoughton Hall was magnificent in size, the clock could be heard from any of the three floors, no matter from what room.

The house had been in a flurry getting the children ready for bed and her brother whisking his wife away for the evening. Even his lordship had retired early into his chambers at the end of this wing. She had quietly followed earlier to learn where she would find him and carry on their discussion from earlier.

Thoughts of her scandalous questions and her mind wandering to what a nude Lord Avonlea looked like, suddenly stirred an unfamiliar feeling in her belly. Dampness settled between her thighs. Even her nipples had stiffened to hard peaks beneath her cotton shift.

How would he perceive her after tonight? Would he deem her the most incorrigible female ever bestowed upon London? Or, would he call her a minx and throw her out of his room? Her only desire was to learn, to educate herself in the ways of pleasure for when her time came to be a wife. To become a wife in name was not an option, nor did she want to play second fiddle to another woman. Yet, the truth be told, Emily desired to get closer with the earl.

Suddenly, the image forever engrained upon her mind of a woman's mouth wrapped around a manhood seemed more of a challenge. The kind of challenge that would certainly scandalize any respectable female. But she desired to know the intricacies of said intimate moments. Perhaps Charles would find it as pleasurable. Emily shook her head and pulled off her covers.

She rose from the bed and put on her slippers and robe. Using the utmost discretion, she opted to leave behind the candlestick and left her room in the dark, knowing all too well it was only the two of them in this side of the house.

Emily gently closed her chamber door and swept down the hall, pausing outside of his room. The glow of the fireplace danced across the floor under the door, but all was silent. Perhaps he was reading from the privacy of the curtained platform bed or standing in the window, basking in the view the west side of the manor offered.

She quietly opened his door and closed it behind her.

No one stirred, nor made a sound.

She took a step forward, parting her lips to call for him.

A soft moan caught her attention and uncertainty crept up her spine. She should not have proceeded, but went on to appease her curiosity. Stealing further into the room, she paused in the corner.

She caught sight of his lordship through the break of the curtains. Charles' eyes were closed, chest exposed as his hand moved beneath the sheet barely covering his waist. *Lord, he's a sight to watch, but what exactly is he doing?*

Emily moved closer, but could not make head or tails of his motions. That is, until he called out, "Emily."

He moaned, then kicked off his sheets.

Good heavens, the sight of him was impressive. Dark, curly hair dusted his chest. His muscles so refined that the creases begged her to touch them. Dampness settled between her thighs again. *What the hell is wrong with me? Did he just moan out my name?*

She could see clearly now as he stroked his manhood.

Emily gasped and stepped back, bumping into a chair. *Drats!*

Avonlea opened his eyes.

She lost all sense of what she had stumbled upon. She should not have been there, no matter how glorious or how beautiful he looked with his eyes closed, or how impressive his body appeared. She would land straight in purgatory for this sin and many others, but she stood at the edge of the platform still.

Charles reached for the sheet to cover himself, as he should, but Emily could not help but feel disappointed at the act of modesty. "You should not be here, young lady. What sort of devil are you, for sneaking upon a bachelor's room as such?"

She pulled away the curtain and smiled upon the shocked earl. "I know this is thoroughly improper, my lord. But please do not let my presence stop you. I want to learn."

He paled and choked at her demand. "Emily, you know not of what you ask. Your virtue is at risk, and your brother would challenge me. Never mind what the duke would say or do if he found out."

"Sir, my lord, I care not for the dictates of proper decorum. You of all people should know that I do not follow the steps of most ladies, nor do I desire to do so. All my life, I have been dictated what to do and say, and now at the first opportunity of discovering what exactly my life would be like after leaving my family, I think not. Please, show me. I want to know what is so fascinating and sinful about the carnal acts between a man and woman."

Emily climbed into bed next to him, her hand caressing the curves of his well-defined jaw, down to his neck and collarbone. His skin was smooth and bristled when her fingers ever so gently brushed against the hairs on his chest. "I think this moment proves I have no desire to give in to regular and proper decorum. You, my lord, are a walking sin. I beg of you, show me how to pleasure you. I want to learn."

He grimaced and shook his head.

"Please."

His member twitched beside her, and she turned to see the purplish crown of his...his...*What did those novels call it? A cock.*

"You realize what this means for you, Emily. If we are caught, you may not have a choice in what happens next. And as it stands, I am already at my threshold for what I can handle where you are concerned."

What in the world does he mean?

He sat up and leaned into her. His cheeks flushed, and he held a gaze of hunger, equivalent to a beggar seeing a sweet roll for the first time in months. His hand rose to slide her shift off one shoulder. "Darling, show me how beautiful those breasts of yours look. I have been dying to know what they taste like," he murmured.

Without hesitation, Emily untied the ribbon holding the front of her shift together. Her breasts spilled over, and he greedily went to work caressing them. His hands were soft to the touch, yet hard when he squeezed. He bent down and took one of her nipples into his mouth. The sensation rocked her. The familiar wetness from earlier suddenly pooled between her thighs once again. She whimpered as he sucked sharp and fondled her other breast.

"Please, my lord, allow me to pleasure you."

"Is that what you desire, love? If it is, then there is no going back. If we are caught, you should know I will be expected to do the honorable thing and marry you. You might even end up a wealthy widow, as the duke may have me hung for this."

"I only want you," she admitted haphazardly as her hands rested on his head, twisting his hair into loose curls.

He removed one of his hands from her and guided her own to the thickness that lie in wait between his legs. He closed his hand around hers, and gently showed her how to pump along his length. His skin glistened with sweat, and he closed his eyes, moaning. She was drawn to his masculine scent and reveled how there was nothing more intoxicating.

Emily followed his instruction and kept at it until he pulled her close and gripped her long hair. "Do not stop, sweetheart. I am just about there."

She continued to slide her palm underneath his, her own heart racing with each passing second. The thought someone could walk in on them at any given moment worried her, but at the same time excited her beyond reason. *So what if my brother, mother, or a servant walks in? His lordship brings out the devil in me.*

All her antics in school could not compare to the world of trouble she would face for this scandalous, sinful education of hers. Purgatory would surely be her resting place for certain, but as long as Lord Avonlea went with her, she would not mind her punishment.

"Emily, do not stop!"

Before she could bat a lash, his lordship grunted. She was sure her brother's wing of the manor heard their foolishness. A wet and sticky substance dribbled down her hand, and the earl exhaled loudly, collapsing back onto the bed. Soon the only sound in the room was his heavy breathing.

"Lord Avonlea, are you well?"

"Perfect," he mumbled as he slipped her shift farther down to her waist. "I could not be better, now that you are in my arms, my sweet."

He did not just call me his sweet, did he? Yes, their moment together had been intense, and she was sure he had not compromised her virtue. *Even more, why did he moan my name earlier? This man will be the death of me.* "Tell me, did I do anything wrong, my lord?"

"Of course not, love. You were perfect, though I am not likely to give you up anytime soon. That, sweetheart, is what it feels like for a man. And now if you will permit, I would like to demonstrate that you, too, can experience the same bliss without losing your integrity."

"Is it not the same, my lord?"

"Of course not, love. Let me show you what heaven can be like for a sweet, deserving angel as yourself, every day, several times a day. You ladies of society need to be reminded you are just as carnal as us men when you aren't busy with the ton."

For the briefest of moments, the sound of his beating heart thundering in her ear gave her comfort, knowing she had done well. She finally knew what it meant to be intimate with another, and appreciated, but now he wanted to pleasure her. She should not allow it, but they had already gone too far. "What would you have me do, my lord?"

He chuckled, his bed shaking in response. "Absolutely nothing, my love. If you have no qualms about removing your shift, I would be able to delight you even further, but please only do so if you wish. I will still be able to pleasure you with or without the gown."

After a moment of contemplating her—their—situation, Emily removed her frock, tossed it to the floor, and laid back.

"That is a good girl. You are beautiful, love. Every inch of you is meant to be worshipped." He rose above her and bent down, gently pressing his lips to hers. The man tasted sinful. She could not help but feel lost with every swipe of his tongue. Yet too soon, he moved to the crook of her neck then through the valley of her small breasts.

That is when his ministrations began.

While his lips closed in around her pert nipple, he slid a hand down the curve of her waist to the apex of her thighs. His touch lingered there while he sucked. His fingers parted her curls and plunged into the warm dampness of her womanhood.

Lord Avonlea's fingers penetrated her inner folds, and the sensation, so new to her, made her shudder. She felt hot, wanton, and unable to control the ridiculous sounds she had begun to make. Lost in the moment, Emily grasped straws, trying to make sense of what was happening to her.

Is this even normal? She yearned for him and could think of nothing else other than this pleasure. Her head swam with nothingness, other than her body reacting. Somewhere in the midst of enjoying his touch, she imagined them together—like this—now and forever. *Shame on me for thinking such thoughts.* 'Twas an affliction brought on by his scandalous talent. But such a wondrous talent should never go to waste.

A kittenish sigh slipped from her lips, and she breathed heavily. Her insides contracted and released in short waves.

"You are almost there, love. Ride it out. Give in to the pleasure and its offerings," he whispered to her in the middle of the haze of lust.

His fingers continued to slide in and out of her while he confused her senses and emotions with his mouth. He had already sucked on both of her nipples and now nibbled on the sensitive flesh beneath her breasts.

Emily's breath shortened, and her insides tensed. He made her mindless with desire. Her heart thundered in her chest, and her skin was ever so sensitive to the earl's heavenly touch. She was blinded by bright light and empty-mindedness. Then, the bed sank next to her when his lordship lay down.

"And that, love, is how a real man pleasures a woman." He wrapped an arm around her and pulled her close. "Mind you, there are more sinful ways to explore, but we shall see what the future holds for us first before I indulge you, my sweet."

For now, all she cared about was being in the arms of this sweet man her brother called a friend. If anyone found out about this mischief, she surely would be locked away. And this riveting man would be called out. She would never let anything happen to him.

Charles was out of his mind for indulging the whims of his host's sister. Hell, Nathaniel would have his arse strung up for being such an ungrateful guest. But Emily tormented every fiber of his being, to the point of being uncomfortable in his own clothing. The damned gel made him want to romp around nude all day and demonstrate how wicked he really could be with her. But Emily needed a husband more than a tarnished reputation.

The only possible way to rectify their carelessness was to get married. Married.

Now the devil had truly done it. He could not simply walk away and pretend *this* never happened. The thought of moving forward without Emily was simply no longer an option. In one night, their passionate embrace had shown him that there was still life after mistakes.

As to the betrothal, it had not yet been announced. Now was the time to persuade her to marry him, and somehow keep her meddlesome mother out of his plans. Nevertheless, it was clear the Duke of Downsbury would not bow out without a fight.

Anger simmered slowly beneath the surface of his thoughts. Her mother and the duke would never agree to dissolve any existing marriage contract between the two, whilst Emily was left in the dark. *However, if they knew of our scandalous night together, what would they think then?* She would be whisked away. So far out of reach, not even Nathaniel would be able to see her. And he, who knows? But Emily was worth the risk. She would be his countess, one way or another.

He awoke shortly after daybreak to an empty bed and a newfound appreciation for the unfamiliar emotion of loneliness. He wondered if anyone had caught her leaving his room, or if they'd even recognize how disheveled her hair had been by the time they were done. *Lord, have mercy on us all.*

Visiting Stoughton Hall had been a mistake. He would never be able to sit at dinner with the marquess again, not without his thoughts wandering back to last night. Or to how truly beautiful Emily had been with him.

He rose from the bed and strode toward the washstand. Tossing on a change of clothes, Avonlea left his chambers. If he stayed on another day, it would be ruinous for all. Stalking down the hall, he found two servants whispering in a corner. His stomach flipped for a moment before he stepped off the staircase. *They could not possibly know, or they would have dragged me out of bed.*

Following the direction of servants leaving the kitchens to the dining hall, he walked, taking his time. The last thing he desired was to enter the room, whilst the others were mid-conversation.

The dowager countess' shrill voice protested from the other room. "I am sure there is something wrong with this tea. Duncan, where in damnation are you!"

He walked in and took the nearest seat available to his old school friend.

"Avonlea, how good of you to join us this morning. You must have slept like the dead. We sent a servant more than an hour ago to wake you, and you did not even stir."

"I slept well, Lord Thompson, thank you for your hospitality. I hope you did not stall your breakfast as a direct result."

"Not at all. We do not stand much on formality here, though my mother would otherwise object."

Emily smiled at him. A blush swept across the apple of her cheeks and down her neck. Her bright blue eyes beckoned to him once again. To embrace her, to touch, to scandalize. Thoughts of their evening made the blood rush to his cock.

The dowager countess swatted her. "Quit making a fool of yourself, Emily. Lord Avonlea, have you no manners? The gel is not available for the plucking. Show some decency, you ungrateful clod!"

"Mother!" Nathaniel shouted from the end of the table. "You will not address my house guest as such."

"Well, if you were not too busy admiring the marchioness's scandalously exposed bosom, you would have noticed *your guest* was making suggestive glances at your sister. Whom, do I need to remind everyone, is soon to be engaged to the Duke of Downsbury. She's to be a duchess and deserves—demands—to be respected as such.

"If no one in this Godforsaken house can give it, then I will have her removed immediately and brought to the duke's estate until they're married. I will not have her debauched in any way, shape, or form." *Yes, she does demand to be respected, but she'll be no duchess. That you can be sure of, Lady Thompson.*

Both the marchioness and Emily threw their napkins and rose from the table.

"I have had quite enough of the insults, Nathaniel. If your mother cannot learn to be civil, then I will be in our chamber until she decides to depart."

Emily did not say a word as she disappeared from the dining hall.

"Well, you've gone and done it now, you wretched woman. Be sure that you are gone from this house when I return downstairs. I will not have you upsetting everyone. Or have you forgotten you are a guest in this house, as well? You may have been lady of the house once upon a lifetime ago, but my marchioness will not be disgraced and insulted in her own home. Dining with us is a privilege you'll have to earn again, Mother."

Nathaniel stormed out the door, leaving Charles with a woman who detested him as much as he did her.

The countess growled and gritted her teeth. For the briefest of moments, the sour woman reminded him of a rabid dog.

There was a reason Avonlea admired his friend. The man had conviction and was not afraid to call anyone out on their misgivings. He gave everyone the benefit of the doubt before passing judgment. And best of all, he loved his wife like no other man.

Charles doubted he would fall to such an affliction, but somehow envied Nathaniel's position. What would it be like for him and Emily if they could marry? Would she love him the same way Isabel did Nathaniel? And would they have as harmonious a home?

Not once over these last few years had he considered the thought of marrying. It was not until last year did he notice how much of beautiful young woman Emily had turned out to be, despite her antics. A house full of children would benefit from a mother who knew how to have fun, but also knew when they were getting into mischief.

He had not much experience in playing with other children as a child, unless his mother took him to tea parties and such. His father, who had passed untimely due to illness before he turned the age of ten and three, did not do much with him either. The man had spent hours poring over his accounts and on social calls with the other gents in his circle.

On occasion, he was invited to learn how to play cards whenever his family entertained. Sadly, those were the only interactions with his parents he remembered.

Their love for each other had been evident in everything they did and said. Not once had he heard rumors of his father straying, and every time his mother attended society events, his father was right beside her. They had always made a united appearance, and much to the ton's dismay, they could never find a scandal to touch his family name.

"Duncan, my good man. Breakfast was excellent. It has been a long time since I have eaten here, and I am pleased to say it still tastes as great as I remember it. Can you please have my horse readied? I will be leaving at once."

"Yes, my lord."

He went to stand, but the countess smacked her palm on the table and glared daggers at him. "Do be seated, Lord Avonlea. I am not quite finished with you yet."

Good grief, how could she not be finished when he was quite done with her and her idiocy? "My lady, not to be rude, but I have important appointments I must keep."

"And I do not give two figs about your appointments. I will only speak my peace once, and the rest will be up to you to decide whether you care or not. You will never be good enough for Emily. She was born to be a duchess, and if you so much as compromise her position in society, there will not be a hovel large enough to hide you. I will find you and ensure your body is never recovered. Now, do what you will with the information, but I have it on good authority, this will be the last time you set your eyes upon my Emily before she becomes a duchess."

"If you are quite done, I will not stand to threats by you or the duke."

The gravity of the situation was becoming quite apparent. The dowager countess was hell bent on elevating her status, and she was using her naïve daughter to do so. Emily would not be safe—not until she was his.

The revelation rippled through his mind. Charles was furious and shocked. Emily would be his. And no matter the cost, he had to expose the duke for the fraud he truly was.

CHAPTER SIX

The Duke of Downsbury paced in his office, shooting his man of affairs a glance. He paused at a sideboard to pour himself a hefty dose of port. "Has there been any word from my solicitor?"

"No, sir, other than his original missive advising Signore Trovatelli was at the dock, waiting for his next shipment."

The duke stifled a groan. He had not expected to be engaged so soon, and he most certainly had hoped another girl would have been ready by now to send off to the Italian pig. Were it not for their previous arrangement, and the possibility of others knowing of their dealings, he would have had the foreigner anchored to the bottom of the Thames.

He swallowed back his entire drink, belched, and returned to his desk. Reaching for a sheet of vellum, he scribed.

Be prepared to send our visitor packing. And do be sure this one will keep him busy for a while. My future bride will not be ready for some time, and I do not want him returning until we send for him.

Be cautious with the delivery as well. Absolute discretion in your next meeting must be key. Neither one of us is prepared to deal with a scandal of this magnitude.

The duke sealed his message with wax, and held it out. "See that he receives this immediately. I am growing terribly impatient with his inability to meet deadlines."

"Right away, sir."

The quiet, middle-aged servant hobbled out of the room to see the missive's delivery. Were it not for his dreadful fall from a horse last year, the duke would have sent the man out on many more duties, as he trusted the man with his life. But fate, as it were, was determined to hinder his success in any way possible.

What he needed was time, and he was running out of it. The quicker he had Emily's dowry, the sooner he would send her packing and buy the

Italian out of his own business. He did not like the idea of working for anyone, let alone some foreigner.

Richard swallowed hard. Fate had gifted him with his wife's tragic accident. She would never learn of his dealings with the chief prosecutor, nor would she ever discover that they were on the verge of losing their estates.

Until this deal with the Italian was finished, he had to keep up appearances. Once he owned all sides of the business, his debts would be paid, and he could return to sampling some of the tons talented ladies.

Thompson's sister would be a problem, though. Considering she lacked experience, his threshold for patience would be tested. Perhaps he would try the same method that he introduced Cordelia too. He remembered her resistance at first all too well.

"Come, my dear, I have a friend I would like you to meet."

"Richard, it is late, and it is highly improper to entertain at this hour."

"My dear, you will learn very fast that nothing is improper in my house. Now, come. That is an order."

She walked toward him warily. Stopping dead center in the hall, she appeared to be listening for which direction a conversation between a man and woman were coming from. When they reached the room, Cordelia questioned her entrance with a glare.

Downbury waved his hand for her to enter. The moment she opened the door, her shriek rang throughout the house. What was supposed to be a discreet liaison with their guests would surely now be speculated by his staff.

"Come now, dear, let us not pretend that the thought of the four of us is not exciting." *He took her hand, pressing it against his cock.* *"I promise, darling, once you have tried, you will never object to entertaining more than myself."*

His duchess broke out into tears. Winston nodded at the Cyprian to approach and console his naive wife. At first glance, the embrace had been meant out of friendship, but when the woman slipped Cordelia's gown down and began to kiss her, he had been most impressed. He loved watching two women caressing each other. Their delicate kisses, embraces, and touching countered the hard fuck they would earn.

The duke had such high hopes for his duchess. Though, when she failed to produce an heir, what else was he supposed to do? Bedding her became boring, too predictable, and her moods irritated him so. His affairs were meant to serve as a distraction for what waited for him when he returned home.

When he first learned of her own dalliances, he desired nothing more than to call out each and every one of the lords that dared touch his property. Then, much to his chagrin, he discovered her condition. The wench had to be dealt with. He could not have his reputation ruined, which was why her exile to the country would have been perfect. Needless to say, things worked themselves out.

Charles leaned back at his chair at White's, carefully scrutinizing the way his somber, gray-eyed friend stared at amber liquid swirling around in his glass. "The brandy is meant to be drunk, or have you lost the taste to drown your sorrows?"

His friend smirked, closed his eyes, and shook his head. "I need to move on, Avonlea. This," he held up his drink, "will not bring her back from her watery grave."

Then, Wycliffe set it down and stared at him. "Why are we really here? I am sure you did not want to meet me to hear about my problems. Though, I do owe you an apology of sorts and my thanks. You did the right thing in dragging me out of Martine's establishment."

An uneasy feeling settled in Avonlea's gut. He had thought of that night many times over and how his friend spoke of the duke. If only he had any knowledge of how troublesome the duke was, he might be able to prove to Lady Thompson that marrying her daughter to his grace was a mistake.

"No thanks is needed, my friend. That is what friends do. And even in the lowest of times, to pull a man up and carry him home is required upon occasion. I do have questions, but not related to your private business with the duchess."

Wycliffe raised his eyebrows then lifted the glass to take a swig. "Carry on then."

"You mentioned that night that the duke meant to do something to her, but instead sent her to the country. What did he intend to do to her, and do you think he's likely to try it again?"

"Good grief, man, I thought you said it was not directly about Cordelia. Christ." He leaned forward and gripped the glass 'til his knuckles blanched. "I have it on good authority the arse was going to put her on the next ship to the continent and sell her to an Italian brothel.

"When her grace confided in me that he threatened to ship her off, I discreetly went to see the port master, who owed me a boon. The gent confirmed, for a parcel of change, there were arrangements in place to have her shipped to the continent where an Italian man would collect her on the shores of Versailles. The manner of business was not clear, but the port master did say it was not the first time."

Blood rushed from Avonlea's face and a chill swept through his body as if he had crawled out of the Thames. "Do you mean to tell me his grace has made those arrangements before Cordelia?" he whispered, clinging to the table.

"Yes. And I doubt he will stop. It is no secret the man is in debt. And a desperate man will go to many lengths to get what he wants."

Charles closed his eyes. *How many women have gone missing over the years?* He could not think of anyone. Yet, if necessary, he could pose the question to the local magistrate. At this point, any information to help break the engagement would be helpful.

"You are absolutely positive the port master identified the Duke of Downsbury as the one making the transactions?"

"How many times do I have to say yes, Avonlea? The duke is indeed up to his neck in a scandal all his own, and one can imagine what he's thinking of doing to the innocent he plans on marrying. Did you know Cordelia came with her own inheritance, and that should she perish before Richard, all the funds would go to him? What do you think now? It all sounds too suspicious, doesn't it? And in addition, everyone in London knows the young Miss Thompson comes with a dowry that includes her inheritance."

Charles put up his hand and refused to hear anymore. He could barely see straight. Fury raged through him. If he did not get his temper in control, he was likely to do something he might regret rather than find a means to rescue Emily before she was sent overseas.

Wycliffe pursed his lips and crossed his arms. "I know that look, Avonlea. It was the same one you gave when you found out what Downsbury had done to the marquess."

"Is it now? This is the look of wanting to a kill a man, yet knowing you can't within the confines of our laws. Pity we do not live in more barbaric times, or I would take immense pleasure in torturing the bastard in any way I can."

"What you need, my friend, is another drink, maybe two." Wycliffe flagged down a server and had another brought over. "This round is on me. Now that you've consoled me, it is my turn to aid you in any way I can."

Avonlea doubted his friend could help him, but the thought gave him comfort, knowing the option was there.

"Mama, was it truly necessary to hide me in the middle of London?"

"Yes, my dear, it was. If that dreaded earl interferes one more time, I will be the least of his concerns."

Emily, for the life of her, could not understand why her mother despised the earl. His lordship had been nothing but kind to her and had shown her mother the utmost respect, until now. And what on earth did she mean she was the least of his worries? What kind of plan was the wretched woman up to?

Emily sat at the writing table in the cozy morning room of Lady Talbot's townhouse, and began scrawling a note to her beloved brother. Someone had to know her mother was up to mischief, and if anyone could stop her, Nathaniel could. She desired he visit her at once, as she doubted she had be permitted to leave without a proper chaperone.

A servant stopped, placing some tea and biscuits in front of her. "Will that be all, miss?"

"Not quite. See that this is sent immediately and, of course, without Mama's attention, please."

"Certainly, ma'am."

There. Now that she had sent word to her brother, she had time to contemplate how to get out of this arrangement with the duke. But every time she thought of him, her thoughts ended up in her evening with Lord Avonlea. His lordship had a wicked tongue to put it plainly. But an oh-so devilish charm, and talented fingers, and…

Her mother dashed into the room, ending the visual she was getting of Avonlea and his impeccable male form.

"My dear, I have it on good authority we will be dining with his grace tonight. Come along, we mustn't tarry. We have some items we must pick up in order to complete your look for the evening."

"But, Mama, we just passed through town yesterday, and only now you want to pick up things?"

"I will not have you looking so paltry and meager. I have had a few more gowns made up and, to clarify, you'll be returning again before the week is out to be fitted for your wedding dress and trousseau."

Emily sighed inwardly. What she would not do to be hidden in a nunnery at this moment. Things were getting far too out of hand, and there was no end in sight she could foresee.

From the moment they returned to town, came home, and changed her gown, Emily could not find a moment of peace. Her dear mama prattled on endlessly. Whether she was to be a duchess or not—the dowager failed to comprehend—the wealth all belonged to her future husband.

That her mother thought that she would be elevated was beyond her scope of understanding. What she did understand was that, the moment a woman is married, she becomes the property of the husband. Losing any voice they may have once had, and no say in how money is spent.

Emily clenched her fists at her side the moment she stepped out of the duke's carriage. She now understood why his palatial manor was held in high regard. Columns, six of them, graced the façade, much like the paintings of the ancient Greek and Roman palaces. The servants lined up outside the door, where they saw to his entrance. "Your grace," Emily and her mother said in unison as they curtsied.

"Come along, ladies. I am sure you will find the food and service stupendous and far more superior than what you are accustomed to. Lady Thompson, if you would kindly follow Myles, I would like to take a moment alone with Emily and show her around. She might as well become familiar with her future."

"Why, of course, your grace," her mother said, following the butler.

His grace extended his hand, offering it to her, and inclined his head. "Allow me to show you around, my little innocent."

She shivered. If he only knew the mischief she and Avonlea had gotten into last evening, he would not think of her in that light. In fact, perhaps telling his grace that their engagement is a mistake would help. Yet a niggle of doubt shadowed her thoughts. She was positive the duke would consider it a relief she had had some exposure to such carnal delights.

When she ascended the final steps of the west wing, the lavishly decorated apartments immediately drew her attention. *Just where exactly is he taking me?* They stopped at a set of double doors guarded by a footman, who then opened them.

"Your grace. My lady." The man bowed and stepped aside.

Emily could not believe what she was looking at. The bedchamber was equipped with what had to be the largest platform bed she had have ever seen. Extravagant linens and silk hung down from the canopy. "Good heavens. Is this my room, your grace?"

"It is indeed. I take it you approve? I, of course, understand your demeanor is of contrast to how modestly you've been living as of late. Though, I assure you, you will be very comfortable here. Now come along, there is another suite I would like to show you."

She followed the duke to the end of the hall where another footman bowed then opened the doors. The room's elegance far exceeded her own. While the bed appeared to be the same in size, the bureau, desk, and the remainder of the furniture were ornately decorated. She suspected she was in his grace's bedchambers. "It is quite large, your grace."

"I know. Not that I need your approval, but I am glad you think so."

He slipped in behind her and wrapped his arms around her waist. A chill crept up her spine, and her skin broke out in goose flesh. She could not have been more disgusted and repulsed by his behavior. His hands wandered up the front of her bodice, stopping at her bosom. He grabbed both her breasts, kneading them hard and making her uncomfortable at how alone she truly was in the moment.

"Have you given my offer any consideration, Emily? Would you like to stay here until we are married? That way I can educate you when we are alone on how I would like things done. *Mmm.* I rather like the idea myself and grow hard at the mention."

She tried to pull away, but his grace was determined to keep her in his embrace. Then he released one arm and pulled up her skirts.

"Please stop, your grace. This is wrong. I do not want to marry you!" Emily struggled to pull away from his strong grasp. Yet every time she pulled back, he leaned in further and harder.

The duke released her, taking her by the hand and leading her deeper into his chambers. She soon found herself staring at a wall of beautiful but nude artwork. "These pieces, I had personally commissioned. They're stunning, and very well depict some of my true passions. There is much to be learned with the carnal pleasures. Once we are together, I plan on taking you every way shown in all the scenes."

She covered her mouth to silence her gasp. Some portrayed numerous women pleasuring one man at the same time. Another was an exact replica of the compromising position she had walked in on nights ago.

Emily felt the duke's heated presence behind her. When she stopped at the next painting, she stumbled back in horror. Heat burned her cheeks. "Good Lord. The men in that painting—how is it even possible for a woman to accommodate so many? You say these pieces were commissioned? Where were they painted? These should be confiscated."

He sneered. "Are you shocked, my dear? Most excellent…These were all painted by individuals who consented to the acts. I do believe they were all done at a local establishment where your beloved earl frequents."

How can he say such lies? His lordship would never stoop to such depths of depravity. "I have had quite enough of this, your grace. I am disgusted, embarrassed, and thoroughly shocked."

He simply laughed. "Get used to it, my dear, for once we are wed, it is my expectation that you will master each of those positions. Of that you can be certain."

Emily's stomach lurched, and she began to feel faint. Tears fell mercilessly, and his grace only smirked at how successfully he held her. "Please, your grace, we've tarried long enough."

He released her after chuckling hard, but just as quickly as he let go, he spun her around to face him. The duke lifted her chin and secured her so she could not move. "I will not be denied, Emily. You may not live here right now, but when you leave after dinner, the arrangements will commence. The sooner you are deflowered, the better, and the easier it'll be for both of us. I have big plans for you, but you need instruction first."

His grace finally removed his hold. "Stay if you want, but if you remain any longer you will not be permitted to leave my chambers anytime soon."

Emily ripped away. She flew out the door and ran as fast as she could until he caught up with her. She turned to him. "I will not be thusly humiliated. If it is all the same to you, I would rather we waited until the marriage bed. Besides, you have not even proposed yet, and just so we are clear, I refuse!"

The duke growled. "You insolent girl. Who do you think paid for that dress you are wearing? You will do exactly what I say, when I say it, and whom with. Am I understood? You are mine. There is no way out of this contract, whatsoever. Once you give me an heir, I will have no other use for you, and you will be free to do as you want. But, until then, I will fuck you as I want, how I want, and as many times as I want."

And there it was. Her future husband, the Duke of Downsbury, talking like a bounder from Covent Garden trying to solicit his soiled doves to the patrons. *Avonlea, I need you now.*

Charles had left White's with Wycliffe hours ago, but when he returned to his townhouse, he could not stop thinking of what his friend had said. His imagination ran rampant with wild and completely impossible things. *But were they entirely impossible given what Wycliffe had discussed of the nature of the threats the former duchess received?* There had to be some truth.

First thing in the morning, he'd visit the magistrate and conduct his own investigation. One, he hoped, would bring down shame and scorn upon the duke. If he could find a way to have the duke's title stripped and leave him powerless, he and Nathaniel would surely have an opportunity to knock some sense into the man.

Tired, frustrated, and still thirsty, Avonlea rang for his butler.

"Sir?"

"The port, man. Where is it? I have been trying to find it and have not yet."

"I will fetch another from the cellar, my lord. Was there anything else?"

He pondered the question for a moment. "Actually, there is. What do you know of girls—women—disappearing without a trace?"

"It happens all the time, sir. In White Chapel, it isn't uncommon—"

"No, no, that is not what I meant. I mean here, in London, ladies of the ton, or girl's fresh out of school some may have thought ran off to the Gretna Green."

The aging man rubbed his chin. "There was a Baron Foster. His daughter of ten and nine was never seen after attending some ball two summers ago. There were rumors she was carrying on with a distinguished gentleman, but no one came forth to confirm who the gent was. Her poor family. The gel was engaged to Lord Broxton's eldest. 'Twas an embarrassment to find out his betrothed had run off."

"Surely, that can't be the only occurrence of a disappearance?"

"There was the matter of the dowager Duchess of Hamptonshire. She was supposedly having an affair with another gent and was last seen at a ball."

How convenient, and all too coincidental, that both women went missing after a dance. If Downsbury was up to his neck in this one, Charles planned to expose him at once. "That'll be all. Now, run and find me some port. I have much planning to do and would like the warmth to settle my rattled nerves."

A quarter of an hour passed before the elderly butler rejoined him in the library. "My lord, are you sure there isn't anything else I can do for you?"

"No, old chap. Go on to bed. I have kept you up long enough."

"Very well, sir, but should you require anything, please ring for me."

Charles gazed into the fire for some time, watching the flames flicker up, dancing the devil's jig. *Just how can I even begin to approach the magistrate about these supposed disappearances?* What were the chances those women were sold to an Italian man in Versailles, to keep silent about the duke's affairs or other crimes he might have committed?

The earl was now entering into dangerous territory, but in the end, if it kept Emily out of the arms of the brutes, then his job was done. Well almost. Until she was his bride, no one would be safe while London's menace was on the loose.

After a night of fitful sleep, Avonlea entered the century old building where the magistrate conducted his business. He approached the reception desk and waited impatiently for the clerk to spare a moment to look up.

The short, stout man lifted his head and pushed up his spectacles so they sat on the bridge of his nose. With a nasally voice, he asked, "Do you have an appointment, sir?"

"I do not."

"And who exactly are you expecting to see without an appointment?"

"The magistrate, of course."

"His honor is not available for random walk-ins. Would you care to make an appointment? But, before you do so, state your business."

"No, I do not have time to come back. It is a matter that is delicate and requires urgent attention."

"Excuse me, gentlemen, perhaps I might be of some assistance," a man said from behind him.

The earl turned to find a tall, lean, and gray-haired gent approaching them. "And who might you be?"

"An excellent question, Lord Avonlea. I am the Chief Prosecutor, William Sayers, at your service. Follow me, and I will see what I can do in the magistrate's place."

Avonlea nodded and followed the man past a pair of French doors and through a long passageway.

"You will have to forgive Byron's manners. The man has aspirations of becoming a solicitor in his late age, so he is a bit hard to discuss anything that is beyond the rules, including making appointments. So, what is the delicate matter you were looking to talk over?"

Something about the man did not sit well with Avonlea. His dark eyes followed every movement. "I am here to discuss some disappearances that might have occurred over the course of two years."

The prosecutor chuckled and poured them brandy. "I had no idea you had become a runner, Lord Avonlea. What has brought on this sudden interest?"

Accepting the amber liquid, Charles took a swig. "I have reason to believe some ladies of society may have been sold to an Italian in Versailles as a means to keep silent. Who else is involved and what the reasons, I do not know. However, I do have every intention of uncovering the truth, no matter the cost. Do you know anything about the disappearances I speak of?"

Sayers went rigid, all the humor from his face lost. "I have no idea what you are talking about, but you are sputtering about nonsense. All my cases are closed and have been closed for the last two years. Some of my cases were of chits running off to Scotland to get married. It is not my business where they go after that or where they take residence.

"If you want my advice, my lord, you must drop this at once. Stirring up trouble will not gain you any favors, and you might ask for more trouble by bringing up embarrassing moments for local noblemen."

Just who does this man think he is? Charles pushed his glass away and stood from the rickety chair. "Mr. Sayers, I know when I smell a rat, and you stink of scandal. I will take my leave now. But know this, if you are involved in any way, you too will be destroyed. I hope for your sake, you have not done something to shame your family as well."

"Is that a threat, my lord? For if it is, I caution you to think wisely before continuing. There are no missing girls, other than the soiled doves from White Chapel and Covent Garden. If you are insinuating I had anything to do with those disappearances, you are mad and have overstayed your welcome, sir!"

Charles rushed out of the office, slamming the door behind him. The situation was far from over, but it all made sense now. Downsbury would have someone to cover his tracks and being friends with the prosecutor was just the way to keep the questions away. *Well, that, and meddlesome lords from becoming suspicious.*

CHAPTER SEVEN

Emily wandered in the garden, taking time to admire the pansies and roses Mrs. Simmons had planted years back.

She often wondered what these great men did when they were home alone. Some of the time, she and the young ladies she gossiped with overheard the comings and goings of mistresses, or the men simply visiting the gaming hells or attending Madam Martine's establishment, all heard through their mothers' gossip over tea.

On one occasion, young Miss Willows divulged her take on the daily accounts of the local men, so her mother questioned her husband's fidelity. When Mrs. Willow's followed him the one day, the driver happened to stop at Madam Martine's. Her mother apparently bullied her way through the house until she found her husband in the throws with two women.

The girls had all gasped at the horror and embarrassment of such a sight. They felt terrible for their friend, but as it were, six months later, Miss Willows had eloped to Scotland. No matter where Emily looked, there was scandal to be found everywhere. Last season with her brother, and now her ridiculous engagement to the Duke of Downsbury.

She plucked a spotted daisy from its resting place, and pulled off its petals one by one. This whole marriage business could not have been a bigger farce. Soon, all of London would be addressing her as 'her grace', the Duchess of Downsbury', while she only wanted to blend in with the background. Emily did not belong in the circle of high society, much less know the first thing about entertaining politicos.

And she would not tolerate her husband's skirt chasing ways.

While she was still a woman with no say in her husband's coming and goings, the last thing she would accept was being the *other* woman. She did not want to be a broodmare for an overbearing prig, a disrespectful clod.

Frustrated, she tossed the limp stem and returned indoors. The house had become quiet. Her mother was up to something. Some days, the woman was worse than a child.

Emily happened upon her room and found her mother packing her trunks. "Mama, what are you doing?"

"What does it look like? I am packing your trunks. We will be heading over to the duke's manor for the remainder of your engagement. When you were off using the convenience before we left, he asked that I bring you as soon as I could. He has already managed to secure your own staff."

Emily shook her head with defiance. "Mama, you *know* I would never ask anything of you, but I think my supposed impending nuptials to the duke are a terrible idea. I would rather not become a duchess at all. Besides, it has not even been announced, and the *clod* has not even proposed."

Her mother straightened, standing there, mouth gaping wide. "You would rather you did not marry the duke!" she shrieked. "And who else do you think will offer for you? Lord Avonlea?"

Yes! She desperately wanted to scream out, and technically, he already had. *Was it so terribly wrong to want someone that felt so right?* Propriety be damned. If she had to give up her station in the haute ton and be shunned for wanting her earl, then that is what she would do.

"Listen to me, you ridiculous gel. You will marry the duke. The contract has been signed, and the nuptials are to take place in one month. You have no other option unless you fall ill and die from consumption. You will marry him, even if I have to drag you to the altar myself." Her mother slammed the trunk closed and rang for a servant. "Have this brought down, immediately."

Then, she turned to Emily, scowling. "Once we arrive at your new home, I would highly recommend you have a bath and rest. You will need every moment of rest you can get. Tomorrow, we will begin shopping for your wedding dress and trousseau. In addition to picking out flowers and such. There is much to do, so do not tarry long."

Her mother turned and stomped her way out. *How has my life spun so out of control? Is this how it had been for Nathaniel and Isabel?*

Downsbury poured over his accounts. He was nearly done paying off a great debt to Lord Bainbridge and his ridiculous loss. It was rather ingenious that he had struck an agreement with the Italian two years prior. Gold for women. All he had to do was pretend to carry on an affair, instruct them in carnal ways, give them some laudanum, and see them off on the boat.

The arrangement had gone rather well, but the bloody foreigner wanted more women, and he could not find any with such frequency without being caught. But when he had sought the friendly assistance of William Sayers,

Chief Prosecutor, they too had struck a bargain and divided the gains and the responsibilities of training the girls.

His butler stood at the door and bowed. "My lord, Mr. Sayers is here to see you. He said it was a matter of some urgency."

"Show him in."

"William." The man had a long face, one that did not hold his usual optimistic demeanor. He normally took pride in the way he presented himself, but now, he appeared as though he had fallen into a barrel of whiskey.

"Your grace."

"What has you in such a state? Your latest case?"

"No. We have a problem, and his name is Lord Avonlea, the Earl of Bridgeton."

Downsbury let the ledger fall to his desk. "What are you talking about?"

"His lordship was by the office earlier, inquiring about open cases of missing women. Do you think he is on to us?"

Impossible. How can he even suspect? All the meetings with Travotelli were held in private at Martine's and on the wharf. In addition, none of the girls would have spoken to anyone else as they were kept in wealth at William's private townhouse. "This is very bad news for us. What do you intend to do?"

"Me? Why should I do anything? This was your brainchild. I cannot simply have someone arrested for asking questions, especially after I invited him into my office."

Blast that damned fool. I would like nothing more than to see his body sink to the bottom of the Thames. "Well if he's already sought you out, I am certain he will try his luck here. Ensure you have a runner at your disposal. I will make sure we have a reason to have him arrested. We cannot have him running amok, spreading vile rumors about a respected member of the peerage."

The prosecutor snorted. "You go too far with that comment, your grace. After those dealings with the Marquess of Stoughton last season, there are many who are still wary of your legitimacy."

"Just make sure your girls are not talking, and all will be well. I will be ending this partnership just as soon as my debt is paid and I take full ownership of this asset overseas. All of this will be over in a snap."

"I truly hope you are certain. If my wife gets wind of this, she will have my bollocks served at the next dinner party."

"Well, if I were you, I would train your wife better. You know the way out. See that you do not visit me so often. If we are being watched, you are only giving them reason to follow you."

This will be over soon enough. The young Miss Thompson's dowry would see to that, and the money he had stowed away would cover the price of procuring the establishment. He could gamble his heart away, fuck who he wanted, and gain a profit from the girls he kept on at the club.

Life was about to improve. And no one, especially an earl, would stand in his way.

The duke got up and walked toward the fireplace. He stared into the dark hollow, thinking of nothing, until a knock at the door roused his attention. "What is it now?" He craned his neck to find the chief prosecutor standing there. "What more could you possibly have to say?"

"I just thought of something...Perhaps we could look into his time serving for the war office. I am sure we will be able to uncover something from his past. Leverage is what we need, and digging up a secret is the solution."

Richard paused. *The man has a point.*

"Well, you have all the connections that you frequently boast about. Find out what you can, and I will do the same. Someone has got to know of his time passed on the continent."

And when you have finally figured out what is happening, it will be too late.

Avonlea waited until no one else was left outside the duke's palatial home. Charles was impressed and stumped as to how the duke managed to keep the manor, considering his finances had taken a bit of a dive last year. *How on earth did he manage to keep cash flowing in?* Unless he really was selling women on the side to the Italian man.

Charles still had much to prove, but luckily, he had convinced Wycliffe to hire someone and seek out the foreign accomplice. With a little luck, and God on their side, they would be able to verify who the man was and where exactly the women ended up.

He approached the door and pounded on it. When it opened, he was met with an ogre of a butler, and a surprised duke.

"What can I do for you, Lord Avonlea?"

The earl ground his teeth, trying to bite back any profane language. "I desire a private audience with you."

"Very well, if you will follow me." Downsbury turned to the butler and sneered, "You know what you must do."

Now, what in the world was is supposed to mean?

Avonlea followed the dolt until they were in his expansive library. He doubted very much the man read anything other than the label of a brandy bottle, but he would soon find out.

"So what is it that you desire to speak of? And be quick about it. My bride arrives today, and we have a wedding to plan."

The word "bride" rolling of the duke's tongue made Charles want to vomit, violently. "I find it hard to believe the chief prosecutor hasn't called yet. Surely, you know why I am here."

"I do not, nor do I care. The only reason why I even permitted you to step foot in my house was to deliver my own warning. Stay away from Emily. Do not think for one moment I have not talked to Lady Thompson in great lengths over your distasteful and disrespect manner of reproach. The girl is to be my wife, and I have no hesitation of disposing the problem at hand."

"And what problem is that?"

"You."

Rage blinded him. The most urgent need to put a hole in the man's black heart became a necessity. "Me?"

"Do not play me for a fool. I have heard of your spectacle at the magistrate's office, and I know of you spending the night at the marquess' home when my fiancée was there. I am not a man to be trifled with." The duke rose from his seat and smirked. He walked around his desk and seated himself at the edge, folding his arms across his chest.

"Nor I. And I will warn you once and for all, if I track back missing women sold on the continent to you, or the prosecutor, you are both finished. Do tell me one more thing before I see myself out."

His eyebrows rose with a speculating glare. "And what would that be?"

"What exactly will you do with Emily once you are bored of her? Will you ship her off to the country as you did your previous duchess, or will you sell her to some Italian brothel? The evidence is stacking, your grace, and you are running out of time before you are caught."

The duke simply sat there and laughed. "I think, once I have plucked her virginity, which I imagine might be tonight when the entire house is asleep—she is after all, due for an education—I might share her with the prosecutor.

"Once we have married and her dowry is mine, I just might sell her. I suppose I should have waited until you were carefully stowed away at Newgate before sharing this, but I must add, even with the small tits she has, I am sure she will make many a man happy. And guess what, there isn't a damned thing you can do about it, because you will be hanged for treason. You are an embarrassment to the war office. Smoke houses and fallen doves? Is it any wonder why you have not been found out yet?"

Charles clenched his fists. Fury raging beneath the surface and the sudden urge to commit a murder was prevalent. He bound from his seat, flying over the desk, and tackled the duke to the marble floor. Straddling Downsbury as the cold marble bit into his knees, he swung his fist back and struck several times.

The duke wheezed and coughed.

Rough hands pulled Avonlea back. He fought them off but to no avail, finding himself hauled off the bastard.

Downsbury struggled to his feet. "That is enough, Lord Avonlea. A runner is already here to take you to jail, and I suspect you will be detained for quite some time."

"You will pay for this," the earl yelled, kicking at the men holding him back. "If you harm one hair on her head, I will kill you with my bare hands."

"And how do you suppose you will do that when you are in prison for accosting a highly regarded member of the peerage, you idiot? The closest thing you will get to murder is a rat, and that will be for dinner. Take him outside and throw him into the carriage at gunpoint. I will not have him frightening the ladies when they arrive, which should be any time now."

"This is not over, Richard." Charles hand throbbed and his head pounded as if he had drunk himself into a stupor. Bile rose from his stomach.

The Duke of Downsbury smirked. "Where have I heard that before?"

The damned fool does not even realize this will only be the beginning.

CHAPTER EIGHT

From the moment Emily and her mother had set foot in the duke's manor, there was an air about the place that something had transpired before their arrival. The duke had not joined them for dinner, and the servants diligently attended to her and mother as if they were royalty. Something was certainly amiss, but she was grateful in every regard that he had not visited her bedchamber as he had threatened previously.

For whatever had kept him away had to be of great import or trouble. Her thoughts wandered to what else he might be doing. Perhaps the rake had gone off seducing another society lady, for which she was eternally thankful for. Ever since her dealings with Avonlea, she had not been able to think of anyone else but him.

When her maid entered her chambers to assist with her disrobing, Emily only inquired about his grace's wellbeing. "Is his grace well?"

The young woman flushed and lowered her head. "If I may be so bold…"

"Go ahead. We are alone here, and I will not say a word to anyone else."

As the maid undid the back lacings of Emily's corset, she whispered, "His grace had a visitor earlier this evening. A Lord Avonlea, or something to that effect. The master and he argued, and they fought. The gent was then carried out and taken to jail by a runner. It was quite terrible. The other servants are worried for you and your safety with his grace. Things were overheard of the sordid type, and while no one will explain to me what was said, I want to caution you."

Good heavens! Jail? What in the world happened? Emily fought tears back fiercely, pressing her handkerchief to the corners of her eyes. She could not let the whole household know how deep her affections were for Charles.

"You are safe to tell me what kinds of things were said. It is pitiful enough I do not wish to be married to him, but if he means to cause harm, I will not stay. If I asked you to help find Lord Avonlea, would it be too much of an inconvenience?"

"Certainly not, ma'am. A few of the others will, too, if I ask them."

"Perfect. For now, if anyone should inquire on my taking visitors, let them know I am unwell. My mother and the duke included. I am even willing to take a draught or something to help pass the time asleep. I also would like some assistance in slipping away to see Lord Avonlea. Mama is planning a trip to town to visit the dressmaker, so if there is a way for me to slip out, I would like to know."

"I will see what can be arranged. My brother occasionally works for the runners. Mayhap, he will be able to assist. It would not be the first time he has helped with something unofficial. Before I leave ma'am, you should know—I have only been employed here for a short period, but it is my understanding the master is very horrible man.

"The servants have mentioned to steer clear, most especially when he has men over late in the evenings. Had the previous duchess been warned, perhaps she might have been saved. Such a tragedy, really. Did you know, she was rumored to be with child?"

The maid curtsied and took her leave in silence. While it was appreciated to be left to her thoughts, the chatty woman could have stayed for a bit longer.

Slipping into her warm bed, Emily wondered how long it would before she escaped the manor. Nathaniel could only hide her for so long before she was found out, so going to him would be out of the question. *There has to be another way.*

What she would do to know what they argued about. Surely it was about her, but there had to be more. *Charles affections for me cannot be the only reason why.* What hold did the duke have over Charles? More importantly—was he injured? Good God! She could not even begin to fathom the discomfort he must be experiencing right now. He deserved so much more. Would this madness never end? Just how low would the duke stoop to set an example?

Maybe the answer to this predicament was to prove his grace had gone mad. But how does one achieve such a feat, without being caught or compromised? The unfortunate thing in all of this was that her mother would deny any allegations too. She would never believe her that the duke meant harm.

Charles sat on the disgusting and slimy floor, wishing he had inflicted more pain on the duke. The wretched bastard would pay dearly for his crimes, and the moment the earl had proof of the whereabouts of those women, the duke's life would be over.

The heavy door down the hall opened and slammed shut. Prisoners hollered obscenities while others rattled the bars of their confines.

"Avonlea, you bastard, you have two visitors. I will be back shortly. We would not want you conspiring anything, would we?" The mangy guard, who looked as if he had not had a bath in ten years and fallen into a tub of ale, disappeared into the darkness.

A young ruffian and Wycliffe, of all people, stood before his cell. "Did the boy come with you, Wycliffe?"

"He most certainly did not. But I get the impression he is here by someone else's request."

The young man puffed out his chest and took off his cap. "My lord, my sister serves the young Lady Thompson and is seeking permission to see you. She also wishes you well and misses you terribly. She desires to dissolve the marriage pact, but they have her detained at the duke's manor."

Christ. She really is there. He glared at Wycliffe, searching for a plan. "Young man, what is it that you go by?"

"Gregory, my lord."

"She may not come here. No proper lady should ever enter such a place. Although, if you stay just a moment, Wycliffe may have use for you yet."

"What are you about, Avonlea?" Wycliffe asked, crouching down.

"Have you already sent someone across?"

"I have."

"How long do you suppose we have?"

"One month."

"That is too long. We must act now. She is to be married in one month, and we need to be rid of him sooner. As it stands, no one will listen to me, and I have a sneaking suspicion they will move me to Newgate."

"What do you have in mind?"

The only thing that will have him hanging on the gallows. "You remember my hunting lodge, do you not?"

"I do. We need to get her there." Wycliffe turned to the boy. "And you are going to help us."

The boy nearly bounced. "My lord, a most excellent plan, too, as the women plan to go dress shopping. We can simply remove the duke's driver, and I can steer the carriage where needed."

"The duke's carriage would be too noticeable. We need something like a hackney coach or a farmer's cart from the market."

"Both can be managed. I am sure the boy can arrange the switch, and I will ride with the lady to ensure her safety. What will you do about Nathaniel? Will you tell him?" Wycliffe asked Charles.

"Not just yet. I do, however, need to talk to him about how delicate this situation has gotten. He has the connections to put someone on this case. There are far too many corrupted people involved, and I need someone who will not dismiss my evidence."

"I will see if I can convince him to visit you."

"Thank you. You are a good friend, and I owe you."

Now if only I could get out of jail, join with Emily, and travel to Scotland.

Hours passed and the earl had not heard a word from the marquess. *Nathaniel would not abandon me now, would he?* Uncertainty flooded the pits of his belly, and for the first time in a long time, he was not so sure he would be able to get out of this situation.

About to doze off, he heard the guard rake his baton along the cell door. "Wake up! You have company."

"I see you have made yourself quite comfortable, Lord Avonlea, though, it would be my suggestion not to get too familiar with these surroundings. I plan on having you transferred before weeks end. Newgate has room for one more traitor," the chief prosecutor announced.

Charles rose from the floor, dazed. "What in the devil are you speaking of? I am not a traitor."

"Of course you are. I have some evidence here—albeit doctored—that proves you were working with the French. Imagine how all of London will react when they learn of the news."

Words escaped him as he tried to think how, or why, they would produce false evidence. But then it dawned on him. If he were not so close to the truth, they would not have gone to such lengths to have him transferred.

"Well, I must be going. I will be informing the magistrate of my discovery this evening. Do enjoy your short stay. I imagine these will be the most comfortable of living conditions until you are hanged."

The moment the door at the top of the stairs closed, Avonlea fell to his knees, burying his head into his palms. If Nathaniel did not come to his aid, he would never see her again. If only he could hold Emily just one last time.

Emily paced her room to and fro. Each night since their arrival, the duke had not made good on his threat, and as each moment passed by, she was grateful. This morning, though, while her mother was busy making plans with the dressmaker for various parts of her new wardrobe, she would slip out the door. She would make her way down the cobblestone streets with her maid and find Avonlea.

A gentle rap at her door alerted her. She stood as femininely as possible and stared like an eagle at who entered. Her maid slipped in and set some linen down on a nearby chair. "Thank goodness it is you. I was beginning to get worried."

"Worried. Why ever for, ma'am? The plan is in place. My brother and his friend will be waiting for us to slip away. I promise you, you will never have to worry about the duke again."

"You are positive our plan will work?"

"Ours will, but let us only hope his lordship will be able to get out of jail in the meanwhile."

The young maid wrapped a shawl around Emily's arms and led her down the hall. Each servant they passed smiled and winked at her. *Good heavens, are all of them part of my grand escape?* If they were caught, their employment would be terminated.

Her mother, already seated in the carriage, glared at her and frowned. "I am not accustomed to arriving late to any engagement. While I understand you are displeased we have moved here much earlier than expected, I will still not have you embarrassing me. So get in, both of you." She tapped the window with her walking stick. "Drive on, and make haste. I do hate being late."

Emily, her mother, and the maid sat there in silence for a half hour until the carriage stopped again in a crowded street. A footman opened the door and assisted the ladies out then escorted them into the shop.

A tall, gray-haired woman, with her hair wrapped tightly into a bun, approached her mother. The woman curtsied. "Lady Thompson, I see you have finally brought our future duchess. A pleasure to meet you, your grace."

"No need for such formality, ma'am. I am not wed, and the duke may yet come to his senses and desire not to marry me."

Her mother glared at her, but the old woman simply laughed. "Do not worry about a thing. I will take your measurements and show your mother a few designs, and then we will begin discussing your trousseau. There are impressive styles coming out of France right now, so I am sure with one of those daring negligees, his grace will be most pleased with your attempt to catch his interest."

"I trust both yours and Mama's judgment. Where would you like to take my measurements?"

"If you will follow me. It is just over here." Emily followed the woman until she was hidden away behind a curtain while her maid and mother waited on the other side. "I have a great many designs we can select, but you have a figure the duke will find appealing and will accommodate my fashionable styles. Do you have a particular one in mind?"

"Not really, ma'am."

"Well, worry not. We will put together the most extravagant thing the ton has ever seen, and you will be the envy of every bride this season." The woman pulled, tugged, and then tossed her measuring tape off to the side. "You may get dressed now. Shall I have your maid come in?"

"Yes, please." The young woman entered while the seamstress wandered off deeper into the shop with her mother. Emily leaned in. "Are we set to go?"

"Yes, ma'am. We should let them know we are looking around."

They meandered about the store until they found the older women hovering over several sketches and swatches of fabrics. "Mama, we are just going to look around."

"Very well, but do try to stay out of mischief."

"Of course, Mama." Emily watched and waited for the driver to become distracted so she could remain out of sight when she left the security of the store.

Then her signal came. A boy tumbled across the street, sending a crate of merchandise flying toward the other side of the carriage. The man hopped out to assist the child.

She reached for the door and glanced back at her maid, waving for her. "Come along. We must go, now."

"I cannot go with you. Otherwise, they will suspect I am up to something, too. Besides, if you are caught and brought back, who else do you think will attend to you?"

"Very well, good luck. I hope Mama does not sack you after this stunt."

"I doubt it. There will be a cart down the road. Look for a boy sitting in the front with a newspaper cap. He will point you in the right direction."

"I cannot thank you enough." Emily snuck out the front, trying to avoid rattling the doorbell. The last thing she desired was to be chased down the street. She lifted her hood and kept her head hung low, avoiding eye contact with even the pushiest of merchants.

She found a cart at the corner matching the maid's description. As she climbed in to talk with the boy, she was grabbed from behind. A heavy hand covered her mouth and kept her from shrieking in surprise. She kicked back, hoping to injure her assailant, but the brute pulled her away and carried her into another carriage. He tossed her in and when she had managed to collect her thoughts, the door had already been slammed shut.

The man pounded on the window, and the buggy began to move away from the busy street and down an alley. "You needn't worry about any harm coming to you. I am merely carrying out Avonlea's wishes. Am I correct in assuming you are wanting to see him again?"

Emily could not find the words, instead she nodded, frightened of what she had started. *What has he done? Was this all meant to look as an abduction?* Good heavens, this was quite the scandal. And since her family was not new to it, the ton would take great pleasure in dragging their names through the mud once again. Her brother would surely be furious, but perhaps this was for the best.

Marrying the duke was no longer an option. And she would be fortunate enough if the earl would ask for her hand, or at least she hoped he would do the honorable thing at this point.

"Madam, I promise you, the earl will join you as soon as he can. He has a private audience with your brother and another solicitor, who will seek his release at once. Things have become slightly complicated with the amount of corruption at the magistrate's office. But, if I know Charles, you will be in his arms soon enough." The well-dressed man bowed. "Lord Wycliffe at your service, my lady."

"Sir, you have yet to advise me on where we are going."

"I am taking you away from London, where you will be safe."

"But what of my brother? Will he know where I am?"

"Absolutely not. Avonlea will let him know you are safe for the meanwhile, and he will return you to your brother just as soon as he has carried out his plans."

What plans? She was going to throttle him. *All this mystery and for what?* "Why will you not tell me where we are going?"

"It is best you do not know."

Lord Wycliffe's blue eyes noted sadness, but held a hint of mystery. There was something different about him, which made her suspicious. Yet, she was at his mercy. *What harm is there in trusting a man who advises that my beloved and I will be reunited soon?* "Can I ask you another question, sir?"

"Certainly."

"Who are you? And can my brother and the Earl of Bridgeton really trust you?"

"My lady, if you are worried I might scandalize you, then worry not. I prefer my women experienced. So you are safe. Besides, I would not do anything to compromise my friendship with Lord Avonlea. He has been a great friend during my times of need. You would do well to remember that."

Emily felt a newfound relief with the comfort in knowing Avonlea was coming for her. She was sure they had a future together, and once they had managed to steer away her mama and the duke, all would be well. *Or so I hope.*

"Rest now, we will be arriving at our destination long after nightfall. I will make sure you are safe."

Oh, to see him. I cannot wait to have him in my arms again.

"Wake up, you blackguard!" the prison guard shouted down the hall. "'Twould appear you're a free man this pathetically dreary morning, Lord Avonlea. Consider yourself a fortunate man with friends such as the Marquess of Stoughton. I was rather looking forward to escorting your arse to the gates of Newgate."

Avonlea stretched his arms over his head and yawned before yelling back, "Whatever are you on about?"

"You are a free man. Lord Thompson is up above, waiting for you. If you should ever find yourself here again, you will find a one-way passage to Newgate's gallows."

Charles shook his head clear, wondering how his little dove had made away. He was sure Nathaniel would grill him once they were in solitude. But for as much as he admired his friend, he would not do anything that would attach the marquess' name to his own scandal. He would resolve this situation once he was free from watching eyes.

He climbed the slimy stairs of the jail to the much more modern section of the facility. He smelled the sweat off his own clothes, desperately needing a bath and shave. He would not even wear these clothes again. They would only remind him of the time spent in the cell below.

"Welcome back to the light, my friend. Let us get you back to Stoughton Hall and cleaned up."

"I should think I would stop at home first."

"That will not be necessary. I had a messenger sent to have some of your things brought over. 'Twas the terms of your release. Consider yourself under house arrest, if you will."

The earl cringed at the thought. He had to get to Emily, and soon, if they were to head to Gretna Green and be back before her wedding. His plan was simple, but did not leave much room for error.

"Very well, it is not as if I am left much choice." He followed Nathaniel out the door and into his waiting carriage.

The moment the cart began moving, Nathaniel folded his arms across his chest and scowled. "Have you heard, then?"

"Heard what, Nathaniel? If you have not noticed, I have been in a cell for these last few days."

His expression turned hard and angry. "Emily has gone missing. Apparently, she disappeared while she was out with Mother yesterday."

"Perhaps she did not want to marry the duke after all?"

"That was no longer her decision to make. She should have come to me. I would have found a way to stop the marriage. Running off will not break the contract. In fact, if she is caught, it will speed things up. The duke is furious and has already procured a special license. The moment she is found, they will be married the very next day."

'Twas as if he had been punched in the gut. "So where do you think she went?"

"I have no idea, man. My mother will not give us any peace. Poor Isabel has begun plotting her death."

Now there was a thought—the marchioness planning the spiteful bag's death. She would have to write a play about it, in the end, so they could mock the demise of Lady Thompson.

"What has you smiling, Charles? I tell you my sister is missing, and you are sitting there smirking."

"I was only thinking upon what you were saying about your lovely wife plotting your mother's demise."

The scowl from Nathaniel's face lifted. "What if I were to tell you I think you know where my sister is."

"And I would have to tell you I know nothing that I can share, yet. She is safe, Nathaniel. I swear it. And she would not have left if she did not have strong objections to the union."

His friend exhaled loudly, clearly not understanding the gravity of the situation. He would have to indulge her brother in his finding, but not until he had had a bath, proper food, and sleep. Until then, no one would know. Wycliffe was also out in the country, keeping an eye on the estate until he could make it there himself, but he would wait to hear from him via messenger as planned.

Soon enough, the lady would be his, and the duke would rot in Newgate in his stead.

CHAPTER NINE

"Wake up, Miss Thompson. We have finally arrived at our destination."
Emily rubbed her eyes to adjust to her surroundings. They were still in a carriage, although it had stopped. The door opened. Darkness had descended in the countryside. A chill seeped down into her bones. She shivered uncontrollably. "Lord Wycliffe, how far north are we? It's cold out here."

"We are really only a day's worth of travel up the Great North Road. And I reckon it is far more frigid the farther north you go. Consider this a balmy climate, if it is your inclination. Nevertheless, let us get you inside and start a fire. There should already be some food and bedding ready for your stay."

Emily was still cross she did not have faintest idea of where she was being held. "Sir, you still have not mentioned where we are."

"We are at Lord Avonlea's family hunting lodge. He will be joining you as soon as he has been released. From there, I do not wish to know what he has planned, but I am positive you will not be marrying that poor excuse for a duke."

Without waiting for a second reminder to get walking, Emily dashed past the earl and waited for him at the door. An elderly gentleman opened it and kindly smiled at her. "Welcome, ma'am. I hope you will enjoy Hastings Lodge as much as the earl's family has over the last two centuries."

Ivy draped over a corner of the home, casting an eerie shadow. Grand wooden doors welcomed visitors. "It is very large, sir."

"It is, and some say it is home to ghosts of centuries past. But I tend to think that after their passing, Avonlea's ancestors loved it so much, they could not part with it. Of course, the spirits are kind. They are only old and noisy. Rickety as m'old bones. Come, come, I will make you some tea. You can warm up by the fire."

She glanced back to find Wycliffe leaning against the ancient oak door, smiling. "Horace, I would appreciate one as well."

"Certainly, my lord. I will have you know, it is a pleasure to serve you both here. When did you say the master would be joining us?"

"In a few days. I will send a message to him at first light and to Miss Thompson's brother, and all will be well."

A cloud of steam from the pot in the hearth rose. They sat warming their hands.

After emptying her cup, Emily yawned. "If it is all the same to you, gentlemen, I really would like to sleep. Are the stairs to the loft where I will be going?"

"No, ma'am. If you follow the hall to the end, the very last room, the master's private quarters is for your particular use. Please make yourself at home. I have had the fire burning for some time now, so it should be warm enough to sleep."

A warmth washed over her, as she realized just how privileged she was. "Thank you kindly, sir."

"No thanks needed, your ladyship. Please call me Horace."

She rose and followed the hall, counting five chambers along the way. The walls were adorned by heads of stags and wolves. Magnificent creatures, though a little too masculine for her liking. Were she to adorn these walls, the earl would return to a lodge that had quilts and family portraits. Simple reminders of family heirlooms and their ancestors.

When she reached the final room, the door was ajar. She pushed through when the warmth hit her in the face. She picked up a candle burning on the sideboard and walked about the area. There, she found lovely furnishings. The armoire had to be at least one hundred years old, as well as the platform bed nestled off in the corner by the window.

On the other side of the chamber was a chest with a note on top. She walked over, sat the candle on the trunk, and picked it up.

Emily, if you are reading this, then you are here because you truly do not want to marry Downsbury. Once I can get out of this predicament, I will join you here at Hastings Lodge, and we will make up for lost time.

Ever since the theater, I have not been able to think of a single moment that did not include you. From the minute you entered my chambers that night, you sealed our fate, and I hope one day you will feel the same way I do. I most ardently adore you, and while I do not know what love is, I am beginning to wonder if I have become afflicted.

I have asked that Lord Wycliffe secure the items in the crate in the event we are able to be together for a length of time. If some of the items do not fit, I apologize, and I will rectify the wardrobe issue as soon as I am able. This may not occur until we have reached our destination north of here, but I assure you, you will be provided with a more accommodating trunk.

Rest easy, my love, knowing his grace will never touch or own you. I will be with you soon.

Your humble servant,
Charles

Emily had already begun to cry at the first line. He really did mean for the two of them to be together. Her heart raced and warmth washed over her. *How will I sleep in such a state of mind?* She moved the candle, set it down on a nearby chair with the note, and opened the trunk.

She riffled through, finding a pair of outdoor slippers, warmer traveling gowns, and other unmentionables. *Does he mean for us to travel to Scotland? How exciting!* They would be married by a blacksmith despite what the ton expected. The duke would surely be displeased, but he could not marry a woman already married. Avonlea's plan was ingenious.

Now she knew why she loved him. The earl was as clever and as devious as she. They were perfect for each other.

"Quit pacing, man. 'Tis plain you have much on your mind. Why do you not explain how much trouble you are in?" Nathanial queried.

"Not just yet. I would rather wait. The walls have ears, and with your mother looming about, 'tis only a matter of time before his grace arrives to further irritate everyone."

"I understand."

Both men stood in the library in silence.

Suddenly, Isabel burst through the door in tears. Her hair, which was normally done up high and angelic, fell down in a frazzled mess. "I want that infernal woman out of here. She is upsetting the staff, the babies, and myself. Nathaniel, I swear it to you, if you do not get rid of her, I will end you both!" She cried into his arms.

Charles winced.

His friend simply held her, consoling the inconsolable, and rubbed her back. Avonlea envied their closeness and desperately needed to hold Emily in his arms again.

He did not have much time to waste, and it was only a matter of time before they were discovered. All he had to do was wait for the messenger, but he could not stay that much longer. If word did not come by dinner, he would have to leave, despite the terms of his release, and race her to Gretna Green. The two of them would have to be back in London in enough time to cancel the wedding to the duke.

His thoughts flew out the window with elder Lady Thompson and the duke barging in to the library. "This is all your fault." The lady waggled her finger at him. "If you had not charmed her when she was already taken, none of this would have come about. She will still be a duchess. I swear it."

The duke stood there and smiled. "Yes, she will still be my wife, despite this infraction. I do not take kindly to false accusations, Lord Avonlea, and it would be best if you stayed out of my way. Or, next time you may not find favorable ears to listen to your babbling."

Rage blinded Charles in that moment. The only thing he could think of was pummeling the duke to a bloody pulp. It took mercy to keep him from accosting the bastard again. "I have done nothing wrong. I only inquired about missing persons. It must have dug up something incriminating if you had me incarcerated so fast. I hope for your sake that my own investigation doesn't turn up anything you do not want the ton to know, because no one, including Emily, will marry the likes of you."

"Enough, Avonlea." Nathaniel placed a firm grip on his shoulder and squeezed, whispering into his ear. "You will explain what this has to do with my sister when they are gone. Am I clear?"

"Of course."

"What are the two of you whispering over there?" the dowager countess asked.

"Nothing that concerns you. Now, both of you get out of my damned house. I will not stand for either of you upsetting my entire household, including my guests. Out with you!" the marquess roared.

His mother countered, lashing out. "How dare you speak to me in such a manner."

"Get out, now."

The butler ushered them out.

After they were gone, the marchioness sighed and flopped onto the dais. "Good heavens, that went well."

"My dear, your sarcasm is ill-timed. Please go check on the children, my love. I will join you as soon as I can."

Isabel nodded and closed the door behind her, leaving the men to discuss the severity of the situation. "I am going to ask plainly, Charles, where is my sister? What are your intentions with her? And what does this investigation of yours have to do with her?"

"You might as well sit down and pour yourself a drink, old friend. 'Tis a tale even you may not believe once I am finished."

"Just start at the beginning. You already know I am a reasonable man."

"Are you quite sure we are alone?

Nathaniel gave him a once over and crossed his arms.

"Fine. Emily is safe at my family's hunting lodge north. She is in the protection of one of my servants, and Lord Wycliffe is keeping watch of the estate. It is my intention to leave tonight to be with her. Once I have arrived, we will be traveling to Scotland. You must know I had every intention of doing the honorable thing. We were—"

His friend held up his hand. "You needn't go into full details, please. Though, the mere mention of doing the honorable thing has me worried."

"My plan was, once we returned from Gretna Green, we would announce our nuptials and, therefore, she cannot marry the duke since she would be already married to me."

"The magistrate can issue an annulment."

"Not if I am alive, and not if there is any chance she is with child." *A child. Christ.* He had not considered what it would feel like to be a father again. Dread began to creep up his spine. He would gladly pay the piper and save them from any hardship if it meant he had to die in their place.

"And what of this investigation? How does any of this apply to Emily?"

"Do you remember that night at White's when Wycliffe had gone off to Martine's?"

"Yes," Nathaniel drawled, rolling his eyes.

"Wycliffe confided in me. Downsbury is not all that he appears to be. I have reason to believe he has been selling women to an Italian man to serve as prostitutes. When I approached the matter, he told me he would train your sister and after her dowry was his, send her off to the continent as well. Wycliffe hired a man to track down the Italian and find those missing women. The more evidence we collect, the better chance we have of removing Downsbury from society."

"Do you mean to tell me that the duke plans to make my sister a whore?"

"Yes. Now do you understand why I went to such lengths to get her away?"

Nathaniel frowning and the tick in his jaw, was all the approval Charles required. *It is set then.* He would leave tonight and collect his bride. To see the look on Downsbury's face when he returned with Emily would be priceless.

"You do realize, if you are caught leaving, you could end up back in jail."

"I do, and while I wish it were not the case, the sooner I marry Emily and return, the better it will be for all. Wycliffe is expecting the gent to arrive at the same time. While we are not entirely sure what the findings will be, we are hopeful the women will be discovered."

"Then do what you must. The moment you arrive, I will take Emily into my home and keep her as best that I can. I truly hope Mother doesn't find you before I do. Lord only knows what will happen from there."

Not that it will matter. By then, it will be too late.

Emily woke up refreshed and eager to see her beloved earl. But, in all reality, it would take him at least a day to get out of jail, if her brother had assisted, and another day's travel to be with her. She did what she could to not unpack anything, in case they had to leave right away.

Her mother must be in a fury and distraught by her disappearance, and heaven forbid what the duke thought. The more she contemplated her actions, she knew she had done the right thing by leaving. The only aspect she had not quite considered at the time was his lordship's love for her. He really did love her. And who would have thought that a gent from her own brother's circle would have tolerated her.

Brushing out her hair, she left the room to join Lord Wycliffe for breakfast.

"I hope you slept well, my lady?"

"Not particularly, sir. I was far too excited at the prospect Lord Avonlea would be joining us soon. Though, I know now, it may take him a few days."

"I am glad you have no illusions as to how bad this can go. We are all taking risks here, and his are the greatest. Did you know they were prepared to send him to Newgate? Downsbury was planning to have him hanged."

Emotion burned her cheeks and suddenly the room felt hotter than purgatory itself. *Do not swoon, you foolish girl. The earl needs you!* "How could I have known such a dreadful fact? Surely, you do not think I would know such things just because I slept under the same roof as the duke? A man only acts out of desperation when threatened. What information does Charles hold over his grace?"

Lord Wycliffe set his spoon down and grimaced. "I should not be the one to tell you this, but you have every right to know. The duke never had intentions of keeping you. He is only marrying you for your dowry, and once he had soiled you, his intent was to send you to work in a brothel for an Italian man."

Emily shivered, suddenly painfully aware that she had been shown a small mercy when Lord Wycliffe took her the other morning. Her mother could not possibly know, or she would not have arranged such a pact with the devil himself. *Or would she?*

Emily would rather take her own life before marrying the devious man. She noticed Wycliffe tapping his fingers on the table. "There is more?"

He nodded. "Unfortunately, Lady Emily, there is. Part of the reason why it has taken us so long to make these arrangements is we are conducting our own investigation, in addition to what the duke had planned on doing with you, there may be a possibility he has done the same to other women. He had also threatened his previous duchess the same way as well."

Emily pushed her chair back, unable to hold her tears. "This really is all too much to take in, Lord Wycliffe. The man is a monster, plain and simple, and my mother nearly married me to him. I will never speak to her again."

"Well, my dear, with any luck you will not have to speak to her again. If we can get you two to Scotland at the soonest possible date, then there should be no reason for you ever to see her again, if that is what you desire.

Try and eat something then get some rest. If you need anything, just call for myself or Horace. When the time comes for the two of you to leave, I imagine you might have to skip a meal or two, and you will need all the strength you can get."

"I am really too upset, Lord Wycliffe. I think I might just lie down for a bit. Would you mind having Horace set aside a small dish for me please?"

"Of course. Go and rest, and I will see if there is any news from London or your brother."

Emily wandered down the hall, terrified for their future. If the duke truly had done some despicable things, he would surely not let this rest. He would hunt them down, murder Avonlea, and most likely marry her anyway. She would never let that happen. She would rather elope with Lord Avonlea and hide away somewhere far on the continent.

Not a really pleasant or ladylike thought, though if it meant that was the only way she could be with her beloved, then so be it. In the meanwhile, his grace needed to be stopped, no matter the cost.

She paced the room frantically. If she had paced any faster, her feet would have made grooves into the floorboards. *What are we to do?* They could not run for the rest of their lives.

Shouting from the front part of the lodge alarmed her. *Charles.* What joy it was to hear his voice again.

"Where is Emily? We must leave at once. There is a chance I might have been spotted."

She ran out the door and right into his arms. For what seemed an eternity, she gazed into the bright, blue depths, certain of his love for her. The man would not fail her.

"We must go at once."

"Lead the way, my love. I do not wish to wait another moment without you."

"Wycliffe, fetch her trunk right away. Horace, thank you for your help. Without either of you, none of this would have been possible."

"Do not get your knickers in a twist, Avonlea. Give me but a moment, and I will drive the carriage. Be warned, we will not be stopping until well after nightfall," Wycliffe said.

It is finally happening. We are going to Gretna Green, and I would not want him any other way.

CHAPTER TEN

Emily leaned into his arms, slowly digesting the journey they were embarking on, and desperately hoping the next few days passed quickly. She found herself completely immersed in listening to Charles breathe, their hearts hammering away in their chests from all the excitement. Soon, she would be Lady Avonlea, and who would have thought Charles would make her the luckiest debutante around.

The carriage rocked along the road at a backbreaking pace, as if demons chased them down the great road. It was a good thing she had not eaten before they left, or she would have tossed her crumpets along the way.

He stroked her hair and hummed a merry tune, which soon faded into nothingness. She fell asleep on his lap, knowing the moment they stopped for the night, she would be lucky if he let her sleep at all.

The next thing she heard was his voice. "Wake up, love, we are at a staging inn for the next few hours."

"Are there enough rooms for all of us, then?" She yawned and climbed out after him.

"Yes. Wycliffe has already gone in and arranged everything. Tricky thing is that we will have to leave before dawn. I have not much time to make up for our separation."

"My love, I would not worry your head about such things. In a day or so, we will have a lifetime to catch up."

"Come then, right this way."

She took his arm, and he led her into the quaint and quiet inn. They were met by the owner, who attended to them in his nightcap and sleeping gown. He walked up the stairs and stopped at the door. "Will you be needing anything else, Mr. and Mrs.—"

"Brown. The name is Brown, and we won't require anything else this evening. Thank you kindly for taking us in at such an ungodly hour,"

Charles added.

The man grumbled and left. Avonlea opened the door with his boot, and after a few moments of scanning the hall, he lifted her into his arms. The very action made her want to squeal with joy, but given the time they arrived, she had to contain her happiness. Within a few strides, his lordship dumped her on the bed. He turned his back on her to lock the door then removed his jacket and shirt.

Emily could not help but admire the statuesque body he donned and could not fathom how many other women may have spent their time admiring it as well. A jealous streak flashed through her unlike any other time before.

"Love, what are you thinking about?"

She shrugged and ignored his question, unlacing her boots.

"No, love. Let me do the honors. Tonight, I want to spend whatever hours we have worshipping you. Every inch of that delectable body of yours, until you cry out my name. You would like that, would you not?"

"I would, my lord. But surely, you do not want to pull off these boots? I can do that myself."

"No, darling, I will tend to that. By morning, you will be completely ravished, from the tip of your head, all the way down to your princess toes. I meant what I said about pleasuring you thoroughly."

Emily's cheeks burned with embarrassment. It was not as if he had not seen her body, and it was not as if she had not seen or touched him before. He knelt before her, unlaced her boots and removed her stockings. He caressed her feet and rubbed her toes for a while until he slid his hands up her legs. His tenderness made him appealing, next to his sense of honor. Though, considering they were not even married yet, they were about to embark on a new scandal.

"Mmm, how I have missed these legs." His hands kept traveling up, until his fingers slid beneath the fabric shielding her sex. His touch made her delirious. "You are wet with anticipation, love. I like that. Now, let us remove the barrier, as you have no need for them now."

He tore the material, which shocked her thoroughly. Then, the earl rose and held out his hands to her. "Up, love. Now, we are going to rid you of those clothes, so I will be able to delight you without further delay."

His fingers made quick work of undoing her dress and stays, until all went tumbling into a pool on the floor. "Aphrodite's beauty pales to yours."

Emily gravitated into his arms. With her chin tipped up and his head lowering, their lips met. The first sweep of his tongue brought back the memory of her slipping into his room at her brother's house, and tonight he was all hers.

Avonlea was ready to combust at any given moment, and the inn would go along with it if they did not slow things down. But Lord have mercy on his black soul. He would take her this night, before their scandalous, makeshift wedding, and before returning to London. The prospect of having her in his bed from this evening forward truly was a blessing in many guises.

He plundered her mouth while he slid his palm along the curves of her backside. Heaven awaited him. Emily was finally his, and she held his heart. Love was a damned ailment. Not only was he in love, he loved being in love with her. A secret he would have to keep from his companions.

His hands followed along the contours of her bottom. He longed to take her from behind and hoped once they were settled, they could explore other positions of copulation.

"I can see you are enjoying the attention as it is meant, love. Tell me, is there anything more beautiful than this moment?"

"No, but a hot bath might be a close second."

He was shocked at her admission and could not help but laugh. "I suppose that answer will have to do." He kissed her again, this time harder, as he caressed her. No matter what he did, his hands and mouth always ended up on her breasts. He loved them, and he wanted to taste them again. He slid down her body and slipped a nipple into his mouth, while he shifted his other hand to her mound.

She moaned at his touch and nips. The sound drove him wild, his cock threatening to burst from his breeches. He had to stop, much to his dismay, to remove them. Then he straddled her and lowered his lips to hers to indulge in her sweetness. She mimicked every swipe of his tongue and moaned into his mouth. His heart quickened in anticipation of finalizing their union. "Are you ready, my love?"

She mumbled something in the haze that was lust. He slipped his hand down her body to prepare her, only to plunge into her slow and deep.

"Allow your body to adjust to my size, love." He observed the wariness in her face and how her body tensed the moment he entered her. "I promise I won't move a muscle until you are ready. Here, perhaps this will help." He teased her folds until her nub was swollen with desire. He continued to rub and pinch with trembling fingers until her breath was ragged.

How he wished his mouth could finish her off, but at that moment, her body tensed, and her soft cry echoed in the room around him. He continued his invasion until he was all the way in.

Merciful heavens. She was tight, and his need to pump vigorously into her raged through his blood. He was ravenous. She made him feel like never before. Her eyes fluttered, and she gripped onto his forearms. "That is it, love, enjoy it. The first time isn't what it will always be like. You will find the more we do this, the more pleasurable it will be."

"Thank you."

Her eyes welled with tears, so he stilled, waiting a moment before he continued to thrust. "Try not to move, sweeting…" But she shifted ever so slightly, and he began to pump into her again. The smell of her sex mixed with his sweat drove him mindless, until his own release exploded. His body vibrated and hummed with the aftershock. He swiped Emily's runaway tear with his finger. "Are you all right, my love?"

"I am."

"Then why the tears? Have I hurt you in any way? If so, for that I am sorry. I tried to be as gentle as I could."

"It was not you, my lord. This…us…it was rather beautiful, and I hope I met your expectations?"

So, she is worried she did not perform accordingly? My sweet, sweet, love. If she only knew how perfect she really was. He had to be the luckiest gent alive. Regardless of how spirited she was, together they would make fine music, in or out of the bedroom.

Charles pushed away from her and crossed the room to fetch the water basin and washcloth. When he returned to the bed, Emily had already covered herself with the sheet. "My lord, I can do that myself."

"Now, now, love, do not be shy. We are about to be married, and we have already consummated our union, so allow me the privilege of wiping you clean. I would be honored if you would permit me to care for you in every regard."

She blushed furiously and gave a worrisome smile as she tossed back the bedding. Tonight would be the first night of many more to come, and hopefully, she would bless their home with many children.

How he wished his parents could see him now. His mother would beat him with her fan for the order of how they went about things, and his pa would probably pat him on the back for a job well done. *Well, with the exception of stealing the duke's betrothed.* That actually may have angered him. In fact, he would not be surprised if the man was rolling in his grave.

"Wake up, love. We must leave now." Avonlea tapped her nose.

Memories of their night together warmed her. She did not know how loving a man could be, how beautiful. And that man was about to become her husband. Every passing second was beginning to feel like a dream. "What time is it, my love?"

"Early enough to make it to the blacksmith before we are apprehended."

"What do you speak of?"

"Your brother sent a servant on horseback, checking all the inns along the way for us. Apparently, the duke is on the lookout for us, and he has also employed the assistance of the chief prosecutor. It is only a matter of time before we are caught. So, we must make haste."

Emily jumped out of bed, throwing on her gown haphazardly. "What do you suppose will happen if we are caught, Avonlea? Do you think they will imprison you? Lord, I hope they do not. I could be with child as we speak." The very thought frightened her. Her, a mother. A child without a father. *Good God! What have we done?*

He only smiled at her. "Do not worry about that, love. We will have time to sort these matters out. But once we are married, you will travel alone to London. Wycliffe will leave you in your brother's care, and I will travel separately. We would not want to be found out only moments upon our arrival. We need time to orchestrate our announcement."

Indeed. Her mother would surely swoon, and the duke would go on a murderous rampage.

They quietly descended the stairs in avoidance of waking the other patrons and slipped into the darkness inconspicuously. He held the carriage door open for her while Wycliffe tended to the horses. "Hop in, love, and get some rest. I will ride with Wycliffe in the front for a bit. We have need to discuss some alternative plans, if things go awry."

Emily pouted. She was hoping she would rest in his arms again, but it would seem fate made her wait until they were married.

Realistically, by this time tomorrow, she would be back in this carriage, traveling alone to London. She shuddered to think who would be waiting for her at her brother's home. Surely, by now, he knew they would be married. Her family, once again, would be marred by scandal. And her mama would disown her and Nathaniel for his betrayal.

Her mama's only regret in life was she did not marry into great wealth. While Papa had done the honorable thing in protecting his best friend's wife by marrying her, knowing full well she would never love him the way she did of her first husband, everyone knew her mother did not think much of the marquess.

She aspired greatly to be elevated in society, and Father had refused to give in to any of the ton's games and gossips. In some ways, she was glad her papa was no longer around. He would be disgraced with the way her mother carried about.

In fact, he would have shipped her to the Americas for an extended stay. That would have learned her.

Emily wrapped her arms around his neck, taking a moment to kiss him. Within a few hours, they would be married and back on the road, homeward bound. "I think I shall close my eyes for a bit longer, Charles."

"A most excellent idea, my dear. Do not worry, all will turn out."

She sank into her seat, leaned against the side, and closed her eyes. *Soon, I will be Lady Avonlea. Soon.*

Later that day, they stood side-by-side, ready to take their vows.

"Are you sure, you are here of your own will, lass? I will not marry you if you are both not consenting," the blacksmith advised, arms crossed. His stance and tone making it quite clear he has had trouble before.

Emily glanced over at her beloved and then back to the imposing man before them. The blacksmith's long red hair and sharp blue eyes penetrated her soul. *Those eyes have lain upon how many couples? How many vows have been exchanged in this same spot?*

While many would oppose these drastic measures at proving their point, necessity drove them to these lengths. "I assure you, sir, I am here of my own volition. In fact, I am more than happy to be wedding this man."

"In that case, let us get the both of you ready." He turned to Lord Avonlea. "Do you have a ring?"

Charles stuttered and finally mumbled, "No."

The blacksmith chuckled.

"To be clear, sir, it was my intention to secure the finest gold for my wife once we return to London."

"That is what they all say. Young miss, if you will follow me, we will get you a proper bouquet. My wife will take you out to the meadow, and you can decide what be pleasing you."

The ceremony, as well as the ride back to London, was a blur of excitement. Once safely stopped at her brother's estate, Wycliffe handed the reins to the stable boy and walked over to help Emily out of the carriage.

"I hope the ride was not too hard, Lady Avonlea."

Emily smiled, appreciating the sound of her married name. Now, if only she had the chance to show her appreciation to her husband.

Isabel rushed out to meet her and quickly folded her into an embrace. "You are back, and married, I hope?"

"Yes, I am. Please tell me Mama is not here?"

"No, she is not, and it is my understanding that Nathaniel has banned her from visiting."

It was a relief to know that her brother had finally stood up to their mother. *And to think, I thought he did not have it in him.* She would have to apologize sometime at a later date, when she was not too preoccupied with finding her husband. "Has Charles returned?"

"Yes, he has." Her sister-in-law then turned to Lord Wycliffe. "The men are in the library. Please go in and join them. They will be happy to know that Emily has returned intact." Then, Isabel grabbed her hand and dragged her in toward the house. "Come, let me order some tea for us, and we can catch up some. I am sure you have all kinds of questions and things you would like to share, no?"

"Of course, but I will be there in just a moment. I would like a few minutes to catch some air, before I return indoors. The long ride has stiffened me, and I would love to stretch out."

"But of course. I will send Duncan when everything is ready. Besides, I am sure your new husband is dying to see you."

Emily wandered into the side garden, which more often than not tempted folks driving by to stop and admire the array of roses, which Duncan maintained over the years. It was often the only place anyone in the house would run off to whenever her mother was in foul mood. Duncan, in most instances, hid her and Nathaniel there until the woman's ire had passed.

Usually, it would take hours, and neither she nor her brother would complain. Between them, Duncan, and their gardener, Mr. Smith, they spent hours learning all the different names of the varieties.

She closed her eyes and took in the fragrant scent. It was so nice to be home once again. The sound of a carriage passing by and stopping seemed to fade into the background. Nothing could ruin this moment of bliss.

"Grab her." a voice said suddenly.

Before she could react, someone pressed a cloth to her mouth from behind. She desperately tried to pull away, but whatever the god-awful smell was had her dozing off.

Her head bobbed up and down as she was carried to a carriage. When she opened her eyes again, the Duke of Downsbury smiled. "Welcome home, dear. We have a wedding to prepare."

She fell into a dreamless slumber.

CHAPTER ELEVEN

"Emily? Tea has been ready for a quarter hour now. Where are you?" Charles heard the marchioness call out.

And yet, he heard no response from his wife. *Where is she? She could not have gone all that far, in such little time.* "Excuse me, gentlemen. I would like to check on my wife. I have a bad feeling."

Footsteps of the marquess and Wycliffe followed, and while he wanted to acknowledge their assistance, he kept walking with speed. Something was wrong, but what it was, he did not know. "My lady...have you seen her?" the earl questioned the marchioness.

"No, I have not. I left her here by the garden and did not think I was gone that long. Truly, I have not the slightest clue where she is. I asked Duncan already, but he swears she never stepped foot in the house."

That is when he noticed a cloth on the grass. He picked up what he thought was Emily's handkerchief and was not surprised to find the initials "R.W." embroidered on one of the corners. He smelled something pungent wafting up from it. *They had to have been watching the house and expecting her return. Ether. I am going to kill that man, if it is the very last thing I do.* "They drugged her."

"Who?" the marchioness asked quizzically.

Her husband jumped in. "Downsbury, I suspect, which means we do not have much time. Wycliffe, when did you say this man was due to arrive?"

"To be frank, he should have ported three days ago. I will ride on to the docks and find out what the delay might be."

"There is no need just yet. There seems to be a rider approaching, as well as a carriage following behind. We might be in luck."

The horse and boy came to a screeching halt. "My lords, Lady Thompson, I send word that you are to be expecting a visitor shortly. Shall I fetch a runner for you, Lord Avonlea?"

"I do not think that will be necessary. But stay on, as you might need to run for one."

"Also, my lords, my sister sent a message. Miss Thompson has arrived at the manor and is unwell. She suspects there is not much time before his grace marries her."

"Gregory, if you will follow my wife, she will make sure you are fed." The marchioness held out her hand to the boy, who reluctantly took it and followed.

Charles pinched the bridge of his nose, hoping the next bit of news would make up for Emily's abduction. If they could only get the proof they needed, then Downsbury would be put away for good.

The carriage slowed, and when it finally stopped at the end of the drive, a portly man, easily ten years older than he, stepped out and shouted an order to whomever was inside to wait until he came back. He walked toward him and Wycliffe while Nathaniel stood his ground and watched from afar.

"Have you any news from the continent, Briggs?" the marquess queried.

"I have, but I have incurred some unexpected expenses. I will need that squared away before we continue further."

"What kind of expenses are you talking about? I gave you sufficient money to take care of everything you needed and more."

"I require more, after being shackled to two whiny women for these past few weeks. Plus, there was their passage, and then there is the matter of my prisoner."

"Prisoner!" Avonlea, Wycliffe and Nathaniel exclaimed in unison, while they pushed their way to the carriage. Avonlea opened the door to find two women, and a foreign man sitting there with a gun pointed at him.

"Nathaniel, you may want to have that boy find that runner now, and any connections you might have to have this one locked up, secretly."

"Briggs, who are these women and this man?"

"The man is an associate of the Italian bastard you had me seek, and the women are the last ones sent to him to work in a brothel. There were others, of course, but he said it was too late. They were either sold or had not survived their first month. Another thing, he said the man we are seeking is already here but did not know where."

Two survivors were surely enough to discredit Downsbury and the chief prosecutor. If he waited too long, then the prosecutor would flee the country to avoid prosecution, which in the end may stall the duke's own trial, and they could not have that.

But if he went there now, without presenting these people to the chief magistrate, then he could very well kiss seeing Emily again goodbye. Married or not, their stunt in Scotland could be annulled, and he would be tossed into prison again, this time for tampering with evidence.

CHAPTER TWELVE

Emily awoke in her chambers, her maid sitting at her side. Nausea overwhelmed her as she sat up, so she lay back again, only to have the young girl prop her pillows up.

"I am so glad you are awake. The duke has been in a foul mood since the day you left. He has stopped in here numerous times to check on you. Apparently, he was worried the ether might have been too much. It has been rumored that some never wake up."

That foul odor and the cloth pressed to her face made her shudder to think of the sort of evil they were. "How long have I been abed?"

"Nearly two days, ma'am. The servants were worried sick. If I may be so bold, did you wind up seeing his lordship?"

"I did, and we were married days ago in Gretna Green. Unfortunately, we have not managed to announce our marriage, as I was taken from my brother's garden shortly after we arrived. Good heavens…Avonlea. Surely he knows where I must be?"

"Yes, miss, I sent word after your arrival. I am still waiting on word from my brother to find out what the plan is, though I imagine once everyone realizes your awake, his grace will push for the wedding on the morrow."

Of course he would. He would not want anyone to get in the way of him obtaining her dowry. Sadly, he would learn soon enough, he was no longer entitled. Now, if only Avonlea could sweep in and rescue her from Downsbury's clutches, then they would be able to carry on as if this nightmare never existed.

Her beloved would find her, they would go on and live happily, and she would give him sons to carry on the Bridgeton legacy.

Emily shook her head to clear the fogginess that lingered. She would have to resort to pleading with her mama, and with any hope, the woman would come to her senses.

Finally well enough to leave her room, Emily threw on a wrap and slid into her slippers. Since her arrival back at the manor, the duke had her guarded at all times. Two sentries were posted outside her door, and one escorted her about. Should she have need to leave the confines of the home, she was to be protected by three footmen and her mother's maid at all times.

She walked down the hall to her mother's apartments. She knocked, then opened the door to find her mother pouring over some paperwork on the desk. "What can I do for you, dear? I have not a moment to spare with all these preparations."

"What are you about, Mama?" She sensed her mother had a hand in her abduction, but thought now might not be the best of moments to discuss it.

"Your wedding, of course. Thomas has gone to the modiste to pick up our order. I am finalizing the wedding meal, and his grace has already made the arrangements for the service. You should be thankful his grace is willing to forgive you for your past indiscretions and grievances."

Emily could not believe what she was hearing. *Good heavens…My indiscretions and grievances?* Clearly, the woman was not right in her head. She was not the one accepting sexual favors the night of her engagement. Nor was she the one knee-deep in a scandal that would rock all of England for its indecency.

She fisted her hands at her side. Trying to keep them inconspicuously out of her mother's eyes. "I simply cannot marry the duke, so you can stop what you are doing!"

"And why is that, you ungrateful chit?"

"Because I eloped to Gretna Green with Lord Avonlea a fortnight ago. The duke cannot marry a woman who is already married."

Her mother dropped the paper she was working with and stood, walked over to her, and slapped her across the face. Emily gasped with surprise. Her cheek burned from the contact.

"You would say anything to get out of this, would you not? Well, I have news for you, you selfish little girl. For years, I have aspired to raise myself in society the way it should have been years ago. But your boorish father insisted we did not need to be a part of that life. And look at me now, I am no one. After you are married, I will be introduced to, and welcomed into, other circles. I might even find myself a new husband who is as wealthy as yours."

And to think, she only considered herself and not my own safety. It was never about finding the right husband for her. It was her mother's sick perversion to being in high society circles. *How could I have been so daft?* Right from the beginning, her mother had pushed and pushed, until she got what she wanted. She did not care about credibility or credentials, her only concern was how deep the coffers were and how it would impact her future. The woman was truly mad.

"If you think I will go through with this, know that you have forever lost your only daughter. I will never forgive you for this, Mama." Emily spun on her heel and retreated to her room without looking back.

"I still do not understand why you want to search the pier. If our main suspect is still at port, what makes you think he will linger around?"

"I do not know, Nathaniel, but something is not quite right."

Charles climbed off his horse and stalked toward the port master's building. The dilapidated shack, at the very least, should have a fresh coat of paint. Perhaps then, visitors at port would not feel like they had arrived at some privateers docks.

Only two ships were at port, and all was quiet aboard both. When they entered the office, something caught his eye. A familiar burgundy coat…and the laugh. He stopped dead in his tracks and shivered. His breath escaped him, and all the memories he sought to keep hidden in the dark recesses of his memory came back.

"What is wrong, Charles?" Nathaniel leaned against him.

"That voice…There are things I never told you about my time on the continent, Nathaniel. Things I can be charged with." He struggled to maintain his composure and sucked in a sharp breath. "I was a troubled man, to put it plainly. Instead of following leads, I passed my time in the smoke houses and brothels. When I traveled to Italy, I met a beautiful woman. She was bright and full of life. I had every intention of bringing her back. The trouble was her employer would not release her."

His friend rested a hand on his back. "There is no need to go on. We all have our demons, and given you have married my sister, I would say you have come a long ways from being the man you were. Let us continue our investigation and move on. I doubt we have much time left before the wedding is to take place."

They walked further into the room and rang the bell. No one attended them, yet the deeper they traipsed, the louder the laughter became. Avonlea stood quietly in a doorway exiting to the back of the pier and watched the familiar man, dock master, and several others playing cards.

A few moments later, Nathaniel joined him, only this time, he cleared his throat, garnering the attention of ruffians.

"You just had to do that, did you not?" Charles glared at him.

"Yes, I did. We very well could not stand in the shadows like two ninny's trying to decide what to do."

Unbelievable! Hell, it is him. The middle-aged, portly Italian still looked the same, with his dark hair long and unkempt. He wore commoner's clothes, even though he was wealthy. *Another man I would like to see dead.* There was simply no way to hide from his past now. "Well, now that you have gone and done that, I hope you are prepared to fight your way out. I am positive I am not leaving without getting my revenge."

"What revenge? I thought we were here to discover more about this Italian. What does that man have to do with anything?"

Avonlea stifled a groan. "Because *that* man is a brothel owner and was the employer of a woman I loved and failed to rescue from his grasp."

His friend gripped his shoulder and turned him until they faced each other. "Do you mean to tell me that he could possibly be the one we are looking for?"

"Maybe, but I can assure you, he will not be leaving alive for what he did to Celine."

The man dressed in the burgundy coat, and three other men rose from their seats and approached them with the surliest of glares. Stares that sent shivers up his spine. *There is that cold, calculating look I remember.*

"Your lordships look too finely dressed for this neck of the woods. To what do we owe this pleasure?" the port master asked, chuckling.

The familiar foreigner snorted. "If it isn't the English *bastardo*...You know, Celine would have made me a handsome profit if it were not for you and the *piccolino* she was carrying."

He did not..."You have no right to bring her into this."

Avonlea lunged for the portly clod, and they both went tumbling down the rickety, wooden staircase. He winced in pain with every step. He would not be surprised if he walked away with a few broken ribs. *How dare he mention her name!* His heart bled for that woman and the child he had never seen. *Christ. If Emily could see me now.* He could still save her, and there was still time to be done with the duke.

Shouting off in the distance pulled his thoughts, and Nathaniel yanked him away from the tangle of limbs at the bottom. "We have to go now. It sounds as if the chief prosecutor is here, and he is not alone."

What? How is that even possible...unless...they're here to deliver..."Nathaniel, he is the one we need. Grab him, and let's go. We must go straight to Bow Street. Now!" The earl managed to get up, but his breath escaped him. Hobbling along, he caught up to Nathaniel, evading whatever company descended upon the pier.

Within the hour, he was likely to be incarcerated again, only this time, they had the proof they needed. And soon, he would be with Emily. His dear, sweet Emily.

The bishop's pause right before the vows unnerved her. Emily's hands trembled at the fact that their ceremony had not been interrupted yet. *What if Avonlea never comes for me? What if I wind up marrying the duke?* She would be married to two men. Surely, that had to be a sin of grandeur proportions.

What would the duke end up doing with her after her dowry was in his possession? Would he keep her around for a while, or would he ship her away as Lord Wycliffe suggested back at Avonlea's hunting lodge? Trepidation shook her to the core.

As the silence became too much, guests began whispering. The Duke of Downsbury appeared annoyed, and she could not help but notice how much he fidgeted. She had purposely held back a moment from delivering her vows. Whispers from the *tons* finest carried throughout the century old church. Her mother stood off to the side.

The bishop craned his head.

Shouting from outside of the church echoed throughout the building. The heavy doors burst open and several men holding it closed fell to the floor, toppling over each other.

An unfamiliar man, followed by several others, walked down the aisle toward them. They wore scowls on their faces, and when they stopped by Mr. Sayers, they stood rigid and ready to apprehend the man. The tallest, dark-haired gent addressed the chief prosecutor. "Chief Prosecutor, William Sayers, you are hereby under arrest for failure to report crimes to the office of the magistrate, conspiracy to committing crimes of slavery."

Emily could not believe what she was hearing. *Can this nightmare be truly over?*

The man walked over to her and Downsbury. "What is the meaning of this intrusion?" the duke spewed. "Do you not see that you are interrupting a very important moment in our lives? How dare you. The magistrate will hear about this."

"Who do you think signed the warrant for your arrest as well, your grace? Richard Waite, Duke of Downsbury, you are hereby arrested for crimes against women and slavery. You are to stand trial for the illegal sale of women to foreigners. We have two witnesses who are prepared to speak against you. Do you have anything to say to your almost duchess?"

The duke spit in the man's face with contempt. "I have nothing to say other than two witnesses mean nothing. You do not have any other evidence."

"Ah. But that is where you are wrong, your grace. We have searched the dock masters' records, and we have searched your home already. Fortunately for us, you did not lock up the most important detail. Your correspondence between the chief prosecutor and the Italian.

"I have to say, for a smart gentleman such as yourself to invest in business prospects overseas, you have proven to all of London how stupid you are. It is just as well your duchess is no longer with us, or is she? We shall look into the circumstances of her death, considering how much we have already discovered."

The duke attempted to run, but the stranger apprehended him before he made it mere feet. "Evading arrest, sir? I do believe that has its own charge, as well."

"None of you will get away with this. I will come back, and when I do, the lot of you will be sorry for crossing me." The duke hissed, trying to point at Charles.

"Is that a threat, your grace? I am certain we can add an additional charge to your ever-expanding list. Have you no idea how much pain and suffering your actions have caused? I do not expect you to care, but the women who did not survive your cruelty deserved a better life, than to perish alone.

"You sir, will not only suffer in purgatory, but I will ensure that your stay at Newgate is anything but comfortable. You will never see the light of day again, unless it is the day they hang you from the gallows. I hope you will enjoy your new home."

Downsbury kicked and screamed, and some guests started to exit the church while others stood and watched with curiosity. Her mother tried to run, but a uniformed man kept her at bay. The bishop could not even form an understandable word in English. "Sinners, the lot of you. Barging into a house of God. May he strike you down."

"Enough," Avonlea said, running toward her. "She is already married. *We* were married a fortnight ago in Scotland, but she was still forced into this marriage. Now, what do you have to say for yourself, Bishop?"

Emily threw herself into his arms while her mother cried out before swooning.

"Come, my love. I have an estate and staff I am sure you will want to familiarize yourself with."

Charles woke with his arms still wrapped around his bride. Not even the light streaming into their bedchamber could do her beauty any justice. Her pale and creamy skin looked ethereal, her red wavy locks splayed across the pillow. He had married a goddess, and he counted his blessings many times over for this second coming of life. Of love.

He kissed her shoulder, squeezing her a little tighter. Home had never felt so complete. He wished his parents could see how happy he was now. They would approve of Emily and, most of all, they would be ecstatic at the prospect that a lady had finally captured his heart.

Who would have ever thought he would see the day where he would marry, a proper lady at that? Ignoring the fact that he had the dowager countess as a mother-in-law. He made sure she was not permitted to come to their house.

His brother-in-law—being the brilliant man he is—gave the crone the option to go on an extended holiday to either the continent or the

Americas, and he did not leave much room for disagreement. Charles found it rather amusing. He would be glad, knowing she would never set foot in London again.

No one had ever expected to see the day where Downsbury was stripped of his title. His holdings had been sold to pay as restitution for the women's lives that would never be normal again. Charles was surprised neither he nor Nathaniel had tried to kill the duke, after how the wretched man had destroyed their dignity.

The last anyone had heard on the subject was that Richard Waite had been transferred to Newgate, and Charles hoped very much that the man would think upon his sins, while he lived happily with his bride.

Would the duke ever think back upon all his wrongs? Most likely not. Though, after hearing that the runners would investigate further into the duchess' accident, one wondered if there was more to the story.

The only thing that had been reported was of the dilapidated carriage being found without a body. One would have expected the riverbanks to be searched. Her body should have washed up or been discovered by now. Nevertheless, even if they did find her corpse, nothing would bring her back.

But for whatever odd reason, he could not stop thinking of her. What if the duchess wasn't dead? *I suppose anything would be better than to learn that her husband was a monster.*

Perhaps, once Wycliffe had settled down, Charles could convince him to go on a ride. He would never disclose his real reason for the trip, but if there was ever a chance for Wycliffe to be happy again, he wanted to be able to help the man in any way he could. Avonlea owed him as much for his own part in the couple's current happiness.

Emily stirred and mumbled something. "Charles…"

"Yes, my dear."

"How glorious is it to wake up in such a state of total bliss?"

"I could not agree with you more. How do you fare this morn, Lady Avonlea?"

She moaned then stretched her arms out. After yawning, she turned to face him. "I am a little sore. Considering my insatiable husband kept me up all night, I am surprised I woke up so early."

"Well, my dear, we did have some catching up to do. All I can say is that I am relieved it is over. With the center of our melodrama out of the country, I daresay we will have some semblance of peace."

The way most marriages should start out. He had a wife that he loved, and her affections were returned. Life was indeed glorious, and he couldn't wait for the day their family would grow. His mother and aunt would instantly get over his choice of a bride, and from that moment on, they would quite swiftly take over Emily's personal space. He was even sure that they would niggle their way into their family home.

Such is the life, though.

"Charles."

"Yes, my love."

"*Mmm*…Say it again, please."

"Say what, my dear? I love you?"

Emily closed her eyes and smiled. "Those were the words. I love you, Charles. May nothing ever come between us."

"Here, here. Enough of this chatter, you appear as if you are ready to be loved again. I wonder, *who* exactly is the insatiable one now, dear?"

EPILOGUE

Blast my head. Here I was doing so well, and I had to stop at Madame Martine's, Wycliffe thought to himself, climbing off his horse and entering the staging inn. Between the galloping of his horse and the thunder rolling above him, his head throbbed. He should have waited until the monsters in his head ceased their roaring.

He sat at small table in the far corner of the inn and rested his weary, wet head against the window. He was close to resting his eyes when a gruff voice rustled his consciousness. "What will it be for today, sir?"

"Aside from something to quench my thirst, your country fare to fill my belly with, and a bed, that will be all."

The man grunted something foreign, or at least it sounded not from these parts, and walked away, disappearing to a side room where dishes clattered. The hunting trip should have waited, but seeing his friend so happy and blessed these last few days renewed the loss he felt for Cordelia.

No one could fill those slippers. She had stolen his heart the first time she had submitted to his rather deviant needs. Were it not for his idiotic notion, sending a message to her through Brimley, the duchess might still be alive, though he was sure he would not have been.

Downsbury would have shot him on the spot, knowing it was truly him carrying on the affair with his wife. But then again, Brimley had lost a great sum of money to the man, so who was to say how things would have ended. All he knew was that he was alone, without the love of his life, and without a single person he could turn to that would not think to toss him out on his arse. With how he liked his women, he would likely spend the rest of his days alone.

In fact, he was rather surprised he had not been sent to jail after the dealings at Martine's establishment. She was happy to serve him in the ways he needed, but offered little in the way of true submission. Martine, in the end, was only hired help, and what he required was a woman who was not afraid to be bound, spanked, or gagged. He enjoyed using the riding crop on occasion, but there was only one person he had used it on.

Wycliffe shook his head. *Get a grip of yourself, man. She's not coming back. Ever.*

The gent brought him a tankard of ale and a trencher of what the man must have thought to be nourishment. "When you are ready, I will have the boy show you up to your room. How long do you expect to stay?"

"I will only be stopping for the night, sir. Has my horse been tended to?"

"'E has. The boy will ready him for you in the morning, after you have eaten."

"Very well. Much thanks for the food and drink."

The man walked away, and the moment Wycliffe popped a piece of dry bread into his mouth, a woman's laugh across room nearly made him choke. *It cannot be...* He shook his head. *No. Now I am hearing things. Hell, I think I need more sleep than food.*

Wycliffe drank his ale in one sitting, took another bite of bread, and pushed the trencher away. He was half way across the room when he saw the woman. Her smile, laughter, and posture had him convinced. The way she tossed her hair over her shoulder—an action the duchess did all too often when they were alone, especially after lovemaking. His body vibrated and hummed with need.

He could not believe in a million years he would have found her. In the middle of the country at that. And in a tavern. She would have never set foot in an establishment such as this previously, so why now?

All this time...Where has she been? Why hasn't she made an attempt to send word? So many questions...I cannot even begin to fathom...

The earl's heart hammered violently in his chest, and his breath hitched. He did not know whether to laugh, be angry, or cry. *Does Downsbury even know she is still alive?*

Time seemed to stop. He stood there until she glanced up from the conversation she was having with a patron. Her head tipped to the side, and when her eyes widened, he knew that she knew.

Christ, it is her.

To be continued...

Her Deviant Lord

PROLOGUE

Wycliff awoke to the sound of a door closing and cutlery clamoring about. His eyes fluttered open, and he turned his head to the side to see dark, beady eyes glaring back at him.

"I see you have awakened from a dead sleep. You had quite the swoon, sir. We were not certain if we should have had a pine box made up." The old woman spoke while tapping at his leg. His bare leg. *Good God! I'm nude!*

He shuddered to think that the old bat had stripped him of his clothes. *Come to think of it...* He searched for them on the chair, then on the floor, but they were nowhere to be found.

Christ. "Woman, what have you done with my shirt and pants?"

"They are off to be laundered, sir. We thought that when you woke, you would care for a bath and clean clothes. We meant no offence."

Of course not. After all, he was the one who had swooned like a woman, thinking he was seeing a ghost.

"If you do not mind my inquiring sir, what had you in a state? Should we summon the village healer?"

"Nonsense, I will be fine. Once my garments are dry and I have fed, I will be on my way."

"Fine, fine, I will go and see to your things. You should know, you have upset quite a few of the patrons, including Mrs. Weylen. The moment she saw you, we did not know if she was going to toss her crumpets either. It was quite the fright, sir. Yes, it was. Should have seen her."

"And where is Mrs. Weylen now? I would like to...*err...*apologize, for my dastardly behavior."

"Oh, she does not live here in town. She be living east of here. Only comes to town to trade goods on behalf of old maid Corinne. The only spinster in these parts. With those two women out there in the middle of nowhere, I am quite surprised no highwayman has abducted the beauty. She's a widow, you know."

A widow, eh? His Cordelia was in hiding, masking as a widow. Or was it entirely all his imagination? "And how long has this woman been here?"

"I imagine for a while. She lost her husband some time ago, and it is only her and…"

His thoughts blanked out. It could not be her. She would have found a way back to him by now, if she had truly survived.

"Thank you, that will be all. My clothes would be much appreciated."

"Very well, sir. If they are not yet dry, shall I find something else suitable to your size?"

He nodded. He didn't want to spend another moment here unless he had to. It was humiliating enough to know what had happened, but to think it was all in vain—over a widow who was not her—did not do a thing for his peace of mind.

As soon as the old woman left the room, he kicked back the sheet and strode toward the tray of food on a table next to the bed. Eggs, bacon, and some lukewarm tea. Anything was better than heading back to his country home on an empty stomach, with his thoughts leaning toward how much of a lunatic he was. Not only was he a deviant lord, he was close to committing himself into an asylum for these visions.

The room lacked the fineries he was accustomed to. A warm fire didn't burn as it should. His blanket appeared to have aged longer than dear Aunt Edith. The painted walls now peeled. Chips curling as if they had been shaved. Staring at the dilapidated structure around him, he thought more on what had driven him to this point in his life.

These were things he didn't think his friends the Earl of Bridgeton and the Marquess of Stoughton would understand, and he certainly was not going to tempt fate. Just how would they handle knowing that an acquaintance preferred to have dominant sessions with his lovers? Expecting nothing less than their full submission, their bodies relinquished to his needs. He loved, adored, demanded to mark their skin in a way that served as a reminder of who they served.

That was one of the reasons why he had fallen in love with Cordelia. She had made his duty to command and master easy. She had given her submission without a question or battle. She had aimed to please him in every regard, and now she was gone. And never coming back.

CHAPTER ONE

B astian Wycliffe, the Earl of Wendelhem, gently tucked Mary Elizabeth's petite hand into the crook of his arm and silently prayed the damned gel would cut their stroll short. For each time he escorted her about, she prodded him to make her his official mistress. A thought that on most days he abhorred, though with each passing day, the benefits outweighed the inconveniences.

He had only just begun to move forward and had spent the last month sober. After the sotted mess he had become all those months ago, he had nearly destroyed any respectability he had left. His man of affairs tended to his properties out of town, while he sorted himself out. He also had to make amends to Madame Martine for his previously obscene behavior.

Not only did he apologize to the brothel owner, but after explaining, in great detail, what his needs were, he paid handsomely for her to assign him a wench who wouldn't take exception to his requirements.

Mary Elizabeth's beauty and feminine wiles distracted him well enough. Her hair as black as coal and pale violet eyes had captivated him the first time she had pleasured him at Madame Martine's establishment. The young woman had been willing to learn how to pleasure him with her submissiveness. Not once did she fuss over being bound, nor did she scold him when he punished her with a spanking for not taking his cock all the way in her mouth.

In fact, since that first night she had entered the room, whenever they were together, the unconventional beauty insisted that she be punished. His cock stirred from its flaccid state into a semi-erect position as she boldly flagged a carriage, stopping the driver.

"You there! Might I have a word with Lady Morton?"

The driver bowed and stepped down to seek permission from his mistress. Lady Eloise Morton, the daughter of Lord Hamish Morton, who had inherited his title and family's meager fortune, had had to endure an embarrassing let down last season. The Earl of Bridgeton had made his intentions clear from the get go, but her dear mama would see the truth for it was. Her precious daughter was to be made a fool of, and he couldn't help but empathize with the girl.

"What do you think you are doing, Mary Elizabeth? This is highly irregular, and I do not approve of how you are blatantly drawing attention to us."

"Why on heaven's earth are you upset, Bastian? I, for one, am extremely pleased with our arrangement, and I always knew that we would have a special bond. One that you obviously do not mind all of London to witness, as we are walking about so openly in Hyde Park." She huffed with displeasure before continuing her rant. "Besides, my dear, I desire to speak with an old friend, is all."

The moment she finished speaking, the carriage door opened, and an un-amused Lady Morton glared at his companion. "What is it that you desire to speak with me about, Mary Elizabeth? I have not got the time to be stopping, nor the patience for your drama. Besides, being seen with you is scandalous enough."

"I simply wanted to point out that what I always told you was true—that I am worthy of being courted by an earl. What do you have to say now at my inability to fit in with the rest of town?"

"Henry," Lady Morton shouted. "Drive on, and do not stop again." The carriage door slammed in their faces.

Mary Elizabeth gripped his arm. All he could do was pat her hand. "Calm yourself, dear. Next time, do try to avoid making a spectacle of yourself. London is hardly a forgiving place, and I suppose that this will be gossiped about tonight whilst she is entertaining company."

"I only meant to—"

"It matters not what you meant. I, for one, could do without scathing gossip for a little while. You, madam, should be grateful for the privacy we are afforded for the time being."

The wench scowled, crossed her arms over her chest, and pouted. "Honestly, Bastian, I have no idea why you haven't moved me into your town house yet. Martine has made it quite clear that if you do not make a decision soon this arrangement will end. There are other lords who will be happy to make me their mistress. Surely you can make a decision on the matter soon?"

Christ! The woman is determined to make me mad. "And I have already told you that I am undecided on the matter, Mary Elizabeth. But let me make amends by taking you to Vauxhall this weekend. I am positive that you will appreciate the entertainment, and perhaps if I can rearrange my schedule, we could continue to the city of Bath. What do you say now of my indecision?"

Her frown faded, and instead he found her lips curling into a mischievous smile. The gleam in her eyes was all the approval he required. Hopefully, the distraction would be enough to keep her insistence at becoming his mistress at bay.

"Mrs. Weylen, are you sure that you really want to go to London?"

"I am. Enough time has passed, and I am eager to see how much has changed since my departure to the country."

Cordelia Waite, formerly the Duchess of Downsbury, watched her companion quizzically. Were it not for the old woman's quick thinking, kindness, and generosity, she and Matthew would have never survived that terrifying night. It had taken days before she had awoken, and many nights after that for her to recollect how she had ended up in the country.

Her blasted husband, the conniving prig that he was, had shipped her off in secrecy for the remainder of her confinement with the expectation that she would give up the child. What he had not expected, however, was that she had a plan all her own.

She had intended to send word to her beloved Wycliffe and deliver the unthinkable ultimatum—trade in all his wealth to travel with her to the Americas and begin a new life together, but when Missus Miller had taken that nasty fall, she had postponed her trip for a bit. The elderly woman needed more help with her trading business, and she would have been the only one who could have cared for her.

Cordelia's love for the earl meant more than all the wealth and power her husband had. 'Twas an unfortunate thing that the Duke of Brimley had been caught in the crossfire. *His poor widow.* She would make amends with the dowager duchess before she left England. The poor dear had a right to know that the rumors of Brimley siring her child were nothing more than gossip.

Although, it was no secret how much of a scoundrel he truly was. The man sorely lacked any scruples and had not one care for those he hurt. One could say the same about the type of marriage she and Richard had. They both had been adulterous, and while she would never apologize for her affairs, she only wished she had found a way to annul the marriage in its infancy. So much hurt could have been avoided. Not to mention the scandal.

Now a year later, she was planning to face Wycliffe and make the proposition she had desired to years ago. And finally announce a little surprise. *But first things first.* If she had heard proper, the dowager duchess was now addressed as the Marchioness of Stoughton, so she had to make sure the driver knew exactly where they were going.

"Has Matthew been readied for our journey, Missus Miller?"

"He has, though he's decided to fall asleep again."

Bah! If he fell asleep now, he will be up all night again. 'Twas terrible enough she had barely slept these last few nights and that tonight would be the same, but if she kept him up now, then he would be sour and restless for their ride into London.

"Very well. Are we ready then to leave?"

"Yes, ma'am."

"Excellent. Please tell Davy that we shall be travelling to Stoughton Hall first, and from there, we will backtrack to the nearest staging inn."

The ride went faster than Cordelia had expected. Matthew slept for the entirety and still slumbered peacefully in her arms. Even despite the rumbling of thunder in the distance and flashes of lightning. When the wagon came to a stop, she handed the babe over to the dour-faced old woman. Her gentle eyes, warm and caring most times, now had a worrisome glare to them.

"Mrs. Weylen, I know not of your previous troubles, but I do not think now is the right time to address them. It appears that hell is about to unleash its fury upon us, and if you do not hurry, the child will get catch the death of him."

"I promise, ma'am, I will not be long. I have only come to say my piece, and then we will be on our way."

Missus Miller waved her arms with impatience as Cordelia climbed down the rickety steps of the carriage and walked the gravel path to the main house. Today was the first time she would witness the grandeur of Stoughton Hall.

About to use the knocker, the door opened before the iron clasp even touched the door. "Can I help you?" the gray-haired, brown-eyed butler asked.

"I was hoping to speak with the dowager duchess…err…I mean, Lady Thompson. That is, if she will see me."

"May I tell her who is calling?"

"My name is, Mrs. Wey…Cordelia Waite, the Duchess of Downsbury."

He glared at her with suspicion. "Just a moment. Please wait here inside—there's a seat just by the alcove—while I see if she is taking visitors."

The marchioness' voice carried into the foyer as she moved closer. "You must have it wrong, Lewis. Cordelia has been dead for some time now. There must be a mistake…"

The marchioness stopped talking the moment she saw Cordelia. Her face paled, and she quickly raised her hands to muffle a cry before swooning into the arms of the butler. A maid walking by the front entrance screamed. Suddenly, all of the house appeared.

When Lord Thompson came to his wife's aid, he glanced at Cordelia and then back to his wife. About to take the marchioness into his embrace, he looked at her again, only this time, he registered who she was. "Your Grace, what are you doing here?"

"I have come to clear my—" *Boom.* The sound of thunder crashed above them. Off behind her, she heard her son wailing as lightning rippled through the sky. She looked back at the wagon as rain pelted it mercilessly. "I have to go now, I cannot stay."

"Your Grace, please, come in. Your servants are welcome as well. Just have the driver take the coach over to the stable."

Cordelia waved to Missus Miller. The old woman transferred the crying baby to Cordelia's arms before she ran off to tell Davy where to bring the cart around.

The marquess ordered the butler and the maid to take his wife to their room, stating he would be along shortly. Then, he addressed Cordelia. "Your Grace, if you will follow me, you can warm up by the fire. Can we provide the baby a dry blanket?"

"You are most kind, my lord."

He waved to another maid, who left, only to reappear with a fresh gown and blanket. "Allow me." The young woman offered to take the now calm babe.

"No, just leave the items here, and I will tend to my son. Thank you."

The maid curtsied and took her leave.

As she undressed Matthew and wrapped him in the dry clothing, she looked up at the marquess and frowned. "I truly meant no harm in my stopping here, Lord Thompson. I know not of what horrid gossip has been spread, or what my husband has been told. All I want is to let your wife know that I had no relations with Henry, nor did I have any designs on him."

Cordelia rocked her son to sleep while she continued. "The fact of the matter is, I have no intentions of ever returning to Richard, but I am in need of your assistance. I need to see Bastian right away. He is the only reason why I have travelled this distance. The earl and I have much to discuss."

Lord Thompson looked at the child and then back to her. "You should know that I do not blame you in any way, however, I am not sure Isabel will say the same. Her life was nearly ruined, and my sisters as well, by your husband. How do you think London will react to learn that you are still alive?"

"I care not for what they think, because they will never learn of my return. Let me assure you, Lord Thompson, once my business with Bastian is finished, I will happily return to my humble life in the country with my son. The accident was providence's way of giving me a second chance at life. And while I had hoped it would have ended differently, I have learned much these last few months."

The marquess frowned. "Your Grace—"

"Please do not address me as such. Cordelia Waite no longer exists. Remember that always. To the world, I am a widow by the name of Mrs. Weylen."

"Very well, Mrs. Weylen. You are welcome to stay here. Get some rest, and know that you are safe. When you are ready, and my wife is calm enough to talk, we shall discuss your plans."

"Thank you, my lord. I am indebted to you." *Though I am sure your lovely wife will not think the same. In fact, I am sure she will turn us out on our arses.*

Bastian scanned the room for where he had tossed his shirt and cravat. There they were, in the middle of the floor, too far out of reach, and more than likely wrinkled from his hastiness. *Blast it! I still have an appointment to attend.* He tucked his manhood back into his breeches, while a very satisfied Mary Elizabeth lay grinning from satisfaction. "Well, don't we look like the cat that ate the canary?"

"Mmm…indeed, my lord. Your masterful skills of pleasure, Bastian, never cease to amaze me. Your wicked tongue, in all its glory, knows how to drive a woman mad. Where ever did you learn all that?"

The question made him chuckle, and while no one had ever sought out such information before, he would never give up his secrets on where he had learned of how to pleasure women. His parents would turn over in their graves if he ever spoke such tales aloud.

What would they say of my visits to brothel upon brothel? What would my mother do if she knew that one of her widowed companions had taken me under their wing and educated me on the needs of women who wished for more than a simple fucking? Who knew that I would not be happy until I bound a woman, spanked her, and used implements to ensure her pleasure?

All this thinking was making his cock thick with need again. And while his companion, Mary Elizabeth, deemed to please him in any way that she could, absolutely no one would whimper, purr, or scream out his name like Cordelia. With a heavy heart, Bastian shook his head to keep thoughts of her out of his mind. *Cordelia is gone. Move on, man!*

With his shirt and cravat back on, he walked over to Mary Elizabeth's bed, planting a heavy hand on her round, creamy arse. "My dear, I need to leave now. Try not to get into any trouble until I come calling again. Am I understood?"

She grinned back at him, her mischievous green eyes indicating that she was prepared to disregard his order and make trouble at a moment's notice. Yet her words sang a different tune. "Of course, my love. I would not dare to ignite your ire. Besides, I have some shopping to do. I have my eye on several new gowns, which I think you will approve of very much."

"Well, in that case, I look forward to seeing them soon."

"Bastian, before you leave, I was wondering if you gave some more thought on—"

The earl pinched the bridge of his nose. *Here we go again.* "Mary Elizabeth, how many times must we go through this? I am not sure having a paid mistress is how I would like to proceed. I happen to like our current arrangement, and I wonder why you do not. If you want more money, I can certainly offer it."

The courtesan scoffed and bounced from the bed to dress. "How many times must I tell you, Bastian? Martine is hoping to draw a more long-term clientele. The woman is set on seeing her experienced girls settled, so that she may begin training others to prepare them for gentlemen of your league. As I said the other morning, if you do not commit to that sort of arrangement, there will no longer be an agreement for either of us."

"Then so be it, my dear. Shall we depart, then, knowing that this was our last moment together?"

She glared at him with a scowl. "You infuriating man!" Mary Elizabeth grabbed her porcelain water jug and tossed it at him. "You cad! Get out! I've had enough of this nonsense…after everything I've done…"

Bastian backed away, watching her fury with increasing fright. He had taken a chance with her, showing her the ways of being submissive to a man's heavy, but loving touch. She could turn around and blackmail him, report their activities to Martine. He could just imagine all of London learning of their tryst and how he prefers to spank women.

Christ! How many people would consider that assault? He could end up incarcerated, or even worse, locked away in an asylum for his deviant behavior. That would top any scandal brought on by the Marquess of Stoughton and his tryst with the marchioness in the pleasure gardens, as well as the Earl of Bridgeton marrying Lady Thompson in Gretna Green moments before she was due to marry the Duke of Downsbury.

I'm doomed.

CHAPTER TWO

Cordelia grimaced as the marchioness joined her in the parlor for tea. She could not imagine how much her ladyship had endured, but knew how vicious London could be and how vindictive her husband was. For what it was worth, she could not have been more pleased when Lord Thompson had divulged that her husband had lost all his holdings and was imprisoned at Newgate.

"Your Grace, you have my apologies for my swooning the other evening."

Cordelia waved off the comment as if it were nothing. "Please, my lady, there is no need to address me with formality any longer. I have renounced any of my associations to Richard and would prefer to be addressed as Mrs. Weylen. However, if you can ever find it in your heart to forgive what I have to say, then I would be happy if you used my name freely."

The marchioness nodded in acknowledgement. "Go on. My husband said you had some news to give me."

"I do not expect you to understand, nor do I expect your forgiveness. For if I was in your situation, I am not certain that I would be so willing to listen. I can, however, be clear in saying that I never, ever had an affair with your late husband. Nor have I ever entertained the thought. Henry owed my husband a great deal of money…or so he said. The night he was caught in my apartments, he was there delivering a message from my lover, the Earl of Wendelhem."

Cordelia stopped to wipe away a tear slipping out of the corner of her eye when the marchioness handed her a square of linen.

"I am so sorry, Cordelia. While some of us have endured displeasure at the hands of your husband, I suppose no one suffered more than yourself. He is a cruel, cruel man. You were with Wycliffe's child, then?"

Cordelia sucked in a sharp breath and nodded, then peered to the door at the end of the room. "Do not worry. Little Matthew is in good hands, I assure you. To be honest, now that I think of it, he has got the earl's eyes." She smiled and her belly fluttered, thinking of the precious gift that was her son. "He does, does he not?"

"Richard is a shallow man and will always seek fortune wherever it is easily made. Perhaps before I depart, I will visit him in disguise. I cannot believe he has received his comeuppance with a vengeance."

"Agreed. However, I wonder what his reaction would be to see his duchess back from the dead. Can you imagine his horror at seeing his duchess while he is dressed like a pauper?"

Cordelia couldn't help but laugh hysterically. To her delight, she would certainly have to pay him a visit. Perhaps if Bastian decided to come away with her, he would join her in making the duke a cuckold. She could see his face now, red with fury and embarrassment. While she was at it, she would tell him how inferior his cock was to Bastian's. The earl's prowess in and out of the bedroom superseded anything to which her husband had ever exposed her.

She had never minded the attention of introducing a second man into their relations. It had surely spiced things up. But not in the way that Richard liked to do things.

To him, a woman was not to be given any pleasure. She was there to serve—to take him full to the hilt, while taking his friend with her mouth. And were she to complain of not receiving any relief, she would be reprimanded with a slap to the face before a third gentleman would join.

Cordelia enjoyed taking a man any way she could, but honestly would have desired just a spanking occasionally.

When Richard had stopped calling upon her, she had been forced to seek other methods of pleasure. At first, she had sought to pleasure herself. It worked, but the effects were minimal, never fully satiating her need for aggression. Then she had met Bastian. The Earl of Wendelhem had wooed her on the dance floor, and then seduced her on Lord Broxton's terrace. Soon, their dalliances became frequent.

The first time they had coupled, she had willingly gone to her knees and taken him with her mouth. After his explosive release, she had demanded that he take her hard and fast. Bastian complied, taking her several times that same evening. Beginning with caution, he introduced her to new positions and promised her a night of total abandon, but with caution.

When the date could be arranged for her to spend another night at his town house, she had learned with expediency that the earl was a whole new category of man. From that day forward, he had become her deviant lord, and she had loved him for all the wickedness he had prevailed upon her.

Bastian stared into the empty glass of port he had just downed. He only drank the stuff when there was much on his mind, and as of this very moment, his rejection of Mary Elizabeth's proposal was a worry.

In a time when much of London thrived on scandalous information, he had no desire to have his personal life splashed upon the pages of the daily. *What I would do to give this all up.* He had no desire to live his life based on the expectations of the *ton.* Quite frankly, the thought of taking residence in Scotland, or even on the continent, was sounding more appealing by the day.

He would have his man of affairs go over the accounts with him. From there, he would be able to decipher which estates he could gladly give up, and then permanently relocate.

He was wealthy enough to take whatever staff he wanted, or even hire new, if necessary. Though the thought of leaving behind some of the most able-bodied staff London had ever set eyes upon worried him, Bastian knew some of them would never agree to move.

The hour was growing late, and while his body was physically exhausted, his mind ceased to shift around possible places to live. Pouring himself another dram of the rich and aromatic wine, he walked over to where he stored his maps.

His travels over the years had been extensive. After university, he had thought it best to learn how other countries maintained agriculture and try to apply the processes to his family's existing acquisitions. There was nothing wrong with their current systems, but if one wanted to continue to make a profit, one had to be willing to expand ideas.

He had opened a map of France and was studying the interior, when his fingers swept across the lines of the coast, toward Italy. *Now, there is a place that has inspired many things.* 'Twas the very place he had learned how to pleasure a woman with his mouth, as well as his first experience with being bound.

Bastian stopped and closed his eyes, ignoring the thickness in his groin increasing by the second. For a moment, he visualized his first impressions of the room and found himself in a memory…

Marble floors were laid throughout the manor. A lush green and vibrant garden wrapped around the terrace. Signora Donatella, a wealthy widow, summoned him to her expansive quarters on the top floor. When he arrived, he found that she was not alone. Her vibrant red hair cascaded past her shoulders, her silk robe open, while a male servant, wearing nothing, kneeled before her.

"Come, come," she said to Bastian.

He approached to find the tanned young man licking her cunt and another disrobing behind her. She held onto a braided cord, which she had wrapped around the young man's neck, as if he were an animal.

"Sit, *mi amore*. You have much to learn, but first I want you to watch."

The other man came up from behind and started caressing her tits. They were large and heavy, yet beautiful. She kissed him and told him she was ready. Then, she dropped her robe and walked over to her bed.

The young man on the cord knelt before her, and she dropped onto all fours. She wrapped her lips around the boy's meager cock, while the other one stroked himself before dipping his penis into her juices from behind. This one reached for a silk scarf and first covered her eyes.

Bastian was aroused, yet did not understand how far she planned to take things. He released his own cock from his breeches and began to stroke, slow but steady.

From behind, the young man pumped into Donatella hard and fast before withdrawing. This time, he entered her posterior, and she moaned. The boy on the cord now reaches for her hair and wraps it around his hand. He, too, pumps fast and furiously. She takes him all the way.

Bastian found himself completely in awe of this display and close to release. Slowing his strokes, he rolled and kneaded his balls as he watched the men climax with a roar.

Not long after, Donatella found her own release with an explosive cry and collapsed onto the bed. The servant removed the scarf from her eyes, and she nodded to the boy whom she had serviced. "You will take care of his needs now. Both of you, in fact. I hope you do not mind, Bastian? In order for you to learn, you have to know how it feels."

The boy approached and reached for his hands, walking him to the dais. He undressed him, finding himself, oddly, even more aroused and curious as to what was going to happen. Bastian's only experience with widows so far had been nothing out of the ordinary.

Once Bastian's pants came off, the young man spread his knees apart. Bastian's cock bobbed in front of him. He lowered his head and began to suck.

Ignoring the fact he had a man's lips around his cock, desire ran hot throughout Bastian's blood. He had started pumping into his mouth, when he felt the man's hand slide beneath his ass. His finger traced up the crease and slightly tickled around the hole. Then, he pulled his hand back and slipped a finger into his mouth while Bastian's cock was still in it.

Bastian was too far gone to even care what the young man was doing. His balls tightened and his legs began to tense. The moment his seed flowed, the man continued to milk him dry, sticking a finger in his ass.

Bastian's nerve endings zinged, making him feel even more confused about this ordeal. The man pulled out his finger and slowly eased back from Bastian's cock. His head spun and his breathing returned to a normal pace.

"How was that, Bastian? Did you enjoy it? I promise you, there is more. Do not get too relaxed. Come here. I want you to practice on me now. On the bed with you, and I want you to kneel on all fours. Diego, cover my friend's eyes. He needs to learn."

Bastian followed her instructions, but decided to do this his way. He had wanted to kiss her from the first time he saw her at the piazza. He had wanted to fuck her tits, suck on them. If he had to do this blindfolded, he might as well learn how to do this the proper way.

He leaned forward and kissed her hard. She moaned into his mouth and clasped the back of his head. Someone reached for his soft cock. *Fuck! Someone is going to suck it while—Christ!* Trying not to say anything, Bastian moved down Donatella's body, using his chin as his guide. Pressing his cheek to the round slope of her breast, he turned precisely at the right time.

Bastian's lips aligned with her nipple, and he drew it out with a gentle tug of his teeth. She groaned. "Bite me harder. Harder, please, Bastian."

He complied before moving to the other. One of the servants continued to suck him off, making him delirious, while the other bent over behind him, cupping his ass. *Christ!* All the sensations were maddening.

Bastian moved down Donatella's voluptuous body until his mouth reached the apex of her thighs. He stopped for a moment and nibbled one side, then repeated the same on her other. Taking another pause, he breathed in the scent of her sex. She was wet, and he could not help wanting to indulge in her taste. Dipping his head, he licked her folds. Slick and sticky, he took in her essence and that of the servant who had spilled into her previously.

It was in that moment, while he delighted in eating her cunt, that he felt the instant sting of something being inserted into his ass. However, the man now sucking his balls made it tolerable.

Up and down, in and out, Bastian's tongue moved. Donatella murmured something in her own heady state before her thighs closed in around his head. As she screamed, he continued to suck her nub and lick up her juices. He spilled into the servant's mouth again.

Collapsing onto his side, Bastian ignored the fact that he had been sodomized and pleasured by another man. He had learned a most vital lesson—women enjoyed sexual congress more than they let others believe. They desired to be bound, blindfolded, and under the proper circumstances, dominated. Women didn't mind submitting, if done properly...

The memory left him hard and in a predicament. He needed relief, and his hand wouldn't suffice, nor did he desire Mary Elizabeth's company.

Bastian set his glass down and strode to the door where his butler stood ready with his coat and hat. "When shall we expect you to return, sir?"

"I am heading to Martine's establishment, Cedric. Go to bed. I know not when I will return."

Tonight he would ask for two women, and while neither would submit to him in the way he'd instructed Mary Elizabeth, he looked forward to being thoroughly distracted.

Cordelia walked with the marchioness through the city streets, wondering if she would truly find anything that would aid in keeping her disguised. For the first time in her life, Cordelia felt guilty, dishonest, and out of place. She kept her head down, avoiding eye contact, and luckily enough, her hood kept her recognizable hair hidden.

"I feel awkward, my lady. This was entirely a bad idea, not to mention bad form."

"Pish posh, Cordelia. However, I have to ask, and please forgive my impertinence. Do you not miss any of this? You owned one of the most sought after wardrobes and a well-designed, elegantly decorated home. Surely the country does not compare to any of town's conveniences?"

Cordelia stopped just outside a supply shop and looked up slowly 'til her gaze met with her companions'. "I do miss it, to a degree, but I am done. That was then. This is now. I have Matthew's welfare to consider."

"You could offer him more, if you returned to your station. While your wealth would not be the same, your son would have the same privileges as any other well-born son."

Isabel raised a valid point, but the fact remained that no one would ignore that her son was a bastard. Bastian's offspring and heir. If people recognized her, what would they say? Would they come up to her and question where she had been all this time? What if they saw her with Matthew? Would they put the details together and see the resemblance?

Panic crept up her spine until the only thing she could think of was leaving. Cordelia clasped onto the marchioness' wrist and started walking back in the direction they had come.

"What in heaven's name are you doing? We still have yet—"

"Please, I will explain…I…we…need to get out of here. I cannot do this. I need my son."

"But Matthew is with my nursemaids. He is in perfect health and in capable hands."

"You would not understand. Please, I would like to leave," Cordelia pleaded as they approached their carriage.

Isabel stared at her with confusion, but stepped into the wagon silently. Guilt washed over Cordelia in waves. She was confused herself. The main purpose of going to town was to find new clothing for her and her son. The marchioness had been generous enough to cover the cost of the items, given she no longer had access to her husband's accounts.

Whatever pin money she had left after the accident, she had stowed away for whatever needs she had and for the expense of her and her son whilst living in the small and cramped cottage.

"Whatever has you spooked, Cordelia?"

"I was afraid. Afraid that someone would recognize me. Honestly, I have no idea why I thought going to town myself was a good idea. I will just send Davy along with Missus Miller, and once they have picked up the items, then I can see to visiting Bastian at his estate. Perhaps Lord Thompson would be able to assist with that. Do you think the marquess would aid me?"

She watched as the marchioness looked down and folded her hands in her lap. "I know not of what he will say upon the matter. However, I am certain he would help you, as long as he had your promise that you mean no harm. Much has transpired, and from what I know, Lord Wycliffe man grieved. He mourned for so long now, that he has only begun to return to society as a man ready to take on the world."

Now what does she mean by that? "Isabel, do you mean to say he is courting another woman?"

"If courting is what you would like to call it…Let me be frank, my dear—the man has frequented Martine's establishment. 'Tis rumored that she is trying to turn her girls into reputable courtesans, and apparently, an offer on some redheaded gel of hers has been made…proposed…Who knows what is true or not? I would caution you to proceed gently. I imagine that man will take ill the moment he sees a ghost from his past."

"That is precisely why I need someone strong with me. I have not ventured to those parts in some time now, and I need someone who will prepare him for the visit. There simply is no other way for us to do this."

Or is there?

The thought had crossed her mind to have the marquess invite him to Stoughton Hall, but it would inconvenience the family even more, and she simply could not bring herself to ask any more favors of them. Having the marquess bring her to Bastian's estate after dark was the only manner on how to deliver her proposal.

CHAPTER THREE

Bastian lay back with his arms crossed behind his head. The two ladies had done a marvelous job taking care of his relief. When he then requested they help each other achieve theirs, he observed with amusement how lovely they looked caressing each other. His cock began to swell again as he watched one of the girls on bended knee licking the others' cunt. The soft moans and hungry lapping made him crazy.

"My lord, you should join us. We should not be the only ones experiencing pleasure."

The invitation had him vaulting from the bed. He picked up the dark-haired girl and placed her on the bed, lying down flat, before turning to the blonde. "You, my dear, can continue what you started. Get on all fours, and I shall fuck your cunt from behind. Perhaps I might even play with your tight little arse." He slapped her on her creamy white rear. "Tell me, Daisy, have you ever had anyone fuck you in the ass?"

She only grinned and then whispered, "No, my lord, I shall reserve that honor for you."

"A most excellent answer."

Daisy crawled on all fours in between the others' legs and began to lap up the girl's juices.

Damn. I can smell her from back here. The sudden need to eat her himself was strong, but for now, Daisy's ass had to do.

Bastian dipped his fingers into her pussy, and then tasted her. It was the most wonderful scent of sex he had experienced in a while. His release, mixed with her juices—heaven. He fingered her again, this time taking a moment to pinch her swollen nub. Up and down his fingers slid, until he planted a smack on her mound. Daisy moaned into the other girl's pussy. The room's essence was purely hedonistic. *God, how I love fornicating.*

"Enough of this, Daisy, I'm going to fuck you hard. No one is to release until I say so," he ground out through clenched teeth. Then, he rammed into her and rubbed her cunt again. Only this time when he withdrew his fingers from her sex, he brought his finger to the puckered hole of her bottom.

In and out, he continued to pump into her, while every so often dipping his finger into her pussy to lubricate her rear until the haze now beginning to fill him became interrupted with the needy moan of the girls. "No coming until I say so, ladies," he growled.

He slowed down his pace until his balls began to draw up close to his body tightly. Bastian slowly and effortlessly slid a finger inch by inch into Daisy's ass. Her cheeks clenched at his intrusion, so he pulled his finger out and slapped her bottom.

"Now, now, sweetheart, I'm not finished." He would wait until he blew his load into her, and then he would ask if she would entertain more later that night.

"Damn it!" His release imminent, he shouted, "Now, girls. Fucking come loud and hard. Daisy, do not stop eating her cunt until I say so."

Pumping furiously now, he tensed as pulled out, spilling his seed over her asshole. When Daisy began to cry from her own release, he inserted his finger into her rear to the hilt. The girl on the bottom bucked beneath them from her own orgasm.

Bastian collapsed onto the bed next to the girl on the bottom with Daisy on top of both of them. Today's romp had certainly been a surprise. And if he calculated correctly, they had been at this for six hours straight. A record, since he and Cordelia had once spent five hours doing the same. His Cordelia had demonstrated her submissiveness to him in a way that touched his soul.

His heart wrenched at the memory. He was done for now.

Shouting in the hall caught his attention as he raised his head from the bed.

The door swung open.

"What in damnation are they doing here? Get out! Now! The two of you," Mary Elizabeth screamed.

Christ! I am in for it now.

"How could you…you…you infernal man! We had an arrangement."

"That we did, my dear. But we ended it because you wanted to secure a more substantial settlement. What we had was nice, but this," he gestured to the air between them, "is no longer an arrangement. Find yourself a protector who will not only satisfy you, but will cater to your every whim. I am sure there is such a man out there who will not hesitate to make you his mistress."

"I do not want anyone else. I want you!" she cried out.

The proprietor joined them. "What is the meaning of this, Mary Elizabeth?"

Tears streaked her cheeks, and all Bastian could think of doing was getting his clothes back on. He rose from the bed and walked to the chair where he had tossed his clothes hours ago.

"Need I remind you, Mary Elizabeth, that your arrangement with his lordship has ended? And need I remind you that Lord Chalcroft is waiting for you in the parlor. He has made a very interesting and promising proposal and desires to go over the details with the both of us. Come along now. Lord Wycliffe is a paying customer, after all, and has paid handsomely to afford the privacy he desires." She turned to him as he buttoned up his jacket. "My lord, if there is anything I can do to rectify this intrusion, just say the word."

"As a matter of fact, madam, there is one thing you can do." He looked over at Mary Elizabeth before returning his gaze to the proprietor. "Have Daisy sent to my town house around six o'clock. I would like to see how she fares outside of this establishment."

"Certainly, my lord, I will have her dropped off and our footman will collect her the next morning."

"No, no, my dear. He may collect her precisely five hours later. Consider it that I am wanting to test out the waters, so to speak."

The madam smiled and winked. "I understand perfectly, Lord Wycliffe. It is a pleasure doing business with you, sir."

"Likewise, madam."

Hopefully, Mary Elizabeth will get the hint that we are through.

As expected, the courtesan arrived at Bastian's estate at six o'clock, wearing a gown of a scandalous red hugging her fine, feminine curves. Her bosom was nearly bursting, and if he had to guess, she probably wore nothing beneath. Something he appreciated, but was not necessary. His only plan for tonight was to see how well she behaved with company present. He wanted to observe her table manners and how well she could think on a whim.

If he was considering on making the acquaintance of another fine female specimen, she would have to be prepared for all that was expected of her. He could not entertain guests and have a companion who was ill-mannered and insulted the expectations of proper decorum. Despite his flair for untamed sexual urges and his need to dominate, he still had to behave like an earl in the eyes of the public. He still had his various tenants and business associates to deal with.

Which is probably what bothered him so much about Cordelia. There was a woman who had impeccable manners and knew how to please him. Unfortunate though that she had belonged to another.

There was not much Bastian regretted in this life. Even coveting the

Downsbury's wife had not bothered him in the least. But he honestly wished that the Duke of Brimley would have ended his life. Things would have been so much easier for them—less complicated and taxing.

That was the only time he had ever considered marriage. But the woman belonged to another, and now she was dead. Fat ounce of good did the situation fare. He physically shook himself. *Stop thinking about her, man.*

"Your home is quite handsome, my lord," Daisy addressed as she walked past him, taking a moment to squeeze his rear. "Do you entertain here often?"

"Sometimes. I imagine now that things have settled, the gents will come calling again, though I do expect to be called to parties and all. If things work out between us, Daisy, and I do say liberally, I am interested in seeing what you have to offer."

The young woman giggled and flounced over to the dais. "Hmm…I have plenty to offer, my lord. The question is—how much more do you plan on corrupting me?"

Wouldn't you like to know?

CHAPTER FOUR

Cordelia avoided much of her hosts once they returned to Stoughton Hall. She wanted to be the one to ask Lord Thompson for his aid, yet she imagined his lovely wife would likely interfere. She wondered how he would react to the request of him escorting her to Bastian's home. Would he flatly decline, or would he feel compelled to do the right thing? The faster she spoke to her beloved, the faster she could return to the country.

Who could have imagined that after all this time, she would have no desire to remain in London? Gone were the days of having to keep up with the latest fashions. Long gone were the days when she felt compelled to appease her husband and entertain the snakes that her husband called friends and associates.

What was once her life was now nothing but a shadow of her past, soon to be forgotten. Matthew was her sole concern now. Not even Bastian could change her feelings on that subject. However, she worried how he would react to learning that he had sired the boy. Trepidation ate away at her as she sat at the breakfast table with Matthew, who happily gummed away at her finger.

His birth had been the loneliest experience of her existence, but the joy that had filled her the moment she had held him for the first time was incredible. Rarely did she leave the babe, and she was not about to do so now.

At that moment, the marquess entered the room with his wife, who only smiled.

"I hope you slept well, Cordelia?" the marchioness asked while picking up a biscuit and breaking off a piece.

"I did, thank you, my lady, my lord."

"Cordelia, we shall have to do something about your addressing us so formally," the marquess added. "I would much rather prefer that you call us by our given names."

"I know you would rather I did, but I will not be disrespecting your station whilst being a guest in your house. I hope you understand?"

He only shook his head and smiled at her. "My wife tells me that you are in need of some help—you want to visit with the Earl of Wendelhem. I should be able to give you a hand, though I imagine we might want to make the trip once it is dark. We cannot have all of London seeing who shows up at his door. Can you imagine it? The news headlines would read along the lines of 'Scandal of the Century'."

Cordelia snorted. "Very true, my lord."

"Excellent. We shall depart shortly after eight o'clock. I am positive that my sister and wife will be more than happy to keep little Matthew entertained while we are out."

"I am most grateful for your assistance and will never forget your kindness."

"Oh, just one more thing, Cordelia. I have sent ahead Davy with one of the maids, while Missus Miller is still resting, to collect the items you tried to acquire the other day. In addition to the country clothing, my wife and I have decided to indulge a bit and we have a little surprise for you later."

Oh! What have they done? Aside from the clothing for Matthew and me, and supplies for the kitchen and spices, what more could I need?

"No need to frown, my dear, I promise you, you'll not be disappointed. Now spend a little time with Matthew. I am sure you'll want to snuggle with the boy before we leave."

How could she not? Nerves and excitement, all rolled up into one fiery ball, threatened to burst forth. She was really going to see him. Finally.

Later that night, they were parked in front of the entrance to the Wycliffe estate. Cordelia was still anxious, but Nathaniel was reviewing the plan. "Now, just remember to keep your head down until we have been permitted entry. Once we are ushered inside and shown into the preferred room for this visit, I want you to stay confined to the shadows. Once Wycliffe is present and comfortable, I will give you the signal."

Cordelia nodded as the marquess ran through her instructions. The beautiful, dark blue gown that he and his wife had gifted her with was reminiscent of the style of gown that suited her the most. Since having Matthew, although she had kept her hourglass figure, she was a bit more top heavy as she was still nursing him. The black velvet cape that Isabel had loaned her covered every nuance of her body that would make her recognizable to the *ton*.

The marquess stepped out of the carriage and helped her down. Cordelia kept her gaze on the cobblestones leading up to Bastian's door.

"My lord, ma'am. If you will follow me to the library, I will see if my master is up for a visit," the butler declared with a scowl.

"I hope he is not too busy? We have much to discuss, and it is very important. Let him know that an audience with him is imperative."

Overly tall and lean, the man had to be near ancient. He furrowed his brows, squinting for only a moment, as if discerning how to deliver—or more accurately, interrupt, Wycliffe. "Very well, sir, please wait here in his library."

"That went well."

"That is only the beginning. I wonder…Cordelia, if you were to stand in the corner by that bookcase…" He pointed to the opposite side of the room where it was dark.

She nodded and made haste before anyone walked in on them.

"Perfect," the marquess commented a short moment before the butler entered.

"His lordship will join you momentarily. He only needs to dress. May I offer you and the lady some refreshment?"

"No, that will not be necessary. I do not plan on staying long."

The butler bowed and left, Bastian arriving soon after. Cordelia noticed that his hair was mussed at the back. *Has he been entertaining a woman upstairs? Has he truly moved on and found another lover?* Her heart sank at the prospect. *How could he replace me so…so…so…soon? It has not even been a full year.*

Her hands trembled beneath her cape, and she could barely stand on her own. How she wanted to throw her arms around him and tell him how much she missed him.

"Thompson! What is so important that it could not wait until morning? Has anything happened?"

"Be easy, man. I assure you, Isabel and Emily are fine. I simply came here to escort a woman who desperately wanted to see you."

He scoffed. "If this has anything to do with Mary Elizabeth, I—"

The marquess nodded, and Cordelia stepped forward into the glowing light of the fireplace. Bastian turned toward her, and when she lifted the hood of the cape, his eyes widened and his mouth gaped before he crashed to the floor from swooning.

"*Oof!* I have to admit, I did not quite expect that response."

Cordelia abandoned her cape where she stood and ran over to him, dropping to her knees. *Good heavens! What have I started?* The man probably thought he was staring at a ghost. "Wake up, my love!" she whispered as the butler walked in.

"What happened?"

"He just swooned. I have it under control. If he was entertaining upstairs, can you see to the lady and have her sent home immediately? He will need some rest, and I am certain he will want some privacy."

"Certainly, sir. I shall have her removed immediately."

So, he was entertaining another woman. How could he... Fury simmered beneath the surface of her calm facade. Why had he never come to confirm if the reports were true? She always knew Richard would never waste a minute on her, but Bastian...They were so close. Kindred spirits. He should have been able to feel, somehow, that she was alive.

Disappointment washed over her. Instead of fawning over his swoon, Cordelia jumped to her feet, walked over to sideboard, and grabbed a bottle of port. Then, she returned to him and began to unscrew the cork.

"Cordelia, what are you doing?"

"Getting him to come out of his swoon."

"With that?"

"Yes. Do you take issue with my course of action, my lord?"

The marquess stepped away and waved for her to continue.

"If you would rather leave, I am quite capable of waking and caring for him."

"I will leave the two alone once I am assured you can stay. Though we should not stay too late."

"And I assure you, my lord, once I have said what I have to say, he will probably want me removed from the premises immediately."

"In that case, I will wait in the hall for you."

Once his lordship closed the door behind him, she dumped the bottle of port over Bastian's face. He sputtered at first, and when his eyes opened wildly, followed by oaths being muttered, he stared at her and jumped to his feet.

"Damnation, woman! You are alive!"

He practically collided into her to embrace her, and all she could do was slap him. Her hand stung from the impact. She instantly regretted her action, but how else was she to express her displeasure at his courting another woman?

Bastian growled at her. "What in the world was that for?"

"That was for not looking for me! And if I were you, I would stay back. I am liable to slap you again for entertaining other female guests."

"Cordelia...please! You have to understand. All of the *ton* thinks you are dead. Hell, everyone thought you dead. The carriage was destroyed."

"But you did not come, not until that night in the inn, and even then, you were not searching me out. Tell me, how many whores have you entertained since my supposed death? Has anyone come close to pleasuring you the way I did so faithfully."

The earl shook his head at her with vehemence. "Sweetheart, had I suspected there was even the smallest chance of your survival, I would have sought you out."

I doubt that. "When you decide to come to your senses, I am only in town for a few more days. I did have much to say to you, but I am so furious with you right now, 'tis best I wait." She walked toward the door.

"Cordelia…wait…" Stay here, love. There is plenty of room."

"I did not travel alone. And, unlike you, I have a responsibility to see to. *Adieu.*" Cordelia opened the door to see the marquess gazing at her with a quizzical brow. "My lord, I am ready to leave."

"Are you certain? You and Wycliffe appear to have unresolved issues."

"Our issues will most likely remain unresolved until I can calm down."

"Very well, come along. I am sure Duncan can fix you a nice tea to soothe you."

Nothing could possibly soothe me. Nary a paddling could not handle. That is precisely what the oblivious earl required—a spanking to make him understand.

"I cannot believe you dumped port on him, Your Grace."

"How many times must I tell you, my lord, stop addressing me as so? Besides, Bastian deserved it. I am tired of being taken advantage of."

The marquess cocked his head to the side as if she had said something trivial.

"What has you so perplexed, my lord?"

"I am just not sure how you think that you have been taken advantage of."

Of course you have not noticed, you dolt. That is because you are happily married and are not paying attention to what is actually transpiring. He has only moved on and forgotten all that we had.

"It matters not, my lord. Now that all the items have been collected, I will give Bastian one day to come to me. Otherwise, I shall forget his very existence. I am simply done playing games, and Matthew will grow up knowing his father died with honor instead of knowing how much of a cad he really is." Cordelia folded her arms across her chest, leaned back into the seat of the carriage, and closed her eyes. As far as she was concerned, the discussion was over.

"Now, just wait on a minute, Cordelia! If you think that man did not mourn you, you do not know Bastian as well as you think you do. That man drowned in his sorrows for many months, risking his own welfare and family fortune. The guilt he carries about your affair, to never rescuing you from the clutches of Richard. You will never know the impact you truly had on him. Were it not for Lord Avonlea, I fear Bastian would have been a lost cause to all."

What on earth is he talking about? Bastian had more sense about him than to drink himself into oblivion. "I know not of what you are speaking. Indulge my curiosity, sir."

The marquess huffed. "Forgive my frankness, Cordelia, but whatever I say now, I say in pure confidence. The Earl of Bridgeton some time ago confided in me that he pulled the gent out of Madame Martine's establishment. 'Twas rumored he has a penchant for binding. He came in one night so foxed that I was asked to remove him. I know not of what transpired, but I do know that his obsession is with you."

He paused for a moment and shook his head. "I tell you, were it not for Bastian, providence only knows what would have happened to my sister. You might as well know that your husband tried to marry her. We later discovered that he planned to ship her off to a brothel in Italy, as he had done to others, and had planned to squander her dowry. 'Twas quite the scandal. Even chief prosecutor, Sayers, was involved in the operation."

"Are you telling me that Bastian had a part in stopping the wedding?"

"He did."

"Pray, where is my husband now?"

"Last I heard, the man was rotting away in Newgate. Albeit, it is now rumored he has come down with some disease, and I would not be surprised if he has passed on."

Passed on…What if Richard has died? Could I even resume a normal life in London? Matthew would benefit from the advantages of it, but I would never be well received again. However, the fact that Richard never went to look for me might be of assistance. This is such a mess! "Is there any way for us to verify his condition?"

Even if they did get confirmation of his death, what did she expect to do? It was not as if she could go back to living in her estate. She had no idea if there was a will, or if he had bequeathed her even the smallest of their properties. Good Lord, there was simply too many things to consider, and not nearly enough time.

"Cordelia, what has you so disturbed? What are you thinking?"

"I am only wondering what, and if, my husband had bequeathed me. Seeing as I was assumed dead, and he is only at his crossroads now, I hardly think that all his assets have been obtained by the magistrate for auction."

"I am not certain either, though, if you were willing to come out of hiding, we should be able to find out if anything was left to you, prior to the accident. Is that something you would like to risk?"

A risk—that is what all of this was. What originally had been one plan, now had been divided into a multitude of mini tasks and assignments. She should just keep with the original idea—invite Bastian to return to the country with her and tell him he had a son. However, she could figure out what her entitlements were and then retreat to the country once London realized that she had never really passed on, but was left for dead by her wretched husband.

While she was not in the market of looking for sympathy, if there was an opportunity to repay the kindness of the marquess and his lovely wife, and of Corinne, the second option would only be the way to do so.

"What I think, my lord, is that running away is for cowards. I shall not run away without truly knowing if I am returning to the country as a penniless dowager duchess. But I shall not grovel for wealth, either. Whilst these last few months have been hard, adjusting to the meager and pauper lifestyle, I still have my health and my son. And both will remain the same, with or without a title."

"If I may be so bold, your grace. I think you are making the right decision. Though, be sure to understand that none of this will be easy. Once London is aware of your return, there will be scathing talk and hatred. Your husband was a vile man…"

"There is no need to remind me of that horrid detail, my lord. I was married to him, after all." If there was one wish she was entitled to, she desperately hoped that her husband had perished. She had no desire to face him ever again.

"Where do we begin? I simply cannot walk into the estate and start ordering about the staff, nor can I summon his solicitor and begin the process. Will you be able to assist me with these things? You have already done so much for Matthew and I, and I would hate to impose on you further."

"Make no mention of it, Your Grace. I will see what my man of affairs can find out for us."

Most excellent. Perhaps things were beginning to look up, after all.

CHAPTER FIVE

Back in his library, Bastian still could not believe his eyes. He called out for his butler, and the man made use of his quick feet. "See that this is cleaned up. And do try to get the stains out, this is my favorite shirt."

"Yes, sir."

Bastian passed the elderly man his shirt and headed upstairs to his room. *Christ! She is alive after all this time.* How he longed to fuck her, but most of all, he could not wait to hold her in his arms again.

However, there was something different about her. In the few moments that he had managed to have a solid look at her, she had appeared a little plumper in the breasts. Not that he minded in the least. He would look forward to fucking those beauties in no time, but it was perhaps the change in demeanor. Something about how she had reacted.

Christ. How will the Duke of Downsbury react to learn that his wife is back from the dead? But wait, her husband has been stripped of his title, and from what I heard last at Whites, it is rumored that he has fallen ill and died. But did he?

This was all too much to digest in such little time. He had to sleep on this and give Cordelia time to calm down. The woman did have a wicked temper. He would wait until tomorrow afternoon to visit the Marquess of Stoughton's estate, assuming she was staying with his family.

He wondered how the marchioness felt about their guest, considering it was rumored that her first husband the Duke of Brimley had an affair with her. He knew all too well, however, that the man had gone to her at his behest to deliver a personal message. Bastian knew he was not the first to fall prey to her feminine wiles, but he knew very well that she had changed her ways once she was with him.

As soon as they patched up this mess the two of them were in, he would look into the duke's state. Were it proven that the man did indeed die in Newgate, he would marry the woman once and for all. If Downsbury still lived, then he would find another way for them to be together.

Bastian stopped outside his door and called down to his butler.

"Yes, my lord?" was the response.

"Before you retire for the evening, have one of my footmen send for my secretary in the morning. I need for him to make some inquiries, most urgently."

Late the next morning, after a fitful night's rest, Bastian readied himself before the looking glass. He tried not to look too fashionable, as his goal was to appear at Stoughton Hall without drawing too much attention. The last thing he wanted was for anyone to stop him and find out why he was decked out to the nines. He had a lady to impress, but most importantly, he had much to make up for.

"Will that be all, my lord?"

"Yes, Cedric. Would you ready my carriage, please? Also, I would like to have the blue room prepared for a lady's visit. It is my hope to return with a companion that you have not seen in quite some time."

"If you don't mind my asking, my lord, who is it that you plan to return with?"

"I cannot divulge that information just yet Cedric, but as soon as I can, I will. The present situation is quite delicate, and it is a matter of urgency that I continue to keep that information guarded."

"Very well, sir, are you in need of anything else while I am in town? I have a list of supplies from the cook, and if I get there early enough then, I will have the pick of supplies."

"Other than my usual, I do not think I have need of anything else."

The valet nodded and departed the room, closing the door behind him and leaving Bastian in the quandary of his thoughts. Would he dare tell her that he loved her? Would she even accept that after the horror she had been through? The only thing he could think of was all the different ways she could tell him "no."

Cordelia would be in her every right to deny him such an honor, yet, he could not imagine losing her once again. This time he would not stop until she was his. Bastian adjusted his cravat and turned to leave his quarters. Hopefully, in a few hours, he would be joined in them by Cordelia.

The house had been dreadfully quiet and lonely as of late. Even despite having Daisy entertain him here, it still did not take away the fact that she was not his Cordelia.

Nothing could change the fact that he wanted his woman back, and he would stop at nothing. If she rejected him today, then he would try again. Bastian would continue to ask her until she agreed.

Cordelia paced her room frantic and worried that she was running out of time. In the meanwhile, Matthew had not slept, nor had the entire household. Her son had cried non-stop all night, eventually waking up the marquess' twins. Her hosts tried to assure her that perhaps he was teething.

A nursemaid had brought in a dram of brandy throughout the night, advising her to dip her finger in it and dab it on his tongue. It had helped, though it did not make her feel any better. Matthew was beginning to run a fever, and without medical attention, who knew what could transpire. She could not bear the thought of anything happening to her son.

Deep in thought, Cordelia failed to notice that the marchioness had entered. "Dear me, Cordelia. You look affright. Let me have one of the nursemaids take Matthew into the nursery for a bit, so that you may rest."

"I could not possibly leave him with someone right now. I may have need to call for a physician."

The marchioness walked over and gently squeezed her arm, smiling. "My dear, if you feel you have need of a physician, we shall have ours drop in. Aside from a slight fever, which I suspect is from teething, I think you will be pleasantly surprised to hear that he is healthy. One of the other ladies I have tea with has just gone through the same ordeal."

Cordelia sighed and walked over toward the window with Matthew in her arms. The lush lawn, a vibrant shade of emerald, wisped gently in the wind. A bright yellow sun illuminated the rolling hills behind Stoughton Hall. "Perhaps a little fresh air will do us good," she whispered to the babe.

"You know, my lady, I think a bout of fresh air is just what I need. Perhaps once I return, I will have a rest, if it is all the same."

"Certainly. When you return to the manor, have Duncan call down one of the girls. Oh, before I forget, I have it on good authority that the Earl of Wycliffe will be dropping by today."

What? Why would he?

Her ladyship continued. "From what the cook said—he is in the middle of making preparations for a permanent house guest."

Cordelia winced. *The man cannot possibly be thinking that I am going to stay at his house.* She rolled her eyes, and inhaled. "It matters not what the man is doing. When he finds out he has a son, I am most certain he will change his mind about everything."

"What makes you say that? All those times we told you that he was a lost soul without you, did you even bother to listen? That man is nothing without you!"

"That may be so, but need I remind you that my husband might still be alive, and if he has any inkling that I am as well, the scandal will begin all over again?"

"You worry too much, Cordelia. Even if your title was restored—which I doubt, as the clod had his stripped—the scandal was his alone. I am not sure what of his estates remain, as I am sure it was all sold off. Besides, I am positive if the man is not yet dead, he shall be soon. Which means you shall be free to marry the earl and carry on with your life, as you intended."

"That may be so, but the more I think on it, do I really want to be saddled with a man? I lived for so many years in Richard's shadow. I do not care to be controlled again." *That is, unless we are talking about in the bedroom.*

Cordelia's mind wandered to another time when the intrigue of her affair with Bastian was the paramount highlight of her week. In hindsight, she was ashamed of her adulterous behavior, but she would never take it back. Bastian had instilled a passion in her which her own husband could not, even if he tried.

Enough of those dreadful memories. "You know what, my lady? I think now is a good time for that walk. I could use the distraction."

"Indeed."

Cordelia swaddled her son, much to his chagrin, and descended the stairs from the guest wing. She heard men's voices, and then she heard *his.* She tried to slip out without being seen, but then Matthew began to cry.

When she reached the final step, the marquess appeared from the parlor. "Is everything all right, Cordelia?"

"Yes, my lord. I was just about to go for a walk. The fresh air will do Matthew some good."

She went to dart past him, but he caught her by the arm. "Would you like to join us for a bit?"

"And who might be 'us,' my lord?"

"Wycliffe and myself. I am sure the two of you could use some time together."

"I appreciate the thought, my lord, but I am in need of the air."

His lips formed a thin line, and he shook his head. "Well, if you change your mind, you know where to find us."

"Thank you, my lord."

Before she could be stopped again, Cordelia dashed out a side door from the servant's wing. And noticed another coach approaching the house. Ignoring the visitor, she walked until she found a glorious apple tree to sit under. She loosened the blanket around Matthew and found that the child had fallen asleep.

Perhaps if I close my eyes for a few moments… Cordelia found every muscle in her body relaxing, and her eyes weighed heavily. *Just a small nap…*

"Who is Matthew? That is not your son's name…"

"No, it is not."

"Then whose child is Matthew?"

"You should speak to Cordelia. The two of you have much to discuss. Besides, 'tis not my tale to tell."

Bastian's stomach flipped. *Who does the child belong to? Why is it not Thompson's story to tell? What the hell is Cordelia keeping from me?* There were too many questions and not enough answers. "Pray, answer me one question. Did I father that child?"

The sudden possibility that he was a father all this time frightened him. And to make matters worse, he had not been there to assist her or bond with the child. Fortunately enough for him, he could make up for lost time.

"Bastian, you have to remember that she has been away all this time for safety. What do you think Downsbury would do if he knew his wife was still alive? Even after trying to marry my sister and all. She probably knows by now how deep in scandal he was. From what I understand, she has been meaning to talk to you, but the opportunity had not been presented."

The marquess paused and rose to pour them a drink. "I can say this, though, from what I know, she may not want to stay in London even after saying her piece."

Not that Bastian could blame her, but how could she not mention this to him before? He could not imagine the burden she had carried all this time. Alone, scared, and completely out of her element. She had spent so many of her years in a privileged society, and then all of it had been taken away so cruelly in an accident.

He would not blame her if his question sent her running back to a village. Perhaps, if she agreed to his proposal, then he would relocate to the country. Cordelia could have her peace, scandal free, and he would be happy just to have her, in any way he could.

"The lady may have wanted to avoid me, but I am going to make sure we talk now. I hope you will excuse me, Thompson? The lady and I have much to discuss." Bastian approached the door when someone knocked.

"How funny," the marquess quoted behind him. "I was not expecting anyone else."

The butler opened the door to reveal a very irritated Mary Elizabeth. Her arms were crossed, and she wore a scowl.

"Christ Almighty!" Bastian grumbled under his breath.

"Lord Wycliffe, I have been searching high and low for you. I cannot believe for one moment you would cast me aside so."

Bastian sighed and shot his friend a weary glance. "I will take care of this. Can you have one of the servants see Cordelia home? Send her on by tonight for dinner. I want to talk first before I am introduced to my son…if he is indeed my son." The marquess nodded and walked away.

"Mary Elizabeth, this is not at all proper. You are behaving irrationally! Come away from here." Bastian grabbed her hand and dragged her back to the hackney. "You called it off, remember? I have no desire to rekindle or revisit our prior arrangement…if one could even call it as such."

Bastian opened the door to the carriage, ignoring the protests from the courtesan. Behind him, the coachman protested too, as she had only hired him for one way. He lifted Mary Elizabeth in and slammed the door. Tossing the driver some coin, he returned his attention to the woman.

"Do not seek me out anymore, Mary Elizabeth. This obsessive behavior is disruptive and not conducive to your line of business. If you do not cease, I will have words with Martine, and I am certain you do not want me to entertain that idea."

"My lord, you would deny me of the only thing I want? It is I whom you do not want to cross. This discussion is not over, Bastian. We will finish it, and soon. Mark my words!" she cried out.

The earl knocked on the carriage to send it on its way. He pitied the next man that sought her services. On second thought, perhaps it was a good idea to discuss these intrusions with her employer, and the sooner the better.

Bastian walked around the exterior of the house until he saw his Cordelia under the tree. He walked halfway up the hill and wondered if perhaps he could sneak a quick glance at the child. Would Matthew have his dark eyes and small nose? He'd be a handsome devil if he had his mother's soft, delicate features too. The need to settle his curiosity rolled beneath the surface. *For now, my love, I leave you in peace, but you have much to answer for.*

The earl slowly approached the sleeping mother and child. With her eyes closed and shoulders relaxed, she cradled the babe who stirred in his sleep. He came closer, and when he bent down, the baby opened his eyes, as if instinctually. After he blinked a few times, the bundled up infant puckered his lips and made infantile sounds. He stuck out his tiny hand from beneath the blanket and held it out for Bastian to touch.

To think, he is mine. Bastian's heart swelled, and he found himself flooded with emotion. Tears welled up in his eyes, and he could not help thinking how beautifully motherhood suited Cordelia. But then the baby scrunched up his face and wailed so loud, as if to alert all of England that the earl had stumbled across them.

Cordelia opened her eyes, and even though she appeared surprised to see him, she cooed the child back to calm.

"I am sorry for disturbing your rest, but the marquess mentioned he had to talk to you about something."

"Oh! Did he say why?"

"No, he did not. I am curious, Cordelia, when did you starting watching children?" he asked quizzically. The last thing he wanted her to know was that he was already onto her little charade.

"Err…The housekeeper had errands to run, and I-I volunteered. Yes, I occasionally do find it good practice to learn such lessons in mothering."

Bastian muffled a laugh. "How about I escort you back? It would be rude of me not to."

She nodded and began to walk ahead of him. He had loved the swagger of her hips before, but now that she had filled out from being with child, he could not wait to take her from behind.

Easy, man. You still have a long way to go. First, you have to convince her to marry you.

Embarrassment washed over Cordelia. What would everyone think of her? Well, not everyone, just a particular earl with a penchant for deviant copulation. The more she thought on the subject, her need to be joined with him again rushed through her. Her desire more intense than anything she had yet experienced.

If they were even to consider reacquainting their former flame, would he receive her the same way? Much of her body had changed since giving birth to Matthew. Her hips were wider, bottom rounder, and her bosom…*Good Lord*. Her amiable bounty of a handful had exploded into a corset-busting situation.

"Slow down, Cordelia. I do not seem to recall this being a race."

"No, but if you said that the marquess wishes to speak with me, I should not keep his lordship waiting."

"Of course not, but we could use this time to talk as well."

"And pray tell, my lord, what is it that you wish to speak with me about?"

He stopped and faced her. His lips pursed, and his posture rigid. "I wanted to let you know that I have my men out, making inquiries regarding Richard's whereabouts. There is a distinct possibility he is on his deathbed, but that is unclear. I should know by the day after next."

Cordelia's belly fluttered with eagerness. If she became a widow, and if he still had anything left, it would be hers to do with what she pleased. Matthew would not have a meager childhood, and she—well, she had no delusions that she would be attending any society balls. Her time for ball gowns, masquerades, and fine dining were over. Nevertheless, she would return the kindness Missus Miller had bestowed upon her.

"Why would you do that, Bastian? What possibly motivated you to make such inquiries?"

"Why else would I do it, Cordelia? Everything I have ever done for you has always been carefully thought out, and with the best of intentions. Do you think I seek to harm you in any way with such information?"

"I know not of what your intentions are, my lord, but I am ever so clear on one thing. Even if he were alive, he has been stripped of his title, as have I. My life cannot be restored to its previous state, nor do I have any desire to be thrown upon the unfeeling and wretched lot that the *ton* is. Should Richard become aware that I am very much alive, I am most certain it will send him into an apoplectic fit."

"How could you possibly know such a thing?"

"Really, Bastian, what would be your reaction, after all the wicked things you have done and having been imprisoned in the meanwhile."

"I would be shocked, horrified, humiliated, to be seen in such a state."

Of course he would.

The sound of a carriage approached. She watched Bastian crane his head and utter an oath. "For the love of—"

"Who is that, Bastian?"

"No one you need to worry about, dear. Run along inside, and try not to keep Thompson waiting."

Cordelia found his secrecy and intrigue about the guest fascinating. "No. I think I shall stay."

"No! I want you to go inside."

"I do not take orders from anyone, least of all you…"

Suddenly, a woman came barreling out of the carriage, marching her way toward Bastian.

"I told you never to return here."

"And I told you our discussion is not over. Who is this woman?" Then, the bold, angry pariah tipped her neck to the side, and her mouth dropped open.

Damnation. I have been discovered.

"She is the duchess…Downsbury's wife…You are supposed to be dead!" the woman exclaimed in horror.

"And you are not supposed to be here. Go home, Mary Elizabeth! I have nothing more to say to you."

Cordelia wrapped her arms tightly around her baby and visualized what would happen. By morning, all of London would descend upon Stoughton Hall. She had to get out of here. There was no way she would drag the marquess and his wife's good name through the mud, as her husband once had.

Before another word could be said, she ran toward the house. When she reached the servants' entrance, she frantically ran to her room and began to pack what she could. Meanwhile, Matthew kicked up a fuss.

In her frantic rush, Cordelia turned to find the marchioness standing by the door, watching her with concern. "Cordelia, what in heaven's name are you doing?"

"Leaving."

"How come? What happened with you and the earl outside? Are things truly over?"

Over. No. They are only beginning, and your good name is about to be scandalized once again. "I cannot say for certain, but if I do not leave this instant, all of London will know by morning that I am truly alive and well. Besides, the rest of my business can be conducted from the country." *More like it has to be.*

She should have seen this coming. Sooner or later, a visitor to Stoughton Hall would have recognized her and alerted the *ton* of her return.

"Can I not persuade you to stay on?"

"My lady, while I am grateful for all that you have done, I cannot, in good conscience, allow any more scandal come to this house. You have gone through enough to last many lifetimes, and I will not play a part in it now."

Guilt washed over her. Perhaps it was best to leave them all now and forget any of this happened. Matthew and she would survive even on the meager allowance of what she earned selling baked goods.

"Allow me to help, Cordelia," the marchioness implored while reaching for the baby.

"Very well, would you find Davy and Missus Miller and tell them to get ready. That we shall depart as soon as the carriage is ready."

"If that is what you wish. I will take Matthew to the nursemaid, so she can watch him while you make the necessary preparations."

When the marchioness opened the door, Bastian's voice carried up the stairs. She had to hurry. She could not find the nerve to tell him now that Matthew was his son.

CHAPTER SIX

"Where is she?" he questioned the servants as he passed them. When he came across Thompson's wife, he took a step back and inhaled. "She is packing, is she not?"

Lady Thompson nodded, and then crossed her arms. "If I were you, my lord, I would begin to make up for lost time now. The scandal is not far behind, and she does not wish to impose. I know not of what transpired earlier, but she is scared, Bastian. We have all suffered at the hands of her husband, so I can understand why she wants to return to the country."

She is running. Of course she is. But to what kind of life would she subject her son in the process?

The marquess soon joined them in the hall. "What in damnation is going on? Duncan was just explaining that he was roused out of the garden because of shouting and found a woman being aggressively put into a hackney coach."

"Ah! What he saw was me tossing Mary Elizabeth in. She recognized Cordelia, and now Cordelia is upstairs packing, trying to leave with my son."

"And how exactly do you know it is your son, and not someone's that she is caring for?"

"For Pete's sake, Thompson, the child has my ears and my eyes!"

"Well, it certainly took you long enough to figure out what was going on. You are not going to let her leave London, are you?"

"Of course not. I had every intention of having her return with me to my house. My servants are already making the arrangements, though I had no idea we would be joined by a child." A surprise he had not counted on, but at least they would both be safe at his house until he knew what to do with Mary Elizabeth. "Thompson…"

"What is it, Bastian?"

Bastian reached into his coat and withdrew some money. "Give this to the man and woman who she arrived with and have them return to the country. There is not much they can do here, and I am certain they are eager to return to their humble lives in the village."

"And what of Cordelia and Matthew?"

"If you would not mind readying your carriage, I shall ride behind them on my horse. The situation requires a firm upper hand, and this is just the way to do so." He turned to her ladyship and dipped his head. "I know I am not in the position to make many demands, but do you have a hooded cape she could use for the ride. I would like to keep her concealed until she is inside my home."

"Certainly, my lord, I shall see to it this instant."

He'd had enough of this scandal already, and it had not even begun. Fortunately for him, the first place people would check was the marquess' home. And if he knew Thompson well, he would leave instructions with Duncan that they were not accepting visitors at this time.

Bastian hoped sincerely that she would agree to stay at his town house, but they would soon find out how much of a fuss she would put up. He would wait outside in the stables and watch the carriage drive away.

"What do you plan on doing about Mary Elizabeth?" the marquess asked, interrupting his thoughts.

"I will be taking a course of action through Martine. This kind of behavior is not only bad form, but is not good for encouraging future business. I imagine Martine will cut her loose, but it is hard to say. I shall be stopping there tonight to conclude all association with the business."

"Are you not concerned at all about how dangerous she may be? The woman obviously is obsessed. What makes you think that once she learns you and Cordelia are seriously involved, she would not do anything harmful to the duchess or the baby?"

Bastian had not considered the consequences until now, nor did he plan on anyone interfering with their future. Mary Elizabeth was emotional woman, driven by impulse, and would likely do something she might regret. The trick was to stay one step ahead of her, every step of the way. If she so much as came within a yard of Cordelia and the baby, he would make sure she never entertained another soul.

"Of course I am, Thompson. How could you ask such a foolish question? I am going to go outside to ready my horse. Just make sure she gets into your carriage. I shall do all the explaining once we get to my house."

The marquess smiled and walked away to deliver commands to the servants. For whatever bizarre reason, Bastian felt happy. Soon, he would have the woman who had long haunted his dreams and his foxed hazes. They would be a family, though that might take some adjustment. Now if only he heard from his man of affairs. The need to learn of Richard's condition was becoming dire.

Somewhere deep down, Bastian hoped that the wretched man had met his fate. He deserved nothing less for all the strife he had created.

"What do you mean Matthew and I will be travelling separately?" Cordelia asked the marchioness.

"All Nathaniel instructed me was to advise you that Davy and Miss Miller will be travelling ahead. He mentioned something that if the weather turned, that at least the baby would be dry."

Cordelia cocked her head to the side, trying to decide how to call the marchioness a liar. But she knew all too well, that after the excellent hospitality they had bestowed on her, 'twas best not to say a word. Though she also suspected that Bastian played a hand in this sudden twist of fate.

A nursemaid stood off to the side, holding Matthew while she and her ladyship talked. The babe began to fuss. "He is hungry. I should probably be on my way. Thank you so much for all that you have done." Cordelia leaned down and hugged her hostess. "Were it not for your kindness, my lady, I fear things might not have gone accordingly."

The marchioness began to weep. "You are welcome back anytime, Cordelia. I know things have been hard for you, but I know that things will improve very soon."

"Somehow I doubt that, my lady, but I will keep an open mind."

The marquess entered and walked toward them. He reached for Cordelia, drawing her into a tight embrace. "Know that we will always be here for you. All you need to do is send for word."

"Certainly, my lord. I cannot thank you enough." Cordelia pulled away, retrieving her son from the nursemaid. The child had started to wail loudly, making the twins cry. "I am very sorry about that."

"Think nothing of it. It just so happens that the twins need to feed now too. Travel safely, and I am certain we will be seeing each other soon."

Cordelia nodded and stepped outside. *Home.* They were heading home, and she could put all this insanity behind her. Finding out if she had anything left from her husband's estate was not worth the scandal and pain. She needed to find comfort in knowing that she could never be the duchess she once was. She had found a new way of life, and one that was meaningful to her.

After settling in the carriage, Cordelia unlaced the front of her gown, bringing her son to her bosom. The child latched on, greedily feeding on her, when a strange thought crossed her mind. Why had the driver not taken the same road that she had travelled up with Davy and Miss Miller? She covered her son while he nursed and reached over to the curtain on the window, shifting to look out.

Why in heaven's name are we headed towar...

Her breath escaped her when she saw Bastian's town house in sight. *Of all the devilish and manipulative things to do, you rake. You had this all planned.* A rush of heat seared her cheeks. Matthew would not be done feeding by the time they arrived. *Good Lord.* She had not exactly anticipated on a short drive, which was the only reason she had decided to feed Matthew on the way. They would simply have to wait in the carriage, stopped outside, until he was done.

No sooner had the thought crossed her mind, the contraption did stop, and the carriage slightly bounced with the driver jumping off. Cordelia looked down to ensure she was covered when the door opened abruptly.

"You, sir, will close that door this instant. I will not step out until we are ready, am I understood?"

The footman blushed from embarrassment, nodded, and closed the door.

Well, that went well. Just as soon as I get in, I shall give that rake a piece of my mind.

"Wait...sir, you cannot open that..."

Before Cordelia could react, the door flung open. Her mouth was open wide, and the sheer shock of being interrupted once again annoyed her. "What is it now? I am not ready!" She pressed her lips together when she noticed Bastian standing at the door.

"Well, this is unexpected. Shall we then?" He turned to the driver and whispered something, then entered, taking a seat across from her. "We shall go for a drive, then. That should give the child sufficient time to finish."

The man has some nerve for imposing himself this way. She gently lifted the blanket away from her son to see him slowly sucking with his eyes closed. This was the moment she loved the most, knowing that her child could drink his fill. She went to cover him, but Bastian reached for her wrist.

"I want to see him." He leaned back into his seat and watched her with a quizzical eyebrow.

"Why do you want us here? What does it matter to you of what becomes of Matthew and me?"

"Cordelia, for the moment, I shall ask the questions. When were you planning on telling me about the baby?"

Cordelia felt shamed for the first time in a long time. She should have sent word to him the instant she had given birth, but life had been confusing enough. To have learned only days after that the *ton* had presumed her dead. Only then did she learn her place in high society meant nothing.

"My lord, I will have you know, it was my every intention to tell you before I left. Nevertheless, that woman...courtesan...whoever she is, discovered me, and that is why I am in a rush to leave. It was my intent to inform you of Matthew and to provide you with the option to come away with us to the country. One can only presume that you have no interest in such notions if you have already committed to a contract with a courtesan."

He scowled at her. She ignored him and lifted the baby. Cordelia struggled for a moment adjusting her gown before he sat next to her and tugged the dress up. His fingers carefully grazed her nipple, then pinched her. Heat washed over her as memories of his touches flooded her brain.

"I have missed them. They are incredible now, too. So full, begging to be touched, nibbled, and sucked. Tell me, my dear, have you missed our interludes as much as I?"

Cordelia tried to ignore her body's betrayal with his advance, but all she could muster was, "Maybe." He laughed, startling the baby. She rocked and cooed him, and then returned her attention to Bastian. "Would you like to hold him?"

His hesitation riddled his face. The man was terrified. "Come now, Bastian, surely you have held a child before?"

Now it was his turn to blush. She looked down at Matthew and pressed her lips to his head. "It is time for you to meet your father, Matthew," she whispered before gently placing the baby into his arms.

Cordelia had not felt this amused in a long time. How could a grown man be so frightened to hold a near sleeping baby? "If it helps, Bastian, I can promise he does not bite…*yet*."

His eyes widened. "Surely, you are jesting."

"I assure you, I am not."

Bastian now frowned, but the moment Matthew cooed, she watched the most beautiful smile form on the earl's face. Bastian's eyes warmed, and the soft lines edging his lips crinkled. The man had one of the most charming smiles that had ever been bestowed upon the ladies of London. *And to think, I have charmed the very rake with his own son.* This would be a memory that would last lifetimes to come.

Bastian stood at his chamber door, lost in the vision before him. Cordelia sat on the edge of his bed, brushing out her hair. Long, precise strokes smoothed out her cocoa-colored locks. Soft waves fluttered past her shoulders, leaving parts of porcelain skin exposed.

The room's temperature rose, yet the fire burned low. He loosened his cravat, pulling it off and tucking it into his pocket. The sheer thought of binding her tonight made his blood rush. His heart thundered in his ears, and the urge to tear off his clothes was instinctual. Tonight, he would remind her of the passion they had once shared. He would finally profess his love, and intentions, and this time, he would never desert her.

He approached slowly, hoping to avoid alarm, when she craned her neck to spy him. "I was beginning to wonder when you would join me."

Bastian watched her lashes flicker in the candlelight. The minx had an unmistakable twinkle in her eye when she was plotting. "Tell me, my dear, what is it that you wish to happen tonight? I can be a very accommodating man."

The bed sank as he sat behind her, only giving them an inch of space apart. Bastian slid her nightgown off her shoulder and began kissing down her neck. With his other hand, he moved to cup her breast.

Cordelia moaned beneath his touch. "I have missed you, Bastian. Do not keep me waiting. I need you to love me. Hurry…" Her voice trailed off as he changed his approach.

"Stand up, love. I will give you what you need, and then we shall discuss how the rest of the night will go."

Lust and love all rolled up into one, and his need to take her soon was imminent. Bastian rose from the mattress and stood before her. She gazed upon him, her eyes filled with arousal and desperate need. He loosened the ribbons from her gown, and when they fell, her bodice opened up, exposing the beautiful, full breasts she possessed.

"They are quite becoming, my dear." How he desperately wanted to latch onto them, and begin to tease her, but the whole purpose of tonight was to begin a new life. He slid his hands beneath the silk fabric, pulling away the robe, allowing it to fall into a puddle of fabric at her feet. Bare as Aphrodite the day she was born, Cordelia embodied all things sensual and sexual.

Without wasting another moment, he drew her into his arms, crushing his lips to hers. Every swipe of his tongue reveled in her sweet, sweet taste. Bastian lowered her onto the bed, stretching her arms above her before binding her to the bedpost with his cravat.

"It has been far too long, my love. Tonight is all for you. May we never be separated again."

Straddling her, Bastian removed his shirt and loosened his breeches. He slid down her body, this time to tease her senses. Showering her with kisses, he left not patch of skin untouched. When his lips reached the contour of her breasts, he greedily sucked on one nipple while his free hand rolled the other. All of his life source seemed to have rushed to his cock. Then, her milk let loose and he drank from her.

Her hips bucked beneath him as he sucked sharply. When he released her breasts, he could smell her arousal.

"To hell with it," he muttered before releasing the confines of his cock, and in one swift movement, he drove himself into her. Over and over again, he thrust into Cordelia, who now wept from pleasure. She cried out his name. How many times, he knew not. All he knew was that to be so fully embedded in the woman he had lost and loved once again, heaven was the only name for the well of emotions building up in him.

His muscled tensed, and as Cordelia released, he pulled out, spilling his seed over the roundness of her belly. Her once lean and slender body had become even more beautiful after giving birth. With any luck, they would have many more children.

Bastian rose from the bed, retrieving a wet cloth from the water basin. He had missed this part the most. The post copulation—the touching, kissing, and even the talking through what they had experienced and what they would try differently.

'Twas a miracle they had found each other once again. All those months of weeping, of being foxed out of his wits and thrown out of White's and Martine's establishments. Good heavens, he had made a colossal fool of himself.

Cordelia meant the world to him, and now that Matthew was here, he would love him all the same. The circumstances of his birth mattered not. The *ton* did not have to know anything at all, nor did they answer to anyone. Bastian then remembered the note his man of affairs had forwarded to him earlier while he was at Stoughton Hall.

He released Cordelia's wrists and rubbed her arms free from the tension. Then he slowly ran the cloth over her skin, wiping his release from her body. "Can I get you anything, my dear?"

She shook her head, but then she frowned. "Do you think Matthew will be all right?"

"Why not, my love? My housekeeper has raised a brood of children herself. He is in quite capable hands, and I assure you, tomorrow we shall ensure he has his own room." Her frown soon turned into a smile. "Here, allow me to pour you some wine. I think you and I have deserved this moment for a while."

Bastian straightened and walked toward the sideboard. Pouring two drams of wine, he returned to the bed and passed her a glass. He sat down, pondering how to bring up her husband. *Will she be hurt, or will she be offended?*

He was staring into his goblet, gaping hopelessly into the claret, when Cordelia's hand touched his shoulder. "Bastian, what is the matter? We should be rejoicing, not mourning."

The earl braced himself for the worst of reactions. "I have received word on Richard's condition. I will show you the letter I received, but first, you must know that I have no intention of losing you a second time."

Before she could say another word, he rose again and retrieved a letter sitting on the mantle of his fireplace. When he returned, her speculative expression went from questioning to worry. Her brows furrowed, and when she held out her hand, he gently passed the paper to her. Instead of hovering while she read the missive, he walked over to the fire to stoke the embers.

"He wants to see me, Bastian! Has he gone mad?"

"That is a possibility. He is, after all, dying. The question is, do we deny a dying man his final wishes? Or do we allow him to perish without closure and live with the guilt of never knowing what it is he wishes to speak with you about."

He turned to watch the pensive look on her face wash away, paving the path to confusion. Exasperated and clearly unsure of what to say next, she stood and strode toward him, only stopping to toss the note into the fire. When her gaze settled upon his, she pursed her lips and stomped her way back to the bed.

The woman clearly needed time to consider the request. In the meanwhile, he would certainly occupy her thoughts in another way. Bastian cleared his throat. "Sweetheart, I think what you need is a good tumble. Let me demonstrate just how much you have missed me."

Now that should get her attention.

CHAPTER SEVEN

Cordelia yawned, stretching her arms out before her. She opened one eye, and then the other, trying to formulate in whose room she was. A moment passed as she bolted from Bastian's room, only to discover that he was across the hall, holding Matthew and reading a book.

'Twas a most beautiful sight to behold. Father and son, alone and reveling in their time together. She had not thought much of how Bastian would take to becoming a father, much less expect for them to bond in such a short time.

She crossed the threshold of the room and swept in behind them, her heart swelling with pride, an unexpected flush of heat rushing through her. Was it wrong to feel so connected, attracted, and satisfied to have a man such as Bastian at her side?

His neck craned to see her approaching. He smiled at her and lowered his head to whisper something to the babe. "I was wondering when you would get up. He's a quiet lad, though he only holds his attention for a short while before he gets squirmy."

Cordelia could not help but laugh. "Surely you jest. One cannot expect a child less than a year to hold his attention long. For heaven's sake," she chided him, reaching for Matthew. "He should be ready to feed right about now."

"The housekeeper has already seen to acquiring a nursemaid on such short notice."

How could he? This is my right. Anger rippled through her that Bastian had taken the choice away from her. "How could you!"

"My dear, I was only thinking of you. The child could use a little separation from you now, and I do not mean to imply a permanent independence. I only speak in the way that you and I can spend some time alone. Cedric is arranging to have Matthew's furniture delivered as we speak."

No sooner had his words quieted, a nursemaid entered the suite and retrieved the baby, leaving her to thoughts of how she would punish him so. She disliked being cross at him, however, Bastian had crossed the line with his interference. She had no intention of them staying in town this long. How could she even begin to ask him to leave this all behind?

He would never leave his wealth and position to be with her and his illegitimate son. She could not believe she had even considered the thought. *How foolish. Foolish indeed. A man of his fortune and nobility would never give anything up for a woman.*

The thought pained her, so much so that she could feel the tears well up in her eyes. Cordelia stepped back and attempted to leave the room, but as soon as she turned he had caught her by the waist.

"Where do you think you are escaping to, my love? I have waited far too long to see you again, and now that we are alone, you are departing."

Cordelia sighed, silently praying to blurt out the words. "Bastian…we…Matthew and I…cannot stay."

"I beg your pardon?" He turned her, ensuring that their gazes met. "Cordelia, whatever do you mean? I thought that we could make our situation…permanent."

How desperately she desired that, but with the small matter of her husband being the obstacle, how could they even begin to make the prospect more than fiction? She loved Bastian with all her heart, but they could never live in harmony in London whilst her husband still survived.

"And pray tell, how exactly do you suppose we will accomplish the herculean task of making this permanent. My husband is still alive. His title was revoked, and all that was mine is gone. Save only for the child that I bore out of wedlock."

"Barely, woman. Richard is barely alive. We shall see him on the morrow and put an end to this madness. You cannot mean to leave me again. I shall not stand for it. I would rather die at the hands of the enemy than let you turn your back on us. Our love. The possibility of our happiness. Do not do this, Cordelia. I implore you!"

The world spun around her whilst she tried to find the words to express her dismay. Surely, he could find it in his heart to forgive her. "I am not sure paying my husband a visit on his death bed is advisable, my lord. If he is ailing from some disease that is contagious, I do not want to pass it along to my only son."

"Sweetheart, Matthew will be the first of many other sons we shall have. Now, come here. We shall settle this nonsense now, so I can get back to being greedy with my future countess."

"Shh! Do not speak such things. It is a bad omen to speak of things in haste."

He *tsked* her and shook his head. "When did you become the superstitious type, Cordelia? I only speak of the truth. After the great moment when the devil takes your husband for all his lust, greed, and sloth, we shall be free to pursue our endeavor."

Cordelia sighed with defeat. Exasperated and slightly relieved, she fell into his arms.

Bastian laced up her stays and fought viciously to keep himself from ripping the bodice away from her. To let it fall at her feet, bend her forward until her chest rested against the vanity, and take her vigorously from behind. Every time the *damned* woman's hips swayed, his cock grew thick and hard. Unfortunately for him, and lucky for her, he had errands to run and business to conduct.

He dipped his head into the crook of her neck. "Mmm…you smell divine, Cordelia. What did you put on?"

"I am not sure. I put on what was left on the table there."

Bastian snickered. It warmed him, knowing the staff was becoming accustomed to having a mistress here. Alongside the fact that he had not seen them about, and when he did, they were in one way or another occupied with Matthew.

He pressed his lips to the soft skin of her shoulder and ran his fingers down the length of her arms. "I know there is much to do before we see Richard, but I think we can steal a few more moments of the day for personal gratification, sweetling."

Cordelia turned to face him, placed a kiss on his cheek, and stepped out of the space. She walked toward the armoire and opened it to find a few gowns already hanging. A gasp escaped her lips, and when she turned to face him again, tears rimmed her eyes.

Bastian closed the distance again, pulling her into his arms. Everything was so right between them. He could not imagine his life without her. "Hush, sweetling. There is nothing I would not do for you. For as long as we are together, you and our son will not want for anything."

She sniffled into his chest. It excited him to see her so vulnerable. "Very well, I shall ravish you later. Let us get you finished here, so that we may enjoy a bit of breakfast before the day starts."

He observed her pull out a dark bombazine dress and press it against herself. "Do you think this will suit?"

"It is certainly dark enough that once we are outdoors, no one could tell who you are. Besides, you have a black evening cloak that will keep you well disguised."

"If you say so, my love. If I may be so bold…"

"Certainly, sweeting, speak freely."

"Well, at first, while I thought seeing Richard would bring some closure, I am not entirely sure it will now. The *ton* is on the cusp of discovering my return from the dead. How do you think the denouncement of his title will affect my status, and that of our son's? That is, once they learn I had a child out of wedlock during my absence."

Cordelia's concern tugged at his heart. He wanted to assure her that her visit would go fine, but he had not the slightest idea as to why the former duke would want to see his wife one last time. Her worry about the *ton* lashing out at her was partially accurate, though he would never permit any harm to come to his family.

"My love, all of us I suppose, in the end, want to free ourselves from the truth. His truth being that he did some horrible things. The man probably had no designs for you in the first place. I suspect that is all he wishes to discuss. I mean to say that he was probably only after your dowry if his recent actions are any indication of what his motivations have been all along." He kissed the top of her head and whispered, "Now go and get dressed, and try not to worry so much. There is still time before we head out to Newgate."

Bastian waited by the door as she finished dressing. When they descended the stairs, a pounding at the door raised their alarm. Cordelia stopped behind him and clung to his waist.

"Do not worry about a thing, my dear, Cedric will ensure whoever it is goes away. Right, Cedric?"

But before Cedric could even open his mouth, Mary Elizabeth came barreling in through the front doors, seething in anger.

"What in damnation are you doing here, woman?"

Mary Elizabeth, in her fury, scowled at the woman hiding behind him.

"You have no business here, woman. Our very short affair ended some time ago, and you go too far this time. Get out!" he roared with displeasure. "Get out and never return to this house, or appear in my presence."

She ran out shrieking like a banshee, and after a few moments, there was silence.

He turned to Cordelia, wiping a runaway tear. "My dear, head on back upstairs, and I will have breakfast brought to you." However, before he could even turn his head, the shouting in the street caught their undivided attention.

"The duchess is alive. Alive, I say. The Duchess of Downsbury was never dead!"

Bastian ran down the stairs in all haste. "Cedric, grab that infernal woman, and gag her if you must. I want her tossed in my carriage. Get it ready. I am going to put an end to this madness immediately."

Bastian glared at the housekeeper who held Matthew in her arms. "See that your mistress receives her breakfast in our bedchamber. After that display, it will be a miracle if she even leaves to visit that wretched wastrel of a man tonight."

The portly woman nodded and scurried away with his son. *Now to end this, once and for all.*

"What in God's name is the matter with you, Mary Elizabeth?"

The cyprian snorted with contempt. "And you choose a disgraced duchess over me. Have you not had enough of scandal, Bastian? I know not of what malady you suffer, as your thoughts do not seem to make an ounce of sense."

"What I do, and who I choose to be with, is of no blasted concern of yours. When will you learn that you go too far? This last event will surely end your employment. I cannot, and will not, have Cordelia's name dragged through the mud, any more than it has been."

"And pray tell, sir, how do you intend to end my employment?"

Surely, she jests. Does she not yet gather that we are headed back to Martine's establishment? No man or woman was safe with the extremes she had gone to today. "Soon, my dear, you will learn my meaning."

A few minutes later, they arrived at the lone house on the lane. The same old, burly man greeted them, holding open the front door. Inside, another gent joined them with one of the house wenches. Mary Elizabeth tried to pry out of his grip, but instead, he passed her to the man. "See that she does not leave this room, nor your sight. I have an important matter to discuss with your mistress. Bring her forth this instant."

The air around him was electric. He was in the mood for a fight, and he would not back down until Martine came to a resolution as to what she planned on doing with the unruly courtesan.

"What is the meaning of all this noise, Lord Wycliffe?"

"One of the girls you employ. You should already know my meaning."

"I most certainly do not, sir. Come into my office for a moment."

Bastian followed the madam into a side room, which already had a guest. Lord Chalcroft sat rigidly and looked cross when he entered the room.

"Have a seat, my lord. It would appear that both of you have complaints regarding my girls, and I wish to resolve this at once. Lord Chalcroft, as you were here first, what is the issue?"

"The issue," he coughed and said hoarsely, "is that I wish to terminate my contract with that bloody wench I paid for. The damned chit is never where she is supposed to be, and when she is, she is a terrible bore."

Madame Martine lowered her eyes to a piece of parchment and pursed her lips. Her attention then focused on him. "Lord Wycliffe, what seems to be your problem? I seem to recall you terminated your services and interest with my house a little while back."

"My concern is Mary Elizabeth. The vexed minx knows not how to take no for a bloody answer. I do not want her in my life, and I will not tolerate this level of harassment."

Lord Chalcroft rose and bellowed, "You mean to tell me, that blasted wench has had her sights on him this entire time? And you still drew up a contract to saddle her on me?"

The madam scowled, licked her lips, and tore up the parchment she reviewed. "Will that satisfy your ire, Lord Chalcroft?" The fat bastard only grunted and left the room, muttering oaths under his breath. "As for you, Lord Wycliffe, I have not the slightest idea about what you expect me to do."

"Then allow me to make this clear for you. We, men, pay a great deal of money for the utmost discretion. And you, madam, have employed a woman who cannot keep her lips sealed. Take care, as I will only speak of this once. The former Duchess of Downsbury has returned, miraculously, and thank goodness she is alive and well. While it is not known what condition the duke is in at the moment, Mary Elizabeth went screaming out into the street after barging into my home, telling everyone she saw that her ladyship was alive."

The woman sighed and now clasped her hands.

"You must understand, under the circumstances, I cannot permit her actions to go unpunished. Either you do something, or I shall have her arrested for harassment. Decide now, as I have other appointments to attend to."

She grimaced and put her hands up in defeat. "Bear with me a moment, my lord. This is the first time in all the years I have been in this profession that I have ever been faced with this decision. I am no fool as to why discretion is required, but I will ask you not to involve any runners. I cannot have my establishment compromised."

Rising from her seat, she walked toward the door, opened it, and motioned a henchman forward. "Please remove Mary Elizabeth's belongings from her room and have Ansen escort her off the property. Seeing as her wages were paid not two days ago, there is no need for compensation."

Madam Martine left the door open and returned to her seat, facing him. "Will that do, my lord?"

Relief washed over Bastian. Never in his life had he ever experienced the need for blood as he did just now. "Yes, it will."

Bastian rose and was nearly out the door when the madam called him back. "Just one more thing, my lord."

"And what would that be?"

"Mary Elizabeth is quite the headstrong chit. If she continues to pursue this fascination with you, you will have to employ a runner. She is not my responsibility any longer."

He nodded, and strode out of the house, never looking back or giving it another glance.

CHAPTER EIGHT

Cordelia fought back the urge to weep as she and her companion followed a guard down the dank, dark corridor. Bastian had squeezed her hand, reassuring her that he was nearby, yet nothing could dull the anxiety that chipped away at her soul.

In a few minutes, she would face the man who had written her off as dead, and even in the eyes of scandal, tried to marry a woman who was already married. A man who was charged, found guilty of crimes, and consequently stripped of his title.

At this point, the mere fact she that did not possess a farthing to her name as a result of his idiocy did not matter. She was here at his request, and with any luck, she would not be in his presence very long. The faster she left this insidious building, she, Matthew, and Bastian, could return to a normal life.

The guard stopped outside the door where another gentleman waited to speak to them. "My lady, allow me to introduce myself. Henry Winchester, your husband's solicitor. Shall we enter?"

Cordelia looked back at her love and frowned. "Dear, would you terribly mind if you waited outside?"

"Not at all, my love. If you have need of me, only call out my name or have Richard's solicitor come for me."

Then, Cordelia turned and entered the cell. It was dimly-lit, and the putrid scent of illness lingered. She lowered the hood to her cloak and sat in a chair next to the ailing duke. She waited in silence until Richard finally spoke."

"So fickle fate is, that she would present me with my wife who is supposed to be dead. Tell me, Cordelia, did you think of me often?"

She desperately tried not to choke on her spit. *The nerve he has.* "No. I did not, Richard. I thought of you as much as you did I."

He snorted, which was followed by a string of dry heaving coughs. His skin, even in the poor light, was discolored. Death would follow him soon, yet not soon enough. "Yes, of course, how I could I expect anything less? I am certain, though, you probably found some confounded village servant to make use of in the meanwhile."

"What I have done while I was presumably deceased is not of your concern. To the world, I was dead, and that time was mine alone. Alone, you wretched fool! How many women did you fornicate with and then condemn to a foreign brothel?"

"Bah!" he choked out. "I did not request your presence to argue. Quite frankly, I am looking forward to be released from this hell into the hands of death. Only then, will I truly have my peace and silence." Richard nodded to his solicitor who then came forward and handed her a note.

Cordelia blinked and whispered to the man, "What is this?"

"Open it, if you will, my lady."

She obliged and read on. Then, her mouth dropped, and she whipped her head back to her husband. "Richard…what is the meaning of this? This was part of my dowry. You cannot tell me that you did not use this money, or sell off my family's estate."

He grumbled beneath his breath, and tried to talk. Cordelia leaned forward to hear what the man had to say. "I could not bring myself to touch something that belonged to someone as cold and unfeeling as you, Cordelia. From the first moment I brought you home, you were nothing but trouble. Is it any wonder that we never had children? Ah! Yes. I know why. Because coming home to bed you was such a task."

He coughed some more, but nothing could hold back her tears. He had finally admitted his disdain for her, and it could not have had worse timing. Fighting back the urge to yell and draw too much attention to her visit with him, she righted herself and gained composure.

"While we are on the subject of revelations, I suppose I shall grace you with one last slice of knowledge before you depart your foul and hateful existence. I was pregnant once, by you. But I lost the child in my second month. I am thankful we were never blessed with such a precious gift as such. I was, however, blessed to have the Earl of Wendelhem's son nine months ago, so what do you have to say for yourself now?"

The man looked positively ill and ready to croak. "Get. Out," he sputtered.

"Gladly, my lord. I hope you rot."

"Let me see you out, my lady." The solicitor offered his arm.

"I am quite capable of seeing myself out. Goodbye, Richard."

By the time she reached the cell door, he was gasping for air. The guard rushed in. "Shall we call for the physician?" the solicitor queried.

"What for? The man is dead," the tall, young guard said with glee.

"Looks like I won this bet."

Cordelia didn't bother looking back. She kept pace until she found Bastian seated down the hall at a guard's desk.

"Cordelia, are you ready?"

"Quite so. Get me out of this…this…cesspool of criminals."

A guard behind her chuckled. "I guess this means I owe you no further debts, Wycliffe."

"Indeed. Come along, my love."

Cordelia followed him. Thoughts of Richard's admission made her skin crawl. *Thank goodness it is over.*

Bastian drew the silent and mournful woman closer to him. He had watched her shiver for a quarter hour now, and he did not know what to make of her silence. *What did Richard say to her, to have her left in such a state?* He wrapped his arms around her as she buried her head into his chest, sniffling and trembling. "My love, what is the matter? Surely, your visit could not have gone so awry?"

She pulled away and gazed up at him. Those dark pools flooded with tears, which now fell mercilessly. "He returned my dowry and the deed to my family's estate."

"How is that so bad, dear? I do not understand the cause for your anguish."

"He could not bring himself to use it, once he realized how 'cold and unfeeling' I was. I cannot believe he actually admitted it to me, but his actions over the years could not have been be any clearer regarding his displeasure in marrying me."

She hugged him and then sighed. "Am I so terrible a person that he did not see fit to use what was part of our marriage agreement? Tell me, Bastian? I cannot understand what I ever did to deserve this treatment. After all I did, *endured,* and in the end, it is not he that is the cuckold. It is I, because I survived and have now returned."

"You, my love, did nothing. The man, right from the beginning, was off. There has always been something off regarding his demeanor and conduct. Even the chaps at White's whispered a time or two about his misgivings. And to be matter of fact, you are not the cuckold, my love. It is he. Now that he is gone, you will have a chance to repair any ill thought of your involvement in his actions."

"I do not see your meaning, Bastian. Society is not interested in hearing from a woman whose title was stripped along with her husband's."

"No. But you are still, by all means, Lady Cordelia Wycliffe. That is to say that you will be, once you marry me. I have always wanted you. And this is an opportunity I do not want to see passed up. Tell me you will marry me, Cordelia. I do want the three of us to be one happy family. I care not for the gossip, nor do I care where we end up living. As long as we are together, that is all that matters."

Cordelia turned away, wiping a runaway tear and returning her attention to him. She slid closer and placed her tiny hand on his cheek, closing her eyes for a moment. "Nothing would give me a greater pleasure than to become your wife, but Richard has only just passed."

"Think nothing of it, dear. Allow me to handle the rest. The man was in prison, and I cannot see a village parson giving us much grief over this marriage." She blinked at him. "What is it, love?"

"A village parson? Do you mean to be married in the country?"

"Quite so. I would rather not have too much attention drawn to the Earl of Wendelhem's wedding. No, I think I should like a private ceremony."

With all their chatting, Bastian did not realize the carriage had stopped outside his house. A footman opened the door, and the dampness of rain wafted into the carriage. He stepped out first, and while it had rained earlier in the evening, puddles still riddled the street.

Bastian lifted his soon-to-be bride and settled her on the doorstep. "Run along and see how Matthew is doing. I will join you shortly. I have some things to discuss with Cedric." She nodded and headed on upstairs. "Cedric, follow me, if you would. I would like a report of the day."

"Sir, about that, there is something you should know."

Bastian stopped at his desk in the library and turned to face the frowning butler.

"My lord, we received several visitors while you were out. All were looking to speak with her grace."

Bastian felt as if the wind had been knocked out of him. There was no way they could put this off any longer. Cordelia needed to make an appearance, and she needed to do it the using the proper channels. He could not allow his household to be disrupted with curious visitors. Bastian walked around the desk and sat down. Picking up a quill and blank parchment, he penned a note before passing it to the aging man. "See that the Marquess of Stoughton receives this first thing in the morning."

"Yes, sir." The butler left him to his thoughts.

Should we marry before the month is out, or should we consider a quick and private ceremony? With visitors already descending upon his estate, the sooner they took care of those details, the better off they were.

Bastian climbed the stairs at a leisurely pace, contemplating how to break the news to his lovely fiancée. Would she scold him for how fast he desired to be married, or would she reject him altogether?

He happened upon Cordelia in their son's nursery as she sat in a chair cradling the sleeping babe, her eyes closed as well. The poor woman had

had a trying day, and tonight had exhausted her. Perhaps he would allow her one night of rest.

He lifted the child from her arms and carried him to his crib, tucking him gently under his blanket. Satisfied that he would not wake, Bastian strode toward his beloved and lifted her from the seat. There was nothing warmer than holding Cordelia and carrying her to their bed. If there was anything more beautiful and consoling, it was being reunited with her after all this time.

Bastian laid her on the bed, taking care to remove her slippers, and covered her with the sheet. In the soft light, he disrobed and joined her in bed, holding her again. Only this time when his eyes closed, thoughts of finally marrying her fluttered about.

"What in the world is all the commotion about, Cedric?"

"I am not quite sure, ma'am. If you will allow me a moment, I shall see what the ruckus at the door is about."

"Certainly, Cedric." Cordelia bounced the happy baby on her knee in the morning room, only to be interrupted by Isabel, Cecily, and Emily barreling through the parlor door.

"Look how beautiful he is," Emily exclaimed. "I can see why you have been keeping him all to yourself."

The ladies sat on the dais, waiting and appearing as if ready to burst.

I wonder what is amiss. "Are you ladies going to share what is going on, or are you going to just sit there as if all of you have swallowed canaries?"

Cecily stifled a giggle. "Isabel and I might have swallowed a canary, but poor Emily looks as if it was an ostrich."

Emily's eyes nearly bulged out of their sockets. She swatted Cecily with her fan, and all the girls broke into a fit of laughter. "Well, if it is an ostrich I swallowed, I do not look forward to pushing out such an oversized egg. Good heavens, there are days when this child means to drive me mad with all its movement."

Cordelia shook her head. *Why did I not introduce myself before to these ladies?* They were all gently bred and looked past her misgivings. The thought made her want to weep. All the years wasted on trying to impress others had left her alone and without the companionship of female company. Company that did not want to compete or impress. Fate had given her a second chance, not only with Bastian, but with *life*.

"Truly, ladies, what engagement do you have planned? Are we to go out? If so, I must find Beatrice, Matthew's nursemaid."

"Yes, we are headed into town for some shopping. I have made an appointment with a *modiste*, specifically for you. It is my understanding that we need some items before the week is out, and she has some already made, which might suit for the occasion."

Good grief! Did Bastian already commence making plans for our wedding without so much as consulting me? The thought made her angry, and she felt betrayed. *Why did he not ask my opinion first? Why the hurry?* "While I do appreciate the gesture, my lady…"

"Pshaw! How many times must I tell you to just call me Isabel? I am glad that you appreciate the gesture, but we are wasting time now. Gertrude has closed the shop specifically for us, as I have asked for absolute discretion. Now run along, find the child's maid, and let us begin our day. We still have so much to do, including meal planning." Isabel winked and rose from her seat.

Cordelia lifted the babe in her lap, propping him against her shoulder, and walked upstairs. Finding the maid, she passed Matthew over. "I hope not to be gone for too, too long, but in the event his lordship returns before I, please let him know that I am with the Marchioness of Stoughton, the Countess of Avonlea, and Miss Turner."

"Certainly, ma'am."

She peered into a looking glass, pinched her cheeks, and fixed some loose strands of hair. She had not been dress shopping for what seemed like an eternity. *Lord, do I ever look terrible.*

She could already imagine what the gossip columns would write up regarding her pending nuptials to Bastian. His name would be dragged through the mud yet again, only this time, they would comment on their lack of regard by marrying so soon. Though, that would only be the tip of the iceberg. The question that remained—would they rehash Richards past crimes, or would they reopen his case and try to find a way to incriminate her in some way?

All were dreadful ideas, and she desperately hoped they were nothing but fodder.

"Come on, Cordelia! We are already late…"

Cordelia raced down the stairs, meeting the ladies at the door. "My apologies, I had to leave some instructions with Beatrice." Before she could say anything to the butler, Isabel pulled her along. *Why do I get the impression that today is going to be a long one?*

She climbed into the carriage last and sat eagerly with anticipation. What color had the ladies decided upon for a gown? Considering she was a widow, and was not waiting the proper time for mourning, surely the girls would not make her wear something as silly as white, or pink, or blue. *Imagine the horror of it all. There would be painted caricatures in the gossip column, along with the ill-timed news.*

CHAPTER NINE

"Your Grace—*err...*I mean, my lady, that is, I know not why you would worry over the color. I will have you know that all my fashions are the latest from France, and widows marry in every color. Though I really do think the maroon gown with the gold trim is a most excellent choice. What do you think?"

The dress fit her newfound curves, and strangely enough, the only thought occupying her mind was how creatively Bastian would get it off. *Hmm...* She could see him now. His hands gliding up her legs. Seeking her wet heat, teasing her until she begged for mercy. He would then tie her to the bedpost, with her back turned him.

Then, he would unlace her gown slowly, sliding it inch by inch off her shoulders. Nipping his way down until his lips reached her bottom. The man had a penchant for spanking. The question was would he spank her with his hands, paddle, or riding crop. Once he'd tortured her enough, he would lean her over and take her from behind. Thrusting hard and fast, then slow and steady.

Good grief. All these wicked thoughts in the middle of the dressmaker's shop was making her damp and dizzy with desire. Her need for Bastian coursed through her veins.

"Ma'am...Your Grace? What do you think of the gown?"

Her companions laughed, probably knowing where her thoughts had wandered off.

"The dress is perfect, Mrs. Hedley."

"Right then, perhaps we shall move onto something special for the evening. I have the perfect garment. If you will bear with me a moment. I have it kept in the storage room," the tall, middle-aged woman said while cheerfully bouncing away.

A moment later, she reappeared, and the girls gasped in shock.

"Oh, my! That is quite…hmm…shall we say…*risqué*," Emily whispered, grinning the whole while.

"Jesu. Risqué indeed. Mrs. Hedley, where on earth…how on earth did you fashion such a sinful piece?"

"That, my dear, is a secret. And allow me to assure you, while everyone knows you and his lordship are not new at this arrangement, I am confident he shall never want to leave your side that night. But I suspect it might end up torn within minutes."

There is a thought. Bastian would indeed tear it off. 'Twould be a waste of something so beautiful and delicate. But Lord, to see his face when he saw the black silk and lace chemise. Her bust would surely be on display for him to torment. Nevertheless, she would enjoy every dashing moment. "I suppose I shall take that as well. I cannot imagine the garment will remain on for very long, but it is a stunning piece, Mrs. Hedley."

The girls now moved about the store, picking up fabrics and holding them against their feminine curves. Clearly, they needed time to shop around.

"Mrs. Hedley, I will indeed take all the recommended items. If you could let the girls know that I will be just outside? I have need for air."

"Certainly, my lady."

Cordelia opened the door, and once she felt the breeze hit her face, she exhaled. The trip had been lovely, yet she could not help but feel trapped. All the attention, the trying on of countless gowns, was overwhelming.

In her time away from London, she had learned to do without and appreciate the humility of being reduced to a peasant. Her life had been simple, almost easier, and she had a finer admiration for those who worked back-breaking chores. Peddling their wares for survival. The lack of frivolity in such an environment made her humble.

As she was deep in thought, dozens of people walked past her, ignoring who she was. Others whispered, but she cared not what they dared to talk about. *Yes, I am the widow of the former duke—the one who had an affair, got pregnant, and then was exiled into the country to have the child. Only to have a terrible accident, and be assumed dead.*

How could no one have thought to look further? They had simply given up. Even Bastian had never explained why he did not come in search for her. Her anger began to return when high-pitched screeching captured her attention.

She turned to see a familiar woman running toward her. *Mary Elizabeth.* The scorned trollop was armed with potatoes and other wares from the market. She began hurling obscenities and objects at Cordelia. A potato hit her in the head.

Horrified and stunned, Cordelia ran off, not paying attention to the direction she was headed. Tears streamed down her cheeks. She needed help, yet no one stopped the angry woman who now fully chased her into a steady stream of carriages.

Tripping in a puddle, Cordelia landed face-first into the street, hoping to die an instantaneous death. *This could not be more embarrassing.* Shaking violently, she attempted to get up, but every time she did, water from another puddle sprayed into her face.

Where is Bastian? I need my son.

A carriage finally stopped, and thick but gentle hands helped her up. Cordelia sobbed into the stranger's arms. Slightly pushing her back, he tipped her chin up. Relief washed over to recognize the friendly face of the Marquess of Stoughton.

"There, there, my dear. Let me help you in, and we shall retrieve the ladies. Once we return to Stoughton Hall, I shall have my servants collect your son. I think you shall be safer with us until Bastian finds a way to deal with that woman."

"Thank you, my lord. I cannot thank you enough."

"Do not give it another thought. We are all here to help you."

Help, a novel concept.

"I hardly have words to express my anger at this moment, Nathaniel."

"I can understand, however, do not digress here. That woman needs to be dealt with. She is not right in the head. She needs to be imprisoned, and that is final. I cannot express enough that your soon-to-be wife and son will not be safe if Mary Elizabeth continues to walk the streets. I implore you…"

Ridden with guilt, Bastian could not help but wonder what would have happened if Nathaniel had not found her in time. To what extent would Mary Elizabeth go to prove that they should be together? The woman was clearly mad, and if he could get her into an asylum he would. *But how? One cannot drop a person off without reasoning, and at this point, she is a jilted lover, nothing more.*

He paced the floor with his glass of port in hand. The fire brightly burning in the library reduced him into a puddle of sweat. All this anger beginning to emerge did nothing for his nerves. He wanted a fight, but he could not hit a woman.

"Calm yourself, Bastian. By now, Cordelia will have had enough time to relax. I would prefer that you kept her and the baby here until you two are married. Perhaps by then, this situation will have been rectified."

The thought had merit, though he would much rather protect her himself. But removing Cordelia from the town house might be the solution, until he could find the opportunity to catch Mary Elizabeth in the act of something socially unacceptable. "An excellent thought, Nathaniel. Do you suppose that we could hold the private ceremony here instead of the parsonage? That is to say, if it would not be a terrible imposition."

"I was going to suggest the same thing. And to clarify, it would be no imposition at all. By keeping the ceremony private, and under the roof of a protected home, there is less risk of your vows being interrupted unnecessarily."

Perfect. Now all he had to do was relay the change of plans to Cordelia, and hopefully she would not be too cross with him. 'Twas bad enough that she had expressed her displeasure in his commencing the plans of the wedding without consulting her first. He did not wish to add further fuel to the fire.

Bastian downed the contents of his drink. "I do not want to be rude, Nathaniel, but I would like to spend some time with Cordelia."

The marquess lifted his glass. "Go on. Enjoy the rest of the evening. We have all had a trying day, and I could use the company of my lovely wife too."

He nodded, and Bastian turned to leave the library. Soon, they would move out of the town house and take up residence in her family's estate. Though, he had not had a chance to examine its condition yet. Her ancestral home should have been passed along to her elder brother, but her parents had wanted to lure the duke in with a proposition that would sweeten the deal.

In the last few days, he had come to discover that the lands in which the estate was located was rich by agricultural means. He supposed that once they were established, and he had the opportunity to meet with the tenants, they could work together in turning a healthy profit. Which would, in turn, provide for future generations of their growing family.

Nevertheless, the first order of business was to get married and get settled. Once things finally smoothed over, he would attempt to convince her to have another son. *Ah, to have a brood full of sons. Brawling, handsome, mischievous little buggers.* Cordelia might oppose having an entire brood of little boys, but he would leave their fate in the hands of destiny.

Happening upon Cordelia in their quarters, he swept into the room with a charming grace. Her eyebrows perked up, speculating his every move. When he reached the edge of the bed, Bastian slowly removed his cravat, gave it twirl, and tucked it into his pocket. "So, my love, where is our darling son at this moment?"

Her lashes fluttered, and she licked her lips. "In the nursery with his maid," she purred seductively.

"Hmm…all this time alone. I think we need to find something productive and conducive to our health, no?"

She nodded and chewed on her bottom lip. "What did you have in mind, my lord?"

What did he have in mind? They could not behave as if there was no one else in the manor, so he had to get creative. And he did not have the implement he preferred to use on hand. "Well, for one thing, you are wearing an impossible amount of layers. Begin divesting yourself. I shall sit here and watch."

There were times in their previous occasions together when she would undress, teasing him until his cock stirred uncomfortably in his breeches. Tonight though, he wanted to savor every moment and take away the memory her horrid experience from earlier.

Bastian worshipped this woman in every regard, and he would remind her as so very shortly. When his teeth would graze over nipples, his tongue sliding over the contours of her belly and his fingers sliding in and out of her. She would not be denied tonight. Her mouth would swallow his cock, and her arse would revel in its entirety when he penetrated her there. The pain would eventually give her pleasure. How he missed her perfectly round bottom.

He pulled out his cock and stroked it as she teased him. Her creamy white shoulders and her full breasts made him ache to bite them and mark her as his. When her garments fell to the floor, and she stood before him nude, he crooked his finger for her to come forth.

She sank to her knees between his legs and took his length into her mouth.

"That's a good girl. How I have missed those perfect lips of yours, my dear. Suck me good and hard, love. I want you to show me how much of a good lass you are."

And a good girl she was. He loved her lips around him, and to think, they would have many nights like this ahead of them. He would do well to remind himself throughout the night, and for the rest of their days, to show her how much he loved her.

CHAPTER TEN

Cordelia sighed at the vanity while brushing her dark hair. In the looking glass, the candlelight flickered, creating an ambience that rivaled any other. The black silk and lace chemise felt exquisite when she slid it over her contours. *Pity that the poor thing will be tattered in a matter of moments, once Bastian lays eyes on it.*

She waited for her husband to return from the gaming room, and with any luck, he would not be too foxed for some loving. After all these years, the heartache, and foibles, she was the luckiest woman alive. She had married the man that she loved and could not think of anything more blissful, other than giving birth to Matthew.

The fire burned with fervor, making her too hot. Perhaps it was her nerves, but something did not feel right. A noise outside—much like crates tumbling down—somewhere below her window, piqued her curiosity. Cordelia looked out but saw nothing out of order. But then again, it was dark.

What could have made that noise?

Somewhere in the manor, doors were opening and closing. A sound that was most welcoming. Her husband would join her shortly, and they could begin making a life with each other. Wedded bliss the second time around.

The bedroom door opened and closed, and then her husband was leaning against the door, grinning like a cat who had caught the prize rat.

"Look at who decided to join me. How do I look, my lord?"

Bastian tried to hide his amusement from her, but she could tell he was quite pleased.

"Ravishing, my dear. The chemise is a work of art, however, if you do not remove it yourself, it will end up torn."

The scoundrel would tear off her gown without a second thought. About to slide it off, she heard the same noise again. "Bastian, I think someone is out there."

"Who on earth would be out here, touring the grounds, at this time of night?"

"How am I supposed to know? I have really have a terrible feeling something is amiss, Bastian."

He came up behind her at the window, wrapping his arms around her. His chin rested on top of her head, and he whispered, "Love, I know not what has you so worried. The marquess' grounds are well-kept, and his house is soundly locked down for the evening. I can promise you absolutely no one will intrude upon us. Beatrice is with Matthew, and the rest of the manor has retired for the evening. Nathaniel went to accommodating lengths to ensure we would have this wing to ourselves for the night."

"I know all of that, dear, but what if that crazy woman is here. Watching the house, and waiting for…"

"My dear, enough of this nonsense." He turned her around so that they now faced each other. "Sweetling, what can I do to prove to you that we are alone?"

All Cordelia could do was shrug. Her imagination was running rampant with a non-existent intrigue. That woman would never dare break into the marquess' home. *Or would she?*

"There you go, thinking again. My love, come to bed, and I will tell you my plans for tomorrow, and then I will ravish you proper."

Removing her gown, she climbed under the sheets next Bastian, who disrobed as if he had less clothing on than she. He pulled her into his embrace and squeezed her tight. Everything felt so right in his arms that nothing could elude the moment or make it devoid of love. Their passion is what Byron wrote about and Shakespeare envied.

"My love, tomorrow after breakfast, I will personally escort you and our son home. From there, you will stay put until I return from checking on your family's estate. I have it on good authority that the grounds have been maintained, and the house is still sound. After I have confirmed its condition and have arranged to have the staff clean it in its entirety, we will relocate there.

"It is my hope that once we are able to call it home, you will organize a dinner party. You are, after all, my countess, and what better way to re-establish your previous credibility than to make peace with society."

The mere fact that her husband was going to such lengths assured her that they were perfect for each other. He made her feel special, a sentiment she had never experienced with Richard. But that was a chapter in her life that she would never gaze upon again. "While that sounds wonderful, my love, right now, I would prefer that we make the most of our wedding night. After all, it could be days before I see you again."

"Very well, dear…Now, where did I leave my cravat? I think we shall tie you to the bed tonight."

Ah! Now, there is the Bastian I remember.

Bastian rode hard for the first few hours, but he knew he would never make it to the house in Leicester in time for sunset. Instead, he turned on the road that would take him to Northampton. Hopefully, he would find a staging inn not filled to capacity for the evening.

When he changed paths, he noticed another rider following from afar. Bastian goaded his black horse into galloping until he disappeared into a thick tree line. For whatever reason, his instinct warned him not to trust the rider.

But why would anyone follow me? This does not add up. It had been years since he had kept up with ill company. He did not owe any debts from when he last visited White's or through some other private affairs he had with a few gents.

Besides, ever since Cordelia and Matthew had returned to his life, he had not been out much, save for only a few drinks with the Marquess of Stoughton and the Earl of Avonlea.

Bastian calmed his mount and watched the rider come to a halt and climb down from his horse. The stout man with brown, scraggly hair grumbled and uttered oaths. He certainly did not appear familiar. *Which means someone hired him, but who?*

The curious earl hid behind a tree and waited for the man to pass him before tackling him to the ground. He pinned the man face-down in the dirt and fallen leaves. "Why are you following me? Who hired you?"

The stranger struggled but conceded to the weight pressing down on him. "That bit o' muslin wanted me to keep you busy, is all. She had matters to take care of, and did not want your interference, guvnor."

"What is your meaning?" Bastian growled, trying to figure out what the man was saying. "What woman are you talking about?"

"She said her name was Mary," he choked out.

"Did she make any mention as to a plan?"

"No, sir, only that she was going to take exception with a certain lady and make sure she was permanently removed from the *situation*."

Bastian could only see red. His chest tightened with fear. Mary Elizabeth intended to harm his countess. *Good heavens…Matthew!* He had to get back to the house promptly. The estate in Leicester would have to wait, or he could send his servants to clean and properly stock the wares if needed.

Home. He needed to get home and swiftly. He would kill the bloody woman if he had to, but there was no chance that she would walk away from this without getting her comeuppance. He climbed back on his steed and rode hard, not stopping until he reached the outskirts of town where the marquess and his family lived in peace. Bastian pounded on the door until a servant answered, sleepy-eyed. "How can I help you, my lord? The family is asleep—"

"What in damnation is all that noise about, Duncan?" Nathaniel came into sight and scowled when he saw the earl standing there. "There had better be a *damned* good reason for this visit, Wycliffe."

"The blasted chit has gone and done it now. I fear for Cordelia and Matthew's safety. She hired a criminal to track me and keep me distracted while she eliminated a *problem*."

The marquess groaned, pinching the bridge of his nose. "Will this madness ever end? Duncan, have my horse readied. I shall see what my connections on Bow Street can do for you, Bastian, but I cannot promise you anything."

"Your help is more than I expected, Nathaniel. I must be off. I have to make sure they are safe."

Nathaniel nodded, and his butler closed the door behind him.

Riding home had never felt so agonizing. Words could not begin to express what he would do if a hair on either of them was harmed. How anyone could take their vengeance on an innocent person and child was beyond him.

As he approached, he heard the fire brigade's bells ringing furiously and saw flames reaching into the sky. Upon closer inspection, he found his town house ablaze. Neighbors, servants, and spectators crowded into the street.

Cordelia! Matthew!

His heart sank and crushed under the weight of excruciating fear until he saw his butler and housekeeper in the street shivering.

"My lord, we do not know what happened."

"Where are my wife and son?"

"We do not know. Beatrice has taken Matthew to her family's home, but the countess we have not seen since supper."

Somewhere behind him, he heard his name being called. When he turned, there was Nathaniel and a runner.

"We are so glad we found you. We ran into a few lads who say they saw someone who looked like the countess accompanied by another woman headed down the street to a waiting hackney. Is Matthew…"

Bastian shook his head and blinked furiously at how surreal this situation had become. "Matthew was taken to our nursemaid's home for safekeeping. As soon as Cordelia has been recovered, I will collect him."

"Allow me to take them into my protection, Bastian. Your servants too. They will need a warm place to stay."

How could he refuse the generous offer? "Certainly. I will be along as soon as I can. I cannot rest until I have found her."

His butler and housekeeper approached. "My lord, I am certain the countess is fine. I know it deep in my heart."

Let us hope so. As I am in no mood for games.

Cordelia shook her head. Groggy, sore, and in disbelief, pain riddled her from head to toe. The gag made her mouth dry, and she would kill or beg for mercy if it meant she could have a drop of water.

The last thing she remembered was that dreadful woman sneaking up behind her in the bedroom. Mary Elizabeth had attempted to choke her. When the countess had slapped the mad woman away, she had taken a lit candle and set the bed and curtains ablaze. After starting a fire in the kitchen, the witch had managed to sneak up the stairs undetected.

Cordelia glared at her surroundings, trying to determine where she was. Nothing looked familiar, nor did the view from outside the window. She could hear the morning hustle and bustle below in the street, which meant she could not have gone too far from home and that she was near enough to the market.

The only question occupying her thoughts was Matthew's safety, followed quickly by Bastians'. *Good heavens…if Bastian had returned last night to find the home afire, he would be having an apoplectic fit. He would be guilt-ridden for having left us alone.* She could not bear the thought of having a life that did not include either one of them.

She was convinced that this was her punishment for her affair with Bastian. It had to be. What else could this purgatory mean?

While deep in a flurry of thoughts about her husband and son, Mary Elizabeth joined her, setting a pistol down next to her on the sideboard. Then, she stalked toward Cordelia and ripped the gag from her mouth before occupying a chair across from the countess.

"What is it that you want from me?" Cordelia screamed, struggling against her restraints.

The woman merely laughed. "The truth is that I do not want anything from you. What I want is for you to die. It appears to be the only way I will be rid of you, once and for all. The earl is mine. We were perfectly matched, until you decided to return to town. With you out of the picture, I will be able to pick up the pieces from where we left off."

"You are mad!"

"Maybe a touch, but after this, you will never see him again."

"If you love him so much, why would you seek to hurt him so? Why would steal his wife from him and kill his son?"

Her captor winced at her words. "You lie!" she shrieked. "Bastian has no children. At least not yet. Once we are together, married, and happily situated away from London, we shall have all the children he wants."

Clearly the woman was beyond delusional. Cordelia shook her head, and *tsked* at her assailant. "You shall never have him. If you think by killing me, you will gain favor with the earl, you are mistaken. When you are caught, and I am certain you will be, they will whisk you away to Newgate. Perhaps, they will even ship you abroad to whatever that place is called…Botany Bay…and you will have to take up your previous profession of lifting your skirts."

"You wretched woman!" Mary Elizabeth howled. She rushed over to Cordelia, slapping her across the face.

Suddenly, the sounds of men shouting and footsteps running through the hallway outside caught their attention.

Cordelia heard the rattling of other doors before they stopped outside of the room. The pounding on the wood shook the floorboards beneath them. "Open the door this instant, Mary Elizabeth!"

Bastian! He had found her. Tears welled up, and relief washed over her.

But then, the door burst open, Mary Elizabeth ran to where she had placed the pistol and pointed it straight at Cordelia.

Bastian, the marquess, and two other men barreled into the room.

"Apprehend her this instant!" the shorter, unfamiliar man shouted.

The moment that Bastian stepped forward, the gun fired. Mary Elizabeth looked horrified before moving back toward the window and throwing herself out.

In the next minutes, Cordelia struggled to understand what was happening around her. All the shouting had faded into somewhere in the distance, and her belly burned. She dared not look at what was causing the discomfort, only realizing that Bastian had fallen to his knees before her and was holding a cloth at her wound.

She tried to speak, but words would not form.

"*Shh*…conserve your energy, my love. We shall get a surgeon to look at you immediately."

This was the last thing she heard before closing her eyes and drifting into unconsciousness.

Bastian paced at her bedside frantically. Cordelia had been asleep on and off for a whole day, and their son was restless. He needed his mama, and the earl desperately needed his wife.

The Marquess of Stoughton had offered them to stay on at Stoughton Hall until his servants had cleaned up their new home in Leicester. Every so often, the marchioness would pop in and check on Cordelia, but she remained asleep. The surgeon had cautioned them that the laudanum would prolong the sleep. Provided that they did not give her any more until she awoke, Cordelia would recover in no time.

The tissue damage was repairable and would not affect her in anyway, should they choose to have more children. There was, however, the distinct possibility that a scar would remain in place of the entry wound.

Truth be told, he cared not if her skin was blemished. As long as he had her in his arms until the end of his days, 'twas all he could ask for.

Suddenly, Cordelia murmured something and her eyes flickered open.

"Conserve your energy, my love. How are you feeling?"

"Matthew…Where is he? Where is my son?" she cried out.

Bastian crouched down next to her. "He is fine, my love. I shall have Beatrice bring him in shortly. He has been quite fussy, and I do not want to overwhelm you with more excitement."

The butler knocked at the door before entering with a companion. "What is the meaning of this, Duncan? The countess is not receiving guests."

"My lord, pardon the intrusion, but this man refused to return another time."

Bastian scowled as his muscles tensed. Rising from his haunches, he approached the familiar man. "What is it that you want, Hugh? I did not realize that you still ran with Bow Street."

"I guess after my last misunderstanding, they decided to give me one last chance. I am here about the countess. A letter was given to me by way of Newgate prison, the women's wing. It is accusing the countess of murdering her late husband in his cell."

The earl laughed hysterically. "Not that you have ever been known to do your job, but if you had sought the guard on duty, you would have known that the countess was never alone with the Richard. Leave now, or you will find yourself without employment by morning. Now, if we are quite done, I have my wife to return my attention to."

"Who said anything about my being done?"

"Honestly, Hugh. If you do not leave now, I will let your captain know about that shady business of yours out of Martine's establishment."

The runner scoffed. "You would not dare."

"Are you certain about that, Hugh? Imagine the headlines—'Runner has an addiction to smoke houses.' I daresay, it would make an excellent read."

Bastian glared at Nathaniel's servant, who had remained present. "Duncan, see this man out. He is not welcome, and I am positive your master will not want to see his face here again."

"Yes, my lord."

Shouting could be heard throughout the house and all the way to the courtyard as Hugh was removed from the property.

"Is he gone yet, my love?" Cordelia queried, coming out of another daze.

"He is. You sound raspy. Let me offer you some water. You must be parched."

She nodded.

He tipped the glass to her dry, cracked lips. The sooner she recovered from this ordeal, the quicker they could resume living their lives in peace. Now that he had his countess, all was right in the world.

"Bastian, tell me, whatever happened to that woman, the one who shot me?"

He groaned loud enough for all the house to hear. "Must I, dear? Truth be told, I'd love nothing more than to put that wretched wench out of my mind, once and for all." Yet, he could not bring himself to keep her from the truth. Cordelia deserved to learn what had transpired after she lost had consciousness, and preferably by him.

"Well, after you collapsed, she threw herself out of the window. Her intent was probably to end her life, however, the good Lord sought to bring her to justice. The idiot landed in a cart with some market wares, trapping her under some crates of fruit, and she was apprehended. The last I heard, she was being held at Newgate, and was bound for Sydney Cove on the next ship."

"What do you mean, Sydney Cove? They really mean to exile her with other criminals?"

Bastian snorted in contempt. "Do not tell me you are sympathetic to her cause."

"No." Cordelia winced and blew out a long, tired breath. "I am just surprised."

"Do not be. She is deserving of her punishment. Now, allow me to bring in our son. I am certain you will be pleased to see him."

Bastian rose from the bed, walked to the bell, and rang for assistance. A moment later Duncan arrived. "Sir, how may I assist?"

"Please have Beatrice bring Matthew in. His mama wishes to see him."

The servant nodded and departed with haste. A few moments later, the sound of a wailing baby approached. The second the door opened and the child came into view, Cordelia raised her arms. Beatrice gently placed the baby into them, and he began to coo.

"Look how happy he is to be finally reunited with his mama. I couldn't have asked for a finer moment. How do you feel, my dear?"

"Incandescently happy, and glad for this drama to have ended. What news do we have from Leicester?"

"Your ancestral home is now ready for us. Matthew and some of the marquess' servants went ahead to prepare the home for our arrival. They have even cleared out a few rooms for any additions to our family unit in the future, and I thought of creating a room just for ourselves. For our particular use of entertainment when we are alone. What say you?"

Despite wincing from discomfort, she managed a smile and stifled a giggle with the baby kicking up a fuss in her arms. "I cannot wait to see what surprises you have in store for me, my lord."

Bastian chuckled. She knew his style too well. He was, after all, her deviant lord.

The End

ABOUT THE AUTHOR

Born and raised in Toronto, Ontario, Layna discovered her love of reading at an early age. She's a bestselling author at All Romance eBooks, and multi-published author of historical, paranormal and contemporary erotic romances. When she isn't devouring salacious romance novels or writing, she enjoys losing herself in researching ancient history and mythology, weaponry, and hiking. She lives in Northern Ontario, with her husband and two daughters.

For updates on her upcoming releases, or to leave her a comment, you can find her at www.laynapimentel.com.

Connect with her on:
Facebook
Twitter

OTHER TITLES BY THE AUTHOR

Shadowed By Sin
His Unexpected Submissive
Hardened Desire
A Gift From Fate

www.ingramcontent.com/pod-product-compliance
Lightning Source LLC
Chambersburg PA
CBHW070549130626
46556CB00001B/82